THOSE WHO BELIEVE

Also by this Author

Mystery/Suspense:

Looking Over Your Shoulder

Young Adult Fiction:

Breaking the Pattern:
Deviation
Diversion
By-Pass

Between the Cracks:
Ruby
June and Justin (Coming Soon)

Stand Alone

Tattooed Teardrops

Don't Forget Steven

Those Who Believe

THOSE WHO BELIEVE

P.D. Workman

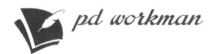

ISBN: 1926500083
ISBN-13: 9781926500089

~ ~ ~ To those struggling with their faith. ~ ~ ~

Acknowledgments

I wish to personally thank the following people for their contributions and knowledge and other help in creating this book:

Beta readers, Dionne Washington, Hanna Krivinchuk, and Hazel Grusendorf.

Tom Grusendorf for editing.

Prologue

NATHAN COULD STILL REMEMBER the first time he was bitten by a snake. He wasn't sure how old he had been at the time; maybe three years old. It was a copperhead, not a rattler. Copperheads were so pretty. Rattlers always made him a bit nervous with their buzz. He suspected that was why they were used in worship services more often. People liked the giddy anticipation that the noise of the rattlers caused.

He'd cried like a baby. But then, he wasn't much older than one. It could be excused. Mama had kissed the bite and swept him up, and danced him around the congregation. The bite burned. Burned like a red hot stove. And it turned a brilliant bright pink. Nathan held it against himself, crying. Mama still held the little copperhead in her other hand, dancing fast to the wild beat of the music. In spite of how much it hurt, Nathan found himself mesmerized by the undulating snake in Mama's hand, the swaying and writhing of her body, and the loud beat of the piano, electric guitar, tambourines, and 'amens' that filled up the room.

Nathan's sobs hitched, slowing down, and he leaned his body backward away from Mama, feeling the pull of the centrifugal force like when they played 'spin me, Mama'. He closed his eyes and let himself become part of the dance, between himself, Mama, and the snake.

Chapter One

NATHAN FELT LIKE THEY were under a microscope as they carried the boxes and suitcases into the house. People were watching. They pretended not to, but Nathan could feel their eyes on him. People on the street pretending to just be walking by. Neighbors looking out through their blinds. There were a lot of eyes.

We're just a normal family, Nathan thought, like a mantra. Nothing unusual here. We're just a normal family, just like everyone else here. Even without the mid-month move, people probably would have noticed them. Billie, his Mama, in a long, flowing black and red skirt, her beautiful dark hair spilling down the back of her white, long-sleeved blouse. And Nathan himself, his hair almost black, toothpick thin and struggling to carry bags and boxes that were as heavy as he was.

They'd made a few trips from the car to the house, when Nathan came out to get another load and saw a girl standing behind their fence, on the outside, watching with undisguised interest.

"Hi!" she greeted.

"Hi," Nathan said back, in a tone that he knew was not very friendly. He went to the car to get another load.

The girl was a couple of steps behind him, following him in order to carry on the conversation. She was a dirty blond, chewing bubblegum with her mouth open. Probably ten years old.

"What's your name?" she demanded.

"Nathan."

"I'm Delia."

Nathan grunted and picked up a box labeled 'kitchen.' He turned around and headed back into the house. She followed him as far as the fence and stopped. At least she had some boundaries. She was still there when he put the box down in the kitchen and went back out to the car, crossing paths with Mama at the doorway. She gave him an impish smile that Nathan supposed was related to Delia. She'd be teasing him later about having a new girlfriend already. As if Nathan had ever had a girlfriend.

"How old are you?" Delia went on when Nathan approached her.

"Eleven."

"Eleven? You don't look eleven," she protested.

"Well, I am."

"You're too small to be eleven," Delia pointed out.

Nathan clenched his jaw and pulled at a suitcase that was wedged between the front and the back seat. He threw all of his weight into it, emphasizing Delia's point about how small he was. Then he tried to wiggle it loose.

"Do you need help?" Delia questioned.

"No."

She climbed into the front seat of the car and Nathan opened his mouth to get after her for putting her nose where it wasn't wanted. She pawed under the front seat and found the release, which allowed her to slide it forward. The suitcase came free. Nathan sighed.

"Thanks," he grumbled, and scooted back out of the car to take it into the house.

He stopped for a rest after putting it down. Moving was hot, tiring work. He had only been working at it for twenty or thirty minutes, but he was already exhausted, ready to just lie down and go to sleep. Nathan leaned on the doorway of Mama's room, breathing deeply and looking for the energy to keep working.

"You okay, sugar?" Mama questioned.

"Yeah, Mama. Just tired."

"There's not too much more."

"I know." He straightened up. "I just need to get me a drink, then I'll be fine."

Nathan went to the kitchen and ran the cold water tap. He scrubbed his hands into the icy cold water, and patted and splashed his face to cool down. Then he put his mouth into the stream and gulped the water down. He was so thirsty. He'd been thirsty even before he started working. Now he was hot and tired and more thirsty.

After satisfying his thirst, Nathan shut off the water and forced himself to march back outside again, to face the girl and the rest of the work.

"Are you really eleven?" Delia demanded. "Really, truly, cross your heart? You're not just teasing me?"

"Really, truly," Nathan agreed. "I don't lie."

"Wow. I thought you were, like, grade three."

Nathan shook his head in disgust. "Thanks."

"But you're older than I am."

Nathan dragged a heavy box containing a terrarium and equipment out of the car. "Uh-huh."

He trekked back into the house, hesitating where to put the terrarium. He ended up leaving it in the sitting room, even though that probably wasn't where Mama would set it up. It was just easiest.

"Just a bit more, Bug," Mama encouraged, as she headed back outside for another load.

Nathan made a noise of agreement, and followed her out. He waited while she took a box out, then they swapped places so that he could pick up the last big box, Mama going back into the house.

"Is that your mom?" Delia questioned.

Nathan looked at her, frowning. Who else would it be? His sister? His gramma? "Yeah."

"She's really pretty."

Nathan smiled, feeling his face warm.

"Yeah," he agreed. "She is."

He started walking quickly toward the house. He could barely manage the box's weight.

"Why's she all dressed up?" Delia demanded to know, following behind him for a few steps.

Nathan pretended not to hear her.

"Well, I think that's everything," Mama said, wiping her sweaty forehead.

Nathan put his box down with a thump. "That's it," he agreed.

"You're such a good helper, Nathaniel," she approved. "I never have to nag you."

Nathan shrugged. "There isn't anyone else to help," he pointed out. "I can't let you do it all yourself."

She gave him a tight hug. "That's my good boy," she said tenderly.

Nathan hugged her back, then squirmed to be released. She held him a few moments longer and gave him a kiss on the forehead, laughing.

"I could just hold you all day."

Nathan's face was hot. He shrugged.

"Do you like that little girl outside?" Mama asked.

"I don't even know her. She's a pest."

"You don't even know her," Mama repeated back to him. "How can you know she's a pest?"

"I just know."

"You will need to make friends. It's nice to have someone who lives close who is close to your age. Even if she is a girl."

"She's not my age. She's too young."

"She can't be that much younger. You should be friendly with her. She can introduce you to the other kids in the neighborhood."

"I wasn't rude to her."

He felt a little squirm of guilt in his stomach when he said it. Well, he hadn't said anything rude. Maybe his attitude had been a little less warm than it should be, but that was because he was working, and he was hot and tired. He just didn't have the time and energy to visit with her right now.

"I'll go lock up the car," Nathan offered.

"Thank you, honey. You're such a good helper."

Nathan went back outside again. He took a deep breath of the air, taking a quick look around his surroundings to evaluate the new neighborhood. It was a warm day, with a bright blue sky. The house that they had rented was small and looked a little shabby. All of the houses on the street were similar in age and size. Some were run down and others were well kept up. There weren't a lot of kids running around. In fact, the only kid other than himself that was out right now was Delia, still watching him with open curiosity.

Nathan went to the car and locked each of the doors, shut them, and shut the trunk.

"It was... nice to meet you," Nathan told Delia, trying to make up for his earlier coldness. "Thanks... for being so welcoming."

She smiled, pleased at this. She kicked the fence lightly with the toe of one of her pink sneakers.

"I have lots of friends," she proclaimed.

"Uh--yeah."

"They're just not out right now. I can introduce you later."

"Sure, that'd be great," Nathan agreed. But inwardly, he recoiled. He didn't want to be a spectacle, a curiosity. He didn't want to be introduced to everyone at once. He just wanted to blend in. Act like he'd always lived there.

"Do you have any lemonade or anything?" Delia suggested.

"No." He looked at her. When did she think that he'd had time to get or make any lemonade? They'd just barely gotten their boxes transferred into the house.

"Oh... do you want some?"

Nathan shook his head. "I don't usually drink lemonade or juice," he said awkwardly. "Just water."

"Ice tea?" she suggested.

Nathan shook his head.

"Just water," Delia repeated, shaking her head like he was crazy. "What about Coke?"

Nathan nodded. "Only if it's diet," he cautioned.

Delia looked over Nathan's frail figure. "You don't need to diet," she observed.

He shrugged and didn't explain. Delia sighed.

"I'll get you one," she said grudgingly, as if he had demanded it rather than it being her who had offered it in the first place. "You wait for me here, okay?"

Nathan nodded. He watched Delia run back to her house, a few doors down. It wasn't long before she was on her way back, three cans in her hands.

"I brought one for your mom too," she explained.

"Thanks," Nathan said. "That was real nice."

He took two cans from her, and hesitated. He didn't really want to take her into the house and introduce her. But it didn't seem polite to just leave her outside and take her offering in to Mama.

"Come on in," he said reluctantly, and turned up the walk to the house.

Delia followed him right on his heels. Nathan found Mama in the front room, poking through the boxes. She looked up, wiping her sweaty forehead with the back of her arm. Nathan handed her one of the Diet Cokes.

"This is for you. From Delia," he explained, gesturing to her.

"Why, thank you, Delia," Mama said enthusiastically. She pressed the cold can to her face. "This is just what I need right now." She popped the tab on the top and took a long swallow. "I'm Billie Ashbury. And I guess you've met my Nathaniel."

"Billie?" Delia repeated, with a line forming between her eyebrows.

"Where I come from, Billie can be a girl's name too," Mama explained.

"Oh. Okay." Delia's eyes were drinking in Mama's unconventional outfit. "You look very nice."

"Thank you. You're very kind." Mama smiled at Delia. "Are you wondering why I'm wearing a dress? On moving day when it could get all grubby?"

Delia shrugged, and twirled around on her tiptoes. "It's very pretty," she observed.

"I'm a pastor," Mama said. "Do you know what that is?"

Delia considered this for a few moments, looking into the few boxes on the floor curiously.

"It's like a preacher?" she questioned eventually.

Mama nodded. "That's right," she agreed. "I'm a preacher."

Delia looked skeptical. "I don't think there are girl preachers," she said, lips pursed.

"Well, there are a lot more around than there used to be. And there's even fewer back home, but when God calls you, it doesn't matter if you're a boy or a girl, you'd better listen."

Delia sipped at her Coke. "Did you hear him call you?" she questioned.

"It's just an expression," Nathan interrupted, irritated that she didn't understand. Misunderstandings led to teasing and bullying, and Nathan was sure that he would be facing plenty of that without people thinking that his Mama was crazy because she heard God's voice calling her. "It doesn't mean she heard a voice."

Mama put a reassuring hand on Nathan's shoulder, rubbing it to let him know that it was okay, he didn't need to get upset over this.

"God called to my heart," she explained to Delia. "I felt a warm feeling about what he wanted me to do."

"Oh." Delia nodded. "Okay."

Nathan looked for a graceful way to end the conversation and get Delia out of there. He gestured to the door.

"I'll walk you out," he offered. "Thanks again for the Coke."

Delia started slowly for the door, looking at him with her brows drawn down. They got to the front door and Delia stepped out onto the steps.

"You don't have any furniture," she observed.

Nathan rolled his eyes. "We'll get some," he said. "You can't exactly fit furniture inside the car."

"Is a moving truck bringing them? Shouldn't it have come today?"

"We're going to buy furniture here," Nathan explained. His hand was on the door and he was working his way toward an opportunity to shut it, so that he didn't have to keep explaining everything to her. "That's easier than hiring movers."

"Oh. Are you getting new furniture right now? Where are you going to sleep tonight?"

The questions just weren't going to stop. Nathan swung the door shut. "Bye, thanks for the Coke," he repeated, as it closed in her face.

Nathan locked it. Standing on his tip-toes, he could see through the peep-hole, and he watched her, standing there for a minute in surprise, then finally deciding to leave. Delia retreated down the sidewalk, which through the peep-hole looked very long and narrow. Nathan let out a puff of air, relieved to have her out of the way. He went back to the living room to see what else Mama needed him to do.

One part of moving that Nathan enjoyed was their tradition of eating their first meal on the living room floor by candlelight. Usually pizza. Of course, cable hadn't been hooked up yet, so there was no TV to watch. They didn't even have a TV yet, Nathan thought ruefully, even if the cable was hooked up. So instead they told each other stories; some of them made-up, some of them memories of other moves and other places, and some of them favorite scriptures or sermons. After the pizza was cleared away, they played cards.

Nathan was happy. Even though he didn't like to be rooted up and have to move again, to start a new school mid-year, and make new friends; he was happy to be with his Mama, with their traditions and memories, knowing that he was loved and cared for. Safe.

It had been a long day, and Nathan had been tired half-way through it. They hadn't been playing cards for long before his eyes started getting very heavy. He had another drink of cold water, but he couldn't keep his eyes open.

Mama laughed. "You ready for bed already, Love Bug?" she questioned.

Nathan nodded, rubbing his eyes. Mama put the cards away and unrolled their sleeping bags out across the living room floor. Nathan crawled inside his as she retrieved a couple of pillows. It felt so good to slide between the warm blankets and rest his body.

"Here, lift your head, honey," Mama coaxed, and slid a pillow beneath his cheek when Nathan lifted his heavy head one last time.

Eyes closed, he felt her sliding into her sleeping bag beside him. He heard a shutter click and groaned, opening his eyes a crack. Mama brought her face next to his and took another picture of them both with her phone.

"We need a picture of our new house," she pointed out.

"Then take a picture of the house," Nathan slurred. "Not me."

She laughed and moved back onto her own pillow. She hummed while she posted it. Then Mama started to pray, her voice rising and falling rhythmically. Nathan tried to stay awake, and got in a couple of 'amens', but he was too exhausted, and fell asleep as she petitioned the Almighty.

Morning came too soon, especially when Nathan knew that with morning came school. He had tried to coax Mama into letting him stay home another day or two in order to help her get the house set up properly, but she wouldn't bend.

"I wish that you could stay at home too, honey," she said in a sad voice. "But you need to get into school right away. You don't want to miss any more than you have to. Your marks haven't been too good, and I don't know where your class is in this school compared to your last one. And you'll want to make friends," she encouraged.

Nathan finished rolling up his sleeping bag and sat back down on the floor, while Mama served up soft, sticky cinnamon buns, still warm from the bakery. Nathan poked at the coiled roll, his stomach in a tight, anxious knot.

"I don't care about friends," he said. "I'd rather be home with you."

She gave him a brilliant smile, and looked back down at her own bun, trying to cut it into pieces with a plastic knife and fork.

"There's extra sauce," she pointed out, tapping the lid of the additional bowl of icing. Nathan wished she had bought something that wasn't quite so sweet, first thing in the morning. He ate a small bite of the bun, swirling it around in his mouth like a wine taster before chewing and swallowing it. "Don't do that, Nathaniel. It's not polite."

They ate in silence for a few minutes.

"I couldn't stay home with you just today?" Nathan suggested. "It's just one day, it won't make that much difference."

"Are you nervous, Bug?"

Nathan shrugged and took another bite.

"It will all be okay," Mama promised. "The sooner you can get used to the new school, the better. I don't like having to make you go either, but that's the way the world works. Parents and children have to be separated for things like school. It's good for you. It will help you to grow."

Nathan took a drink of water. He was always so parched in the morning. He felt like he could just drink a whole jug of water. "Why can't I do homeschool?" he questioned. "Other people do."

"I know... and I'd love to do it with you... but..." she struggled for words. "Even though other people do it, it can be a sort of red flag for the authorities... it makes them suspicious... we need to..." she trailed off.

Nathan knew without her finishing the sentence. They needed to be normal. They couldn't have the authorities looking at them with suspicion, investigating, thinking that they needed to take a hand. He nodded his understanding and pulled his bun into smaller pieces.

"Are you going to eat that? Or just worry it to death?" Mama questioned.

He looked up, pushing it away from him. "I'm not really hungry. My stomach's all knotted up."

She nodded, making a sympathetic noise. "I'm not surprised. But it will all work out. You know it always works out, if we follow where the Spirit leads."

"I know, Mama. I try to believe," he confessed, "but my faith isn't as strong as yours."

She took one of his hands in each of hers. "Not yet, baby. But you're young. I didn't get my call until I was older. You've always been guided and protected by the Spirit, even when you were just a babe in arms."

Nathan nodded.

"When you're as old as me," Mama went on, "you'll have way more faith than I do now."

Nathan swallowed. His eyes grew hot with tears at her assurance. He sure didn't feel that way himself. He felt like his faith was just a blade of grass, blown around by every breeze. He wanted to be strong like she said, but he wavered at every little thing. He wavered.

Mama let go of his hands, and finished eating her bun. She started to pick up the debris, and Nathan pitched in, folding what was left of his bun into a napkin and throwing it into the garbage bag with the rest. Mama rubbed him on the back, in between the shoulders.

"All right, baby. It's time to go to school."

He didn't argue or cajole her anymore. He just picked up his backpack, already all packed for school, and slid it onto his shoulder. Mama dug around in her purse, and handed him a few dollar bills.

"There you are, you get whatever you like for dinner, okay? I don't even care if it's all junk food. Just make sure you get something to eat."

"I will," Nathan agreed, pushing it deep into his pocket so he wouldn't drop it.

She led the way to the door, and Nathan went outside while she locked up. Mama gave him a quizzical look as he stood on the sidewalk and stared at the house. "Is something wrong?" she questioned.

"No. I'm just trying to memorize it," Nathan explained, repeating the house number to himself several times and looking for any features of the house that made it different from the other houses on the block. White picket fence. Fake shutters. The right-hand one had a big knot hole in the corner that made it look like someone had taken a bite out of it. Like a bite out of a gingerbread house, Nathan told himself. That was something he wouldn't forget.

"I'll pick you up after school," Mama said. "You won't get lost."

Nathan nodded. "Okay. But I'll have to be able to recognize it."

"Number forty-two," she pointed out. "You can remember that."

"Forty-two," Nathan repeated. He turned slowly away from the house and walked toward the car.

Chapter Two

"HOW OLD IS HE?" the woman in the office repeated, looking over the counter at Nathan.

"He's eleven. Grade six."

"He doesn't look like grade six," the woman said doubtfully. "Are you sure?"

Mama sighed and opened her wallet to find Nathan's birth certificate. She laid it down on the counter. "Look," she insisted, pointing at the date on the card. "I know how old my son is!"

The woman eyed it for a moment, then took the wallet card, together with all of the forms that Mama had filled out over to the copier and ran everything through. She shuffled back to the counter, giving Nathan another disbelieving look, and carefully divided the papers that she had copied between herself and Mama. She studied the papers, and looked over them at Nathan.

"If Nathan will just sit on one of the chairs," she gestured to the visitor seating along the front wall of the office. "In a few minutes, one of the staff will take him to his classroom."

Nathan took a deep breath and took a couple of steps toward the chairs.

"Nathaniel Ashbury," Billie said in a warning tone, and Nathan froze, and turned back toward her. "Don't you tell me you're not going to give your mama a hug and kiss good-bye."

Nathan rolled his eyes and gave a little laugh, and stepped back over to her to give her a brief hug and kiss good-bye. But she grabbed him and held him tight, half-smothering him with her grip.

"Oh, baby," she crooned. "You be good. It'll all turn out, you'll see."

"I'll be fine, Mama," he protested, fighting to pull out of her grip. Looking up at her face, he saw that tears had welled up in her eyes, and she was struggling not to let them show.

"I'm a big boy," he told her firmly. "I've started at new schools before, and I've always been just fine. Now you go home and you go shopping for some furniture, and start getting the house together for us. So we can sit down to supper at the table and thank the Lord for all our blessings."

"Amen," she agreed. She squeezed his hand, and hurried out of the office, her head down so that no one would see the tears.

Nathan sighed deeply, and swallowed his own tears. He chose a chair and sat down. It was sort of embarrassing to be sitting there by himself, waiting. He might not have ever been at that school before, but he knew instinctively that this was where the troublemakers sat while they were waiting to talk to the principal or one of the other staff. If you were in trouble and got sent to the office, this was where you sat, on display, until someone dealt with you. He was acutely aware that any students walked behind him down the hall as they moved to their classes would think that he was in trouble for something, instead of just waiting for someone to take him to his class.

"Nathaniel Ashbury?"

Nathan jumped at the sound of his name. He looked up and saw a man standing there looking at him, and looking at the sheet of paper in his hand. Nathan rose quickly to his feet.

"Nathan, sir. I go by Nathan."

"Nathan, then. Good to meet you. I'm Principal Falstaff."

Nathan offered his hand, and they shook firmly. Nathan's hand was swallowed up in the principal's grip.

"A very well-bred boy," Falstaff complimented him. "Shall we take you to your class?"

"Yes, sir. Thank you."

Falstaff motioned to the office door, and Nathan went out ahead of him. Then the principal took the lead.

"You have English first," he said. "It's already started. Then phys ed. I guess you'll be sitting phys ed out today, since you don't have gym clothes yet. But you'll at least see where everything is."

Nathan nodded. Phys ed was not his favorite subject. Lots of boys lived for it, he knew. A chance to burn off excess energy, to move around instead of having to listen to a teacher lecture. But Nathan was too small, too weak, and tired too quickly. He was bound to be at the bottom of the class and made fun of behind the teacher's back, if not by the teacher himself. English was better. He decided to focus on that. He followed the principal through several twists and turns, and quickly got turned around.

"Mrs. Davis is your teacher," Falstaff went on chattily. "She's a real gem. You'll like her. All of the students like her."

Nathan nodded.

"Now, I don't know where you are in your studies. Whether your last school was ahead or behind where we are, or what order you covered your units in. If you are having trouble, I want you to let me know. My door is always open. And you can talk to your teacher. We have a resource room available for those who are behind for one reason or other and need some special tutoring. I don't want you to be embarrassed to use it. What looks worse, using the resource room so that you can get caught up to grade level, or refusing to be seen there and failing the grade?"

"Right," Nathan agreed.

"Your mom said that you might need some extra help..." She'd made them think he was slow too. Could things get any worse?

Falstaff led him up to a closed classroom door. He knocked briskly and opened it. The teacher at the front of the room fell silent and looked inquiringly in their direction, wanting to know what was going on.

"Mrs. Davis, you have a new transfer student," Falstaff announced, in a voice much louder than it needed to be. "This is Nathaniel--Nathan--Ashbury. He's joining us from..." the principal trailed off and looked at Nathan to fill in the details.

"Hi," Nathan greeted Mrs. Davis and the room at large. "Where do you want me to sit?"

"Well, let's see," Mrs. Davis was a tall, slim, flaming redhead. Nathan didn't even know that hair came in that bright a color. "We'll have to get them to bring in another desk for you, because they are all taken. But for today, Bly Munro is sick, so you can take his seat." She gestured at one in the back. Bly Munro must have been a big boy, because his desk was huge, bigger than any other in the room. Nathan slid into the chair and sat up straight in order to see over the desk. The room was alive with giggles.

"That's enough," Principal Falstaff warned, quieting them. "Well, enjoy yourself, Nathan. Welcome to our school."

Nathan nodded. The principal withdrew, pulling the door behind him with a bang. Mrs. Davis looked at Nathan for a minute.

"You'll need some books," she said, more to herself than to Nathan. She moved to a cupboard at the back of the room and rifled through it, pulling out several textbooks and workbooks. "Do you have a pen or pencil?" she questioned.

Nathan nodded, and dug into his backpack, feeling warm and lightheaded. When he leaned over, bright lights started popping in front of his eyes, and he had to brace himself and straighten back up for a moment, waiting for the feeling to pass. Mrs. Davis put the books on his desk.

"You'll have to hang onto them for today. We don't have lockers, and I don't have a desk for you to keep them in yet. Today we are in this one," she pressed her index finger down on a purple-spined textbook. "Page fifty-two. Keep up the best you can and I'll talk to you later to see where you are. Okay?"

Nathan opened up the book and looked down at the page. Mrs. Davis went up to the front and picked up her lesson where she had left off. The book appeared to be new. Not a beaten-up hand-me-down, pages falling from the spine, like you got at some schools. Nathan's last school had been quite poor. In a poor neighborhood, with too little school funding. There had barely been any intact textbooks. It was nice to have a brand-new textbook, with no swear words written in the margins. It meant that no one had circled all of the answers in the exercises either, but Nathan would have to live with that.

There were whispers around him, and Nathan glanced around. Some of the other students were eying him. There were still some suppressed giggles. Nathan imagined that he looked pretty comical, his skinny body stretching up as far as he could reach to see the teacher over the top of the massive desk, his feet swinging free two inches off of the floor. He felt like a child playing at being an adult. He ducked his head, trying to ignore the giggles.

Phys ed went about how Nathan had expected. The coach had looked him over critically, eyes analyzing him like he was something broken.

"What did you do at your last school?" he questioned. "Basketball?" There were snickers from the class, but the coach was serious. "Volleyball? Anything?"

"Knitting," a loud whisper interrupted the coach's query.

The entire room broke down into loud guffaws. The coach grinned, shaking his head. Nathan stood there in front of the class, wishing that he was invisible. His ears and face were hot, and he knew that everyone would be able to see how uncomfortable he was up there, his face flaming red. Other suggestions were made. Chess. Baking. Picking flowers.

"That's enough," the coach advised, deciding that the joke had gone far enough. "Five laps for everyone. That should quiet you down a bit."

With groans of complaint, the other boys got up and started running a circuit of the gym.

"Boys!" the coach said with a shrug. "So... nothing? Gymnastics? Rope climbing?"

Nathan shook his head. He had one unit that he'd enjoyed at another school, but he wasn't about to share it with the coach.

"All right... well, we'll just try to involve you however we can. You know what you need for gym clothes?"

Nathan glanced around at the other students, and nodded.

"Your mom will have a list. We have gym every day, so be sure to get it as soon as possible. You don't want to be sitting out." He started to turn away from Nathan. "Sprints?" he suggested. "Long jump?" the words kept coming, even though the coach had already turned away and was no longer looking at Nathan. He didn't know whether he should answer, or just let the coach keep making more suggestions to the air.

Nathan wandered over to the bench at the side of the gym and sat down. He watched the other students running around the gym, wondering who would give him a hard time, and who would leave him alone. He didn't expect anyone to actually stand up for him or become his friend. He just wanted to know who the bullies were. The fastest boys, jocks who would look down at him. The fattest ones, who felt like his stick-thin figure was an indictment of their lifestyle and strength of character. The ones toward the bottom of the pecking order, who were looking for someone to pick on, someone smaller and weaker that they could tease to make themselves feel better. It would be the middling boys who would leave him alone. Average kids who weren't fighting to get on top or to stay off the bottom, but who just went through life without having to worry about who was going to try to flush your head down the toilet.

When phys ed was done, Nathan followed the other boys back to Mrs. Davis' class for social studies. Nathan stopped at the water fountain to drink, even though he hadn't worked up a thirst by running or playing basketball. He got a series of scowls and nasty looks from the boys who had been working out for taking such a long time to drink his fill. But he was thirsty.

Chapter Three

B Y THE MIDDLE OF social studies, Nathan could hardly keep his eyes open. He tried to focus on the text and what Mrs. Davis was saying, but his eyes just got more and more blurred. He rested his chin in his hand, both elbows propping him up on the desk, and closed his eyes. Every few minutes, he would drift off to sleep and jerk back awake. He rubbed his eyes and tried again to focus on Mrs. Davis. He found her watching him. After she gave them their workbook assignments, she walked to the back of the room where Nathan sat. She crouched beside his desk, coming down to his level.

"Have you done this already, Nathan?"

Nathan shook his head.

"I thought maybe that's why you were having such a hard time focusing."

Nathan shifted uncomfortably in the desk. "No... I guess I just didn't get a good enough sleep last night. I was trying to pay attention."

She nodded. "Well, be sure to get a good enough sleep tonight then, won't you?"

Nathan nodded. "Yes'm."

"Okay. Give the workbook a try," she said, taking it upon herself to open his workbook and point to the set of questions that he was supposed to be doing. "Let me know if you can't figure it out."

"Yes'm."

Luckily, it wasn't long until lunch. Nathan needed to get up and move around or he was going to be lying on his desk drooling all over the workbook. He tried to read over the workbook questions, but couldn't focus on them. He didn't want to ask Mrs. Davis for help so soon. He planned instead to take the workbook home and get Mama to help him get through it. Finally, the lunch bell rang. Everyone got up and streamed toward the door. Apparently they were dismissed without Mrs. Davis having to tell them to go. Nathan got to his feet and stretched his arms and legs, opening and closing his hands and wiggling his toes to try to wake them all up. They tingled with pins and needles.

Following the general flow of the other students, Nathan found his way first to the boys' room, and then to the cafeteria, which was across from the gym. There wasn't enough room for everyone to sit down in the cafeteria, and students moved across the hall into the gym and sat on the floor. Nathan lined up, and looked to see what was on the menu. He put a black bean taco on his plate, and a package of roasted chickpeas, and headed for the checkout.

"You didn't take five," the woman at the register said, motioning him back.

"What?"

"Take five. Go back and get your five."

Nathan shook his head, and looked at the other students and their trays to try to sort out what she was talking about. What did take five mean?

"He's new," a blond girl who towered over Nathan told the cashier. "I'll show him."

Nathan gave her a quick look. She was tall, wore a dark blazer, and some kind of loose bun at her neck. She had a few pimples on her face. No makeup. She gave him a smile. "Nathan, right?"

Nathan nodded. "Yeah."

"Summer," she introduced herself.

"So what am I supposed to do?"

She touched his arm to guide him back over to the food counter. "One, main course. You got the taco, so you're okay there. Two, vegetable. You don't have any vegetables."

Nathan considered, and picked up a bundle of celery wrapped in plastic wrap.

"Three, fruit."

Nathan added an orange to his tray. He looked at the food on the counter. "And is four a dessert?" he questioned.

She gave him a smile. "You got it," she agreed.

Nathan shook his head. "I have to have a dessert?"

"They're not bad," Summer said. "They make them healthy, you know, but they're all right."

"I have to?" Nathan pressed.

She nodded. "Yeah. It's not like you couldn't use it," she pointed out, her eyes flicking over his thin body.

Nathan picked up a granola bar and put it on his tray.

"And five, extra," Summer said, indicating the roasted chickpeas that he had already selected. "Now you got your five."

"Thanks for your help," Nathan said.

She smiled and lined up behind him at the cashier. "What happened to your hand?" Summer asked.

Nathan didn't have to follow her gaze to know what she was talking about. But he looked down at his deformed forefinger holding the tray anyway. It was lumpy and crooked and had no nail.

"I had an accident when I was little," he said.

"Yeah? What happened?"

Nathan shifted his grip on the tray, sliding his finger underneath. "I was really little," he evaded. "I don't remember very well."

"You must know what happened, though."

Nathan got up to the cashier, and she looked over his tray and accepted his money. Nathan stood and waited for Summer, since he had nowhere else to go and no one else to sit with or talk to. She was the first person to reach out to him, and he would hang around with her if he could. He looked down at his tray as she rejoined him.

"Do you want my granola bar?" he questioned.

She glanced down at him. "You don't have to give me something just because I helped you out," she said. "That's not why I did it."

"I don't want the granola bar. If you want it, have it."

Summer considered. She swept a loose lock of hair over her ear, and made up her mind. "Okay," she agreed, and took it off of his tray. "Thanks."

They both stood there for a second, not sure what to do next. "Do you want to come sit with me?" she questioned.

Nathan shrugged. "You don't have to offer," he said, "just because I gave you my granola bar."

Summer laughed, breaking the tension. "You're funny," she said. "Come on, come sit with me. I'll introduce you around."

Nathan followed her out of the cafeteria. A glance through the doors of the gym showed that it was almost full now as well. There were students starting to line the halls, sitting down with their backs to the wall to eat. Summer led him down the main hall, and sketched a wave to a group, mostly girls, sitting close to the water fountain. She seemed like she knew where they would be, and they were expecting her. It must be their usual lunch spot.

"Hey," Summer greeted. "Everybody, this is Nathan. He's a new transfer, just started today."

They variously nodded or said hi.

"How old is he?" demanded one of the boys who was hanging with them, a lanky, dark-haired boy with a red baseball cap on backwards. "He looks, like, five or something."

Nathan sighed. He should be used to it by now, but every time he started a new school, he kind of hoped that he would have hit a growth spurt and people wouldn't all think that he was too small or too young for the grade that he was in. It got discouraging. Mama said that he was fine, and some boys were just late bloomers. His daddy had been short when he was a boy, but he'd caught up when he was in high school.

High school was a long way away.

"I'm eleven," he said. "Grade six."

Summer glanced sideways at him and nodded. She pointed to the various members of the group, telling Nathan their names, and in some cases something about them. Nathan knew that he wouldn't remember half the names, but in a few days, he'd start to recall them. He nodded at Summer, appreciating the introductions.

"Nice to meet y'all," he said.

There were giggles from a couple of the girls. The boy with the red cap shook his head. "Where y'all from?" he questioned, and Nathan realized that he was mocking Nathan's speech.

"Here and there," he said with a shrug. "Would y'all believe I was born in the South?"

There were louder giggles from the girls, and an appreciative smile from the boy. He gestured to the floor beside him. "Saved a place just for you, Nathan-from-the-South. Pull up a piece of floor and make yourself comfy."

Nathan sat cross-legged and balanced his tray across his lap. "What was your name?" he asked the red-capped boy.

"Malachi. You can just call me Mal."

"Like from the Bible," Nathan observed.

Malachi frowned at him. "Yeah," he acknowledged curtly.

He looked over at Nathan's tray as Nathan started to unwrap his taco to eat. Then his eyes went to Summer's tray as she sat down to visit. He raised an eyebrow. "You're already giving gifts to your girlfriend?"

Nathan looked at Summer, his face getting warm. "I don't like sweets," he explained. "You want my dessert tomorrow?"

Mal grinned, looking pleased. "Heck, yeah! I'm nuts over the chocolate pudding, when they have it."

"You got it," Nathan agreed. "Tomorrow you can have my pudding."

He bit into the taco and chewed. It was good. A little bit spicy, but not crazy hot. His stomach was growling and complaining, having only had a few bites of sweet bun that morning, and it felt good to get something into it.

"You could use some fattening up," Mal commented. "Looks like you've been on a hunger strike or chemo or something. What's up?"

Nathan shifted uncomfortably, and took a couple more bites of his taco without answering. He hoped that Mal would be distracted by one of the other conversations going on around them, and not notice that he hadn't answered. But Mal kept looking at him expectantly. He raised his eyebrows.

"Well?"

"Nothing. I've been sick, is all."

"Sick with what?"

"I don't really want to talk about it," Nathan said, taking another bite of his taco.

Mal's eyes widened. "You don't have... AIDS, do you?" he question, inching away from Nathan slightly, as if his touch might contaminate.

Nathan just about dropped his taco. He put it down on his tray. That was all he needed--Mal to start a rumor that he had AIDS. "No!" he said firmly. "I don't have AIDS. It's nothing like that. Just something I was born with."

His stomach squirmed a little at the fib. But the doctor did say that it was in his genes. That was sort of like being born with it.

Mal eyed him warily, not quite believing it. Nathan glared back. "I don't have AIDS," he repeated.

Mal shrugged.

Nathan went back to eating his taco. He didn't really taste it now. He just knew he had to get something into his system. They were sitting near a garbage can, and Nathan watched student after student toss their untouched fruit and vegetable portions into the can. He wasn't really hungry anymore, but he ate his celery and orange anyway, just because he felt bad about so many people throwing theirs out.

Summer was nudging Nathan, and he startled and looked over at her. He hadn't been listening to the conversation, just thinking his own thoughts.

"Where do you live?" Summer questioned. "Maybe you can walk with one of us after school."

Nathan shook his head. "My mama is going to pick me up--"

"Your momma?" Mal interrupted, snorting. "Your momma is gonna pick you up? Does she still change your diapers too?"

"Mal!" Summer objected, giving him a stern look. "Be nice! Nathan's new; you don't want him going home thinking we're a school full of jerks, do you?"

Mal smirked and didn't answer.

"Then quit being one," Summer chided. "I like the way Nathan says 'mama.' I think it's cute."

Nathan's face burned. He hadn't been embarrassed by Mal's display, but Summer rushing to his defense made him feel extremely self-conscious.

"Don't you stop calling her that," Summer warned. "Just 'cause of jerks like Mal."

"I don't plan to," Nathan agreed. "She's always been my mama, that's not going to change just because I moved somewhere they say 'mom' instead. She'll always be Mama to me."

"Good," Summer approved, resting her hand on Nathan's arm briefly. A couple of the other girls giggled a little. Summer let go of Nathan's arm, but she gave him another smile.

The other boy in the group, who hadn't spoken before now, addressed Nathan as Summer went back to talking to the other girls. "She's not your girlfriend, you know," he said in a low voice that Nathan could barely hear over the sounds of a hundred other students talking in the hallway.

Nathan frowned in confusion. "I know that," he said.

"She's nice to everyone. And she's not allowed to date."

"I just met her," Nathan protested. "I hardly know a thing about her!"

"Doesn't stop you from crushing on her. I'm just telling you now so you know. She's not available."

"And if she was?" Nathan questioned, sensing jealousy under the friendly warning. "I wouldn't have a chance because you're interested?"

The boy's smile was a little sheepish. "Maybe," he hedged.

Nathan shook his head, rolling his eyes. "I don't think you need to worry about it," he advised. "Girls don't generally fall for this." He gestured to himself.

"You never can tell with *nice* girls," the boy said.

The afternoon wore on. School always seemed long, but first days were worse than usual, and Nathan was losing the battle to stay focused and not give in to the intense tiredness that engulfed him. He'd been to sleep in plenty of time the night before, but that didn't seem to make a difference. He could have put his head down on the big desk and just gone straight to sleep. It was a battle not to. Mrs. Davis walked by him during the last period class.

"How's it going, Nathan?" she questioned.

He shrugged and rubbed at his eyes. "Okay, I guess. Long day."

"You look beat. I hope you sleep better tonight. It's always hard in a new place, though, isn't it? It takes a while before you feel like you can call it home."

Nathan nodded. "I guess maybe I'm still tired from the car trip," he explained. "We were three days in the car. And then trying to set up the new house. I'm bushed."

"Well, maybe have a nap when you get home, before you try to finish your homework. Get a little bit of energy back."

"Yes'm," Nathan agreed. He stretched, trying to keep his body awake.

Mrs. Davis nodded her bright red locks, and moved on to talk to another student. Nathan sat there, pinching himself, biting his cheek, and watching the big clock on the wall, waiting for the class to be dismissed. Most of the other students worked away in their books, but a few like Nathan were just sitting there, watching the clock and waiting for their release. Nathan looked at Summer, who sat a few seats away from him. Her head was bowed over the page, and her pen flew quickly back and forth. She was smart. That's who he should call on if he had trouble with the work. He wouldn't mind sitting next to her on the porch, close together, working through his homework problems. Nathan felt his face flush a little just thinking about it.

At long last, the dismissal bell rang, and the room erupted into noisy chaos. Mrs. Davis tried to yell over the noise, reminding everyone about what work they needed to have done for the next day, a group assignment that they were supposed to have done, and an upcoming quiz, but her words were drowned out. Nathan could barely hear her even when he tried, and the rest of the students weren't trying at all. They just chattered on, putting their books away and packing their bags. Summer looked up and saw Nathan as he walked toward the door. She smiled and walked next to him.

"So your mom--your mama," she corrected herself with a warm smile, "is picking you up today?"

"Yep," Nathan agreed. "I expect we might have to go out and run some errands. Pick up some supper. We're still just getting everything set up."

She nodded and hitched her backpack up higher on her shoulder. "Why did you have to move?" she questioned. "Did your dad get transferred or something?"

"I don't have a daddy," Nathan said. "Not anymore. It's just me and Mama."

"And was it because of her job?"

Nathan shrugged. "Sometimes you have to just go where they say," he said, not really answering her question properly. It was easier to be vague and just let her think that she had it right.

Summer nodded understandingly. "That must suck." They walked on for a minute in silence. "I hope you like it here. It's a good school, and Mrs. Davis is really nice. She does a good job."

"Sure. It's nice," Nathan said. It certainly wasn't the worst school that he'd gone to. It was a sight better than most of them. And even if he didn't like it, he wouldn't be there forever. Sooner or later, they would be on the move again, and starting at another school, and this one would be a distant memory.

"What street do you live on?" Summer questioned as they walked down the main hall toward the door.

Nathan opened his mouth and just about gave his last address. His brain stalled, and tried to think of what the new one was. He frowned, trying to make himself remember.

"It's okay," Summer laughed. "You just got here. You'll learn it!"

Nathan rolled his eyes. "Ask me tomorrow," he said. "I'll figure it out."

She giggled and nodded. They got to the door and burst out into the sunlight. Nathan squinted and shaded his eyes at the sudden bright assault of light. "Sheesh. It's like walking out of a crypt," he said.

Summer rubbed her eyes, and he could see tears squeezing out the corners. "Oh boy," she gasped. "That stings. My eyes are so sensitive."

"You should wear sunglasses."

"Yeah."

Nathan looked around, trying to remember which door he had gone into the school through, and where Mama would be picking him up.

"Usually the parents line up over there," Summer said, pointing to the side street, traffic moving slowly down the hill. "You want me to come with you?"

"No, I can manage."

"Okay. See you tomorrow, Nathan."

"Bye."

She walked away, and after watching her for a moment, Nathan turned and headed toward the street. He saw their old clunker partway down the hill, and walked down to it. Mama smiled at him through the window, and reached across to open the door for him. Nathan slid his backpack off of his shoulder, sat down, and held it in his lap, arms wrapped around it. He gave a deep sigh and rested his head on the backpack like it was a pillow.

"Long first day?" Mama questioned sympathetically.

"Yes'm. Long, long day."

"Well, the first one is always the worst. Things will be better tomorrow."

Nathan rolled his shoulders. "What did *you* do today?" he questioned.

"I miss you so bad when you're at school!" Mama exclaimed. "I never could understand all of those mothers who say how happy they are to get rid of their kids during the day, or at the end of summer vacation."

Nathan clearly remembered his first day of kindergarten. Mama had been devastated about having to take him to school and leave him there. She had cried and hugged and kissed him. He'd initially been excited to go to school like a big kid, but by the time that she had left, he'd been crying too. She posted pictures of him online, miserable tears running down his face. *My brave little kindergartner.*

"I know," he said, patting her on the arm. "I missed you too. So tell me about your day."

Her face relaxed. "Well, I got us some furniture. I went early, so they even delivered it already. You can sleep on a real bed tonight, and eat supper on the table."

"Wow, that's fast. I didn't think we'd have anything until tomorrow, at least. How did you manage that?"

"Just sweet talking. Called about a cable hook-up, and they'll have it in this weekend, they said."

Nathan nodded. His eyes wanted to close, and he rubbed them. "Sounds like a good day," he observed. "We'll be all set up and unpacked in no time."

She nodded, smiling. "I put out some resumes. Took them around to different places. I think I've got a good chance of a job at the stationery store. They were really positive. I think I'll get a call-back."

"Wow, that would be great," Nathan approved. "They pay all right?"

"The pay would be good. And then whatever I can take up in collection. The rent here isn't so high. This could be a real nice place to grow up."

A nice place to grow up. Nathan wondered how long they'd actually be there. He licked his lips. He looked out the window, blinking. "Are we going home? I thought it was closer."

"I thought we'd get us some supper first. You must be starved."

Nathan yawned. "Mostly tired. Don't have much appetite."

"But you ate dinner, right?"

"I told you I would. What are we getting?"

"How about pizza? You always like pizza."

"Sure," Nathan agreed. "Did you already order it? Or do we gotta wait?"

"It'll be quick. Twenty minutes."

Nathan groaned inwardly. Twenty minutes felt like twenty hours. He just wanted to get home and to lie down and relax. Maybe, like Mrs. Davis said, if he had a nap, he'd get enough energy to finish his schoolwork. And then he could go to bed, and he wouldn't be so tired for school tomorrow.

Mama pulled in at the pizza joint a few minutes later. "You going to come in with me?" she questioned.

"I just need to rest my eyes a bit," Nathan said. "Is that okay?"

She looked disappointed, but she left the keys in the ignition and climbed out. "Listen to the radio if you like. I'll try to be quick."

Nathan nestled into the lumpy backpack and closed his eyes. Just to rest for a bit.

The next thing Nathan knew, Mama was shaking him gently by the shoulder, calling his name. "Nathaniel! Wake up, sleepyhead! Come on, time to wake up, sweetie."

He lifted his head and looked around. It took a moment to get oriented. Mama pushed a pizza box into his hand. "Here, I need you to hold that. Take it. You got it?"

Nathan nodded, gripping it and keeping it level while she climbed back into the car and settled in.

"See, I told you it wouldn't be long," Mama said.

"Hardly had time to blink," Nathan agreed, rubbing his eyes sheepishly.

Mama laughed. "You are the silliest boy. But I love you. So, tell me all about school now. You heard about my day. Did you make some friends?"

Nathan stared out the window. "I met some people," he hedged. "I don't know who all will be my friends, yet. But I met a few. It seems like a good school."

"The reports I read were all very positive. That's why I tried to find a house in this area. There's good things going on at that school."

"You'd be happy with the dinner in the cafeteria," Nathan advised her. "Everything's real healthy, and they make sure you're eating a balanced meal. Fruits and vegetables and everything. They've got a real system going."

"I read about that!" she agreed. "It was one of the first schools in the state to get rid of all of the junk food, start buying and making fresh, and educating the students on eating healthy. That's real good, I'm happy about that. Maybe you'll be able to start feeling better, putting some meat on those bones."

"Yeah, that'd be good," Nathan agreed.

"We'll say a special prayer at supper today. Ask the Lord to get you healthy again. Heal your body."

Nathan glanced over at her, not turning his head, just looking out the corner of his eye at her. They had already had lots of prayers for his health. He had a sneaking suspicion that the Lord didn't want to heal him. He thought it might be due to his own lack of faith. The Bible said you needed faith to be healed, and Nathan's wavered. He wasn't a strong believer like Mama. Oddly enough, she thought that he was, thought that he was even more righteous than her. He felt guilty when he thought of all of the things he did that she didn't know that. Or thought of doing. Or thought of other people. He was far from the perfect little boy that she thought he was. So she had faith that he could be healed. Even though Nathan didn't believe it anymore. The doctors said this was something he would have for the rest of his life. But Mama read him stories about people who had been healed miraculously. Not just from the Bible. She read him stories that she found online, about people who had been healed by prayer, or fasting, or laying on of hands. The doctors called it 'spontaneous,' but it was surely a miracle.

"You can never go wrong by praying," he said.

Mama nodded vigorously. "That's what I always say," she agreed. "You can never go wrong with prayer."

The smells of the pizza filled the car, and pretty soon, Nathan's stomach was growling despite what he'd thought earlier. He actually was hungry. Nathan wished fleetingly that it was the first sign that he would be healed. But he didn't dare believe it.

Chapter Four

NATHAN WOKE UP DISORIENTED, not knowing where he was, or when it was, or what he was doing there. He sat up and looked around the dark room, but could only make out vague shapes. He was lying on something soft, with slightly scratchy material, with a blanket over him. But it didn't feel like a bed. And it was too soft to be his sleeping bag. He felt around, and swung his feet off the edge of the couch. It was a couch. Nathan tried to marshal his thoughts and make the connections. He had fallen asleep on the couch. But where? And when was it?

It was dark, so it was night. Still time to be sleeping. But his bladder was sending powerful signals that he was going to have to get up, or end up in wet clothes and blankets. He stood up and reached his arms out far in front of him to keep from banging into anything. He found the wall and followed it around, looking for the door. He kept bumping into things and stubbing his toes. He didn't feel any closer in sorting out where he was and getting closer to the bathroom, and that was a problem.

"Mama? Mama!"

He heard her stirring.

"Mama? Where are you?" Nathan called.

"Nathaniel? What's wrong?"

She turned a light on somewhere. Nathan blinked, able to see some dim shapes, but still disoriented. A hallway light went on, as footsteps came toward him, and Nathan squinted and shaded his eyes against the sudden light. He hurried down the hall, eventually identifying the bathroom and rushing in. He flipped on the light switch and shut the door quickly behind him, even though Mama was calling his name again, asking what was wrong.

After relieving himself, Nathan sighed and wiped down the toilet where he had splashed. He washed his hands and opened the door. Mama was standing right on the other side.

"Nathaniel? Are you okay?"

Nathan nodded. "I didn't know where I was," he said. "I just woke up, and I couldn't see anything or remember where I was."

"I'm sorry," she stroked a curl of Nathan's hair. "You fell asleep on the couch and I just covered you up. I didn't think about you waking up and not knowing where you were."

Nathan tried to cover a yawn. "It's not your fault," he said. "Just a new place."

She gave him a hug around the shoulders. "Well, let's get you settled in your bed this time. There's a night light in there, so you can see a bit if you wake up again."

Nathan agreed, and they walked together to his new bedroom. He hadn't even seen it with the furniture in it yet. They had eaten supper, and Nathan fell asleep on the couch without even going to see his room and how Mama had fixed it up.

"A bed, yay!" he said with a little cheer, making her laugh.

"Yay!" she echoed softly. She pulled back the covers for Nathan, and he climbed in. She tucked him up and kissed him on the forehead.

"All right, Love Bug. You go back to sleep, okay?"

"Yes'm," Nathan agreed, his eyes closed. "I'm already there."

He felt a light stroke across his cheek, and then he was asleep again.

Then it was morning. Nathan stretched sleepily, enjoying the warmth and coziness of his new bed. He looked around the room, taking in the details that he hadn't been able to see the night before. A blue and white quilt covered him on the bed. There was a chest of drawers, the surface distressed, but still serviceable. There were blue curtains on the window. And a study desk in the corner, at the foot of the bed. No chair yet, but there were chairs around the kitchen table, and he could borrow one of them.

"Honey, I told you it's time to get up," Mama prompted, appearing in the doorway again. "Get out of bed and get ready."

Nathan drew in a long breath, and slid his feet off of the bed to get up. He was still in his school clothes from the day before. Nathan's stomach clenched. "I fell asleep and didn't get my homework done," he said.

Mama waved her hand. "I'll write you a note."

"I should have gotten it done. I can't believe I just went to sleep."

P.D. WORKMAN

"Don't worry about it, sweetie. You didn't do it on purpose. We'll get you caught up. But there are going to be some bumps in the road while you adjust to the new school and the work."

Nathan didn't relish the idea of giving Mrs. Davis the note saying that he hadn't done his work. He reluctantly stood up. "Okay, I'm up," he pointed out. "I have to get changed."

She nodded and closed the door. "I'll get breakfast on," she called from the hallway.

"What did you get?" Nathan called. "Could I have eggs? Or oatmeal?"

"I'll make eggs," she agreed, and he heard her footsteps retreating to the kitchen. Nathan quickly undressed, threw his clothes on the floor near the door, and pulled on a fresh outfit. He combed his hair without looking at it, and wandered out to the kitchen as the eggs were sizzling.

"Mmm, smells good, Mama."

She nodded, getting out the plates. "What do you think of this?" she questioned, looking down at her navy blue dress and holding her arms out slightly from her body.

"For...?"

"For an interview. If the store calls me back."

"Sure. It's nice." She was waiting for more, and Nathan thought about it, trying to figure out what she wanted to hear. "Professional," he offered.

Mama smiled. "Good."

She went back to the eggs, and in a few minutes was sliding them onto the plates. Toast popped out of the toaster, and she put a slice on Nathan's plate.

"I don't want toast," Nathan protested. "I mean--no, thank you, ma'am."

"Just eggs won't hold you over. I'll get some jam to put on your toast."

Nathan opened his mouth to stop her, then changed his mind. She was already set on getting the jam out. There was no point in arguing it. He started to dig into the eggs while she brought over jam and honey and set them beside him.

"Wait," she said, stopping him. Nathan stopped, and then folded his hands expectantly. He should have known better than to start eating without some kind of prayer over the food. "No," Mama said, grinning. She pulled out her phone and framed him with it. "First real breakfast at the new house."

Nathan held still for the shot, smiling the best he could, then rolled his eyes when she lowered the phone. "Now can we eat?"

"Now we can have blessing."

She sat down on her chair and joined hands with him to offer a prayer. Nathan's eggs were getting cold by the time they started eating. And it was so late that there was no time to eat the toast anyway.

Nathan wasn't able to find Summer or anyone familiar before school started. Then he made several wrong turns before he managed to find Mrs. Davis' classroom of the day before. The bell had rung a second time by the time he managed to find the classroom, and walked into the room late, behind everyone else, soaked with nervous sweat. Mrs. Davis was trying to settle the class and quiet them down for their first lesson. She looked over as Nathan walked in.

"Make it okay, Nathan?" she questioned.

His face got hotter still, and he nodded. He stopped and stood there, wondering where he was supposed to sit. The big desk that he had occupied the first day was now occupied by its owner, apparently no longer sick. Bly Munro filled up every inch of the seat; in fact, his large bottom slopped over the edges like a full water balloon.

"They brought in another desk for us," Mrs. Davis reassured him, and she directed him to a desk right at the front of the class. As usual, shortest students in front, so that people could see. You couldn't very well put a guy like Bly Munro in the front, where he would eclipse the view of the board for half the class. Nathan slid into the seat, stowing his backpack underneath.

"Thank you," he murmured.

"Good. Now, if I could get everyone to settle down. It's time to begin."

Conversations around the room petered out and the other students started to open up their books. Nathan looked around to see what text they were opening, and followed suit.

The first class had been English again, which Nathan was beginning to think was one of his better classes. He'd always liked to read, and he did fairly well in English without having to put a lot of work into it. It was certainly less confusing than math, and less boring than social studies. And then there was phys ed...

Nathan traipsed down toward gym with the other boys. Nathan didn't try to walk with Summer, since the girls' locker room was down a different hall than the boys'. He lagged behind a little, not eager to go to the class. Mama had spent yesterday buying furniture and getting things set for the house, so he still didn't have his gym clothes. Nathan supposed that if he'd been eager for the class, he could have just taken any old t shirt and pair of shorts to use until he got the prescribed school gym strip. But since he wasn't eager to join the class, he was fine with sitting on the sidelines.

"What's this I hear about you sitting in my desk, shrimp?" a voice growled from behind Nathan.

He startled and turned his head to look at Bly, his heart dropping to his stomach. "I'm sorry," he said. "It wasn't like I picked it, Mrs. Davis just put me in it because it was the only empty seat yesterday and they didn't have another desk for me yet--" Nathan sputtered to explain.

"How do you think I feel, knowing *your* skinny butt was in my desk, getting your stinkin' cooties all over--my--" Bly could barely seem to speak, he was so angry over the invasion of his personal space. But then without warning, his face broke into a wide grin, and the reason that he couldn't speak was because he was laughing and snorting uncontrollably.

Nathan stared at Bly, completely confused. "What--?"

Bly rubbed at his eyes. His face was bright red and blotchy. He swore weakly. "No need to wet your pants, shrimp. I'm just kidding," he said in a high, unsteady voice, trying to control his mirth.

Nathan tried to smile, but he knew he must look as confused as he felt.

"I'm just pullin' your leg," Bly said. "I don't care if you sat in my desk."

He wiped at tiny tears in the corners of his eyes, still snickering and snorting. He cursed several times, as if that might help him to settle down. "Man, you looked terrified," he said. "What'd you think, I was gonna eat you for dinner?"

Nathan swallowed. "Well..."

Bly slapped him on the back, almost knocking Nathan to the floor. "I promise. I'm harmless. I just couldn't resist," he explained.

Nathan let out a long sigh, trying to recover his composure. He wasn't about to be beaten up or bullied by the biggest boy in the school. It was just a joke. The two of them were straggling behind the other students. Bly was breathing heavily, and not just from laughing. He swung his arms, trying to speed up a bit.

"I got asthma, and the medications make me put on weight," he explained. "I didn't used to be so fat. But at least it didn't keep me short, like some kids," he drew himself up, looking proud of his towering bulk. "What about you? You got asthma?"

Nathan shook his head. "No. Just short for no particular reason." He paused, thinking about it. "Actually, my mama says that my daddy was short when he was a young'un. She thinks I'll catch up in high school."

Bly nodded, his breath coming in short puffs as they tried to keep up with the rest of the group. When they reached the locker room, Nathan stopped.

"I don't have my gym clothes yet," he explained. "So I gotta sit out."

"Lucky dog," Bly growled, and made his way down the stairs to the boys' locker room.

Nathan headed to the gym, and sat down on the bench he had occupied the previous day. The coach saw him come in, and shook his head.

"You don't have your uniform yet?" he questioned.

Nathan shook his head.

"I told you that you have to get it quickly. We can't have you sitting out every day because you haven't got it yet. I'll make you play in your street clothes if you don't get what you need."

Nathan stared down at the floor. "My mama had lots of other things to do yesterday," he explained. "Getting furniture and unpacking and everything. And she's looking for a job, too."

"Well, just see to it that she gets you your gym strip soon. Or you're going to be walking around in sweaty clothes for half the day."

Nathan nodded. It was only a couple of minutes before the faster students were finished changing and trickling into the gym, talking and visiting. The coach waited, looking at his watch. After a few more minutes, as latecomers hurried in, he demanded:

"Is that everyone?"

"Munro is still down there," one of them replied.

The coach rolled his eyes and shook his head. He got the class doing some warm-up exercises, and eventually Bly came into the gym. His body strained to escape the too-small gym uniform, and he was puffing more than ever.

"Hey, Coach, I dunno if I should participate today," he started to say, making his way across the room to where the coach was standing.

"You're participating," the coach replied briskly. "Unless I hear you wheezing, there's no reason for you to sit out. You need the exercise," he said pointedly.

"It's just 'cause of the medication," Bly protested, smoothing the t shirt over his stomach as if he could just tuck his bulk away beneath it.

"It's more than just that," the coach disagreed. "Get out there and start warming up. Run two circuits."

"Two?" Bly protested with a groan.

"Everyone else is doing five, and they're half done already. Get to it."

Bly jogged over to the circuit station nearest to him, and started to do clumsy jumping jacks. He looked over at Nathan, watching from the bench, and shook his head. Within five minutes, Nathan heard Bly's breathing change from labored gasps to wheezing. The whole gym heard it, and many of the other students stopped and turned around to look at him. The coach jogged over to Bly, who was standing bent over with his hands on his knees, face cherry red.

"Use your inhaler," he told Bly firmly.

Bly just stood there, wheezing. Nathan felt his own chest getting tight and felt like he couldn't get enough air. He clenched his hands into fists, anxious for Bly. Very few students were working on their circuits anymore, standing around to watch the drama.

The coach patted at Bly's pockets and pulled out the asthma puffer. He held it up to Bly's face.

"Here you go, breathe it deep," he instructed.

Bly took the inhaler and put it in his mouth. Nathan wondered how he could get the medicine down into his lungs when he was wheezing so hard.

But in a couple of minutes, Bly's breathing had eased. The redness started to fade from his face and neck.

"Thanks, coach," he said, and took a step toward the bench where Nathan was sitting.

"No, you finish your circuit," the coach insisted. "I don't care if you walk it. But you should be fine now that you've had your inhaler."

Bly stared at him with dismay and disbelief. "I can't."

"Yes, you can. You're breathing fine now. You should be taking your inhaler before class to prevent an attack in the first place."

Bly coughed. He looked at the coach pleadingly, hoping for a reprieve. But the man stood firm.

"Like I said, you can walk it if you think you could trigger another attack. But finish the circuit."

Bly reluctantly went back to his warm-up. Everyone else went back to their circuits, although there were frequent glances toward Bly. Nathan watched him work slowly through the assigned circuit. Even though everyone else had done five and Bly had only done one, he was the last one to finish and shuffle back over to the group seated on the floor waiting for further instruction.

Nathan knew more of the students now, but during the lunch hour he still found himself alone, wondering where to go and what to do. Bly was off with his friends. He guessed that Summer was off with hers. He went through the line in the cafeteria, being sure to get his 'five,' including the chocolate avocado pudding that Mal had said that he liked. He looked around the cafeteria seating, but already knew there would be no seats free so late. He went out into the hall, and looked for the spot that Summer and her friends had chosen the previous day. Summer saw him looking at them and motioned him over.

"Hey, Nathan. Come and sit with us."

He gratefully joined them. Without a word, he put the chocolate pudding on Mal's tray. Mal touched it, and looked at Nathan with pursed lips.

"You keep it," he said, pushing it back toward Nathan.

Nathan was surprised. "You said you liked the chocolate pudding. That's why I got it for you."

"I changed my mind," Mal said.

Nathan studied him. He remembered the conversation from the day before, and his stomach clenched into a tight knot. "I told you, I don't have... that," Nathan said in a low voice, trying to keep the others from hearing the conversation.

"That's what you say," Mal agreed. "But I've seen pictures of guys that have got it. And that's what you look like."

"You can't tell by looking at someone!"

Mal shrugged. "I don't want it. You have it, or throw it out."

"I didn't even open it. Even if I did have something contagious, I haven't touched it. It's safe."

"Take it!" Mal told him sharply.

Nathan took the pudding back off of Mal's tray. The others had looked over to see what the problem was. Nathan swallowed.

"Anyone want an extra dessert?" he questioned hoarsely, offering it up.

"I'll have it," volunteered Simon, the other boy who had been bugging Nathan about Summer the day before.

He reached over and plucked it from Nathan's hand, before anyone else could get it. Mal elbowed him.

"Hey! What? You snooze, you lose, Mal."

"I don't want it. And neither do you."

"Who are you kidding? Of course I want it."

"He's already got his germs all over it," Mal said. "You want to catch what he's got?"

Simon looked at the container, puzzled. "What are you talking about?" he questioned. "It's still sealed. What would I catch?"

"I don't have anything contagious," Nathan protested. "You're not going to catch anything."

But Simon had already lost his enthusiasm, looking at Mal uncertainly. He handed the pudding back to Nathan yet again. Nathan shook his head and didn't offer it to anyone else. His stomach felt sick over the whole thing. Why would Mal say something like that? Nathan had never done anything to hurt him. They barely knew each other. Even though Nathan was only half-done his dinner, he felt too sick to his stomach to finish. He stood up and dumped his tray into the nearest garbage can and walked away. He heard Summer's voice behind him.

"What happened? What's wrong?"

He kept going. Summer scrambled to her feet and followed behind Nathan, grabbing at his arm. "Hang on, Nathan. Hey, don't worry about what those guys say, they're just being jerks. Don't take off..."

He shook loose of her grasp, and ducked into the restroom, where she couldn't follow. He stayed there for the rest of the lunch hour. When the class bell rang, he considered just staying there in the bathroom for the rest of the day. No one would bug him, and he wouldn't have to listen to boring classes, and he could get a drink or use the toilet whenever he wanted to.

But he didn't have the courage to follow through. Mrs. Davis would want to know where he was, and when he didn't come back, they'd call Mama, and then she would be all upset and wanting to know what was going on. It was better to just fly below the radar, to pretend that everything was fine.

Nathan walked down the column of cars to Mama's. As he got in, a group of boys walked by behind him, laughing and talking, and he heard one of them say 'momma' in a high, childish voice. He glanced over at them as he got into his seat, but didn't see anyone there that he recognized. Was he just being paranoid, or were they laughing at him? Had word already gotten around what a mama's boy he was?

He pulled the car door shut, and avoided Mama's welcoming kiss. "Hi. Can we go?" She looked at him, hurt and surprise in her eyes. Nathan looked over his shoulder. "There's other cars that want to pull in," he pointed out, as if that had been his reason for saying it in the first place.

She pulled the car away from the curb without a word. Nathan watched as they drove by the group that had just walked past him. He still didn't recognize anyone. But that doesn't mean that they didn't know him. He had to remember several hundred new faces. They only had to remember one.

"Can I take the bus home tomorrow?" he questioned.

"Well, I suppose. Why? You don't like me picking you up?"

Nathan looked for a good excuse. "It's just extra gas," he said, "and all your time. I can walk from the bus. It's good exercise, and it helps me unwind at the end of the day."

She was silent, considering. "I don't mind picking you up," she said tentatively.

"I know... but I need some time to myself at the end of the day, to relax. Talk to God for a spell."

Mama nodded. "That's a good idea," she admitted. "It's always a good idea to share with the Lord at the end of your day."

Nathan nodded. They were both quiet for a few minutes.

"Better day today?" Mama questioned as the silence drew out longer.

"Yeah, I'm feeling lots better," Nathan said, squirming inwardly at the lie. But he could be excused for lying in order to make her feel better, couldn't he? He didn't want her fussing and worrying, as she inevitably would if she realized that he was having a hard time fitting in right away. He wasn't quite as tired as he had been the previous day, but still felt like all he had the energy left to do was to go home and lie down.

"That's good. I was worried yesterday that I had made you do too much. You aren't strong enough for it."

"I was just tired. I'm okay now."

"You sure?" She looked over at him. "Ya'll still have big black circles under your eyes."

"I'll be fine."

"I sure hope so. I'd never forgive myself if moving was too much and made you sick. I just want to keep you well and safe."

"I know. I'm okay."

As they arrived at the house, Nathan remembered about phys ed. "Hey... do you think you could get my gym outfit? The coach says he'll just make me run in my clothes if I don't have my gym strip."

"Oh, I keep forgetting it." She looked at her watch. "I'll go now and see what I can get. Will you be okay on your own for a while?"

Nathan nodded. "It's good for me," he told her. "I need some 'lone time now and then."

She gave him a smile and a laugh. "Do you have your key so you can let yourself in?"

Nathan checked his pocket. "Yes'm. Right here."

"Good. I'll see you in an hour or so."

Nathan nodded and got out of the car. "See you soon then."

He watched her drive back off, waving at him. He turned to go up the sidewalk into the house.

"Hi, Nathan!"

Nathan looked up and saw Delia skipping down the street. He nodded. "Hi, Delia."

"You're going home, huh?"

"Yep," Nathan agreed. What else was he going to say? Of course he was going home, she could see that plain as day.

"You went to school today?"

Nathan nodded, walking slowly up the sidewalk.

"Me too," she let out a dramatic sigh. "What a looong day."

"Was it? Mine too." Nathan stretched, trying to shake of his sluggishness. "I think I might lie down for a nap."

Delia shook her head vigorously. "A nap? Who wants a nap? I want to play! I've been waiting all day!"

Nathan shrugged. "Well, I didn't sleep too well. I might need a nap."

"I hate naps. I hate sleeping."

"Oh. Uh-huh."

Nathan was halfway up the sidewalk now, and not sure how to end the conversation. It wouldn't be polite to just walk into the house and shut the door. But he wasn't sure what she really wanted out of him.

"Oh, there's the witch," Delia said.

Nathan looked at her, startled. "What?"

"The witch," Delia pointed to a woman two doors down, who had just come out of her house to take out the garbage. She was an older woman, like someone's grandmother. Her hair was a reddish-brown, not grey or white. Even from the distance they were away, her face appeared to be deeply wrinkled, and her eyes were black hollows.

"She's not a witch," Nathan dismissed. "There's no such thing as witches. Not real ones."

Delia looked at him. "If there is, she is one," she asserted.

Nathan rolled his eyes and shook his head slightly. Was she serious? A witch? "Why do you think she's a witch?" he questioned.

"She lives by herself, and she's so ugly. And she has a black cat. She doesn't like kids, or anyone visiting her. She always wear black, and she cooks stuff that smells really weird. Potions."

"Sounds like she's just a lonely old woman," Nathan observed. "She's not a witch."

"She can predict the future," Delia insisted. "And she puts a curse on you if she doesn't like you. If she catches you trespassing on your property or something. One boy *died*."

"Died of what?" Nathan questioned.

"Died of a curse. I told you."

Nathan watched the woman walk back from her garbage can. She walked slowly; he thought she might be holding a cane in her hand, but couldn't see through the fence. She glanced over in Nathan's direction and Delia squealed and dove behind the short picket fence, out of sight.

"You're silly," he proclaimed.

"That's what you say. Until she curses you."

"You've been watching too much TV."

Delia's eyes lit up. "I saw a show about witches on TV."

"Yeah, I'll bet you did," Nathan agreed. He watched the neighbor lady go into her house again. Delia got to her feet. "She's just a lonely old lady. You should be nice to her."

Delia stood on the lower cross board of the fence. "You'll see," she promised.

Nathan nodded. "I have to go inside now," he said. "I have homework to do."

"Okay. Bye."

"Bye."

Nathan let himself into the house and shut the door behind him. He relished the peace, taking a deep breath of the quiet atmosphere. It might not be home yet, but at least it was quiet.

Chapter Five

NATHAN WAS DREAMING BEFORE Mama shook him awake. He tried to hang onto the dream, to remember what it had been about, and groaned. It had been a nice dream. And he was still tired. He wanted to go back to sleep and keep dreaming it.

"Wake up, Nathaniel. It's time to get up, honey."

Nathan tried to remember what day it was. He worked through the days in recent memory, trying to untangle the threads. "It's the weekend, Mama," he protested. "I want to sleep in."

"You've already slept in, baby. And yesterday you slept almost the whole day. It's time to get up now."

If he'd slept all of yesterday, than today must be Sunday. Nathan forced himself to sit up, rubbing his eyes and trying to convince himself that he'd had enough sleep and would be able to get through the day without being tired today.

"That's a good boy," Mama approved. "You get up, and we'll have a nice brunch together, okay?"

Nathan nodded and scratched his leg. "Okay. What else are we doing today?"

"We'll have church. Praise God on his Sabbath."

Nathan got up, shuffling toward the bathroom. "Are we going out to church, or staying home?" he questioned.

"Staying home. We'll get a congregation, but I haven't had time enough yet."

"Okay. Be out in a minute," Nathan said, and shut the bathroom door behind him.

He took a long time in the shower, knowing that Mama would need some time to get brunch together. Brunch usually meant pancakes or french toast. When he got out, Nathan could smell sausages. He wrapped a big towel around himself and pattered down the hall back to his room. He pulled on a t shirt and bluejeans, and combed his hair, and headed for the kitchen.

"Hi, baby. Feeling better now?" Mama greeted.

"Yes'm," Nathan said. And it was true. He felt like a real person for the first time in days. He'd really needed the weekend, just to sleep and get some energy back.

She glanced over her shoulder at him, smiling. But when she looked at him, her brows drew together in a frown. "You need to get your Sunday clothes on," she said.

Nathan groaned. "Not yet!"

"Today is the Sabbath. I want to see you in your worship clothes. All day."

"I don't want to spill breakfast on it," Nathan tried. "I'll dress after."

"You'll change now, young man. You know that. Ain't that always been the rule?"

Nathan nodded, but she wasn't looking at him anymore, her attention back on the stove. "Yes'm. I guess so," he admitted.

"Well, that isn't going to change because we moved somewhere new. Now go get dressed."

"Yes'm," Nathan sighed. He turned around and headed back for his room. He saw Mama's laptop on the table as he walked by. "Mama!" he complained.

She turned around to see what he was upset about, and smiled when she saw the image on her screen. "I can't help it," she said with a giggle. "You're so cute when you're asleep."

Nathan read the words she had posted beside the picture.

"You can't come in and take pictures of me when I'm asleep," he protested.

She shook her head. "I don't know why you're so embarrassed," she said. "It's not like you sleep in the nude, or in your little undies or something."

Nathan's face got hot. "Mama--you wouldn't!"

She laughed at his expression. "I wouldn't do that," she agreed. "I don't post anything that might be taken the wrong way. But that," she looked fondly at the picture of Nathan fast asleep, his hair awry, mouth open, and a dribble of drool down one side of his chin. "That is just cute, Bug."

"Don't take pictures when I'm asleep," he pleaded again.

Mama smiled and shook her head. Nathan headed back to his room. He reluctantly took off his casual clothes, and looked in his closet for the neatly-pressed, long-sleeved white shirt. He pulled it on, yanked on his black pants, socks, and dress shoes. Feeling tired just from that, he sat down on his bed and opened his drawer to look through his ties. He picked out a nice bright red one, and tied it loosely around his neck. Before going back out to the kitchen, he looked in the mirror to comb his hair again and tucked in his shirt.

Nathan walked back into the kitchen as Mama was putting dishes on the table. She looked up to see him, and smiled broadly.

"That's better," she approved. She walked up and took both his hands while she looked at him. She adjusted his tie, snugging up the knot to lay right against his throat. Nathan swallowed and loosened it slightly. "I have such a handsome boy," Mama said. She gave him a tight hug, and kissed him on the cheek.

"Thanks," Nathan said, his voice coming out a bit gruff. He patted her on the back. "Brunch looks great."

She released him and turned around to survey the table.

"It's going to be great," she agreed. "I love our Sunday brunches together."

"Me too," Nathan agreed. After making sure that everything was on the table, Nathan pulled Mama's chair out for her, sliding it forward as she sat down.

"Thank you, sir."

Nathan sat down, and folded his hands for prayer.

"Would you like to offer it today?" Mama suggested.

Nathan cleared his throat and nodded. There would be lots of opportunities to pray today. He might as well take an easy one. He gave a brief thanks and blessing, and then they were ready to eat.

The cable had been hooked up. Nathan didn't remember the cable man getting there, it must have been while he was sleeping on Saturday. Mama flipped through the channels, and they found and watched a couple of worship services. The second one was just ending when the doorbell rang. They looked at each other. Mama got up and answered the door.

Nathan heard Delia's voice. "Can Nathan come and play?"

"No, not today," Mama advised.

"Is he still sick today?"

Nathan vaguely remembered that the doorbell had rung several times on Saturday, and he supposed that at least one of those had been Delia inquiring after him.

"No, but today is the Sabbath."

"What's that mean?"

"It's our day of worship."

"Oh... so you're getting ready for church?" Delia inquired.

"We're worshipping at home today."

"Oh... for how long?"

"All day," Mama said, with a smile in her voice.

"All day? Whoa."

"Would you like to come in and join us?" Mama questioned.

Nathan expected Delia to say no, but she was apparently up for anything, once. "Sure," she agreed.

Mama stepped back from the door, and Delia entered. She came into the sitting room. "Wow," she observed, looking Nathan over. "Don't you look spiffy!"

Nathan felt his cheeks flush. He scratched the back of his head. "Uh, thanks."

"So," Delia looked around the room. "What are you doing?"

"We were just watching one of the TV services," Nathan explained. "But now, we'll probably..." he trailed off, looking at Mama for guidance.

"How about some scripture stories?" Mama suggested.

"Okay," Nathan agreed. He motioned for Delia to sit down, and she sat on the couch close to him. "Do you have a favorite Bible story?"

Delia considered. "Yeah, how about the one about Noah?" she suggested.

Nathan grinned. "That's one of my favorites," he said. "Lemme show you some pictures I have from it, and then Mama can read it to us."

He went to his room and examined the shelves, eventually pulling out the illustrated stories that he was looking for. He went back to the sitting room, and sat beside Delia again.

"Here, look at these," he said, opening it up and thumbing through to find the pictures of Noah and the animals.

"Ooooh," Delia crooned, looking over the gorgeous spreads. "Those are so beautiful. You can see... every hair and feather..."

Nathan flipped the pages slowly, giving her lots of time to look at each picture. Mama started to read the story from the Bible. Nathan sat back, closing his eyes and envisioning it. He'd seen all of the pictures, could see them in his head, Mama's words bringing them to life.

Nathan became aware that Delia was poking him. He jolted upright. "Amen!" he declared.

Delia giggled. "You fell asleep," she accused.

"I wasn't asleep," Nathan protested. "I was just imagining it. All those animals... it must have stunk."

She giggled again. Mama stood up, putting the Bible on the shelf. "I think we'd better do something active, and wake Nathaniel up," she suggested.

"I'm awake," Nathan insisted.

"Come on. On your feet," she encouraged.

Nathan got up and stretched, trying to suppress a broad smile of embarrassment. Mama was fiddling with the stereo, and Nathan knew what was coming. He motioned for Delia to get up too. She stood up, looking nervous because she didn't know what happening next.

The music started up, loud and fast. Mama bumped the volume back down a bit so that they'd be able to hear their own voices. Mama and Nathan started clapping, and it didn't take too long for Delia to get the idea and join in. They all clapped to the rousing beat, and Nathan and Mama sang out the refrains. Delia managed to get a few 'amens' in, even if they were off-beat. At the beginning of the third song, Mama grabbed Nathan and danced with him. They shook to the beat, and whirled around the room, sometimes holding hands and sometimes apart. Nathan managed to make it to the end of the song, then collapsed on the couch, huffing and puffing and holding his hand over his pounding heart.

"Hallelujah!" he finished, with an arm-pump.

Mama laughed. Her face was pink and glowing. She motioned to Delia. "Come on, dance with me," she suggested, as the next song started up.

"I don't know what to do," Delia protested.

"Just do as the Spirit moves you! It don't matter, just give glory to the Lord!"

Delia jittered to the beat, looking around self-consciously. Mama clapped and stomped and spun around. Delia copied her movements slowly, awkward and off the beat. Nathan tried to clap to the beat to encourage her, but was exhausted from his dance. He hummed a little to the song, watching the girls spin around the room, rejoicing with the music.

Mama only lasted one more song, and then she collapsed next to Nathan and gave him a big hug. Delia stopped dancing and stood there laughing.

"That was fun!" she said. "What else are we going to do?"

Mama ruffled Nathan's hair, looking down at him. "I think Nathaniel's going to need to lie down a spell." She kissed the top of his head. "He tires easy lately," she explained softly, as if Nathan couldn't hear her if she spoke quietly.

"Is he sick?" Delia questioned. "What's wrong with him?"

"The Lord tries all of us," Mama said. "Nathaniel's challenge is infirmity in his body. Do you want to pray with me for him?"

Delia twisted her fingers together, shifting her feet around. "I don't know how to pray," she said. "I mean... I know you talk to God, but I don't know the right way..."

"Come here." Mama held her hand out toward Delia, who came closer and let Mama take her by the hand. "There ain't no wrong way to pray. Whatever comes into your heart is right. It doesn't matter what the words are, it doesn't even matter if we can understand the words. It's *all* right."

"Maybe this time, you could pray," Delia suggested.

Mama nodded. "Ya'll come here. Hold hands together."

Nathan and Delia joined hands with each other and with Mama. Mama raised her voice to the Lord, praying for Nathan's healing. He concentrated on her words, trying to hold them in his heart. If he just had enough faith, maybe he could be healed. They'd read lots of stories of people being healed. Watched them on the TV, too, and seen some in person. He knew his faith was small and weak, and prayed for it to grow bigger. Jesus said that faith the size of a mustard seed could move mountains. Nathan thought that his must be about the size of a dust mote. He needed faith like Mama's. Faith that was strong.

When Mama said 'amen,' Nathan and Delia echoed her. Nathan opened his eyes and saw that Delia had tears in her eyes. He looked away.

"All right, Bug," Mama said. "We'd better let you rest now. Say 'bye' to Delia."

Nathan nodded at Delia. "See ya."

Delia gave a little wave. "I had fun," she said. "Thanks for letting me come."

"Everyone is always welcome at our worship," Mama said. "I'd love to be able to get my own little congregation going. You feel free to join us any time, and invite your friends and family."

"I will!" Delia agreed. "Bye, Nathan."

"Bye."

Delia headed out the door.

"Do you need a hand?" Mama asked Nathan. "Or do you want to lie down on the couch?"

Nathan considered just laying there, not having to move anywhere, and sighed in frustration. "I gotta get a drink and use the john." Mama held out her hand to him, and Nathan climbed to his feet with her assistance. "That was a great dance," he told her.

She smiled back at him. "It was," she agreed.

She walked him to the bathroom. "Okay now?" she questioned.

Nathan nodded. "I'll be fine, Mama."

"Okay. Holler if you need me."

Nathan didn't sleep the rest of the day away, but was back up in an hour or two. They didn't dance again, but read their scriptures together silently, played softer gospel music, and talked.

"Do you think you got that job at the store?" Nathan questioned.

"It was a good interview. I think I will."

"That will be good."

"It's a manager's job, not cashier, and the hours are good. Mostly while you're in school."

"Will it give you enough time for church work too?"

"If it doesn't, I'll find something else."

Nathan nodded.

"What are you going to do? Ring doorbells?"

"To start with, probably. Start seeing who is interested. Maybe Delia will be able to bring along someone else next time. She seemed to have a good time."

"That's because you're such a good dancer," Nathan said, snuggling up to her on the couch.

"My boy has always loved the dancing," Mama declared, putting her arm around him and giving him a squeeze.

Nathan murmured his agreement.

"You can invite your friends from school, too," she reminded him. "Anyone you think might be interested."

"When I get to know people a bit better," Nathan said, and smothered a yawn. "I don't know who might be interested yet."

"Well, it never hurts to ask. The worst they can say is no."

The worst that they could do was to tease and bully him about it for as long as they went to school together. He'd seen it before, and he would be pretty careful before ever inviting anyone out to services again. He had to be sure that they would really want to come, before he'd do that. Certainly not in the first week that he knew them.

Chapter Six

ONDAY NIGHT, SUPPER WAS homemade instead of takeout. Well, it was cooked at home, anyway. Mama hadn't actually made it, but had heated it herself. One of these days, she would get some time to start cooking again, when her whole day wasn't taken by getting them settled and comfortable in the new house and finding a job.

"What have you heard about the lady that lives a couple doors down?" Mama questioned, motioning in the direction of the neighbor.

Nathan looked up from his supper at her, his shoulders tensing. "What lady?" he questioned. He looked back down at his plate, pushing the potatoes around and spearing a few peas.

"The lady that lives two doors down, toward Delia's house. She walks with a cane. Have you heard anything about her?"

Nathan shook his head. "Not really. Where would I hear anything?"

"Maybe some of your friends know something about her. What kind of person she is."

Nathan shrugged his shoulders. "Delia maybe mentioned her once." Mama looked questioning, waiting for more. "Just silly kid stuff. You know, she's an old lady and she doesn't go out much, so little kids think she's a witch or something." He shook his head. "She looks lonely to me."

Mama nodded.

"Why?" Nathan asked. "You want to meet her?"

"I was already by there today, dropping off invitations." Nathan glanced over at the small stack of invitations to their family worship services beside Mama's computer. "I just wondered. She seemed... odd."

Nathan swirled his fork in his mashed potatoes, then pushed his plate an inch or two toward the center of the table.

"Everybody's odd. Aren't we supposed to be peculiar people?"

Mama laughed. She pointed her fork at him. "You're right there, Bug," she agreed. "No, I just wondered... She said she knew that we were going to be moving in, and was glad to see that we'd arrived... And she already knew that I was a pastor... It was a little unnerving."

Nathan nodded. "So she already heard about us from the other neighbors."

"You would think so... but I didn't get that feeling. I got the feeling... I don't know. I just got a weird feeling over there. Watchful-like. I can't describe it."

Nathan tapped his fork on the edge of the plate. "Is she going to come to worship?" he questioned.

"I don't think so. Eat up, honey."

"I can't. I'm full up." Mama looked at his plate. "I ate most of it," Nathan pointed out.

"You need to eat to keep up your energy. You need your vitamins."

"I know. I ate, but I'm full."

She picked at her own food. Nathan could tell that she was thinking about something, worrying it over in her mind. Still about the neighbor?

"Did you have gym today?" she questioned, in an obvious attempt to change the subject.

"Yes'm. Every day," Nathan agreed. "They say on the radio that all the schools are dropping phys ed, but we have it every single day."

"Did your uniform fit? What did you do?"

"Basketball. Lots of drills and stuff to warm up, and then a few minutes playing."

"I always liked basketball in school. Did you have fun?"

Nathan grimaced. He'd sat out as much as he could, only subbing in when he was forced to. He wasn't tall enough to shoot. Didn't have the strength or stamina to guard or block anyone, or run to the end of the court. The other players were pretty disgusted with his poor showing.

"I'm not very good at it," he admitted.

"But did you still have fun?"

Nathan shrugged. "Maybe once I get to know them better," he waffled.

He'd sooner sit on the sideline with Bly Munro and the other non-athletic boys and just watch the action. Bly had brought a note from his doctor saying that he wasn't allowed to do any vigorous exercise, which Bly was claiming as pretty much anything. Nathan didn't have a doctor's note, but the coach had obviously already recognized his limitations and wasn't pushing him as hard as he would other students.

"Her name is Chandra," Mama said out of the blue. "What kind of a name is Chandra?"

"Who?" Nathan questioned.

"That lady," she said, motioning toward the neighbors again. "Her name is Chandra Mullenny. That's just a weird name."

"It doesn't mean anything," Nathan said. "Lots of people have weird names. Maybe her mama read it in a book or something."

"She said she knew I was going to get that job. How could she know that?"

"Maybe she knows someone over there, and they said they were going to hire you," Nathan suggested.

"I got a real creepy feeling when she said it. Her eyes when she looks at you... it's like she's looking into your soul."

Nathan shifted uncomfortably. "I don't think it's anything to worry about, Mama. Really. Don't get yourself worked up over it."

"No, no I'm not..." she trailed off.

"We're just supposed to love our neighbors. I don't think God cares if they have a weird name."

"No," Mama agreed. "But he cares if they are fortune tellers or diviners." Her eyes were distant, the rest of her supper forgotten.

Nathan stood up. "I'll clear," he offered.

Mama looked startled, and handed him her plate. "Thanks, honey. You're always such a sweet boy. Such a good helper."

Nathan scraped the plates into the garbage, and loaded the dishwasher. He put the rest of the serving bowls in the fridge. Mama was still sitting at the table, not paying any attention to him.

"I guess I'll go do my homework," Nathan said. "Do you want anything, Mama?"

"Would you hand me my Bible, sweetie? Thanks."

He picked up her well-worn scriptures from beside the computer and handed them to her. He went to his room and pulled out his workbooks, feeling a sense of unease.

At lunch the next day, Nathan looked around for a seat. As usual, there weren't any in the cafeteria.

"There you are, Nathan! Come sit with us!"

Nathan turned at the touch on his arm. It was Summer. He looked down at his feet.

"No," he said, swallowing hard. "I'm just gonna sit by myself."

"Why?" Summer demanded, her voice going up a notch.

Nathan just looked at her. He wasn't one to talk about people behind their backs, but he figured she should be able to figure it out on her own. Summer frowned.

"Because of Mal? I know he can be a jerk sometimes, but..."

Nathan raised his eyebrows, waiting. Why should he hang around with a guy who was a jerk? Why would he sit with someone intent on bullying or ostracizing him?

"We've always hung around with him," Summer finished lamely. "I don't know. He wasn't always like that..."

Nathan looked around for somewhere to sit down. There still weren't any empty seats. He took a step toward the door to go to the gym. Summer fell in beside him.

"He used to be real quiet," Summer said. "Like you. He was nice. But... I dunno... hormones, or his parents' divorce, or something... he gets in these dark moods, and he lashes out..."

"I don't want to be around him," Nathan said. "If you want to hang out with him, that's fine. But not me. I don't need that kind of friend."

Summer looked at him with sad eyes, giving him one more chance to see how much she cared and to change his mind. But Nathan held fast. He'd lived lots of different places, and there were jerks all over. It was best to avoid them. Seeking them out was not a good idea.

"Okay... well..." Summer trailed off. "I guess I'll see you around, huh?"

Nathan nodded. "See you in class this afternoon."

They broke apart. Summer headed back down the hall to where her group of friends usually sat, and Nathan tried the gym. It was floor seating only, no chairs or tables, but nobody seemed to care. That's just the way that it was.

"Nathan, my man!"

Nathan looked around for the source of the voice. He saw Bly sitting on the floor in the corner, bending over his lunch tray. Bly motioned for him to come over. Nathan hesitated at first, but in spite of Bly's mock-anger when they had first met, the boy seemed to be pretty laid-back and easy to get along with. And he didn't appear to have many friends himself. Bly patted the floor beside him encouragingly.

"Come on. Pull up a floor."

Nathan conceded, and went over to sit with him. Bly took a big bite out of a black bean burger, spilling lettuce and tomato back onto his plate. He watched Nathan open up his lunch bag.

"You didn't get anything at the cafeteria today?"

"No." Nathan took out a chicken salad sandwich. "If I go there, I have to get a bunch of stuff that I don't want to eat. If I bring it from home, I can eat what I want."

Bly nodded. "Just don't let the supervisors get too close a look at it," Bly warned. "Or they'll make you take the other stuff anyway. All lunches are supposed to be up to code, whether they're from the cafeteria or from home. And they'll send home a note telling your mom that she's got to include fruits and vegetables and all, or get fined."

"Seriously?" Nathan demanded. "You've got to be kidding!"

"Nope," Bly shook his head. "Most of the parents are in the know now, so they don't watch as closely as they used to. But if they see you eating a bag of chips, or that you don't have a fruit in your lunch bag or something... well, your mom ain't gonna be too happy."

Nathan shook his head. He folded over the top of his lunch bag as he ate his sandwich, so that the supervisors wouldn't be able to see what else he had, or didn't have.

"That's crazy," he said.

Bly nodded. "I don't have any trouble getting my five," he said, grinning.

Nathan looked at Bly's tray. He didn't have a ton of food. You might think that someone as big as Bly ate three times as much as anyone else. But if Bly did, he didn't eat it for dinner. He didn't have any more than one food from each of the five categories.

"You don't have that much," he countered.

"No." Bly sighed. "The doctor says I gotta lose some weight, or my asthma's just going to keep getting worse. And maybe I'll have heart trouble and crap too. So I'm on a diet."

Nathan took a bite of his sandwich. "That sucks," he agreed.

"Now you, on the other hand," Bly looked Nathan over. "You're never going to have to diet a day in your life, are you?"

Nathan shrugged. "You can't tell what's in the future."

"But you've got a pretty good idea."

Nathan shook his head. "I don't know what will happen," he repeated.

"What are you eating? Maybe we should trade lunches. I'll eat yours and lose weight, and you can eat mine and put some fat on those bones."

"Chicken sandwich," Nathan said not making any move to trade.

Bly sighed and took another big bite of his burger. He apparently wasn't actually interested in trading either.

When Nathan got home after school one day later that week, the house was empty. He had expected Mama to be home, but she had warned him that if she got a call for an interview, she would have to go. He took the bus and he had a key, so he didn't need her. He just kind of liked her to be there when he got back from school. She'd always tried to be there for him after school.

Rather than sitting in the empty house, trying to do his homework, Nathan sat on the front steps and watched the activity in the neighborhood. Not that there was anything much to watch. Delia was playing with some of her young friends in the little stand of trees in the middle of the crescent. A couple of people were out mowing lawns or doing yard work. The neighbor lady from two doors down was again taking her garbage bin out to the alley. It must have been heavy, because she appeared to be struggling with it. Nathan watched her, wondering if he should go over and offer to help her.

Then he saw her stumble and fall, and the bin went over with a crash. Nathan jumped up off of the front step and ran over. His feet hardly seemed to touch the ground on the way, and in a few seconds he was by the woman's side.

"Are you okay? Let me help you up," he offered.

She shook her head, looking confused. "Where did you come from?"

Nathan moved the bin away a few inches, collected her cane, and hovered over her, holding out his hand. "Let me help you," he offered again.

She took his hand, but she was heavy and he couldn't do much to help her get to her feet. She took the cane out of his hand, and leaning heavily on it, she managed to pull herself to her feet. Nathan tried to right the garbage bin. It clanged and was very heavy. He braced himself and lifted it upright, but it was off-balance and wanted to just fall over again if he let it go.

"I'll take this out," he told her, and he pulled it along over the uneven bricked pathway to the gate. There was a hollow where it had previously resided, and when Nathan maneuvered it into place, it settled. He shook it a bit to settle the contents, and when he pulled back experimentally, it stood on its own without tipping back over again. Nathan went back through the gate into the yard, latching the gate behind him. The woman was still standing there on the pathway with her cane, looking a little disoriented.

"Are you okay?" Nathan asked her.

"Yes. Yes, of course, I'm fine. Who are you?"

"Nathan Ashby, from down the way. You met my mama the other day."

"Oh, the pastor woman," she said, nodding. She looked Nathan over with a frown.

"I know, you were expecting someone older," Nathan said. "But I am older. I mean, I just don't look my age. Because I'm small."

She laid her hand on his arm softly, giving him a smile. "You are just right," she said. "Not a thing wrong with you."

Nathan smiled at that. Oh, there was plenty wrong. But he was happy to have her accept him as he was, instead of insisting that he couldn't possibly be eleven.

"Thank you, ma'am," he said politely. "Can I walk you into your house? Make sure you're okay?"

"What lovely manners. Yes, you may."

He walked slowly beside her, his arm on offer if she wanted to lean on him. But she used her cane and seemed to be well enough without him. He walked with her all the way into the house, and she sat down in her sitting room, sighing as she settled into the couch. Nathan looked her over. He couldn't see any scrapes or bruises from her fall, though her slightly reddish-brown hair was a bit in disarray and had some leaves stuck in it. Her watery blue eyes were steady and alert. He supposed there was no need for an ambulance.

"Do I meet with your approval, young man?" she questioned.

"Yes'm. I'm sorry, I just wanted to make sure you were okay."

"That's very gentlemanly of you. Would you like to sit down for a moment?"

Nathan realized that his legs were shaking, and that his dash over from his house had left him feeling drained and lightheaded.

"Yes'm," he agreed. He sat on a straight-backed chair with a padded seat, and took a deep breath.

"You look more shaken than I feel," she observed.

"You scared me," Nathan admitted. "Ma'am," he tacked on at the end.

"You can call me Chandra," she told him. "No needs for ma'ams and missuses."

"Chandra," Nathan echoed awkwardly, feeling like he needed to at least put a 'miss' or 'missus' at the beginning. "My name is Nathan."

"Nathan is a nice, sensible, strong name," she approved. "Your mama seems to think you're just the best thing since sliced bread. And I must say, you make a good first impression."

Nathan's face warmed a little at that. "Mama's always going on about me," he said, shaking his head a bit. "She does overdo it a bit."

She laughed. "Well, she's certainly smitten with you, that's for sure."

He nodded, looking down. "So... you're okay?" he questioned. "If you want, I can come and take your bin out every week. That one was really heavy."

"I've been clearing some things out. It isn't usually that heavy. But it's a very kind offer. I'm fine," she added as an afterthought. "Really, I don't think I damaged anything."

"Good."

"You're a little pale," Chandra observed, sitting forward on the couch. "Can I get you anything? A drink of juice, maybe?"

"No, I'm fine. Just... a mite tired."

"Tired? A boy your age shouldn't be tired at this time of day. Young people have so much energy!"

He didn't explain. "I should be getting back. If Mama gets home and I'm not there, she'll be worried."

"All right," Chandra agreed, using her cane to help her to her feet. "I'll just walk you to the door." When Nathan opened his mouth to object, she held up her hand. "I will be just fine, walking you to the door. I may not look it, but I'm really quite strong."

"Okay," Nathan acquiesced, and he walked to the door with her.

He took a quick look around as they left the sitting room, which was a little dark because of the drawn blinds and curtains, but friendly and comfortable with little pictures and knickknacks, to the hall, lined with portrait collages, to the doorway with a welcome mat and a place to sit to take off your shoes.

"You have a very nice home," he told her as she opened the door for him.

"Thank you, Nathan. And thank you for coming over to help me today. I hope you're feeling better soon."

Nathan nodded and headed down her walk, down the sidewalk, and back over to his own house. Mama's car still wasn't in front of the house, so she hadn't missed him while he'd been helping out Chandra. There was a patter of running feet, and Nathan turned around to see Delia running up to him.

"You went into her house?" Delia demanded. "What was it like? Is she a witch? What happened?"

"It's just a normal house," Nathan said, laughing at her questions. "No boiling cauldron over the fire. Just a normal person's house. And she was very nice. Not like a wicked witch at all."

"She still could be," Delia pointed out. "Witches aren't always like that. They can act nice and they can disguise themselves."

Nathan smiled and shook his head. "She's just a normal person, Delia. Just a normal old lady, probably somebody's grandma."

"She's weird," Delia insisted. "You'll see."

Chapter Seven

AFTER SUPPER, NATHAN WAS outside again, this time looking for Delia. She was down the street with some of her friends, drawing chalk pictures on the sidewalks. Several house-widths of sidewalks had been covered with stick men, fanciful pictures, and hopscotch squares.

Delia looked up from where she was crouched, working on a rainbow with the colors in the wrong order. "Hi, Nathan!"

"Hi." Nathan was awkward. She was friendly with him, but he didn't really consider her a friend. It was awkward approaching her like this. "Um, my mom wanted to know if you want to come over again. For worship."

"Sure!" she agreed. "What time should I come on Sunday?"

"Actually... we're having a prayer meeting tonight, and she thought you might like to come too."

"Tonight?" Delia questioned, looking puzzled. "In the middle of the week?"

He shrugged and cocked his head to the side slightly. "We don't just worship on Sundays," he explained. "We pray and all on the other days too, and we like to have a worship meeting in the middle, so it's not so long between having other people over. It just helps people remember... you know, their faith."

Delia considered. She looked at the other girls who were playing with her. "Do you guys want to go to Pastor Billie's prayer meeting? Remember I was telling you about Sunday?"

They all looked at each other. "Yeah, let's," agreed one of the other little girls.

So the third one nodded that she would join the others.

"Great," Nathan said faintly.

They left their chalk on the sidewalk, and he led them back to his house, feeling a little like a mother duck leading her ducklings all in a row behind her.

"Do your folks want to come?" he asked Delia.

"Uh, I don't know... my mom might come."

"Why don't you ask her?" Nathan suggested.

So they stopped and waited while Delia ran into her house to ask her mother as well. In a couple of minutes, Delia came out with her mother, who was dressed in blue jeans and a t shirt. She looked at Nathan with an uncertain smile.

"You must be Nathan."

Nathan nodded, and politely offered his hand. "Pleased to meet you... um... Missus..."

"Clay," she filled in. "Dorianne Clay."

Nathan squeezed her hand, and released it.

"Delia's told me all about you," Mrs. Clay said with a self-conscious laugh. "And about what a great time she had with you and your mom on Sunday."

Nathan started back off toward his house. "We had fun," he agreed, not sure what else to say.

A few more houses down the street, and they were home. Nathan led everyone into the house. Mama was in the sitting room with another couple that Nathan didn't know, and smiled broadly when they came in.

"Welcome," she exclaimed. "Looks like you did a good job, Nathaniel! Come on in, everyone, and tell me who you are."

Names were exchanged, and Mama introduced Nathan to the other couple, who apparently lived across the street in a basement apartment.

"This is a great little group to start with," Mama gushed, looking happily around at everyone. "Thank you everyone for coming! We'll get started right away, unless you know of someone else who might be coming or might want to come if we knocked on their door?"

No one offered any suggestions, so they started. "Shall we start with a scripture story?" Mama suggested.

Delia nodded. "Last time we did Noah's ark," she told her friends.

"You told us!"

Delia's mother shushed them. "Listen, now," she prompted.

"It's okay," Mama smiled. She looked around at them. "How many of you have ever heard of the witch of Endor?"

Nathan's heart sank. He swallowed, trying to shake his head at Mama. She didn't notice or didn't want to. Everyone else looked at each other blankly.

"How about Daniel in the lion's den?" Nathan suggested.

"Yeah, I like that one," one of Delia's friends piped up.

Mama opened her Bible and started to read. Everyone was quiet, listening to her. Their eyes went back and forth to each other, but they listened to the words and tried to understand them.

"Do you understand what Saul did wrong?" Mama questioned, looking around.

There was silence for a few minutes.

"He shouldn't have gone to a witch," Delia offered finally.

Mama nodded. "That's right, Delia. The Bible tells us 'There shall not be found among you anyone who practices divination or tells fortunes or interprets omens, or a sorcerer.' Saul shouldn't have gone to the witch of Endor, and we need to make sure that we don't allow diviners or fortune tellers or any other kind of witch to be among us, either."

"There are no witches," Delia's mother protested, with a bit of a laugh. "We don't believe in that."

Mama shook her head. "No one who tells fortunes?"

"Well, not really... the horoscopes in the newspaper, maybe... I guess some people do it, but I don't know anyone who does."

"No one who seems... strange... like she might harbor evil spirits...?"

Everyone shook their heads. Delia looked at Nathan, her eyes wide. Nathan shook his head slightly at her. She kept quiet.

"What about some music, Mama?" Nathan suggested. "I think it's time for some praise."

Mama didn't say anything, frowning. Nathan went over to the stereo and picked out a CD. He couldn't suppress a smile as the music started to beat and fill the room. Mama didn't stand up right away, so Nathan grabbed Delia by the hands and pulled her to her feet. She started to dance with him and clap her hands. She motioned to her friends to stand up and join her. They looked self-conscious at first, but in a couple of minutes, were laughing and clapping and twirling around the room.

Mama started to smile, and she stood up and grabbed Nathan away from the little girls to dance with him, then let him go, and went over to Delia's mom and the other couple.

"Join us!" she invited, and then broke off into the chorus of the song, lifting her voice up over the music and laughingly inviting Nathan to sing with her. He knew the song and the others didn't, so he quickly joined in. The little girls were quickly picking up on the words, and if they couldn't figure out what came next, just clapped and whooped and whirled around happily.

Nathan dropped back to his seat. Smiling, he continued to clap until his arms grew too tired, and he just sat there, watching them, and drinking in the music. Eventually, the others started to slow down and stop dancing too. Mama seemed to be back to her usual cheerful self, and led the little group in prayer. Afterward, everyone shook hands and chatted to each other like they were old friends, their earlier unease forgotten.

"There's a bowl by the front door," Mama said, "where y'all can leave any offerings that you feel moved to give. We surely appreciate anything. Sunday we'll have worship, and you're welcome to join us again. My door is always open to my brothers and sisters in the gospel."

Everyone started to move toward the door. Delia tapped Nathan's bicep with her fist. "Thanks for coming to get us," she said. "I sure like the music!"

He smiled at her. "Thanks for coming, Delia."

The house was quiet once again. Mama straightened away the chairs, and picked up her Bible, stroking the worn cover. She went over to Nathan and ruffled his hair.

"How you doing, Love Bug?"

"Okay. You know, you scare people talking about witches."

"People need to know, Nathaniel. They need to know there are still sorceries among us."

"But not the first week," Nathan countered. "They'll think you're some kind of nut."

She looked at him, frowning. Eventually, she nodded slowly. "Milk before meat," she agreed. "That's what Paul said. Not before they are able."

Nathan nodded in agreement, then rested his head back and closed his eyes. "You always want to go too fast," he said. "You gotta go slow for people, teach them one bit at a time. These are folks that don't even go to church most of the time."

"You're right as usual, my little man. They're not ready for that yet. We've got to teach them the love of the Lord first. Bring them into the fold."

"Yes'm."

"You'd better get off to bed. Do you need a hand?"

"No, I can manage," Nathan said. It took a few seconds to persuade his body to get going again, but then he levered himself out of the couch and shuffled off toward the bathroom.

Nathan heard footsteps behind him as he waited at the bus stop to go to school. He turned his head and saw Delia coming up. He smiled at her. Delia smiled back, but her forehead was knotted in concentration. Nathan left her to her own thoughts.

"Do you think that Mrs. Mullenny is a witch?" she questioned after a while.

Nathan sighed. "No. I think she's just a nice old lady," he said. "I don't think there's anything wrong with her."

"But your mom does."

"She didn't say that," Nathan reminded her. "She said we need to watch out for people who are trying to predict the future, or whatever, she never said a word about Mrs. Mullenny."

"But I think she could be," Delia said.

"No. You don't even understand the kind of witch Mama is talking about. She doesn't mean like on Harry Potter or something, waving around a wand and casting spells and turning into a cat, and all that. She means... people who mess around with the devil's power. Working against God."

"I know," Delia insisted. "I'm not a baby. But you haven't lived around here for long. You don't know some of the weird stuff about Mrs. Mullenny."

"I've been in her house. There wasn't anything out of the ordinary."

Delia rolled her eyes at this. "You think she would leave things out for everyone to see? If she was doing devil-worship, do you think she'd do it in the front room?"

Nathan was taken aback by this, and had to admit that she had a point. If Chandra Mullenny was a witch, she certainly wouldn't advertise the fact. Unless she was reading palms for money or something like that.

"So why do you think she might be a witch?" he asked Delia, turning it back on her.

Delia scrunched up her mouth and considered. They both watched for the bus, now running late, to arrive. "Well... she always wears black. That's weird, right?"

Nathan shook his head. "Kids that are goth always wear black. It doesn't mean anything, just that she likes black clothes."

"*She's* not goth," Delia said.

Nathan's mouth twitched. "No," he agreed. "But there's lots of reasons for wearing black other than being a witch. I don't think real witches wear black all the time."

"She has a cat. Witches have cats, right, even real ones?"

"I don't know. Lots of people have cats that aren't witches." Nathan squinted at her, remembering waiting outside Delia's house for her to get her mom for the prayer meeting. "You have a cat, don't you?"

Delia giggled. "Yes."

"Are you a witch?"

"No! But my cat's not black."

"Oh," Nathan nodded. "Only witches have black cats."

She giggled some more.

"Or," suggested Nathan, "maybe the reason she wears black is so that the black cat hair doesn't show up on her clothes."

"Maybe," Delia agreed. She shook her head. It was a few minutes before she said anything else, obviously thinking twice before making any other suggestions. "I've heard that she doesn't just have a cat, though. She has spiders and snakes and rats and stuff too."

"Do you believe that?"

Delia sighed. "No."

The bus finally pulled up, and Delia and Nathan got on. There were no available seats. There never were. So they hung onto the poles and stood.

"I just think it's weird," Delia said. "She never goes out. She always stays home. Even gets her groceries and everything delivered to the house."

"Lots of people are like that. Sometimes people have a phobia of going out. Or they don't like being around other people. Or they're sick or hurt."

"Or they're witches."

"I don't think so."

"She makes potions. You can smell them when you go by her house sometimes. Weird smells and fogged up windows and stuff. That's not normal. Normal people don't make potions."

"Some might. Making tea and using herbs and stuff. Maybe she's a naturopath."

Although Nathan knew that Mama would be suspicious of anyone like that, too. She believed in herbs for healing, but anyone else who used them was subject to scrutiny. It all depended on whether they were following God or the devil in using herbs. And it was hard to tell, sometimes.

"What's a naturopath?" Delia demanded. "Someone who can, like, control nature with their brain?" By way of demonstration, she held her fingers to her temples and made a face like she needed to go to the bathroom.

Nathan laughed. "No. Just someone who uses roots and herbs and natural things for healing. Lots of people use herbs. I bet your mom does too."

"Well, she doesn't cook them into potions."

Nathan stared out the window. "Well, I don't think Mrs. Mullenny's a witch. I think you're just being silly about it. She's just a lonely old lady, that's all. Just a normal, lonely old lady."

Chapter Eight

IT HAD BEEN A long day at school, and Nathan was glad to get home at the end of the day. Mama's car was parked in front of the house. Nathan walked up to the door and paused on the doorstep, catching his breath, before going inside.

The smell of baking filled his nostrils when he stepped into the house. Nathan breathed it in. He loved it when Mama cooked. It wasn't really home until she had started baking again. He went into the kitchen and looked over the mess scattered over the counters and table. Mama turned around to look at him.

"Hi, honey. Did you have a good day?"

"It was fine," Nathan said. He looked at the dark, shiny loaves on the table. "Banana bread?"

"Banana bread with chocolate chips," Mama agreed. She sighed, looking over the loaves, and over the chaos that ruled the rest of the kitchen. "What a mess."

Nathan thought about offering to help to clean up, but his heart was pumping hard and he was already out of breath. He pulled out one of the kitchen chairs and sat down. Mama started to pick up the flour and other various ingredients to put them away. Moving the ingredients out of the way revealed an open box with a picture of a mouse on it. Nathan frowned at it.

"Do we have mice?" he questioned.

"You cannot let unclean things pollute your house," Mama said solemnly. "Let no unclean thing come near you."

Nathan swallowed. "Yeah," he agreed. "So you're going to kill them? The mice?"

She raised an eyebrow at him, and put the box of poison under the sink. "Do you need to lie down for a while?" she questioned. "Or are you doing all right?"

"I'm okay, I guess. Why? Did you want me to do something?"

She looked at her watch. "I've been called back at the store," she said. "I think that the call-back is to give me the job. I'm praying it is. I don't have supper ready yet, but..." she looked around the kitchen. "What I need, is someone to take one of these loaves to that neighbor lady. You know, that Chandra whatever."

"Mrs. Mullenny," Nathan offered.

"Yes. You think you could do that for me?"

Nathan looked at the loaves on the stove. "That won't take but a minute," he said. "I could do that."

"She might invite you in. An older lady living by herself, she might want some company for a mite. It's fine with me if you spend a little time over there. Make sure she knows who we are, so she won't be afraid to enjoy the bread. See what she's like."

Nathan nodded and got up. He went over to the bread cooling on top of the stove. He reached to take the middle loaf.

"No, not that one. The one on the end is for Mrs. What's-it."

Nathan moved his hand over to the last loaf and looked at her questioningly. "This one? They all look the same."

"That one rose a little better than the other two. You take her that one."

Nathan wrapped it carefully in plastic wrap. It was still warm from the stove. His mouth watered. He had been pretty good about giving up sweets, but Mama's baking was more than just a sweet treat. It was an expression of her love. Comfort food. Mama watched him wrap it in silence.

"Okay. I'm going out," she said, rinsing her hands in the sink and drying back off. "Make sure you've got your key so you can let yourself back in again. All right?" Nathan nodded. She leaned in to give him a kiss. "Bye, then. Hopefully I'll be coming home to tell you I've got the job, and we can celebrate."

"Bye. Good luck!"

She left, and Nathan looked down at the wrapped loaf in his hands.

A few minutes later, Nathan was standing on Chandra Mullenny's porch, again looking down at the warm loaf of banana bread. He could smell it, even with the wrapper on. Hints of chocolate mixed in with the banana. And maybe a touch of cinnamon as well. It was intoxicating. He didn't usually have much appetite, but he knew what Mama's banana bread tasted like.

Bracing himself, Nathan reached up and pressed the doorbell. There was no car parked in front of the house, but he hadn't noticed before whether Mrs. Mullenny had one or not. He waited, looking over his shoulder at the street as he wondered if she was even at home. Eventually, he could hear footsteps inside, and then the doorknob turned and the door opened just a crack.

"Yes?"

"It's Nathan, from down the street, Mrs. Mullenny," Nathan said. "I brought you something from my mama."

She opened the door further and looked at him, smiling. "I told you, it's Chandra," she reminded him.

"Yes'm. I mean, Chandra, ma'am. She made you banana bread," Nathan lifted the loaf slightly to show her.

"Oh, how very sweet of her," Chandra said. She opened the door the rest of the way. "Come in, come in."

Nathan entered, and again looked around her front hall, and a few minutes later was seated in her sitting room.

"So, how is your mother doing?" Chandra questioned. "I haven't seen her again, since that day she came by."

"She's gone to a job interview tonight, or she would have come herself," Nathan explained.

"Oh, good for her."

"She thinks she's got it, and this is just to let her know."

Chandra nodded. "She's been very quick in finding something. Sometimes people are looking for weeks or months before they manage to pin something down."

"We don't have much saved, especially with the move costing money," Nathan said. "So we needed to find something right away."

"Well, she's done very well. She'll get it."

Nathan shifted uneasily at the prediction. He looked down at the banana bread, still in his hands. He should have handed it to her to put in the kitchen, instead of sitting down with it.

"You keep looking at that banana cake," Chandra commented.

Nathan's face burned. A trickle of sweat started to run down his back, and he looked at Chandra, at a loss as to what to say.

"Maybe you would like a slice?" she suggested.

Nathan swallowed. "Oh, Mama kept one for us too. This one is for you."

"There's no way that I'm going to be able to eat all of that all by myself. I'm going to need some kind of help, and I don't get a lot of visitors." Chandra stood up, and shuffled over to him to take it from his hands. "You wait here, and I'll slice some for you."

"No, really, it's for you," Nathan insisted.

"I'll be right back."

Nathan watched her go, and sat there with nothing to hold anymore, and looked down at his hands. Now what was he going to do? She wasn't going to let him out of eating some of the sweet cake. It would look strange if he refused to have any. The sweat continued to drip down his back, even though it wasn't hot in the room.

It was a few minutes before Chandra got back, with a lunch plate holding a couple of pieces of the banana bread, and a glass of milk. She handed them to him without a word, and put a coaster on the coffee table in front of his knee. She sat back down, smiling at him.

Nathan looked around the room for something to talk about. There were a few pictures of a young man, smiling in a friendly way at the camera.

"Is that your son?" he questioned, nodding to one of the pictures.

"Yes... he's passed away now."

"Oh..." Nathan rubbed his forehead. "I'm sorry. I didn't mean to..."

"It's all right. He's not entirely gone... I can still see him."

It seemed like a bizarre thing to say. Nathan had known people who had died, and that wasn't one of the things that people usually said. They said 'he's still in my heart' or 'I think about him every single day' or 'you never stop missing them' or things like that. They didn't say that he wasn't entirely gone and they could still see him.

The smell of the banana bread teased at Nathan's nostrils. He broke off a small piece that had a couple of chocolate chips in it, still melted. He put it in his mouth and closed his eyes, savoring it. It melted away in his mouth, spreading over his tongue.

"That looks good. I'm glad you're enjoying it," Chandra said.

He opened his eyes to look at her. He smiled nodding. "You should have some," he encouraged.

After he swallowed, there was a very bitter, metallic taste in Nathan's mouth. He took a swallow of milk to rinse it out, but it persisted.

"Later," said Chandra, with a peculiar smile that made Nathan think that she wasn't going to. She was just saying it to make him happy.

"My mama knows how to make banana bread," Nathan said encouragingly.

He took another bite of the bread, hoping that the sweet chocolate and banana would wipe out the bad taste in his mouth. For a moment, the cloying sweetness covered it up, but as soon as he swallowed it was there again, a nasty, horribly bitter aftertaste. Nathan struggled not to make a face, to keep his expression pleasant and not react to the taste. He took a couple more gulps of milk.

"What do you mean," he said, trying to distract her from watching him eat, "when you said you can still see your son?"

She was silent at first. She had a slight frown, and watched him closely. Nathan felt compelled to take another bite of the cake. "What do you know about time travel?" she said finally.

Nathan choked on the last bite he had taken. The cake lodged in his windpipe for a moment, then shot back up, stopped by his hand over his mouth, when he coughed. He swallowed strenuously to get it down. He coughed a couple more times, clearing the crumbs out of his windpipe.

"Time travel?" he echoed finally.

"Yes," she nodded. "Do you know anything about it?"

"Do you mean in a machine, or something? Or what?"

She smiled. Nathan took another drink of milk, draining the glass.

"Humans really don't know very much about time," Chandra said. "We're governed by it. We live in a world that is bounded by time. But we don't really understand what it is, its nature, how to manipulate it."

"With a machine?" Nathan squeaked.

He looked around the room for a hidden camera. This had to be some kind of a joke. People didn't really talk like that about time travel. She had to be crazy, if she thought that he actually believed it. Or if she believed it.

"We don't need a machine to manipulate time," Chandra said in a low voice. "Just our minds. Do you know how little of our brains we actually use?"

Nathan nodded, but couldn't speak. Chandra looked at one of the pictures of her son, and then stared off into space. Nathan waited for her to say that it was a joke. That she was just pulling his leg.

"Have you ever read 'A Wrinkle in Time'?" she questioned.

Nathan shook his head. He'd seen it in a display at school, but he'd never read it. Chandra pursed her lips. "In that book, they talk about wrinkling time and space to get from one place or time to another. Folding it so that you don't have to go all the way from point A to point B, but just jump from one to the other without traveling all of the intervening time and space."

Nathan thought about that. "But that's a book," he said. "That's not real."

She raised her eyebrows. "What do you know about time, other than moving from your birth to your death in a straight line?"

"Well, I dunno. Nothing. It's, like, the fourth dimension or something. But nobody can time travel."

"You already are traveling. The trouble is, you only know how to go in one direction."

"You can't travel any other way," Nathan insisted.

"'A Wrinkle in Time' is pretty simplistic," Chandra said. "I want to challenge you to think a little bit deeper about it."

Nathan chewed on the inside of his cheek. He wished he had more milk to try to wash the taste in his mouth away. But he didn't want to ask, and he didn't want to distract Chandra from this line of discussion. He knew that she couldn't possibly really be able to travel in time--other than in the usual direction--but he liked that she wanted to discuss it more deeply with him, to challenge his brain. Even if he did only use a small percentage of his brainpower.

"Okay..." he said.

"We'll start with the nature of space. Can you put something big into something smaller?" she asked him.

Nathan shook his head. "No, of course not. It won't fit."

"Are you sure?"

"How could you?" Nathan challenged.

She gave him a little smile. She left the room for a moment, and came back with an assortment of bowls and a shopping bag stuffed with other shopping bags.

"So you can't put a bigger bowl into a smaller bowl, right?" Chandra questioned, handling the bowls and demonstrating.

"Right," Nathan agreed with a smile.

"But you can put one of these bags into even the smallest bowl," she went on, and she folded a mesh bag into a small bundle, and put it into the cereal bowl.

"Right."

"So is the bag bigger or smaller than the bowl?"

"Smaller."

"And if it's smaller than the smallest bowl, then it's smaller than all of the others too, isn't it?" she questioned.

Nathan nodded. "Sure, yeah."

She took the mesh bag out of the bowl and unfolded it. Then she took all of the nested bowls and put them into the bag. Nathan just looked at her.

"Then how do all of the bigger bowls fit into the smaller bag?" she questioned.

"Well..." Nathan frowned and tried to put it into words. "You can change the shape of the bag."

"And the size?"

"No, the bag stays the same size."

"Then how can it be bigger and smaller than the bowls?"

"Because it can be crunched up, or stretched out."

"But it still occupies the same amount of space," Chandra said. "And isn't that what size means?"

"Yes..."

"Then how can it be bigger and smaller, if the size doesn't change?"

Nathan shrugged hopelessly. "I don't know."

Chandra took the bowls out of the bag and put them to the side. She picked out a few other bags and spread them all out on the floor in front of her. "Which is the biggest?" she questioned.

"The red one."

"And which is the smallest?"

"The mesh one."

"You're sure."

"Yes."

"You can tell which is bigger and which is smaller, even though you can't tell me what bigger and smaller mean," she teased.

Nathan nodded.

Chandra took the red bag and folded it up small, putting it inside the next larger bag, and so on, until all of the bags were inside the mesh bag, which was the smallest.

"So can you put something bigger into something smaller?" she questioned.

"Yeah, I guess," Nathan admitted.

She smiled at him. "You understand space and matter, because you can see and feel them. Or at least, you think you can understand them. But you can't even tell me the most basic rules about matter and space, like defining bigger and smaller. But you think you can tell me the rules of time?"

"But you can't do that with time," Nathan pointed out. "All you can do with time is travel in one direction from birth to death."

"That's all that *you* can do. How do you know that I haven't learned how to manipulate time just as easily as I can manipulate my bags?"

"It's not the same."

"How do you know that time, and space, and energy aren't like matter? How do you know that they can't be folded, contained, or nested? How do you know that I can't travel backward or sideways? Or jump from one time to another? Just because you've only ever travelled forward, that doesn't mean that's the only way."

Nathan tried to puzzle through this. He looked at the bags that she had stuffed into a little bundle, and at the bowls. His mouth was dry, and when he tried to lick his lips and work up a little spit, they just dried up worse.

"But you can fold the bags with your hands," he said. "What would you use to fold time?"

"What do you use to travel forward through time?"

Nathan was stumped. "I don't know. Nothing. We all just travel forward through time."

"Does everybody travel forward at the same pace?"

"Yes."

"Do they?" Chandra persisted.

Nathan thought about it. How did you measure how fast you traveled forward in time? Time was constant. Everyone went through it at the same pace. But what about someone with an aging disease, like that kid he'd seen on TV who was an old man even though he was only eight? Had he traveled forward faster? How could you measure if your perception of how fast time moved forward was the same as someone else's perception? When he was younger, time had seemed to take much longer. Christmas vacation had felt like months, it lasted forever. Now it seemed like it had hardly begun and it was over. Nine o'clock had been late, and it seemed like the night drew on and on.

"I don't know," he admitted.

"How do you know you have never travelled backward, the opposite way?" Chandra questioned.

Nathan laughed. "I think I'd know if I'd gone back in time," he said.

"Would you?"

Nathan shrugged, holding his hands out wide. "Yeah."

"Do you remember when you were a baby?"

"No."

"Probably not for the first two or three years, at least, right?" she questioned.

"Yeah, probably three."

"So how do you know you didn't travel forward and backward when you were a baby and a young child? Maybe that's how long it took you to learn to always go forward in time, just like a child learning to walk, taking one step forward at a time."

Nathan had a queasy feeling in his stomach. It felt like the banana bread was roiling around in there, bubbling and frothing. He suppressed a burp. "Wouldn't parents notice if their baby was traveling back in time?" he said.

"Why would they? They have already learned to travel forward in time. They wouldn't be aware of the baby going backward, because their time would only go forward."

Nathan shook his head. "That's just... weird. You don't really think that babies travel back in time, do you?"

She just raised her eyebrows again and didn't answer.

"You can't time travel," Nathan asserted. "You're just making stuff up."

"Have you ever had *déjà vu?*" Chandra questioned.

"Yeah."

"What does it feel like?"

Nathan tried to put it into words. "Like, you've been there and done that before."

"Why do you feel like that?"

"I don't know... everybody does sometimes."

"How could you remember the future if you can only travel one direction?"

"You can't really. It's just a feeling."

"Have you ever had it really, really strong?" Chandra questioned.

Nathan nodded.

"Was it really just a funny feeling?"

Nathan shook his head slowly. He was convinced that it had meant something. He wondered at the time whether it was some kind of revelation; God trying to tell him something. It was so strong, he could remember every detail of what was happening to him as it happened.

"How can you remember the future?" Chandra repeated.

"I don't know."

"Are you still sure that you've only ever travelled in one direction in time, at one consistent pace, and everybody else is doing the same thing?"

Nathan stared down at the banana bread left on his plate. He was hyper-aware of the seconds ticking by, slower and slower as if to mock his perception of what was real. He felt like his brain was getting overloaded. It was too big to think about.

"No. I dunno," he said. "I just don't know anymore."

"So if you have travelled other directions in time before, then maybe with some practice, you could become more skilled at it. Get better control over it."

"People can't control time," Nathan protested. "We can't just change it, manipulate it like some shopping bags. If you could travel in time, you'd need machines, or powers, or something."

"You *can* travel in time," Chandra reminded him. "Everyone travels in time. And maybe everyone travels through it in different ways. When you were a baby, could you walk?"

"No."

"And to a baby, something like that must have seemed impossible. Getting up on two legs and walking around? How about reading? How old were you when you learned to read, do you remember?"

"Kindergarten, I guess."

"And when you looked at big books with lots of words in them, did you ever think that you would ever be good enough to read like that?"

He shrugged.

"It seemed pretty impossible, didn't it?" she prodded.

"Yeah."

"I've seen some amazing feats on television and on the internet," Chandra said slowly. "People who can do incredible things with their bodies or minds. Or both. People who can control their bodies, or manipulate them in astonishing ways. Things you would think were impossible. And brain feats like memorizing hundreds of digits of pi, or calculating long mathematical functions. And things like telepathy and telekinesis..."

"Those aren't real," Nathan said immediately. "They're not proven."

"There are a lot of things that aren't proven that are still real," Chandra said. "You ask your mama about that. She believes in God and miracles, doesn't she?"

"Yes'm," Nathan agreed. Mama had a great faith in miracles and signs.

"You hear many stories of things that are miraculous or unexplainable. Does that mean that they are not real? Can you really disprove that sometimes people communicate with each other without words? Over long distances, without even seeing each other? You've heard miraculous stories about that, haven't you?"

Nathan nodded. He put the plate he was still holding down on the coffee table.

"So if all of those things are possible for us to learn to do with our bodies or brains, then why would we not be able to learn to manipulate time, or our existence or progression through time? Is it really that far-fetched?"

"If it could be done, then people would have done it. They'd be able to tell us about it. Tell us how to do it. But nobody can."

"Would you believe someone who told you that they could?" Chandra questioned with a bubbling laugh.

Nathan laughed too. "No!" he said. "I *don't*."

She sat looking at him and smiling for a long time. Then she stood up and picked up his glass and plate.

"It's been very pleasant talking to you," she said. "I don't want to be keeping you from home for too long. Your mom will get home from that interview and be looking for you."

Nathan stood too. He looked at the banana bread on the plate as she headed back to the kitchen. "You'll have some of that, won't you?" he questioned. "So I can tell Mama that you liked it?"

"It looks lovely," Chandra assured him. "You tell her thank you very much for me. That was very kind of her. And I enjoyed visiting with you, too."

Nathan nodded, and he headed back toward the front door. She joined him there to see him off.

"Come and visit any time, Nathan."

"Okay. Thanks."

Nathan walked back home slowly. He felt like the gears in his brain were stripped, skipping and stuttering as he tried to think about the things that Chandra had said. Whenever he thought about the possibilities that she had suggested, part of his brain rejected the new ideas and tried to shut him down. Nathan stopped in the kitchen and took a long, long drink of water. Then he headed to his bedroom to try to work on homework until Mama got home.

He didn't even remember getting to his bedroom.

Chapter Nine

NATHAN DREAMED THAT HE was back at the old church, before the pastor had died. He was listening to the pastor's fire-and-brimstone sermon, a little bit scared by it, but excited about the rest of the service to come. He joined in the 'amens,' hoping that the sermon was almost done so that they could sing and dance. Mama had brought a tambourine for him so that he could really join in with the music.

Chandra was standing next to him and put a hand on his shoulder.

"What did I tell you?" she questioned. "How did you get back here again?"

"I wanted to dance," Nathan said. "So I came back."

"Easier than you thought, isn't it?" she questioned.

"Only when I'm dreaming. I've never come back here when I was awake before."

She smiled knowingly.

"I used to be able to dance for a long time," Nathan said. "Before I got sick."

"But not anymore?"

"No. Now I can only dance one song. I get too tired."

She was shaking him by the shoulder. Nathan pulled away, too tired. He wanted to stay asleep, he was too tired.

"Nathaniel. Come on, baby, wake up."

Nathan groaned. "Mama..."

"Wake up, I want to talk with you."

Nathan sighed, and forced his eyes open. Mama sat on the side of the bed, waiting for him to wake up.

"It's not time to get up yet, is it?" Nathan questioned.

"It's not even bedtime yet, silly. Come on, you can get up for a little while. I have news for you."

Nathan scrubbed at his eyes. "You got the job?" he questioned, grinning.

"I got the job!"

"Good work!" Nathan cheered. "You did a really good job getting something right away." She smiled too. "Chandra said you would get it!"

As soon as he said it, he wished he could take it back. Mama's eyes got wide.

"I mean--I mean... she hoped you'd get it," Nathan amended. But Mama was already upset.

"That woman," she said, in an angry tone. She marched out of the room. Nathan slid off of the bed and hurried after her.

"Mama!"

She went to the sitting room window, and looked out between the slats of the blinds, prying them apart. Nathan stood behind her.

"What are you looking at, Mama?"

She turned around and didn't answer.

"Are we going to celebrate?" Nathan questioned.

"What?" she questioned distractedly.

"You said we would celebrate if you got the job. So what are we going to do?"

She looked out the window once more, and then turned around to face Nathan. "I'm sorry, Bug... I'm just... I thought I heard a siren."

He saw her glance toward Chandra's house. "There's no siren," he said. "Everything is quiet."

"Did she eat the banana bread?"

Nathan swallowed, not wanting to lie to her. "She said it looked really good. She said to tell you thank you."

"Did she eat some?" she persisted.

"We ate a little bit while I was there," Nathan said.

She looked at him sharply. "You ate it too?" she questioned.

"A little bit," Nathan said. "I love your banana bread. And she said she couldn't eat it all by herself."

She chewed on her lip, looking at Nathan. Then she turned back around and looked out the window again. Nathan went into the kitchen and started looking through the cupboards and fridge. It was still pretty meager. He put a couple of slices of the banana bread on a plate for Mama, and poured her a glass of apple juice. For himself, he grabbed a handful of nuts and a glass of water.

"Mama. Come on in," he called. "Let's have our celebration snack, now."

After a minute, she joined him in the kitchen. She looked at the snack that he had prepared and smiled faintly. "You're such a thoughtful boy," she said. "Don't you want any banana bread?"

"I had some earlier," he said. "I don't want any right now."

She sat down and took a bite of the banana bread and a sip of her juice. "That's pretty good stuff," she said. "I have to admit."

Nathan smiled. "Sure it is," he agreed. "Your baking is always good."

"She'll like it," Mama said. "I'll bet she eats the whole loaf."

Nathan nodded. "I'm sure she will. No one could resist it."

He could see that she wanted to get up to go look out the window again. She kept glancing over that way, and shifting in her seat.

"When do you start working?" Nathan asked.

Mama's eyes focused on him. "First day is tomorrow! I'll drop you at school, and head over. How's that?"

"That's great. I'm sure glad you got it."

"Me too," Mama agreed, taking a big bite of her banana bread. "The Lord blesses his faithful."

Nathan nodded. "It was a blessing," he agreed. He was silent for a moment. "You believe in miracles..." he started.

Mama cocked her head, looking at him with a smile. "We've seen many miracles. You know that."

"There are lots of things that we don't understand. About the universe, and the way that God works."

"That's true."

"You think that... anything is possible, if God is in it?"

She nodded slowly. "Of course. What are you thinking about?"

Nathan held up his hands in a shrug. "It's a big universe," he said.

Mama nodded. "Yes, it is." She reached for her Bible laying on the table, and held it between her hands, as if warming up frozen fingers on a hot water bottle. She opened it up and flipped through the thin pages, looking for a familiar verse. She didn't read it out loud like he expected her to, but mouthed the words to herself and closed her eyes in a silent prayer. Eventually, she looked back at Nathan again.

"You are my miracle," she asserted. "How are you doing; you feeling okay?"

Nathan nodded. "Just a little tired."

"You want to go back to bed?"

Nathan chugged down his water. "Would you come read to me?" he questioned, nodding to the Bible.

Mama nodded and touched his hair, curling a lock around her fingers. "Of course, Love Bug. Did you get any schoolwork done?"

"No. I'll try to do some in the morning." He shifted to get up. "Is the school going to start calling you? I try to get it done, but sometimes, I'm just so exhausted..."

"I know. You just do what you can. I'll deal with the school. Come on, let's get you to bed."

Nathan headed back toward the hall. Out of the corner of his eye, he saw Mama's head swivel toward the front window again. But she didn't go look out again. She followed Nathan, and when he climbed into bed, she snuggled up beside him and opened her Bible. Nathan closed his eyes, but tried not to go to sleep right away. Mama started to read the familiar passages, her voice soft and soothing.

Nathan awoke with a start. The room was only dimly lit by his nightlight, and a dark shape hovered over him. He gasped, heart racing.

"Shh, it's okay," Mama said. She laid a soothing hand on his shoulder, then stroked his hair. "I didn't mean to wake you up."

Nathan propped himself on his elbows. "What is it? What's wrong?"

"Nothing is wrong, sweetie. I was just checking in on you to make sure you were okay."

Nathan blinked and rubbed his eyes, trying to focus on her. She was in her nightgown, her hair mussed from sleep. Nathan looked over at his alarm clock. It was two in the morning.

"Was I dreaming?" he questioned, lying back down on his pillow again. "Was I calling out?"

"No, no. I was just checking to make sure that you weren't sick. Because you weren't feeling well earlier."

Nathan frowned, trying to remember.

"Go back to sleep," Mama soothed. "It's okay. I didn't mean to wake you up."

"Okay," Nathan agreed. He closed his eyes. "Love you, Mama."

"You too, honey. Sleep well."

She stayed by his bed for a few more seconds, and then left the room, her bare feet making faint shuffling noises on the floor. Nathan laid awake for a while, thinking about her. Then he fell back asleep.

Nathan had made a quick trip to the boy's bathroom before getting to his class, but he had also stopped for a long drink at the fountain, and his bladder was uncomfortably full. He looked at the clock on the wall and shifted in his seat. He didn't want to interrupt Mrs. Davis' lesson in front of the whole class to ask for permission to leave, but he wasn't sure he could hold out much longer.

He tried to distract himself by reading over what she had written on the board. He opened up his workbook and looked over the questions that they would probably be working on once she finished the lesson. The seconds ticked by. He crossed his legs and bit his lip, hoping to distract himself with the pain. Finally, he raised his hand.

Mrs. Davis looked over at him, smiling approval that he had volunteered to answer a question.

"Nathan?"

"Umm--can I go to the restroom?" Nathan asked.

There were giggles around the room. Mrs. Davis sighed in exasperation. "Honestly, Nathan. You leave this room way too often. You need to listen to this. If you miss steps, you're not going to understand what we are doing. You need to wait until I'm done. About ten minutes, okay?"

Nathan swallowed and nodded. He tapped his pencil eraser on the top of the desk. He was in agony now, and Mrs. Davis still went on. She seemed to be talking even more slowly than she had been. Bly put up his hand to ask a question, confused, and a couple of other hands shot up with further questions. At this rate, Mrs. Davis wasn't ever going to finish the lecture.

Nathan couldn't hold it any longer, and jumped out of his desk, running for the closed classroom door, wrenching it open, and belting down the hall to the bathroom, fumbling with the button and zipper on his pants on the way there.

Nathan barely made it to the urinal closest the door in time. He sighed in relief, and closed his eyes, letting the tension fall away. It was enough of a struggle just fitting in at a new school and trying to make friends. The last thing he needed was to pee his pants in class. To be branded the boy who wet his pants in sixth grade. Nathan shuddered at the thought. There would be no mercy.

When he finally finished, he zipped up his pants and washed up, and walked back to the classroom at a more moderate pace. He stopped at the water fountain to moisten his parched mouth, and when he looked up, he saw Mrs. Davis standing just outside the classroom watching his return. Swallowing hard, Nathan walked up to her. He looked down at his feet.

"Sorry," he apologized. "I just really had to go."

"Stay in the classroom at lunch. I want to talk to you."

"Yes'm," Nathan agreed.

It was still another period before lunch hour. Nathan sat worrying throughout the class, his stomach sick with tension. Detention for going to the bathroom when he didn't have permission? Would he have to take a note home to Mama? Apologize in front of the class? Write lines or an essay for the principal? He kept his eyes down, not wanting to catch Mrs. Davis looking at him during the period. What was he going to say to her? At one point she asked him a question, but Nathan hadn't been following the lesson, and he just shook his head.

"I dunno."

There were snickers from others around him. He'd probably just missed a really simple question, but Nathan barely even knew what subject they were on. His face and ears got hot, and he kept looking down at his desk, waiting for the torture to be over.

At last, the bell rang, and there was a rush for the door. Nathan stayed at his desk, slowly closing up his books and putting them away. He really hoped that Mrs. Davis wouldn't keep him in for too long, because he had to pee again.

Mrs. Davis brought over a tall stool that she sometimes used, and put it in front of Nathan's desk. She sat down.

"Nathan."

Nathan swallowed and looked up at her, pressing his lips together hard to keep from showing his emotion. His eyes were hot with tears. Mrs. Davis looked at him, but she didn't appear to be angry or frustrated this time.

"I'm sorry I told you no, Nathan. I'm glad that you just went and didn't wait until it was too late."

He was surprised and embarrassed by his teacher apologizing to him. He nodded and looked down again, his face warm, sweat trickling down his back.

"I'm really concerned, though. Do you want to tell me what's going on?"

Nathan shrugged. He wasn't sure what she wanted to know. Or what he wanted to reveal.

"I think that you're sick, Nathan. Am I right?"

Nathan cleared his throat to answer, but the muscles in his throat were too tight to form the words. He swallowed and shrugged.

"Do you want to tell me about it?"

He cleared his throat again. "It's... it's private," he said hoarsely.

She looked at him, knowing that she wasn't allowed to insist on him telling her. Students had their right to privacy. "You're in the bathroom ten times a day. Your focus and attention are all over the place. You have half a dozen homework assignments outstanding."

Nathan nodded.

"The coach says you barely have any energy in phys ed. He's afraid you're going to faint or collapse if he makes you do anything. You don't look well."

Nathan wasn't able to answer her. Tears started to escape from his eyes and run down his cheeks. She reached out and took one of his hands in hers. "I want to help you, Nathan. I wish you'd talk to me about it."

He shook his head, the tears flowing faster now. Nathan sniffled.

"I've left messages for your mother to call me, but she doesn't return them."

"She's--been--busy," Nathan managed. "Moving in."

"That's understandable. But I'd really like to talk to her. If we had a better understanding of what was going on and what we should do..."

Nathan nodded.

"It's really important," she reiterated.

Nathan wiped at his leaking nose with the back of his hand. Mrs. Davis got up and went to her desk, returning with a box of tissues, which she put on his desk in front of him. Nathan pulled a few out and wiped his face. She waited, and Nathan just breathed, trying to calm himself down and get the sobs under control. When he managed to slow them down so that he was almost breathing normally, she spoke again.

"Are you being treated by a doctor, Nathan?"

Nathan shook his head. "That's private," he told her again.

Her mouth formed a thin line. A crease appeared between her eyebrows. Nathan tried to decide if he should say anything else to her. If he told her no, she would have Child Services on them, before they'd even finished getting moved in properly. If he told her yes, she might detect the lie and be even more concerned. He wished he could reassure her by telling her that Mama was praying and laying hands on him, and if they just had enough faith, God would heal him of his sickness. Mama had helped to heal others. But Mrs. Davis probably wasn't a believer, and would just think that was silly or irresponsible.

"I'm... being treated..." he said carefully. He didn't say 'by a doctor.' He didn't say it was his Mama or his pastor. It wasn't a lie, exactly. He just let her think what she wanted to about it.

"That's a relief," Mrs. Davis said, her worried expression smoothing. "I am very concerned for your welfare."

Nathan nodded dumbly. He shifted uncomfortably and crossed one leg over the other. Mrs. Davis' sharp eyes caught the movement. She nodded, sliding off her chair.

"Go ahead. Please be sure to let your mother know to call me. We really need to talk. In the meantime, I'm going to assign you some time in the resource room; we'll get the teacher there to help you with some of the stuff that you're falling behind in. I'll see if I can get you there during gym time, and kill two birds."

Nathan got up, nodding and mumbling his thanks, and dashed off down the hall.

Chapter Ten

MAMA PICKED NATHAN UP after school and was not happy at Nathan's report of his talk with Mrs. Davis. She shook her head angrily, scowling.

"We hardly even get here, and she's already poking her nose into our business. What's wrong with people? Why can't they just mind their own business and leave us alone?"

She stomped on the gas, and Nathan steadied himself, feeling nauseated at the sudden acceleration. "Maybe we should just homeschool," he suggested. "Some people do that. Then I could sleep in, and I could do the work while you're at the store, and you could help me after work..."

She shook her head at this. "It doesn't get rid of them," she said. "Homeschooling is just a red flag for the bureaucrats. As soon as they see it, they're digging to see what kind of dirt they can find. Making up nonsense and not letting people practice their own religion. The Constitution guarantees us the right to practice our religion! They can't govern that. Separation of church and state!"

Nathan nodded, feeling miserable. He held his backpack in his lap, hugging it tightly to himself. He knew that they were being tried, and that everyone had to go through trials. But it seems like his trials were a lot bigger than most people's. Mama would say that was because he was so righteous, the devil had to try his faith all that much harder. But Nathan couldn't help but wonder if it wasn't because he had done something wrong. That there was something in his life he needed to fix, before he could be healed and get away from the scrutiny of those who would interfere with their lives. He put his head down and closed his eyes, both because he was exhausted and because he wanted to search out those flaws within himself, and to offer them up to God. He wanted to promise to be a better person, if in return God would make things easier for them.

Mama eased off of the gas pedal, letting the car decelerate. She touched Nathan gently on the shoulder. "Are you okay, Bug?" she questioned. "I'm sorry, I didn't mean to make you feel bad. It's not your fault this is happening. Are we still okay?"

Nathan nodded. "It's okay," he murmured.

"Did you have a bad day today? Are you not feeling well?"

He shook his head. "Kinda rough."

She ruffled his hair and rubbed his back as she drove. "Just because of Mrs. Davis? Or other things too?"

"I just... don't feel well. It's not Mrs. Davis. She's really nice, you know. She's just worried."

"It doesn't help for you to be stressed out. It always gets worse when you're upset or pressured."

He knew it was true, but couldn't seem to shut the feelings off. He couldn't stop being worried about Mrs. Davis and what she would say or do, and what the conversation she had with Mama might go like. And that they would have to move again, without even getting settled in here. If anything was stressful, it was moving.

"We'll get you home, and you can have a nice, relaxing supper and evening. Then you'll feel better."

"Yeah. I'm okay."

He closed his eyes again and tried to relax as she drove the rest of the way home. She sent him to his room for a nap before supper, and Nathan fell into bed, happy to comply. But even though he was tired, he couldn't sleep, and eventually he got up to keep Mama company in the kitchen while she made supper. He wandered in and said 'hi' while she hummed to herself, stirring a pot on the stove. She looked over her shoulder.

"What are you doing up again already? Couldn't sleep?"

"No."

He sat down at Mama's computer and moved the mouse to bring it to life. On the screen, he saw a picture of himself as he'd been sitting in the car, hunched over his backpack, eyes closed. It almost looked like he had two black eyes, and his arms were so skinny he could hardly look at them. He hadn't even known that she'd taken his picture in the car. Nathan intended to open a new tab to see the evening's TV schedule, but without really intending to, his eyes tracked the words posted beside the picture.

'The new school has ALREADY started a pattern of harassment of my Love Bug. I can't believe how they insist on digging into our private lives and trying to force us to stop practicing our religion! Can't they just leave a poor sick and disabled boy alone for once???? Pray for me and little Nathaniel.'

There were already comments starting to come in under the post, most of them sympathetic and properly outraged. Nathan stared at the post and read it through again. He felt sick again, fighting against the bile that rose in his throat. He got up and hurried to the bathroom, and hunched over the toilet bowl, retching and spitting out the sour, burning bile. Mama left the food on the stove and hurried in to check on him.

"Oh, baby... are you okay? Are you going to be all right, sweetie?"

Holding his stomach, Nathan nodded. He tried to stop the retching and give his stomach a chance to recover. Mama rubbed his back soothingly. After he'd knelt there for a few minutes, shaking and sweaty, she encouraged him to get back up.

"Come on, let's get you into bed. I'll get you some ginger ale to settle your tummy, and you just try to relax and recover, okay?"

Nathan let her help him to his room. "No ginger ale," he said. "I'm okay. I feel better now. Just water."

"I'll get you both," she promised.

He lay down and let her tuck him in, but he couldn't settle his brain to go to sleep. He kept thinking of that picture of him and Mama's comments going out to all of her old friends and parishioners. Sick and disabled. Referring to him by pet names and telling everyone about their private lives. *Poor little Nathaniel.* He was glad she didn't know the details about him nearly peeing his pants, or she'd be posting that too. Mama returned with a couple of glasses for him. Nathan took a sip of the water and put it down to wait and see if his stomach would be able to tolerate it or not.

"Do you want something to eat?" Mama questioned. "Would you be able to keep it down, if I got you some crackers or something?"

Nathan shook his head. "Not yet," he said.

"Okay. Are you going to sleep?" she asked.

"I don't think I can right now."

"I could put some music on for you or something."

Nathan realized he never had checked to see what was on TV. "After I rest for a bit... we could see what's on. I can lay on the couch."

"Sure. I think The Bachelor is on tonight."

"That's *your* show," Nathan complained. Even though he actually quite liked it. It was their guilty pleasure. They both knew the show promoted immorality, and they shouldn't be watching it, but they both loved it. It was romantic, with the red roses and beautiful suits and dresses.

Mama gave Nathan a knowing smile.

"Well, maybe we can find something else on," she suggested.

"No... it's okay. You can watch Bachelor. I don't mind."

Mama laughed. "All right. You rest for a little bit and make sure your stomach's settled down. Then I'll come get you when it's time for the show to start."

Nathan nodded and settled back. "Okay," he agreed.

The next garbage day, Mama asked Nathan to take the garbage out to the back lane so they wouldn't miss the pick-up. He dragged the big wheeled bin back behind the fence. Glancing down the alley, he saw that Chandra's bin wasn't out yet, so he walked over and entered through the back gate. The bin was sitting over by her back door. He knocked on the back door.

He waited, a hollow feeling in his stomach. What if something had happened to her? What if she was dead, laying in there all by herself? What would he do if she didn't answer? If she never answered? He remembered the bitter, metallic aftertaste of the banana bread that he had brought her. Surely once she tasted it, she wouldn't finish it. She'd have a bite or two and throw it out before it could do her any harm, wouldn't she? But sometimes old people didn't have very good taste buds anymore. What if she couldn't taste it like Nathan could?

He knocked on the door again, and rang the bell. A few more minutes passed, and he knew that something had happened to her. She was sick, or dead, and was not going to come to the door.

The door swung in suddenly, making Nathan jump. He saw Chandra standing there with a frown on her face, and his knees went wobbly with relief. She was okay. She was still alive.

"Nathan?" Chandra questioned. "What are you doing here? I'm sorry, I went to the front door. I don't usually get anyone at the back."

"Oh, yeah," Nathan said. She'd had to walk all the way to the front and then the back, with her bad leg and cane. He hadn't even thought about that. "It's just that it's garbage collection day, and I saw your bin wasn't out. I was going to take it for you, but I thought I'd see if you had anything else to put in it before I do."

"How thoughtful of you! I completely forgot what day it was." She got an impish look, her eyes sparkling. "That's one of the dangers of time travel. It can result in a bit of disorientation."

Nathan shook his head, pretty sure that she was teasing him. He put his hand on the bin. "Did you have anything else, then?" he questioned.

"The kitchen's just about full. Step inside for a minute and I'll get it."

It wasn't cold out, but Nathan accepted her invitation and stepped in the back door to wait for her. Everything was neat and tidy. The mat was vacuumed clean, gardening shoes lined up neatly to the side. Some plaques with cute animals and homilies hung on the wall. There was a shoe scraper shaped like a hedgehog that looked like it had never actually been used.

Chandra returned with a small garbage bag in her hand. "Thanks so much, Nathan. You're such good neighbors."

Nathan nodded. "It's no trouble."

Nathan took the garbage bag and went back outside. Throwing the bag into the bin, he dragged it all out to the back lane and placed it the prescribed distance from the back fence. Then he went back in through his own back door. Mama looked at him.

"What took you so long? Is everything okay?"

"Yeah. I just took Mrs. Mullenny's garbage out for her too."

"Oh." She stilled, thinking about that. "Did you see her?"

"Yeah. I knocked to see if she had anything else to put in the bin before I took it out. She was there, and she said thank you."

"She was there," Mama repeated.

Nathan shrugged. "Yes'm."

"Did she look sick?"

"No, she looked just fine. Just the same as usual."

Mama rubbed the center of her forehead, her eyes going back and forth like she was reading a book. Her voice was very soft, not intended for him, just a reflection of what was in her mind. "...these signs will accompany those who believe..."

Nathan watched her face closely, until she turned away from him. It was smooth and blank, trancelike. She went down the hall toward her own room for something. Nathan stood there, watching her retreat. He knew the scripture she had murmured by heart. It was from the Book of Mark.

'And these signs will accompany those who believe: In my name they will drive out demons; they will speak in new tongues; they will pick up snakes with their hands; and when they drink deadly poison, it will not hurt them at all; they will place their hands on sick people, and they will get well.'

Nathan bit his lip, considering. Did that mean that Mama no longer thought Chandra was a witch? Now she thought that Chandra was a believer, like them? Thinking about it, Nathan went to get his school bag and to prepare for school.

When Mama got her first paycheck from the store, she picked Nathan up after school, smiling widely, obviously excited.

"Are we going to celebrate?" Nathan questioned. Usually that meant going out to dinner or going on some other special date together.

"I already got something to celebrate," Mama said, looking at him coyly.

"What?"

"You have to find it. It's at the house."

"What did you get?" Nathan demanded. "Is it food? A computer? What did you get?"

"I'm not telling. You have to find it."

"Is it big or little?" Nathan demanded.

"I'm not telling. You have to find it."

"Can you eat it?"

She laughed, and covered her mouth. "I'm not telling," she insisted. But her reaction had already given him the answer to that question.

"Can you wear it?" he tried.

She laughed harder. "I'm not telling, Nathaniel! You have to look around when you get home and find it."

"Is it hidden? How big is it?"

She pressed her lips together and shook her head. "I'm not telling. You'll just have to figure it out."

Nathan shifted in his seat and pulled the seatbelt around him. Mama was giddy with excitement, and it was rubbing off on him. He didn't even know what to be excited about, but her mood was infectious.

"I can't wait. Tell me!"

She shook her head, smiling widely. Nathan could hardly wait to get home. Mama loved to surprise him with little presents. It made her almost more excited than it made him. He watched out the window, impatient with the traffic that he usually didn't pay any attention to. It seemed like it was taking longer than ever to get home.

"You'll see," Mama assured him.

They finally made their way out of the rush hour traffic, and pulled up in front of the house. Nathan took his time getting up to the door, even though he was excited. He didn't want to burn all of his little remaining energy off in a sprint for the door, and then not be able to search properly for the present. Mama moved ahead of him up the sidewalk and unlocked the door. She went into the kitchen to work on supper, pretending that she wasn't paying any attention to Nathan's search for the surprise. But he noticed that she didn't get anything cooking while he was looking.

He made a quick circuit through the house first, looking for something obvious. But it wasn't that big. He tried a search of his room next, checking under the pillow, under the bed, and in the drawers and the closet. Nathan sat down on his bed, dizzy from bending down to look under the bed, and puffing a little from the search and his excitement.

Where was it? Mama had laughed when he'd asked her if it was something that you could eat, so he didn't think it would be in the kitchen. He didn't think that it would be in her room or in the bathroom. That left the sitting room. After getting his breath back, he went to the front room, and looked for the hiding place. He looked through the shelves and cupboards that housed their books, CD's, and DVD's. He sat down and looked around the room, trying to identify something that was out of place. Mama peeked in through the doorway.

"Haven't found it yet?" she teased.

"No. Not yet."

"Keep looking. You're getting warm."

Nathan got up slowly, and walked a slow circuit around the room.

'You're getting warm,' she had said. Was it a clue? He felt warmth on his arm as he walked past a shelf, and stopped and looked. The terrarium was radiating heat. Nathan bent down to look at it. He hadn't noticed during his search that it had been plugged in, the light and the heater turned on. He searched through the branches and landscaping, then finally spotted a couple of inches of scales, well-camouflaged in the back. He reached up to open the lid.

"Leave it for now," Mama warned. "Give it a chance to get accustomed to its new home."

He left the lid alone.

"What kind is it?" he questioned. "I can't see it."

"Crote," she said. "Red diamond."

"Is it pretty?" Nathan tapped lightly on the glass. "I want to see it."

"Very pretty," Mama agreed. "But you'll have to wait. I don't want to aggravate it right now. Quit tapping."

Nathan obeyed. He knew snakes didn't like you thumping on the glass. He'd grown up around them.

"How big is it? Full grown? Is it a boy or girl?"

Mama laughed. She sat on the couch and patted the cushion beside her for Nathan to sit down. He sat and watched the terrarium, hoping that the snake would decide to show itself.

"Female. Juvenile, but not a hatchling. About half-grown."

"You didn't tell me you were getting one!"

She smiled.

"I wasn't sure if it was going to come through or not. You never know if something is going to happen."

Nathan's stomach growled, and Mama looked at him.

"Does that mean you're hungry for once?" she questioned.

"Little bit," Nathan admitted.

"Well then, I'd better get to work."

"I'm not *that* hungry," Nathan warned. "Just a sandwich or something."

"You'll have to do better than that. We're celebrating, remember?"

Chapter Eleven

"THEY'RE GOING TO FIND you."

Nathan's eyes were heavy, he couldn't open them properly to identify the voice. "What? Who's going to find me? Who's there?"

He was standing on a big rock on top of a hill, looking out at the sunset. Looking down at the edge of a wooded area. Everything seemed dark and secretive. There was something hiding in the trees. Something watchful and malevolent.

"Where's Mama?" Nathan demanded. "Mama? Who's there?"

"They will find you," the mysterious whisper repeated.

Nathan rubbed his eyes, turning in a circle, trying to find the speaker. "Mama? Who's there? What's going on?"

There was a movement in the woods, and Nathan was drawn toward it. He didn't know why, but he needed to get down there, to find out. Something was in there. Was it the voice, or was it the 'they' that the voice was speaking of? Nathan was afraid. The wind whispered through the trees, and he looked around. He was in the trees, with no memory of how he had gotten down there. Had he run? Flown? Nothing was making any sense.

"I'm going to find you, Nathaniel."

Nathan awoke with a start. He was sweating heavily, his pajamas soaked. He still felt the unease of the nightmare, felt like someone was watching. Although he hated to get out of bed to change, exposing his body to the cool night air, he knew that he had to; he'd never be able to get back to sleep in the clammy, damp clothes. Nathan pulled back the blinds slightly in order to be able to reach the handle that he would wind to close the window, so at least there wasn't a cold breeze blowing on him. A shadow moved across the yard, making him jump.

It was just because of his dream. He was seeing things and was so jumpy because of the nightmare. Dreaming that people were watching him, searching for him. It had just scared him into thinking that there was someone in the yard. He strained his eyes at the shadows, waiting for a further movement, waiting for something that he could identify as a human shape. Or an animal. Or a tree swaying in the wind. Nothing. After a while, he dropped the blinds back into place, without reaching over to close the window. He felt too exposed. As Nathan changed out of his damp clothes into something warm and dry, he heard noises outside. Stealthy movements through the grass and twigs.

Afraid to look out again, afraid of what he would see, Nathan lay back down again and pulled the blankets up over his face. There was nothing there. It was just his dream.

It was all just the dream.

Nathan got off of the bus after school and walked up to the house, noting immediately that Mama's car was not in front of the house. He let himself in with his key, and looked around for a note. It was stuck to his bedroom door. Mama used to leave notes on the fridge, because that was the first place that Nathan went when he got home from school. But now the first place he went was to bed for a nap or early bedtime.

'Was called in for an extra shift. Mrs. Mullenny has invited you over for supper. You can stay there until I get home.'

Nathan had to shake his head at that. Now that she'd decided that Chandra was a believer instead of a witch, it sounded like they were suddenly best friends. Now she was encouraging him to go over there to visit. He put his backpack down in his room, and headed over to Chandra's.

He didn't have to wait long at the door this time. She must have been watching for him, and was there to open the door almost before he finished knocking. Nathan stood there with his fist raised, surprised.

"Come in, come in," Chandra encouraged. "I was delighted when your mother asked if you could come over after school for a visit. Come right in and make yourself at home."

Nathan stepped into the house and could immediately smell something cooking. It had a sort of a seafood-y smell that made him feel nauseated. He gulped and followed Chandra into the sitting room. She looked perplexed.

"I was just working in the kitchen..." she started. She seemed to want to keep him company, but she couldn't very well entertain him in the sitting room and make her supper at the same time.

"I could visit with you there," Nathan suggested. "In the kitchen."

She hesitated at first, but then nodded. "Yes, of course. Come on in. That makes a lot more sense."

She led the way to the kitchen and Nathan followed. He chose one of the straight-backed wooden chairs and lowered himself into it, closing his eyes for a moment to rest. He knew that he should offer to help her with the supper preparations, but he was too tired and needed to sit down. He wasn't sure he had the energy to rip lettuce leaves just then. Chandra went over to the stove and stirred a big stew pot. Nathan caught himself smiling. He could just imagine Delia's reaction to Chandra brewing up some sort of weird concoction in a big pot on the stove. She would be more convinced than ever that she was a witch.

"What are you making?" Nathan questioned.

"Frogmore stew."

Nathan's stomach twisted and lurched. He was already tired and shaky after a long day at school, and nauseated by the seafood smell. The suggestion of frogs put him dangerously close to the edge of being sick.

Chandra turned away from the stew pot and smiled at him. Nathan attempted to smile back and look interested. "I can't eat wheat and have some other allergies," Chandra said. "So I'm always on the lookout for recipes that are new and interesting and don't have any of the things that I am allergic to in them. There's a whole world full of delicious foods that the pizza-and-spaghetti crowd will never experience!"

She turned back to the stove and turned down the burner.

"Frogmore stew isn't much to look at, but it really is quite tasty. Still... it's not what I would have made for a preteen boy who wasn't used to different foods, if I had known ahead that you were coming."

Nathan made an interested noise.

"You're from the South, though," Chandra said. "Maybe you've had it before?"

"No."

There were a number of traditional southern foods that Nathan had no intention of trying. Anything with intestines or brains in it, for starters. He wondered uneasily what all was in Frogmore stew. Chandra sighed and got out a couple of plates, and ladled stew onto them. She placed one of the plates in front of Nathan, and went back across the kitchen to get eating utensils. Nathan stared down at the stew. It looked like a pile of garbage. Pieces of corn on the cob, whole potatoes, shrimp, hunks of sausage, and some kind of legs. Nathan didn't think that they were frog legs, but shuddered just the same. His stomach did flips, and he didn't know how he was going to manage to eat any of it.

Chandra handed him his utensils, and looked at his face. "Are you okay?" she questioned.

"I'm just... not feeling very good," Nathan said, poking one of the potatoes with a fork and wondering whether it was going to taste like seafood too. He swallowed hard.

"Do you want something else?" she questioned.

"No, no, it's okay," Nathan protested weakly.

"That's very polite of you. Now be honest with me. I could make you something else. I can't make you a sandwich, but... maybe baked beans from a can?"

Nathan nodded, his face burning. To his relief, Chandra picked up the plate in front of him and moved it off of the table. He put his head down on his folded arms, resting on the table, though he knew it was probably rude to do so. He heard Chandra using the electric can opener.

"My son used to like wieners in his beans," she said. "I could cut up some of these sausages into yours."

"No thanks," Nathan said. "Just beans by themselves."

She nodded and proceeded to put some in a bowl to warm up. He remembered that she had said that her son was dead. Had he been a soldier? Or killed in a car accident? Nathan was curious, but afraid to ask. Delia had said that Chandra always wore black, and Nathan had never seen her in anything else. Maybe that was in mourning for her son. People didn't really do that anymore, but that didn't mean that Chandra couldn't, if she wanted to.

Chandra took the beans back out of the microwave and uncovered them. Without further fuss, she put the bowl in front of Nathan, as he sat up again to make space. Nathan kept his eyes focused on the beans, averted from her Frogmore stew. Chandra didn't offer grace or any words of thanks, she just started eating. Nathan sat there awkwardly for a moment, then said a hurried prayer in his head and took a bite. He chewed for a long time, much longer than necessary to get the beans down. His stomach calmed a little, but he still couldn't eat very much. After a few spoons full, he was trying to figure out what to do with the rest of the beans.

"You don't like them?" Chandra questioned.

"No, I do, they're good. I'm just... I can't eat much at a time. I don't have much appetite."

Chandra put a bite of stew in her mouth, considering this.

"Are you doing chemotherapy, Nathan?" she questioned. "I have a friend who had a cancer scare and had to do that, and it was so hard for her to eat anything."

Nathan shook his head. "No. I don't have cancer."

He looked at her for a moment, feeling like he should add something. Then he shrugged, looking down at the nearly-full bowl of beans.

"Well, that's okay. Don't feel like you need to eat all of them. I should have asked how much you wanted before I dished it up."

"They're good," Nathan said. "I just... can't. Can I use your bathroom?" Chandra nodded.

"Just down the hall, there," she pointed.

Nathan retreated to the silence of the bathroom. He used the toilet, and thankfully the smell of the stew was much less there. The beans stayed down. Nathan washed his hands and splashed cold water on his face. He went back to the kitchen.

"I'm going to go home," he said. "I need to do my homework, and maybe lie down a bit. Sorry I can't stay and visit longer."

Chandra gave him a reassuring smile.

"That's okay, Nathan. I'm glad that you came over to see me. You let me know if you need anything while your mom is gone okay? I'm happy to help, and you've been such a good neighbor to me."

"Thanks," he said. "I'll... see you later, then."

And with that, he went home.

Mama was late getting home, but Nathan was awake when she got there. She came in and sat with him on the couch, putting her arm around him to pull him close and kiss the top of his head.

"So, Bug. Why don't you tell me about your day today? I want to hear every little thing."

Nathan considered. He wasn't about to tell her about Chandra's stew. For all he knew, it might set her off to thinking that she was a witch again, like it would Delia. So he steered clear of that, and thought about school.

"Today I had gym instead of resource room," he said. "I guess resource was full up. But Coach got a student teacher, and I did yoga with her, instead of basketball. So I didn't get too tired."

"Yoga?" Mama repeated, frowning.

"Not the hard kind," Nathan said, "where you get all hot and sweaty. Just stretching... it actually made me feel good..." he trailed off.

Mama's face was tight; her look made him nervous. He swallowed, and bit his lip, waiting for her to speak.

"Yoga is a religious practice," Mama said, drawing back from him to look him in the face. "A non-Christian religious practice. You know better than that!"

"But--it wasn't!" Nathan protested. "It was just stretching, and balancing and stuff. There wasn't anything wrong with it. There wasn't..." he shook his head, trying to understand. "It wasn't religious."

Mama got up and walked a few steps away, then turned back around to face him. "Do you think the devil is going to make it obvious? He wants to hide it, drag you in slowly. It is Hindu. They worship other gods--many gods--and animals and trees and nature."

"But it was just exercise. Just phys ed!"

"Did you put your hands together in prayer?"

Nathan stopped biting his lip. His stomach flipped. He couldn't truthfully tell her that he hadn't put his hands together like he was praying. The teacher had even called it 'prayer position'. But he hadn't *been* praying. Had he? Could you pray to another god without meaning to?

Mama took a step closer to him, her eyes hard and angry. She saw the answer in his face without him saying anything. "Did you bow down?"

Nathan nodded. "But..."

He hadn't bowed down to any idols. It was just an exercise. Nathan's eyes were burning. He hadn't intended to do anything wrong. He had thought that it was just an exercise class. The thought that he had been participating in a non-Christian religion made him feel sick.

"Did you raise your arms up to heaven? Did you prostrate yourself? Did you bow to each other? Did you mock the resurrection by lying in corpse pose and then arising?" she fired the questions at him rapidly, giving him no chance to answer or protest.

The tears started to leak from Nathan's eyes. He swiped at them. "Mama... I didn't mean to do anything wrong."

"The Bible says 'Thou shalt have no other gods before me.' You know the scriptures, Nathaniel. You know better."

"She didn't say anything about other gods. I didn't know!"

"I can't believe that the school would try this," Mama muttered, and she paced back and forth, her eyes wild, her movements jerky and angry. She suddenly stopped and whirled to face him again. Her face was sheet-white, like she'd just seen a ghost.

"Did they tell you that you could heal yourself?" she questioned.

Nathan held his arms folded over his stomach, knotted with cramps. He knew what she was talking about as soon as she said it. The teacher had talked about the healing power of breath, and sending energy to all of his cells, all over his body. She had encouraged him to reach deep down inside to identify the energy of the parts of his body that needed healing, and to breathe into that place. To imagine his body working together perfectly, the way that it was meant to. She said that he could do that. He could harness the power of his body and his mind to heal himself.

When he didn't answer, Mama put her hands up to her face, crying out. "No, Nathaniel! Only God can heal you. Only faith in the one true God! If you are trying to heal yourself with your thoughts and that pagan practice, you are drawing on the powers of the devil! You see how quickly he pulls you in!"

Nathan smeared the tears now coursing down his face. He had felt the strange power. The confidence that the yoga gave him. The feeling of awareness of his own body that he had never experienced before, and of power within it. He knew the word for that kind of feeling. Carnal. And that meant it was from the devil, as Mama said, and not from God.

"What am I supposed to do now?" he questioned, sobbing, his feelings beyond his control. "I didn't mean to, Mama. I didn't know."

"I know," Mama said slowly. She sat back down next to him and gave him a hug. "I know, baby. They deceived you and they trapped you. But now you let the devil in. And that's not easy to fix."

'This kind goeth not out except by fasting and prayer.'

Nathan read the words again. He could barely keep his eyes open anymore. The letters blurred on the page. Kneeling by the couch, he closed his eyes and bowed his head, praying for forgiveness for participating in the pagan worship of other gods.

"Nathaniel!"

He jerked awake. Mama shook him by the shoulder.

"You need to stay awake," she insisted. She turned the music up louder. "Come on. Come dance with me."

"Mama, I can't," he groaned.

"You can. God can give you the power. Come on."

She pulled him to his feet. Nathan clapped to start out with, getting the beat and trying to work up the energy and excitement he needed to join in the dancing. Mama sang the chorus loudly in a chirpy voice, trying to get him into it. But Nathan's body just dragged. He was so tired.

"Come on," Mama grabbed him by the hands and danced.

Nathan tried to join in, bouncing and moving his feet, but it was like he was in concrete.

"Shake off the chains," Mama encouraged. "It's the devil that's slowing you down. Shake off the chains and move your body."

Nathan shook his body, and tried to dance. His legs gave way and he fell to his knees. Mama knelt down next to him, giving him a tight hug.

"Pray, Nathaniel. Pray for Him to take away the evil spirit."

Nathan rubbed his aching eyes. "I am, Mama. But I'm so tired. Can't I go to sleep now?"

"We need to drive it out, Nathaniel. You let it in, and we have to drive it out. Weaken it by depriving it of sleep and food, and pray for it to leave," she urged.

"I am..." Nathan swayed giddily. "I'm trying, Mama."

He overbalanced and toppled to the floor. Mama put her hands on him, praying, and the sitting room faded from sight.

When Nathan woke up, he knew he had been asleep a long time. The room was bright. He was in his own bed. He didn't know if it was the next day, or even longer. His eyes were sticky and gritty, and a headache pounded in the back of his head. He felt sluggish and dull. Nathan rubbed the grit out of his eyes, and turned over, seeking sleep. He didn't have to try for long.

The next time he awoke, the room was dim again. Mama was shaking his arm gently.

"Nathaniel. Nathaniel, can you wake up?"

He struggled to open his eyes to look at her. She sat on the edge of the bed and waited for him to fully awaken. Nathan rubbed his face drowsily.

"Is it night or day?" he questioned hoarsely.

"It's evening. I'm sorry to wake you up... but I was worried. We need to get some food in you."

Nathan was cold and tired. He didn't want to eat. His body felt shut-down.

"Come on, Bug. Let me help you up."

She pulled him up by the armpits, positioning him in a sitting position with a pillow behind him. Nathan wondered fleetingly if he would ever get too heavy for her to move around like that. Some of the kids in sixth grade were over a hundred pounds. Some were taller than their parents. But Nathan still felt like an eight-year-old, like he was stuck in a child's body.

Mama picked up a bowl from the nightstand, and held a steaming spoonful in front of Nathan's mouth. "Eat," she insisted. "You need to eat to get your strength back. You haven't had anything in days."

He accepted the spoonful. It burned his mouth. Chicken soup. Even though he hadn't been hungry, it felt good to eat. She was right, his body was starving, even if his stomach hadn't woken up yet. She held another spoonful in front of him, and Nathan blew it. Gently, so it wouldn't spill down his chest. Then he swallowed it.

It took a long time to eat the soup, one small spoonful at a time, but Nathan felt energized by it. His stomach was happy. He started to feel warmer. He put his head back, closing his eyes.

"Mmm. That's better."

"Have some more," Mama said. "You haven't eaten half of it."

"Not now. I'm full."

"Just a few more bites?"

"I can't. I'll have more later."

"Okay." She put the bowl down and sat there, looking him in the eye. "How do you feel?"

"Good. Just tired."

"All better...? Like yourself again...?"

"It left me," Nathan confirmed. "Did you see it leave?"

She hesitated. "I didn't see it... but I felt it. I knew, when you collapsed, that it had left. We drove it out. It couldn't stay in you any longer."

Nathan nodded, his eyes still closed.

"Only... I was afraid I'd lost you too. I was so scared, Bug. So scared."

"It's okay now."

"Yes. It's all okay now," she agreed.

Summer ran up to Nathan as he approached the school.

"Nathan! Are you okay? I missed you!"

She gave him a hug. Soft and fleeting, but it couldn't be denied that she had hugged him in her joy of seeing him again. He couldn't stop the blush that rose over his cheeks. She took his hand for a minute.

"So are you okay?" she demanded.

Nathan nodded. "Sure. I'm fine. I was just sick for a few days."

"The flu or something?"

Nathan shrugged. "Something like that."

"I was so scared that something had happened, and we wouldn't see you again."

He shook his head, bemused by her intensity. He liked Summer, but they didn't spend much time together, didn't talk to each other much. They hadn't shared the lunch hour together since those first couple of days. Nathan ate with Bly, or went out for a walk and ate by himself.

"I missed you too," he said lamely.

"Come on, the others will be glad to see that you're back."

Most of her friends did seem happy to see Nathan, but not like she was. Not so intense over it. Mal didn't smile at him, but just looked him over suspiciously, as if evaluating him. Nathan grew uncomfortable.

"I should see if I can talk to Mrs. Davis before class," he told Summer, excusing himself. "So I can find out what I missed."

Summer's smile fell away. She sighed. "I guess," she agreed. "But can we spend some time together later? Lunch, maybe?"

Nathan shrugged. He glanced at Mal. "I dunno. We'll see."

Summer followed his gaze to Mal and scowled. "He's not going to bug you," she said firmly. "Are you, Mal?"

"Did I say anything?" Mal questioned, his mouth turning down in a scowl.

"See?" Summer said to Nathan.

"We'll see," Nathan repeated, and he walked away from them.

Mama's car was gone when Nathan got home from school, and he didn't feel like being alone, so he went over to Chandra's house. Not to eat this time, just to visit.

"Ah, there is my friend," Chandra said, when she opened the door. "Come in, come in." She studied him closely, her pale blue eyes concerned. "You're looking a little worse for wear. You've been sick?"

Nathan nodded.

"Yes'm. A bit."

"You don't look well at all. Come in and sit down. Can I get you anything?"

"No. I don't need anything. I just didn't want to be alone."

Nathan led the way into the sitting room, and sat down, closing his eyes for a moment to take a breath. Chandra didn't sit down, hovering over him.

"You're sure I can't get you anything?" she pressed. "Do you want to lie down? My Kenneth's bed is free, no one uses it anymore. It's all made up with fresh sheets."

Nathan rubbed his eyes. "Well, maybe if I laid down for just a few minutes, I'd get a bit more energy," he admitted.

"This way."

Nathan followed Chandra down the hall to her dead son's bedroom. Nathan looked around curiously. It was done in navy blues. All of his possessions were neat and tidy. It was dusted. But still it felt cold and empty. Nathan moved toward the bed. His eyes caught on a small terrarium on the bedside table, and he leaned closer for a look.

"What's... oh!" He'd been expecting it to be empty, or to house a small lizard or frog or something, and was startled at the big, hairy spider. "You have a spider," he observed.

Chandra laughed. "Yes, I suppose I do," she agreed. "Although I never think of it as mine. It's Kenneth's."

Nathan sat on the bed and studied it. "What's it's name?" he asked.

"Her name is Bubbles."

Nathan laughed, and Chandra smiled at his reaction. Nathan looked around the room, and saw there was a large terrarium by the door that he hadn't seen when he walked into the room. He got up and walked over to it.

"Oooh."

Chandra looked over his shoulder. "It's a boa," she said.

"Yeah," Nathan agreed. "Nice. Can I hold it?"

Chandra reached past him to open the terrarium. "You like snakes?" she questioned.

Nathan nodded. He put his hands into the terrarium and carefully picked the boa up. "It's a little thin," he observed. "Hasn't it been eating?"

"Not since Kenneth died."

"Oh," Nathan stroked the snake's scales. "Poor thing. It misses him." He watched the boa wrap around his arm. The snake's tongue flicked in and out. Chandra looked at him with sad eyes.

"I don't really like the cold-blooded creatures," she said. "So she hasn't gotten a lot of attention."

Nathan nodded. "They still have feelings," he said. "They get... used to their handlers."

Nathan started to feel lightheaded, and lurched back over to sit on the bed, which suddenly seemed much further across the room than it had previously. He put his hand down on the mattress and lowered himself to sit on it.

"Are you okay?" Chandra questioned.

"I'm not sure," Nathan admitted, touching his forehead. "I feel... weird."

"Weird how?" she got closer to him.

"Just really... dizzy... and I can't... catch my breath."

She took the snake out of Nathan's hands. "We'd better put her back."

Nathan put his head in his hands, resting his elbows on his knees. "It will pass..." he said.

"Nathan... maybe I should call your mom," Chandra suggested.

"I don't know..." Nathan swallowed. "Maybe some water..."

"Sure. Hang on a moment."

She moved out of the room as quickly as she could, which with her bad leg and cane was not very fast. Nathan waited, the pain in his middle growing. His thoughts were fuzzy. Not just tired and fuzzy, but really disoriented. It was hard to focus on reality. He held his stomach.

"Chandra?" he called out, scared.

Before she could turn around, Nathan hit the floor on his knees, throwing up. That was the last thing he remembered.

Chapter Twelve

HE WOKE UP ON a gurney with a paramedic leaning over him. Nathan tried to sit up and look for Mama, but was unable to get up. He shook his head at the paramedic.

"No. No, leave me alone!"

"It's okay, Nathan. We're here to help. Can you tell me what happened?"

"No. No, please leave me alone. Let me up!"

"It's okay, Nathan. Can you tell me when your last dose of insulin was?"

"No. No insulin."

"You're diabetic, right?" the paramedic questioned, frowning at him.

"Yes."

"Your sugar is sky high. When did you take insulin last?"

Nathan shook his head. "No. I don't take insulin."

The paramedic shook his head. He checked the IV that was already draining into the back of Nathan's hand. Nathan couldn't see what he was doing.

"This will help you to feel better," the paramedic said.

"No!" Nathan protested.

"Shh. Try to just stay still and calm. You'll stabilize faster if you are calm."

Nathan turned his head. "Where's Mama?"

"They're trying to contact your mom right now. She'll meet us at the hospital."

"I want Mama. Don't do anything."

"It's okay," the paramedic soothed. "We'll talk to her really soon."

Nathan must have fallen asleep or passed out again. He didn't remember anything of the ambulance ride. He didn't wake up again until some time later. He could hear Mama's voice raised, arguing with a man nearby.

"You didn't have any right to treat him! You need permission before you can do anything."

"We have the right to provide life-saving measures," the voice responded. "All we did was stabilize him until we could get a hold of you. He was in crisis. He might not have even made it to the hospital without insulin and the other life-saving measures that were provided. I don't think you realize how seriously ill your child is."

"We don't use medicine. We heal through faith."

"Have you been told before that he has diabetes?"

"His body is sick," Mama said. "But God can heal him. With faith. You can't heal him. You can only treat him."

"We are required by law to treat him. If you object to that, you're going to have to file a court injunction. He is going to die if we don't treat him."

"I haven't given y'all permission!"

"I will have him apprehended by Child Services, and then they will give their permission to treat him."

"You can't do that!"

"You know I can. The nurse will bring you forms to sign. If you will give us permission to treat Nathaniel, then I won't have a reason to call Child Services, will I?"

"You can't heal him," she pointed out.

"No. But I can keep him alive. I can give him a normal life." The curtain beside Nathan's bed was drawn back, but Nathan kept his eyes closed. "Look at him. He's emaciated. You're starving him to death. His cells can't get sugar without insulin. He's in ketoacidosis. His organs will shut down. How long has it been since he saw a doctor or had any insulin?"

"We have been praying--"

"Prayer is not enough," the doctor's angry voice rose impatiently. "Prayer won't make his body start producing insulin again. You need to treat him."

Mama's voice was sullen. "If I sign your papers, y'all won't call Child Services?"

"I won't call Child Services if I'm convinced that you are going to care for him properly. And that means keeping up the proper insulin protocol."

"You can't force me to give him insulin."

"Then Child Services will remove him."

There was a period of silence. Nathan held his breath.

"Fine," Mama said finally. "Bring me the papers."

"Good."

"*Now* can I sit with him?"

There was no answer, but the doctor must have given her some kind of indication, as Nathan heard the rattle of the curtain and the scrape of a chair on the floor beside his bed. He opened his eyes and turned his head toward Mama.

"Nathaniel," she pressed his hand and stroked his hair. "How are you feeling, baby?" Her voice cracked.

"I'm sorry, Mama," Nathan said, squeezing her hand. "I told them no. I told them I didn't want insulin."

"Shhh. It's okay. Don't you worry about that. Don't worry about anything. You just need to rest now."

Nathan lay still for a while, not saying anything. She continued to hold his hand, humming very quietly, so he could barely hear her. Her eyes closed, and he knew that she was praying. Eventually her eyes opened again.

"Are you going to be in trouble at work?" Nathan questioned. "Because you left early?"

"When my son was being rushed to the hospital? No, they make allowances for that sort of thing," she said with an ironic attempt at humor. "My shift was almost up anyway. I wanted to be home to spend the evening with you."

"I'm sorry."

"You didn't do anything wrong, Nathaniel. You don't need to be sorry about anything."

"That doctor is going to make me take insulin. Are we going to have to move again?"

There was a frown line between Mama's eyebrows. She shook her head. "We can't move again right now. I don't have the money. We just barely got moved in. We'll just have to manage it the best we can." Nathan opened his mouth, and she touched his lips, stopping him from speaking. "And don't say you're sorry again."

Nathan didn't.

Nathan was starting to feel better when Chandra came to visit him. By that time he'd been moved to his own room, much quieter than Emergency and Intensive Care had been. He'd been sleeping a lot, and with the insulin and whatever else they were putting in his IV tube, Nathan's body was starting to recover. He wasn't so thirsty all the time, and was starting to overcome the exhaustion.

Mama had stayed with him as much as she could, but she had to go back into work again, and Chandra had offered to come and sit with him for a while to keep him company. So they all agreed, and the next time that Nathan woke up, she was sitting there beside his bed, reading a book. Nathan must have made some noise or movement as he woke up, because she looked up from her book at him.

"Well, hello there, sleepyhead."

"Hi."

"How are you feeling?"

Nathan shrugged and sat up a little bit. "I'm doing better," he admitted.

He felt guilty about feeling better. It was such a relief to feel some energy start to return to his body, such a relief for the diabetic symptoms to start fading away with a carefully calculated regimen of insulin. But he felt guilty about it. Like he had turned his back on Mama and on God. He felt worse about allowing them to give him insulin than he had about participating in the yoga at school.

"That's good. You gave me quite a scare."

He thought about how it must have been for her, him collapsing like that, and her not knowing what was going on. "Yeah... sorry for puking on the carpet..."

She shook her head, smiling. "I raised a son. I've dealt with it before. I was more concerned about you than the carpet."

Nathan nodded. They were silent for a few minutes.

"I have to ask... did you know that you were diabetic?" Chandra questioned.

Nathan nodded.

"But you weren't taking any insulin at all? Why not? Couldn't you see what it was doing to your body?"

Nathan tried to sit up, and she adjusted his pillow and helped him keep his IV line from pulling or kinking.

"We... don't believe in medical treatment," he explained.

"You don't believe it in. You mean you don't believe that it works? I don't understand."

"We only believe in faith healing. We believe that God can heal you, if you have enough faith."

Chandra stared at him. The bags under her eyes were more pronounced than usual, giving her a distinctly witch-like appearance.

"Nathan... you could have died. Right there in my house. Do you think God doesn't want you to take care of yourself? Don't you have to do everything you can, and leave the rest to him?"

"When it's your time, it doesn't matter whether you seek medical treatment or not," Nathan said. "If it's your time, God will take you. If it's not... if you have faith, and do what he wants... he'll prolong your life."

There was silence, and Nathan swallowed and looked away. He'd said the words. He'd explained it as Mama would have. But inside his head, his own brain fought against the idea. Nathan wanted to live. He didn't want to die on the floor in Chandra's house, or in his own bed at home. He didn't want to pray, and wait and see if God would heal him, taking away the burning thirst and exhaustion. He was a hypocrite for saying the words when he doubted them, when he couldn't overcome his own doubts and carnal desire to live, no matter what the cost to his soul.

"Are you upset that I called the ambulance?" Chandra questioned.

"No."

"I can't believe that your own mother would stand by, and watch you waste away. I would have done anything to help my son."

Nathan looked back at her. "What happened to him?" he questioned softly.

She stared off into the distance, not seeing Nathan. "He suffered from depression. He got that from me, I've always struggled with it..."

"What happened?" Nathan asked.

"He took his own life." Chandra's voice was anguished. "He got his depression from me, and I was so wrapped up in my own problems, that I didn't realize how dark things had become for him. I should have been able to see it. If I suffered from it myself, how could I not see it in him?"

"There was nothing that you could have done," Nathan said.

"Of course there was! We could have tried medications. Counseling. Helping him to deal with his problems at school, or whatever else he was going through. If I had paid attention, I could have prevented it. And I wouldn't have lost him." She shook her head. "Instead, I thought he was just a little down after breaking up with his girlfriend. I thought that encouraging him to get out more, to sleep and eat right, take some herbal remedies, I thought that would be enough. I was so blind."

"Kenneth wouldn't want you to beat yourself up over it," Nathan pointed out, feeling sorry for her.

Chandra sighed. "That's why I can't understand your mother letting this happen. I wouldn't have stood by and let Kenneth die, if I had known. I would have done everything in my power to save him."

"What does it profit a man to save his life if he loses his own soul?" Nathan asked.

"Do you think God would punish you for taking medication?" Chandra demanded. "How could that be wrong?"

Nathan looked out the window. He couldn't see much, other than a little corner of sky. It was clear blue, with no clouds.

"I'm sorry," Chandra said after a while. "I shouldn't be challenging your religious beliefs. I'm just trying to understand them."

He looked back at her. "We've seen miracles," Nathan explained. "We've seen the signs that follow the believers. Mama's faith is so strong, and she has healed people, by laying her hands on them in prayer."

Chandra's eyebrows rose. "Oh?" she said skeptically.

"She has. People with cancer, or paralysis. Littler things too, but we've seen people on their death beds get up and walk."

Chandra studied Nathan. She didn't seem to know what to say about this.

"When you see signs and miracles, how could you not believe?" Nathan said.

"I don't now. That must have been a very powerful experience."

Nathan nodded. A nurse came in with a lunch tray. "Hello, Nathan. Time for you to eat," she said with a pleasant smile. She stopped to check his chart before taking the covering off of the tray. Nathan saw the orange 'diabetic' tag on the cover.

"I'm not hungry yet," Nathan said.

She shook her head and wheeled the table over in front of him. "You need to eat at regular intervals to get your sugars under control. And now it is time to eat."

She looked at Chandra sitting in the visitor chair. "Is this mom?" she questioned.

Nathan and Chandra both laughed.

"No, just a friend," Chandra said.

"Oh, okay. Well, I need to spend a little time with Nathan talking about his diet, if you want to take a little break."

Nathan looked at her name tag, and realized she wasn't a nurse, but a nutritionist.

"I'll just go get a coffee," Chandra agreed. She stood up and looked down at Nathan, both of her hands resting on her cane. "Can I get you anything? Some pop and chocolate bars?"

The nutritionist's mouth dropped open. "Nathan can't--" she cut herself off when she saw that both of them were grinning. "Oh, I can see I'm going to have to keep an eye on you two."

Chandra made her way out of the room. The nutritionist sat down with Nathan. She pulled out a little flip chart book and put it on the table next to his dinner. "We need to talk about the things that you can be doing to help control your sugars," she said.

Nathan nodded. "I try not to eat stuff with sugar," he said. "The desserts at school, and juice and stuff."

"That's a good start. So let's go over the things that you should be eating, and portion sizes. You get started eating your lunch," she gestured at it. "You're very malnourished. You understand that when your body can't use sugar, it starts to cannibalize your fat and muscle for energy instead?"

Nathan shrugged, looking down at his plate. He took a few bites of his meal.

"Do you have a blood glucose monitor? Someone else will be talking to you about how to monitor your sugar so you know how much insulin you need."

"No."

She pulled out a notepad and jotted something down. "We'll make sure you get one. The doctors will help you to sort out how much insulin you need on a regular basis to maintain, but you'll need to understand what to do if your sugars are too high or too low."

Nathan nodded.

"Okay. So let's talk about portions and some of the rules you should be following."

She opened up the flip book to the first page.

Nathan shifted around restlessly. He picked up the book that he'd been reading, but he'd finished it, and didn't feel like starting it over again. They hadn't turned on the TV channels for the small TV mounted in the corner of the room. He couldn't see anything but sky out the window, even when he was sitting up. The bed next to him was empty. Though he didn't know if he'd have been brave enough to start up a conversation with a patient that he didn't know even if it was occupied. Starting to overcome the fatigue from his diabetes, he no longer felt like sleeping all the time. He was restless to actually get up and do something.

There was a knock on the open door of the hospital room, and he turned to see who it was. Summer stood there with an older woman. "Hey, Nathan," she greeted, coming into the room. "How're you doing? Are you up for some company?"

Nathan nodded. "Yeah, come on in," he invited, and gestured to the unoccupied chairs next to the bed.

"This is my mom," Summer gestured to the woman.

"Hi, Nathan," Summer's mom greeted. She pulled one of the chairs back from the bed, setting it down against the wall at the foot of the bed. "I'll just sit out of the way over here. You guys go ahead and visit and pretend I'm not here."

Nathan nodded. "Thanks for bringing Summer to visit."

Summer pulled the other visitor chair closer to Nathan's bed. She touched his arm lightly. "So how are you?" she questioned. "Are you doing okay?"

"Feeling a lot better now," Nathan said, again with that twinge of guilt over relying on medicine instead of having the faith to be healed. "I should be back at school in a few more days."

"You sure scared us." Summer shifted. "Oh, I have a card." She looked over at her mother, who rifled in her purse and pulled out an envelope. Summer went and got it from her, and handed it to Nathan. "Here. It's from the whole class."

Nathan opened it up, and smiled at the cartoon on the front. He opened the card and looked at all of the names and doodles inside.

"Cool," he said. "Thanks a lot!"

"I thought you were going to die," Summer said. "We heard that an ambulance had to take you to hospital, and then you were in intensive care. I knew how sick you looked, and I thought..."

Nathan shrugged, looking down at the card to avoid looking her in the face. "I have diabetes," he admitted.

"Oh..." her voice was surprised. "So... your sugar got too high?"

Nathan nodded. "Yes... if it stays too high for too long... you can get really sick."

He looked back over at her. Summer nodded. "My cousin is diabetic and has to take insulin shots. Is that what you have to do?"

"I guess so... now."

She looked him in the face for a moment without saying anything, and Nathan grew uncomfortable. "What?"

"You're looking better, you know. Your eyes and everything. You don't look so tired."

"I'm getting my energy back," Nathan agreed. "Maybe I'll actually be able to sit through social studies without falling asleep."

She snickered. "Don't count on it. Social studies puts everyone to sleep."

Nathan laughed. "Okay. Maybe not social. Maybe math."

Summer wrinkled her nose. "Maybe. So that's why you can't eat the desserts in the cafeteria? Because of the sugar? They shouldn't make you buy stuff that could make you sick!"

Nathan shrugged. "It's okay, I've been bringing my own lunch anyway. Maybe now, since everybody's going to know... they won't make me."

"Yeah. I don't want them to make you more sick."

"I wouldn't eat it, even if I had to buy it."

"I guess." Summer looked around the dismal little hospital room. "So this looks pretty boring. What have you been doing?"

"Not much. Sleeping at lot. Mama and my neighbor come to visit. And I have lessons. You know, on how to manage my diabetes. I had a book," Nathan indicated it on the side table. "But I finished it now."

"Do you want some more books? I could get some from the library."

"Sure," Nathan said, "that would be really nice of you, if it's not any trouble."

Summer looked at her mother, who nodded. "Of course you can," she agreed.

"Yeah, that would be good. It's kind of boring, just laying here."

"I bet," Summer agreed.

"How's my Love Bug?" Mama's voice rang out as she entered the room. She stopped short. "Oh, you have visitors."

Nathan felt his cheeks flush over Summer hearing Mama use his pet name. "Mama!"

"What? Does that embarrass you? I didn't know you had anyone here."

She came the rest of the way in, and looked questioningly at Summer.

"This is Summer, Mama. From my school class." He held the card out to her. "She brought me a card from everyone. Wasn't that nice?"

"It surely was," Mama looked over the card, and smiled at Summer. "What a sweet thing you are."

Summer smiled and scratched her ear, looking away. Mama looked Nathan over.

"Nathaniel's looking awfully piqued," she said. "He should be resting, having a nap. Y'all don't want to make him sicker."

"No. We'd better go," Summer agreed. She looked over at her mother. "I guess it's time to go, Mom."

"Are you sure you don't want to spend a little longer? We just barely got here. Nathan seems to be holding his own."

Nathan looked back and forth at the mothers, not liking being stuck between them. "I'd better get some rest, like Mama says," he said.

Summer nodded and went to her mother. "Bye, Nathan. Get better soon, okay?"

Nathan nodded. "Thanks for coming."

They left the room. Mama sat down in the chair. "Now it's just you and me," she observed.

"Do you think I can go home soon?" Nathan questioned, leaning his head back.

"In the next day or two, probably. Then you might still need a few more days recuperating at home before going back to class."

"I'm already feeling better than I was when I was going to school."

"That's good. I'm glad you're feeling better."

But she looked a little sad when she said it. Nathan knew she was thinking about being forced to treat him. He had to bite his tongue from telling her he was sorry again. He knew she was tired of him saying it.

"So... tell me about work," he suggested. "How's the job been going lately? Is it good?"

Mama put on a smile. "It is good," she agreed. She proceeded to tell him all about an upcoming sale that they were preparing for. Nathan listened with his eyes closed, and didn't fall asleep.

Nathan had missed at least one Sunday worship while he was in hospital. He was still having problems unravelling the timeline and thought it might actually have been two. And he didn't know for sure if Mama had still held a midweek prayer meeting or not.

He woke up in the morning without Mama having to come in and wake him up, and he stretched, feeling focused and energetic. The contrast to how he felt when he wasn't taking insulin was incredible. He took a deep breath, and climbed out of bed. He dressed in his Sunday clothes without being told, and went to find Mama. She was sitting on the couch, with the sun shining on her hair. She was reading her Bible, and looked up at Nathan as he came in.

"There's my handsome little man. How are you doing, sweetie?"

"Good. Are we going to have brunch?"

She smiled. "I'm glad to see you interested in food." She stopped for a minute, frowning, as if remembering the reason he was feeing better. "Well, what do you want to eat?"

"Bacon and eggs?" Nathan suggested.

"And pancakes?" she asked.

Nathan hesitated, thinking about it. "I could have two pancakes. But no syrup. What would I put on them?"

Mama considered for a few moments. "Blueberries?"

"Yeah, I could do that," Nathan agreed.

"Okay, then. We'll do brunch."

"Good," Nathan said happily. "What time are people coming?"

"Not until the afternoon. And you're up early, so we have lots of time."

"Early?" Nathan looked at the clock in the kitchen. "It's ten."

"Compared to how late you've been sleeping lately."

"Oh. I guess."

She closed her book. "I'll get started. We'll eat in a half-hour or forty-five minutes."

Nathan's mouth was watering and his stomach was complaining loudly at the smells coming from the kitchen. He heard Mama starting to put plates on the table, and then she called him to come eat.

"Okay," Nathan said. "I'll be there in a minute."

He took out the little pouch from the hospital, and laid everything he needed out on the top of the dresser. First he pricked his finger and put the bloodied test strip into the little computer that measured his blood glucose. The doctors had programmed it so that it flashed his level, and then the dose of insulin he was supposed to use.

He turned the dial on the insulin injection pen, and closed his eyes and held his breath to inject himself. It got a little easier every time. The first time, he'd been so scared to inject himself that his hands had been shaking, and it had taken half an hour to work up the courage to do it. Now he was getting used to it, it wasn't such a big deal. He put the used needle in his sharps box and went out to the kitchen for brunch.

Their little worship group seemed to grow a little bit each week. The sitting room was starting to get a little crowded, even though they had intentionally rented a home with plenty of space for seating. Maybe sometime soon, they would need to find space to rent in another church or community center or something. Mama would be so happy about that.

Delia was there, though her mother hadn't made it this time. Some of her other little friends had come along as well. There were a few neighbors that had come before, and a couple of them that Nathan didn't know. He was a little disappointed that Chandra hadn't come. He got the feeling that she wasn't really religious, but he thought maybe she would want to come anyway, just for the company and for Nathan's homecoming.

Quiet music played while everyone arrived. Then they talked a little about a lesson and the scriptures that Mama had read the previous week, and Nathan tried to keep up with the discussion. He hadn't been there, but he was familiar enough with the scripture Mama had used to follow what they were talking about. But what he was really waiting for was the music.

The little girls had picked out the Bible story of Jesus raising Lazarus from the death. Nathan listened to Mama's reading and commentary and the ensuing discussion. Mama looked at him a couple of times during the reading, her eyes sparkling. She could tell how impatient he was for the music. Finally, the story was done, and the girls were finished looking through the picture books, and it was time for singing and dancing. Mama put on one of Nathan's favorite CD's, and he was on his feet immediately, raising his voice with the music and clapping his hands. The girls were quick to join in as well. He wasn't so embarrassed to be dancing in front of them anymore. They were just part of a bigger family now. Nathan held Delia's hands and danced her around in circles, then let go and just shook and danced by himself. He just lost himself in the music, until Mama switched it to something slower. He looked at her, disappointed to have the dancing end so soon.

Mama just looked at him.

"You've danced for half a dozen songs," she marveled. "Look at you!"

Nathan felt warm and happy. His shirt was drenched with sweat, and he was pleasantly tired after the heavy workout, but not exhausted. He twirled around once again, spinning in a tight circle for a dozen turns, until he was too dizzy to stand. Mama took him by the arm and guided him back to his seat, where Nathan sat waiting for the room to stop spinning around him.

"Wow, you were really good today!" Delia exclaimed. "They sure must have fixed you up at the hospital!"

Nathan was torn between being happy to feel so well again, and guilty for denying his faith and taking medicine. He just smiled at Delia and shrugged.

Mama led the prayers, and afterward, people started to say their goodbyes and trickle out. Nathan saw Delia off at the door. He shut the door after everyone was gone, and picked up the collections bowl. He took it into the kitchen and put it on the table.

"It looks like we got a good collection," he said.

"It went way up when you went to the hospital," she told him.

Nathan went back into the sitting room. Mama came in while he looked in the terrarium. "Can I, Mama? I want to hold it," he said.

She hesitated. "I don't know if the time is right."

"I feel moved. Come on, turn on the music," Nathan urged.

She still hesitated. Nathan had never known her to be so reluctant to let him handle serpents before. He went over to the stereo and turned the music back on. He danced and clapped. He didn't look at Mama, but after a few minutes, she danced with him, and then went to the terrarium and removed the top. Nathan's heart raced. He danced closer, clapping to the music. She lifted the snake up out of the tank and danced with it. Nathan danced around her, the music getting faster and more frantic. He reached for the snake, and she relinquished it. The snake's head reared back for a moment, but Nathan stayed relaxed and just kept dancing and belting out amens and hallelujahs. The snake wrapped its tail around his arm. Nathan watched its glinting scales. He raised it over his head and closed his eyes.

As the music ended, he danced back over to the terrarium and let the snake slither out of his hands back into its den. He put the top back on the terrarium. He turned to face Mama. Her eyes were shining.

"I didn't think you'd be able to," she explained. "I thought, with the insulin, you wouldn't have the protection."

"I still believe," Nathan said. And he did. Maybe not as strongly as he should. Maybe he still couldn't reconcile how much better he felt with the medical treatment with his faith. But he still believed. It was still a part of who he was.

"Of course you do," Mama agreed. She gave him a hug. Nathan steadied himself on the top of the cabinet the terrarium sat on, suddenly dizzy. "Oh. Are you okay?"

Nathan pressed his hand to his forehead, trying to shake it off. "Yes, I'm fine."

"You overdid it. You need to lie down," she said. "You're feeling better, but you can still do too much."

"Too much," Nathan repeated. His brain was thick like sludge, and he couldn't think straight. They had told him something at the hospital about if he got too much exercise without planning his insulin doses carefully. But he couldn't think of what it was, or what he should do about it. "Yeah, I did too much."

"You should lie down," Mama repeated.

"No. I'm supposed to do something."

She was trying to keep him steady, but Nathan was afraid he was going to pass out.

"What are you supposed to do?" Mama questioned urgently. "Take more insulin?"

"No... no. The opposite. Too much exercise. Burns up sugar. But what am I supposed to do?"

Nathan was shaking. He was afraid that he was going to pass out, or puke, or something else. What was he supposed to do?

"You need more sugar?" Mama demanded, not understanding. "I thought you weren't supposed to have sugar."

"Yes. I need sugar," Nathan agreed, grasping at her arm. "What should I do?"

"Come on."

Mama slowly walked him to the kitchen, and put him carefully into one of the kitchen chairs. Nathan lurched, just about falling back out of it.

"Just stay there," Mama encouraged. She went to the fridge and came back with a glass of juice.

"I'm not supposed to have juice," Nathan argued.

"You said you need sugar. Drink it."

He couldn't find the words to argue with her further. Mama held it up to his lips, putting her other hand behind his head to keep him steady and prevent him from pulling away.

"Just drink a bit, Bug. Come on."

Nathan drank the juice that she dribbled into his mouth. It was only a few minutes before the confusion started to clear, and Nathan started to relax again.

"Okay?" Mama questioned. "Is it better now?"

Nathan nodded. "Yeah. Thanks."

She looked relieved. "I was afraid it was the wrong thing. Because you're not supposed to have sugar."

"Yeah." Nathan ran his fingers through his hair. "But if I get too much insulin, or too much exercise, then I might swing the other way. Then I need sugar. Juice or a hard candy, they said. I should always have a couple of candies in my pocket or something."

"So you're okay now?"

"I'll go check my levels in a minute. I just want to sit here a minute first."

"Sure, baby. Wait until you're sure you're okay."

He rested his elbows on the table, cradling his face. "You should have taken the classes at the hospital," he told her. "Then you'd know what to do."

She just looked at him. Going to the classes would mean that she agreed with treating him, and she didn't want to treat him. She would do it because they forced her, but she didn't have to go to the classes and admit defeat.

But she had just treated him. She'd just given him sugar for his hypoglycemia.

Chapter Thirteen

NATHAN HAD TO STAY a few minutes after class for Mrs. Davis to walk him through the new problems that they were working on in math. Nathan paid close attention to her instructions, and after a try or two, he was doing them himself. Mrs. Davis smiled at him.

"That's really good, Nathan. I was worried how long it would take you to catch up after being sick, but you've done really well." She looked at his face. "I can see the difference in you. You're much more focused now. And not so tired."

Nathan rubbed his chin. No more falling asleep at his desk anymore. It was so nice to have enough energy at the end of the day that it didn't hurt to walk to the car or the bus.

"Thanks," he said. "I am feeling a lot better."

"I'm very glad. I think you've got this, so I'll let you go. Say hi to your mom for me."

Nathan nodded. At least Mrs. Davis was still treating him nicely. The coach, on the other hand, would hardly say a word to Nathan, or let him do anything in phys ed, even though he was feeling better now. Nathan heard in a round-about way that Mama had called the school after the yoga class, and really blasted them. The student teacher had been sent away to another school. The coach was given some kind of warning. And he didn't want anything to do with Nathan. Nathan felt bad about that, but it wasn't his fault that Mama had been so angry. It was the coach's fault and the student teacher's fault that they had thought it was okay to involve him in some pagan ritual worship. They shouldn't have done that.

He grabbed his bag and his jacket and went out to look for the car, as Mama was supposed to be picking him up. He got in, and she gave him a quick squeeze around the shoulders and kiss on the cheek.

"Hey, Bug. How was your day?"

Nathan shrugged. "It was okay. Still getting caught up on stuff that I missed."

"Well, you missed a bit of time, it's going to take a while to get caught up. Don't be too hard on yourself."

"Yes'm. I know."

"I think we should go out tonight, what do you think?"

Nathan considered. There wasn't really any reason not to go out. He was feeling better now, so he didn't need to go home and sleep. He was getting the hang of managing his insulin and felt more confident about going out to eat and maintaining his sugar levels in the right range. He didn't have anything else to do, other than schoolwork.

"Sure," he agreed. "As long as I have time for my homework. What do you want to do?"

"I thought maybe supper and a movie."

He was a bit surprised that she'd suggest a movie on a school night. "I'd better do my homework first, then," he said. "I won't have time after."

"Sounds good."

She drove for a few minutes in silence. "So..." she said. "I wondered about what you wanted to do for your birthday?"

"Oh. I dunno. I get to choose what to eat for supper, right?"

"Of course you do! And I thought you might want to have a party, invite a bunch of your school friends over."

"Well..." Nathan rubbed the back of his neck. "I don't really have any friends to invite."

She looked at him, frowning, then looked back at the road again. "You have friends," she said.

Nathan was silent.

"What about that girl who came to see you at the hospital?"

"She's nice to everyone. We're not really... we don't do anything together, spend any time together. She's just nice to me. And I can't just invite one girl over for a party. She'd freak out. Or her mom would."

"But she's not the only one. Delia, down the street..."

"She's only nine or something. I can't invite a little kid!"

"There must be others," Mama said. "Who do you hang out with at lunch?"

"Bly sometimes. Usually, not anyone." Nathan sighed. "I don't need a party, Mama. We can do my birthday together, just you and me. A party is just a big hassle for you."

124

She didn't say anything, driving with her eyes straight ahead, her lips pressed tightly together. Nathan thought her eyes looked teary.

"Don't be sad about it, Mama," he said. "I don't need a big party."

Nathan had hoped that Mama's worries over his birthday and the non-existent friends and birthday party would blow over quickly. They had each other, and that was all that they'd ever needed. But she seemed to be obsessing over it. She kept making suggestions about how he might make friends at school, telling him he should have someone over after school, and bringing it up in every conversation.

He was used to her going a little over-the-top when it came to his birthday. She always had some big surprise planned. In spite of his irritation over her fussing about his lack of friends, he was looking forward to his birthday and what she might have in store for him. His birthday fell on a Saturday. Nathan went to bed Friday night, his mind whirling. She hadn't given him any hints as to what she might be giving him. He hadn't seen any signs of it around the house. There were no mysterious packages, no areas of the house that were off-limits. What was he going to find when he woke up in the morning?

It took a long time to get to sleep, and he thought that he would wake up again too early, like Christmas morning when he was a little kid. Then he would lay there in bed, watching the clock and waiting until it was late enough to wake Mama up. But he surprised himself by sleeping in. When he finally woke up, he rolled over and stretched and yawned, eyes still closed. He remembered instantly what day it was, and sat up, sliding his feet off the bed.

He opened his eyes when his toes touched something rubbery and bouncy instead of the floor. For a minute, he just gaped.

The room was filled with balloons. Not just a dozen balloons on the floor, but what must have been hundreds of balloons filling every inch of floor space, packed several layers deep. And there were helium balloons too, some of them floating all the way up to the ceiling, and some of them tied down with weights so that they floated at various heights between the layers of floor and ceiling balloons. Nathan had no idea how Mama had had the time to blow up so many balloons, and managed to fill his room with them without him waking up.

"Mama!" he called.

She came to the doorway of the room, and looked at him, suppressing laughter. She held her phone out in front of her, filming him. "What is it, Bug?"

Nathan laughed. "My room is full of balloons!"

"Oh, is it?"

"Yes!"

"I wonder how that happened."

"How am I supposed to get out?"

"Just walk through them," Mama suggested. "Although, you might notice that some of them have things tied to them, or messages inside."

Nathan grabbed the string of one of the helium balloons that floated near the bed. The weight on the balloon happened to be a pink cellophane package of nuts, the barbecue ones that he especially liked.

"Oh! Thank you!"

One by one, he grabbed the weighted balloons to check out the prize at the end of each string. Little treats that he liked, books, pens, and knickknacks. After wading through the room to retrieve each one, he looked down at the floor. Mama had said that some of them had messages inside. He picked up a balloon and tried to peer through the balloon to the inside. He couldn't see anything. He shook it and couldn't hear anything. He looked at Mama.

"How do I know which ones have messages?" he questioned.

She shook her head. "What do you think?" she questioned.

Nathan looked helplessly around the room. "Do you have a pin?" he questioned.

She smiled and handed him a sharply-pointed letter opener. Nathan stabbed at the balloon in his hand, and after a few tentative jabs, it popped. He looked in the broken pieces and didn't find a note.

"I wouldn't stab towards your hand," Mama advised. "I don't want you to hurt yourself."

Nathan started randomly stabbing balloons around him, creating chaos as they flew into the air, bumped each other, and burst. He spotted a piece of paper, and scooped it up.

'Dear Nathaniel, I hope you have the best birthday ever!' it read, followed by a name that he didn't recognize.

Nathan read it out. "Who's that?" he asked Mama.

"A friend," she said cryptically, with a smile.

Nathan continued to pop balloons, occasionally finding messages similar to the first, sending him birthday greetings, but followed by names that he didn't know. He grew increasingly frustrated.

"Who are these people?" he demanded. "Are they from your work?"

"No. They're friends."

"Your friends?"

"No, yours."

He shook his head. "I don't know these people!"

He stopped popping balloons, a sick feeling building in his stomach. He pushed his way through the remaining balloons out the door and down the hall to the bathroom.

"Shut off the video, Mama."

She lowered her phone, tapping the screen. Nathan went into the bathroom and shut the door. He sat down on the seat of the toilet and breathed deeply. He wasn't sure what was going on, but he was liking it less and less. What was going on? Who were all of these people that he didn't know? They certainly weren't his friends, like Mama stubbornly repeated. He would have to be firm with her to get to the bottom of it.

Nathan splashed cold water on his face and combed his hair. Then he went back out to confront her. "I want to know who all those people are."

She looked at him for a minute, then shrugged. She motioned for him to follow. Nathan walked behind her into the kitchen and her laptop. Mama tapped in her passwords, and clicked a few times, eventually opening up a social media site. She scrolled through and pointed to a picture that she had posted, of Nathan when he was in hospital. Nathan read the caption.

'My poor Nathaniel's 12th birthday is coming up, and when I asked him about having a party, he said he had no friends. Between us moving around so often, and his health problems and learning disabilities, he hasn't been able to make any friends here. Please help me to make this the best birthday ever by sending likes and birthday greetings. Please share with all your friends!'

Nathan looked from the screen to Mama in disbelief. She smiled proudly. Nathan looked back at the screen. Five million views. Two and a half million likes. Seven thousand comments. Nathan's stomach was tied in knots. He felt angry and embarrassed and afraid all at once, like Mama had thrown a bucket of cold water over him. His eyes burned and his throat constricted. He didn't know what to say or do.

"Nathanial? What do you think? Look at all of those people who want you to have a happy birthday! You have millions of friends!"

He whirled around to face her, his face burning hot. "I don't have millions of friends!" he shouted. "Those people don't even know me! A friend is someone you do things with and like being around. None of those people are my friends!"

Mama's brows drew close together. She looked perplexed. "What are you so angry about?" she questioned.

"Because you just told five million people how pathetic I am!" Nathan pointed out. "Now the whole world knows I'm a reject!" He shook his head, the tears spilling down and flying off his face. "I can't believe you would do that to me!"

Her jaw dropped in frank astonishment. "But sweetie. I wanted to make your day nice for you," she protested.

"Then buy me a present! Take me out somewhere! Don't make a--a freak show out of me!"

"No, that's not what I was doing," she protested, distressed. "It was a gift, to make you feel better!"

The phone rang. She turned to answer it, and Nathan stalked away, back to his room. He shut his door and went to work popping every last balloon. He ignored the papers. He didn't pick up the balloon corpses. He just kept stabbing and stabbing and stabbing every last one of them, until the floor was covered with their shriveled bodies and congratulatory notes. He threw the letter opener down on the dresser and sat down on the bed, shaking with emotion. He listened for Mama's voice and could make her out still talking to the caller on the phone.

The sick feeling kept growing. How was he going to go back to school? Everyone would know about this. They would all be making fun of him or feeling sorry for him. The poor boy with no friends.

When his shaking didn't subside, Nathan checked his blood sugar. Alarm bells rang on the little computer. As well as the prescribed dosage of insulin-- higher than he'd ever given himself before--it flashed a little plus sign that meant he was supposed to see his doctor or go to emergency. He shoved it back away in the little pouch and angrily prepared the insulin dose.

That done, Nathan went to the bedroom door and opened it, listening for Mama's voice. She wasn't talking anymore. He opened the door the rest of the way to go find her, sorry for blowing up when she thought she was doing something nice for him. But the phone rang again. Mama picked it up, and Nathan listened to her side of the conversation.

"Yes, it is...? Yes, today is the big day...! He was very surprised when he saw the balloons... I'll post the video... I hear him still popping balloons now... Um, I don't know, I think he'll be too shy for an interview..."

Nathan withdrew to his room, shutting the door quietly. An interview? She was posting the balloon video? Who was she talking to?

Five million views...

He heard the phone ring again. How many people were going to call today? Every time she hung up the phone, it rang again.

Five million views.

In another hour or so, Mama tapped on his door and poked her head in.

"You'd better have some breakfast, Bug."

Nathan got up off the bed and walked through the puddles of broken balloon bits. "Who keeps calling?" he questioned.

"Oh, just some of the people who wanted to make sure that you had a good birthday. Everybody wants to know how it's going. I don't have the phone number on my profile, but people are managing to track me down anyway." She shook her head, smiling. "But I turned the phone off so we can have a nice quiet breakfast together."

"Thanks," Nathan said. "And thanks for all of the birthday surprises. That was... really... amazing."

She nodded. "There have been donations too. I had to set up an account that people could e transfer money into, and there have been a ton of donations. You think about what you would really like for your birthday, and we'll get it for you. Whatever you want."

"Whatever I want?" Nathan repeated. "How much?"

"If you ask for something that's more than is in the account, I'll let you know. Think about what you really want."

"Like... a computer for myself?"

She nodded. "If that's what you want."

Nathan thought about that. Though Mama often got him presents or treats, he rarely got to choose for himself. She liked to surprise him, and if he asked for something specific, then it wasn't a surprise, so she didn't want to do it. And her idea of great gifts weren't always the same as his. Maybe something good could still come of the fiasco. He could get his own computer. Or something else.

After a breakfast of bacon and eggs, Mama turned the phone back on, but let the calls go through to voicemail. She did some posting on the computer, and Nathan didn't want to know what she was writing about him now, or how the entire universe would respond to his waking-up-to-balloons birthday video. He wandered into the sitting room to look at the snake. She was sunning herself on a rock today, more visible than usual. She didn't hide or rear up when Nathan pressed his face close for a look.

There were cars honking outside, and Nathan looked out between the blinds of the window to see what was going on. There were several vans with the names of TV stations on their sides and small satellite receivers on top. Nathan gulped.

"Mama?"

"What is it?" she questioned, without coming to see.

"I think you better look outside."

"What's wrong?"

Nathan shook his head in disbelief, even though she couldn't see it. The reporters didn't approach the door immediately, but talked a bit to any neighbors that were on the street, even Delia and her friends. Then one eventually came up to the door and rang.

"Can you get that, Nathaniel?"

"I think you'd better," Nathan said.

"I'm right in the middle of..." she trailed off as she worked on her computer. The doorbell rang again. "Oh, for goodness sake! You can't get that?"

She rushed past him, impatient, and pulled open the door. The reporter introduced himself, and for a few moments, Mama didn't say anything.

"Can I come in?" the reporter questioned.

"Um... no. How did you find me?"

"We'd like to get a shot of Nathaniel, and maybe talk to the two of you for a minute about what it's been like, your post going viral and attracting so much attention, all of the wonderful birthday wishes that Nathaniel has been getting..."

"No... Look, my phone number and address are supposed to be unlisted. No one is supposed to have them. There are... people that we don't want to be able to track us down."

"Ahh." The reporter lowered his voice, as if these people might be somewhere close by. "We can arrange for studio use, or some other anonymous setting. Then we can protect your interests and still give our viewers a little peek at the happiness that this campaign has brought little Nathaniel for his birthday."

Mama stepped out the door onto the front step with the reporter, pulling the door shut behind her so that Nathan could no longer hear what was going on. He watched Mama through the window, talking to him animatedly, and the other reporters standing nearby, watching and listening to everything they could catch. Even though Mama said that she didn't want people to find them, Nathan had a feeling that the reporters would be getting more than enough information from her. She never had been very good at keeping a low profile.

Nathan looked at the other reporters again. There was one man standing among the TV vans that looked familiar, but Nathan couldn't identify where from. He didn't look like a reporter. Nathan didn't think he recognized him off of any TV news program. It was from somewhere else. The man stood very still and quiet, watching and listening to everything around him. He was a handsome man, with sort of wavy hair, a couple day's whisker growth, and a young face, even though Nathan would put him at least in his forties. He just looked out of place.

They had continued to be inundated with phone calls and reporters at the door. Mama pretended to be annoyed with it, but her eyes were sparkling and she kept going back onto the computer to answer questions and post pictures. They put a sign on the door stating 'No Reporters,' and the assaults on the door wound down. Nathan was in the sitting room reading a book for school when there was a quick, almost hesitant half-ring of the doorbell. The reporters had tended to be quite aggressive, so Nathan wondered who it was now. He went to the blinds and peeked out again. A glimpse of the blond hair told him that it was Summer. He went to the door and opened it.

"Hi," Summer said. "A little birdie told me it was your birthday today." She blushed pink.

Nathan shook his head and motioned for her to come in. "Better not stand out there, with all the reporters," he warned.

Summer glanced over her shoulder at the car that her mother sat in. "Just for a minute," she said. "I can't stay."

Nathan nodded. She came in and Nathan shut the door after a quick glance around. The man who had been watching the house earlier--who never had come up to the door and rung the doorbell--was gone. Nathan looked at Summer.

"It's been sort of a mess," Nathan said holding his hands out in a helpless shrug.

"Yeah. I've been seeing it on TV."

Nathan groaned.

Summer looked sympathetic. "Yeah," she said again.

Nathan ran his fingers through his hair. "Man. What a mess. I don't know how I'm going to go to school on Monday. Everybody... everybody's going to know, and be making fun of me. Like things weren't bad enough already."

They went into the sitting room and sat down.

"Has it been that bad?" Summer questioned. "At school, I mean. I didn't think it was that bad."

"Not for you," Nathan said. "You've known everybody forever, and you've got lots of friends. It's not the same, me coming here partway into the year, and being so sick and everything. You're about the only person who talks to me."

"But they haven't been bullying you," Summer said. "Right?"

"Not so bad. But now... now they've got lots of ammunition. I couldn't be much more obvious."

"Why did your mom do that? Didn't she know...?"

"That's just Mama. She thought it would be great for me. I'd feel happy because all of these people suddenly decided they were my friends. But now... everybody knows... she's just made everything so much worse."

"I saw one guy that said he was sending you guys to Disneyland for a week."

Nathan stared at Summer. "What?"

"I guess your mom didn't tell you that yet."

"I don't think she'd ever go."

"And people are talking about giving you scholarships, and investments, and all kinds of stuff. There are YouTube videos of people singing 'Happy Birthday' or encouraging you. One guy had printed out all of the comments back to your mom, this morning, and it was a pile of paper this deep!" she held out her hands to demonstrate.

Nathan groaned.

"It's up over eight million views now," Summer said. "Everybody's going and posting because today's the day."

Nathan rubbed his eyes. "It will all stop tomorrow and be old news, right?"

"All the talk shows and late night shows want to get you on, to talk to you about how this has changed your life. They keep showing the video of the balloons over and over."

Nathan shook his head. "The balloons were clever. But all those messages from people I didn't know..."

"It's kind of creepy," Summer suggested.

"Yeah. I wish I could just wake up and find out that this whole thing was a nightmare, and that it is my real birthday morning, and Mama got me a pair of socks..."

Summer laughed. "Is that what you want?" she questioned.

"I might get a new computer. I don't know yet. But I didn't want eight million views."

"That's pretty crazy," Summer agreed. "Whoever thought that someone I knew would go viral?"

"Yeah."

Summer took a small box out of her jacket pocket. "I got you this," she said. "I know it's not a scholarship or a trip to Disneyland or something, but it's from a real friend."

Nathan took it from her. He unfolded the end and slid out a small digital picture frame.

"You can put your own pictures on it," Summer said. "It's just a small one, but you can load hundreds of photos at once."

Nathan saw that it already had batteries in it and turned it on. There was a smiling picture of Summer. He looked at her, and she blushed again.

"I dunno. I put a picture on it to see if it worked. You can delete it, and put your own pictures in it."

"I like it," Nathan said. "Thanks a lot!"

He hesitated for a minute, wondering if he should give her a hug to say thank you. What was appropriate?

"Nathaniel, did someone come in?" Mama questioned, and appeared in the doorway. She saw Summer sitting there. "Oh, it's you. I thought I heard voices."

"Oh, hi Mrs. Ashbury. I just stopped by to wish Nathan a happy birthday. I should be heading out, my mom's waiting in the car."

Mama came into the room and looked down at the picture frame, still displaying Summer's picture. Summer was blushing furiously.

"You can load all kinds of pictures into it," she explained. "I know you like to take pictures..."

"How would you know that?"

"Well, you know... I saw the birthday postings for Nathan... and you have lots of other pictures of him in your profile, and selfies and all. So I figured... a digital photo frame, where he could see lots of them at once, instead of only being able to put one photo in the frame."

"That was very thoughtful," Mama agreed.

Nathan switched the frame off again, and slid it back into the box. Summer stood up, and moved her hands around like she didn't know where she should put them.

"Well, happy birthday, then. I guess I'll see you Monday."

"Thanks," Nathan told her again. There was no way he was going to hug her now, in front of Mama. He didn't think that shaking hands was appropriate, so he just gave a little wave. "See you."

He walked her to the door and let her out. He turned back around to face Mama.

"What a nice girl," she said. "You see, you should have invited her over. She wanted to give you something."

Nathan shrugged. "I told you she's nice," he said. "But she's nice to everyone, it's not just me. We're not... special friends or anything."

"Boyfriend-girlfriend?" she asked.

"No," Nathan said, sweating. "I don't have a girlfriend."

"Well, you be careful. She's giving you pictures of herself, that means she's interested. And you're too young to be in a relationship."

Nathan nodded his agreement. "It's just a little gift. You can take that picture off."

"You don't know what her beliefs are. You have to be careful of girls who will try to lead you astray. They can be very... tempting."

Nathan swallowed. "Yes'm. But we're not boyfriend-girlfriend. I promise. We're not."

She nodded. "Be careful," she warned again. "That girl has designs on you."

Chapter Fourteen

MAMA PUT A FEW bills in Nathan's hand, giving him a curious look. "Where are you going to go while I am picking up the computer?" she questioned. "I thought you would want to come with me to make sure I got what you wanted."

Nathan motioned to the printout he had given her with the computer model that he had picked out. "It's all on there. I don't need to come."

"But where are you going to go?" she questioned.

"It's a secret. A surprise," he said, giving nothing away.

"I'm not feeding anything," she warned him, "or cleaning up any more cages. So it better not be something live."

Nathan shook his head. "It could be..." he told her mysteriously. "But it's not."

That just made her frown more, trying to figure out what he was up to. Nathan grinned.

"Go to the store," he ordered. She was going to buy the computer at her own store, which meant that she got the employee discount. Just because they were given the money for free, that didn't mean that they weren't going to take care of it just as carefully as if she had earned it herself.

Mama walked away, shaking her head. Nathan waited until she was out of sight before turning around to buy the surprise.

Nathan had kept his surprise carefully hidden in layers of boxes and bags, so that Mama would be unable to guess what it was. He waited until after supper, and then disappeared into his room. He knew that Mama would think that he was going to set up the new computer, but that wasn't what he was doing. He changed into his best Sunday suit, with a black bow tie, looking in the mirror to make sure that nothing was out of place. Then he unwrapped the layers of bags and boxes to reveal the one perfect red rose.

Mama already had the lights dimmed and was studying her Bible to prepare a message that she was going to give at the next worship. The Sunday worship after Nathan's birthday had been more crowded than usual, and if the attendance kept up, they would be able to move to a larger meeting room pretty soon. Nathan just wasn't sure how many of them were there for worship, and how many just wanted to get a look at the celebrities.

Mama looked up, startled, when her eyes caught a movement in the doorway.

"Oh sweetie, you scared me." Her eyes narrowed at Nathan's good clothes. "What are you doing?"

Nathan walked into the room, right up to her. Then he took the rose out from behind his back. "Will you accept this rose?" he questioned, just like on The Bachelor.

Mama took it from him, with a great big grin. "What is this for?" she questioned with a laugh.

"Because you always try to do nice things for me, and treat me so well. I don't think I'll ever be able to find a wife who is as special as you are."

He'd written the words out and practiced them. He knew that she would ask, and had to have an answer for her.

"Oh, Nathaniel. That's the nicest thing that anyone has ever said to me. Do you know what a special boy you are?"

"You're my best friend, Mama. Thank you for taking such good care of me."

She grabbed his hand and pulled him toward her. "Come here, you."

Mama pulled him down onto the couch with her and gave him a big hug and a bigger kiss. "You are the absolutely sweetest boy. I was so lucky to get you as a son."

After they had spent some time cuddling and talking and Mama went back to her studying, Nathan returned to his room. He put on his pajamas and turned on the computer. He didn't have a long time before he had to get to bed, but he could hopefully get some of it set up.

The time passed much more quickly than expected, and Mama had already told him to get to bed a couple of times before he was starting to get things set up the way he liked them.

Signing into his social networks had probably been a mistake. He had never really participated that much in them, but they were connected to Mama's account, and since her little campaign to get him friends, he had been overwhelmed with requests and random posts. He pretty much just refused all requests and barely scanned the comments posted on his wall by strangers. He'd figured out how to turn on some of the privacy controls so that only his established friends, like Mama, could post on his wall, but it had taken a while to delete as much of the other unwanted posts as he could.

The computer pinged, and Nathan saw the alert for another friend request. He was going to reject it, but then realized that it was for Allan, one of Bly's friends at school. They had talked a few times, and Nathan thought that he would be okay to have as an online friend. He seemed like a nice enough guy. He approved the request.

"Bed now, young man," Mama ordered, coming into the room. She caught him by the arm and pulled him up from his chair.

"I was just finishing," Nathan protested. "I'm getting ready now."

She gave him a little shove in the direction of the bathroom. "Brush teeth, pee, and go to bed," she ordered.

"What about prayer?" Nathan questioned saucily.

She smacked the back of his head very lightly. "Of course say your prayers. But I want to see you getting ready."

"I am, I am."

When he got out of the bathroom, she was back in the kitchen or front room, and Nathan went over to his computer to shut it down for the night. There was a new posting on his wall, from his new friend Allan.

'Hey, whazzup, Nathaniel?'

Nathan shook his head. He quickly typed. "Just logging off. See you at school." He shut the lid of the laptop just as Mama was coming down the hall again. He looked up. "It's off," he pointed out.

"Good. Now off to bed. You shouldn't be staying up so late."

"I know. I'm sorry, it just took longer than I thought."

"Well, it can wait until tomorrow. Let's see you in bed."

Nathan climbed into bed. She tucked him in and gave him a peck on the cheek. "Thank you again for the rose, Love Bug. That was such a thoughtful surprise."

Nathan smiled, feeling warm and satisfied. "I just wanted you to know how special you are," he said.

"All right. Off to sleep now."

She headed toward the door and shut off the light. Nathan closed his eyes and tried to go to sleep.

When Nathan got up the next morning, he knew he probably shouldn't turn on his computer, since he needed to have breakfast and get ready for school. But he decided to only do a quick check on his e-mail and social networks. They were new accounts, so it wasn't like there were going to be a lot of messages to read.

On his wall was another post from Allan.

'Hey, can you meet me before school at the mall?'

Nathan hesitated. 'Don't know. Where? What time?'

Allan must have been online right then. His post back was almost immediate. '8:00 by Sam's?'

He wasn't sure if he would be able to talk Mama into dropping him off at the mall before school. She wasn't going to be too keen on it. And he'd have to get going soon. 'I don't know. I'll try.'

He didn't wait for any further reply, just shut his computer and quickly got ready for school. Mama was surprised to see him in the kitchen so soon.

"You're up and at'em today," she observed. "Hungry?"

"Sort of," Nathan said, and busied himself with getting some cereal. "One of the guys at school needs some help with some homework," he said. "So if I could get there early..."

"Oh. Well, I'd better get moving then. I've just been dallying this morning."

"Thanks."

She left to get dressed, and Nathan sat down to eat by himself. He finished the cereal in record time and went looking for her. She was dressed and brushing her hair. "You ready for me already?"

"Yes'm. If it's okay."

"I'll just take a few minutes..."

Nathan impatiently watched her fixing her hair. Though Mama was usually on time for things, she didn't move fast, and trying to hurry her up always resulted in an argument, making them later instead of earlier than usual. So he swallowed any protest or encouragement, and just waited.

Mama was just about finished getting ready, looking for where she had put down her keys, when the smoke alarm started to scream shrilly. "Oh, no!" Mama gasped, "I forgot I had something in the oven!"

Nathan hurried in ahead of her. The smoke in the air blurred his vision, it burned his eyes and throat. Nathan waved his hand back and forth in front of his face, trying to clear the air in front of him, and approached the oven. He threw open the door.

"Use a glove!" Mama called out, and Nathan drew his hand back, realizing that in his panic he was about to use his bare hand to pick up a hot pan. He fumbled around on the counter for one of the oven mitts, and reached into the oven to take out the smoking pan.

"Here, take it outside," Mama said, opening up the back door and trying to wave the smoke out the door. She let Nathan by with the smoking, hot pan, and Nathan went down the steps and put it on the pavement where it wouldn't burn anything else. He looked in dismay at the blackened, smoky mess.

"What was it?"

"Some breakfast muffins," Mama said. "I got the idea for them on a pin board online..." She sighed. "I forgot they were even in there, when you said you had to go."

Nathan headed back into the kitchen. "Sorry," he said. "I guess you'll have to try them again another time."

"Yes, I will."

She started opening the kitchen windows. Nathan turned on the exhaust fan over the stove. He picked up a towel and started flapping it, trying to clear the smoke out faster. Mama came over and turned the oven off.

"At least we hadn't already left. Burning the house down would probably not leave a good impression on the landlord."

She started scrubbing the top of the stove, where there was a dark, smudgy ring around one of the back burners from the venting smoke.

"Oh, dear," she muttered. She looked inside of the oven as well, shaking her head.

"It'll be okay," Nathan said.

"I suppose. You'd better bring them back inside," she said with a nod toward the back door. "I don't want any critters getting into them once they cool."

"Why would they?" Nathan laughed. "They're burned to a crisp."

"You never know. They could."

He went back out and tentatively touched the pan, which was now cooling. He took it back inside and dumped the muffins into the garbage. Mama took it from his hands, and attacked the burned-on bits.

"Mama, maybe that can wait until later..." Nathan suggested.

"No, you have to get it off while it's still fresh. It will harden more and the pan will be ruined."

"You could put it in to soak..."

"Then it will get rusty. I'm sorry, Bug, but I've got to take care of it now."

He watched her for a couple of minutes, and looked at the clock. "Maybe I should catch the bus," he suggested.

Mama looked up at the clock, wiping her forehead with the back of her arm. "Oh, look at the time. You can make it if you catch the last bus. You'd better run."

Nathan nodded. He grabbed his school backpack, gave her a kiss, and took off. The bus was just pulling away from the curb as he arrived at the bus stop, but the driver saw him and stopped and waited.

"Thanks," Nathan breathed, and he held onto one of the straps and waited for his breathing to slow back down again. At least he had the energy to run for the bus. That was something to be thankful for.

When the bus drove past the mall, it was already past eight, so he didn't bother to get off and see if he could find Allan. Nathan's eyes were drawn to a man who was in the parking lot walking away from the mall, who stared at the bus as it went by. He thought it was the man who had been standing outside the house with the reporters on his birthday. Nathan thought again that he looked familiar but couldn't place him. Maybe it was just someone who lived in the neighborhood, so he happened to be in places where Nathan was.

As it turned out, the school bell was ringing just as Nathan got off of the bus, so he had to run again to get to his class on time. He didn't have a chance to look for Allan or apologize to him. At lunch time, Nathan looked for him.

"Where's Allan?" he asked Bly.

"I don't think he's here today. He was sick."

Nathan frowned. "Sick? No, he was here today... he asked me to meet him at the mall before school."

Bly frowned, taking a couple of bites of his chili and bun. "What are you talking about? You didn't see him."

"No. He messaged me. But I didn't get there when he wanted me to be..."

"Allan doesn't have a computer."

Nathan frowned at him. "What? But he messaged me. He must be using his mom or dad's computer."

"No, he's totally banned. His folks caught him with some... bad downloads... and he's not allowed to be online at all."

"But..." Nathan shook his head. "He must have been able to use one somewhere. Maybe the library or something."

"I told you, he's sick today. He's at home."

"That can't be."

"He didn't message you. Maybe somebody spoofed his account, or hacked it 'cause he hasn't been on lately. It couldn't have been Allan."

Nathan scratched his chin, trying to take this in. Bly patted him on the arm. "Sorry, amigo. Who knows what creep you were talking to."

Nathan shuddered. "Yuck. Don't say that."

Bly laughed and shook his head. "I bet you're getting lots of attention, after all that stuff on TV and all."

Nathan nodded. "Yeah, too much. But I thought that it was Allan... I thought it was okay."

"You'd better block him when you get home."

He was anxious the rest of the day, not getting much out of his lessons, just wanting to get home and get on his computer again. Mrs. Davis gave him a look when she tried to call on him during math and he had no clue what she was talking about.

"Pay attention, Nathan," she warned. "Are you feeling all right today?"

Nathan ducked his head and nodded. "Yes'm... sorry... I just... got distracted."

"Focus. This is important stuff."

Nathan looked over the gibberish on the board, and nodded as though he understood it and had just been temporarily distracted. He tried to pay attention and unravel it, but he just couldn't pick up the thread of the lesson. He was relieved when the final bell rang and he could get out of there. He gathered his books together and held his breath as he walked by a group of other boys in grade six. Boys who were twice his size, at least. As he expected, they spotted him and immediately started in on the comments, mocking him for being such a loser with no friends that his mama had to pay people to be friends with him. The usual. Nathan ignored them and just kept walking. He glanced over the cars waiting to pick students up, and not seeing Mama's, he got on the bus. He hadn't really expected to see her there. He thought he remembered that she was working late every evening of the week. It was inventory time, and that meant that everyone had to work extra hours. As expected, her car was not in the front when he got home.

But someone else was.

It was the wavy-haired man again. He was waiting in front of Nathan's house. Who was this guy, and what did he want? He had never rang the doorbell, hadn't approached Mama to try to get her to answer questions for an interview. Was he the online impostor? He had been at the mall, where the impostor had tried to lure him. What was his interest in Nathan? Had he seen the stories about Nathan and decided he wanted to meet him in person? Nathan's stomach squirmed uncomfortably. Rather than let the man see him, he ducked into Chandra's front yard, and rang the doorbell, trying to stay out of sight. Chandra let him in.

"Nathan! It's good to see you, neighbor. Did you just come for a visit?"

She let Nathan in, and he looked out the window of the sitting room, to see if he could see the man from there.

"There's a man hanging around outside my house," he explained. "I don't know him, but I keep seeing him around. And today, there was someone online, on the computer, and he was pretending to be this guy from school, but it wasn't him..."

"Whoa, whoa. Slow down a bit. Who is this guy?"

"I don't know. It's probably nothing, but... it's like he could be stalking me or something."

She looked alarmed. "Have you talked to the police about this?"

Nathan shook his head. "I haven't even told Mama. He just keeps showing up, and then on the computer today..."

"Stay calm," Chandra said. "It's probably nothing to worry about. But let's call the police just to be sure, and your mother."

"Don't call Mama at work. She's doing inventory, and I don't want her to lose her job or something."

"Well, I'm calling the police." She took him by the arm. "Come on, sit down and relax. It will probably be a while before they actually get here." She looked out her front window. "Where is this guy? Can you see him?"

Nathan peered out the window, and pointed. "Right there."

Chandra looked out, and they both watched him for a minute. He stood there waiting, looking around, trying to appear casual. Chandra nodded her head.

"He's not from around here. I don't recognize him."

"I saw him when all of the reporters were around. And then today at the mall, after someone online pretending to be a guy I know asked me to meet him at the mall. I can't go home while he's there."

"I agree. I'm going to call the police."

She went into the kitchen to make the phone call. Nathan heard a few worried words here and there. She hung up and came back in. "They're going to send someone over. Are you sure you don't want me to call your mom?"

"No. I'm safe, she would just worry."

Chandra nodded and sat down on the edge of the easy chair across from Nathan. "Do you want anything. A drink of juice...?"

"No, thanks."

They both sat there, unsure what to say or do. Every time one of them started a conversation, it fell flat. Both were watching out the window every minute or two, waiting to see what the man would do, or when the police would show up. Nathan's ears caught the siren of the police car first.

"They're coming, I think."

Chandra listened. "Why would they have their siren on?" she questioned. "Won't that just..."

As they watched, the man swiveled around, listening to the approaching police car. He cut through Nathan's yard into the back, out of sight. The police car pulled onto the street and cut its siren, but it was too late. He was gone. Officers got out of the police car and looked around the house, going around back and looking up and down the street. Eventually, they made their way over to Chandra's house. She started for the door so that she was there by the time they rang the doorbell. Nathan hung back behind her, listening.

"You were the one who called in a suspicious person?" the tall police officer questioned.

"Yes. You spooked him when he heard your siren," Chandra chided.

The officers looked at each other. "Well, I'm sorry about that, ma'am. We were just trying to make the best time we could through traffic. Did you see which way he went?"

"He cut through the back yard. Then I couldn't see him anymore."

"We took a look, but couldn't see any sign of him in the back yard or lane. Do you mind if we come in for a minute?"

Chandra let them in, and they all went into the sitting room. The tall policeman eyed Nathan. "Is this your grandson?"

"No, it was my house that guy was hanging around," Nathan explained. "I didn't want to go home while he was there."

"I see. Did you have any reason to think that he might be a danger? People do go out for walks..."

"He wasn't walking," Nathan objected. "He was just camped out in front of my house. I saw him there before once, and he just kept watching and never came in. Then today I saw him at the mall, where I was supposed to be. I think he's... you know... stalking me."

"He probably lives in the neighborhood."

"Then why would he be standing in front of my house?"

Chandra interposed. "I've lived in this neighborhood for twenty years, and I've never seen him before. Nathan said that someone was trying to lure him online. Tell him about that, Nathan."

Nathan rubbed the back of his head, a bit embarrassed. He didn't like the word 'lure.' That suggested a pedophile or something.

"I just got a new computer," he said, "and set up my accounts yesterday. This person sent me a friend request, and it was the name and picture of one of the guys I know at school, so I said yes. He wanted me to meet him at the mall this morning, but I couldn't get there when Mama burned the muffins. But when the bus went by the mall, I was watching for him, and I saw that guy," Nathan nodded toward the window. "Then I found out later that the boy I thought it was, he's not even allowed on the computer. So it couldn't have really been him."

Both officers were writing down notes. The tall one looked at Nathan. "Well, it sounds like you were right to be concerned. Can you describe him to us?"

Nathan did his best.

"Great. We'll see if anything pops when we check for pedophiles in the area," the tall one said. "You never know, we could be lucky. We might have some photos for you to look at."

Nathan nodded. "Okay."

"I'd like to get a look at your computer too. Can we go over to your house now?"

"Yessir. Thanks." He got up to go with the officers. "Thanks for helping me out," he said to Chandra.

"You know I'll help you any time, Nathan. If there's anything you ever need, you just ask. If I can do it... I will."

The two officers took Nathan over to his house, and he unlocked the door with his key. He looked at the name badges of the officers. The tall one was Petrovic, and the older one Andrees.

"Is your mom around?" Petrovic asked.

"She's at work. They're doing inventory, and I didn't want to get her in trouble asking her to come home. I knew I was safe at Chandra's--Mrs. Mullenny's--so I didn't want to make her worry."

"You'll need to tell her about it when she gets home, so she can help you to stay safe. Keep the doors and windows locked, and let us know if you see or hear anything suspicious. If you see or hear this guy again, call 911."

Nathan nodded. "Okay."

"Good. Let's have a look at your room. Is that where the computer is?"

"Yessir. This way."

He took them down the hall to his room. The computer was still sitting there, closed, and he wasn't sure at first what they wanted to see, if he should boot it up or just give it to them. He looked at Petrovic.

"Boot it up for us," Petrovic prompted. "I want to have a look at this guy's account. We might need to take the computer with us, but let's start with just a look."

Nathan nodded. He turned it on and waited for the password screen. Petrovic sat down on in the chair without invitation. Nathan navigated to his wall where the fake Allen had posted to him. In addition to the exchange that Nathan had seen, there was an additional note.

'Where are you???'

Nathan shivered. Petrovic read through it, and clicked on the fake profile, making notes of what he found there. He pointed at the pictures. "This is a picture of your friend?" he questioned.

"Yeah."

"And you talked to him and he said he hadn't messaged you?"

"No. He was sick today and didn't come to school. But Bly, he said that Allen isn't even allowed to go on the computer, or use his mom's or anything. So it couldn't have been him."

"Unless he did get access without permission. But it's odd that he wasn't even at school, if he wanted to meet with you. We'll have to talk to him. Do you think it was some kind of prank or practical joke?"

"I dunno. Maybe."

"You had any trouble lately with bullying or teasing?"

Nathan bit his lip. "I get picked on some. Especially after..." he trailed off, trying to think of how to explain it. "My mom posted some personal stuff on her account... and it got millions of hits... so I've been getting a bunch of attention over that."

Andrees turned and looked at Nathan, with a frown of concentration. "You're the birthday boy," he said after a minute.

Nathan sighed. "Yeah. That's me. And that guy--that man outside--he was here on my birthday, outside watching the house with the reporters. I looked out the window and saw him, just on the other side of the fence."

Andrees wrote something down. "Have you had any other trouble?" he questioned. He looked out the window on the other side of Nathan's bed. "Anyone else hanging around? Anything strange happening?"

Nathan considered. He remembered the dream he had of the prowler outside. "No... I don't think so. I had a weird dream, and when I woke up, I thought someone was in the back yard, outside. But it was so dark... it was probably just my imagination."

"Maybe," Andrees allowed. "Do you know when that was?"

"Not really... a few weeks ago."

Petrovic motioned to Nathan. "I'm going to tweak your privacy settings a little, make sure your firewall is set up properly and that you have an antivirus program watching for trojans. Is that okay?"

"Sure," Nathan agreed. "I don't know how to do all that stuff."

"We'll just make sure that it's as safe as possible. But we can't be one hundred percent sure that it's all secure. You're going to have to be careful. Don't say anything online about where you are, or what you're out doing, when you're away from the house. Don't approve any friend requests from anyone you don't know. I wouldn't even accept any requests from anyone you think you know for a couple of weeks. It won't hurt them to wait. But you can't be sure that this guy isn't your friend on several different accounts, so don't assume that just because we get rid of one profile that he's not lurking here on another one."

Nathan nodded. "Okay."

"What about your mom's computer? How secure is that one?"

"I don't know. Probably not great. She said she didn't have her phone number or address anywhere, but a lot of people still tracked us down here." He shook his head. "She posts all kinds of stuff online, all the time."

"I want you to unfriend her. We don't want crazies looking at the stuff that she's posting and then linking up to your account. You might want to just not use any social media for a while. And then when you do, set up completely new accounts. Use a pseudonym that you only tell your friends. We'll try to talk to her about being careful what she posts, but it sounds like that might not be very effective."

"Yeah."

"Okay. Let me play with this a bit more. When is your mom home?"

Nathan looked at the time. "Hmm, another hour, maybe."

"I think we'll stick around and talk to her. She needs to know what's going on, and that will give me a chance to look at her computer too. You can't really give me permission to look at hers."

"Thanks."

He wasn't sure what to do while Petrovic worked on the computer. He stared out the window. "Do you think he's dangerous?"

Andrees shook his head. "I don't expect so. Most of the time, it's harmless. Just a fan that saw you on the internet or on the TV, and wants to get a look at you, make sure you're okay, maybe get your autograph or give you a birthday card. I wouldn't worry too much about it. But you do want to be careful. You did the right thing in not approaching him, and going to your neighbor's. Just be alert, keep your eyes open."

When Mama got home to a police car outside the house and two policemen inside, she went immediately into panic mode. "Nathaniel! What's wrong? What's happened? Are you all right?"

She threw her arms around him, then changed her mind and held him at arm's length, studying his face.

"It's all right, Mama," he told her. "Everything's fine. It's just... there was this man hanging around, and I got worried."

Her eyes searched his. She looked at the policemen. "Is everything all right? Did you catch him?"

"He left before we got here, ma'am. But it does sound like Nathan had reason to be concerned. We'd like to talk to you about it. And maybe look at your computer too, to make sure that he hasn't hacked it."

"Hacked it...?" She sat down on one of the kitchen chairs with a thump. Nathan and the officers filled her in on details. Nathan described the man once more.

"Do you recognize the description?" Petrovic questioned.

"Did he try to talk to you?" Mama demanded. "Come up to you?"

Nathan shook his head. "No."

She sat back, thinking. "We just moved in here... we can't afford to move again..."

"I don't think you need to do anything that drastic," Petrovic assured her. "I don't think that you are in any danger here. You should be on the alert; keep your doors locked. We'll run some patrols through the area, watch for him. There's no indication that it is anyone other than a fan. Someone trying to get a good look at Nathan because of his internet celebrity status. As things quiet down, he'll probably go away again. But he hasn't actually done anything illegal or threatening."

"He'd better not," Mama said darkly. "He'd better stay away from my baby." She looked at Nathan. "If he tries to talk to you, you go the other way. Understand?"

Nathan nodded. "I know," he agreed. "I won't talk to him."

Mama poked her head into Nathan's room later on in the evening. "Hey, you. You need to be getting to bed soon, Bug."

Nathan leaned back in his chair and stretched. "Yes'm," he agreed. "I will soon."

"No more trouble on the computer?" she nodded to it.

Nathan shook his head. "No. But I've been staying off of the social networks. I'll just use it for schoolwork." Nathan looked at his pile of school books.

Mama came into the room and picked up the reader on his desk. "An adaptation of H. G. Wells' 'The Time Machine'," she read and raised her eyebrows at Nathan.

"We are studying early science fiction. So we had to choose something from Jules Verne or H. G. Wells or those guys."

She put it back down on the desk. "What do you think about it?"

Nathan considered. "It's interesting. Do you think that time travel is really possible?"

Mama shook her head. "No," she said flatly. "God controls the movement of time. We can't do anything about it."

"So you don't think that someone could build a time machine...?"

"No. I don't."

"What if some people could travel backward and forward in time without a time machine," Nathan suggested. "Just with the power of their brain."

Mama rolled her eyes. "I would say they were probably insane and should be locked up."

"But there's lots we don't know about time, and how it works..."

"I know all I need to about it. Only God controls the progress of times and seasons. He can roll back the shadows or end the world. Only he knows the beginning and end of time."

Nathan blinked at this. "Roll back the shadows?" he repeated.

"Yes."

"Can God roll back the shadows?"

"He did it in the Bible. He made the shadow on the sundial of Ahaz go back ten degrees. He also made the sun stand still for Joshua."

Nathan rubbed his arms, prickling up in goosebumps. "So he can turn back time, or make it stand still."

Mama shrugged. "He can do whatever he wants. But that doesn't mean that we can control time. Human beings can't stop the earth from rotating, or the progression of the seasons, or anything like that. We are bound by time. Only God can operate outside of it."

Nathan put his chin in his hand. "That's cool." He fingered the book. "But you don't think that we could manipulate time, if we understood it. There isn't any way."

"Scientists can do a lot of things... but they can't change time. Just like they can't create life. They'll never be able to. They're not God. That," she tapped the cover of the book. "That came out of someone's imagination. Just like the three little pigs." She smiled at him, her eyes sparkling. "Just because someone writes about pigs building themselves houses and talking, that doesn't mean they really can."

Nathan nodded. "Okay."

"Now, off to bed."

He closed his notebooks and put them all in a neat pile. In bed fifteen minutes later, he lay still, his eyes closed, pondering on the idea of God turning back the shadows.

Chapter Fifteen

WHEN NATHAN TOOK HOME the forms from school on the grade six outdoor education program, Mama was one of the first parents to volunteer to go along to help out. Nathan was glad that she was letting him go to the camp, but was anxious about her going along with him. He was already the target of teasing about being a mama's boy due to the birthday fiasco. He'd hoped that it would eventually just fade, but with her coming to supervise at the camp, there would be plenty of opportunities for further embarrassment.

"You have to treat me just like the other kids," he warned her in the car on the way to the camp. "You can't be giving me hugs or lots of attention, or coming into my tent or anything."

"I'm not going to embarrass you," she told him with a tolerant smile.

He was already separate from the rest of his class, arriving in the car with his mama instead of saying goodbye to her as he got onto one of the big yellow buses at the school. But there were other parents who were helping out too, and they'd be driving their own kids in. What was the point in paying for charter fees for the kids whose parents were driving in anyway?

"It's just..." Nathan struggled to explain in a way that wouldn't hurt his feelings. "I don't want the other kids to think that I'm a baby. You have to let me be independent while we're at the camp."

"I can do that," she assured him.

Nathan sat watching out the window, wondering. It was the first camp she'd even let him go on. Lots of the kids went to camps every summer, or with Scouting programs or something. It was Nathan's first campout with anyone other than just Mama.

He was glad to get out of town, away from the mysterious stalker. The police had traced the suspicious computer profile, and it hadn't belonged to Allen, but it also hadn't belonged to the mysterious man. It had, in fact, belonged to a woman, one who had seen Mama's postings and wanted to meet him in person. She was good enough at hacking to set up a fake profile for someone else in his class, hoping that Nathan would know him well enough to accept his friend request. They had given her a warning, and so far Nathan hadn't had any other suspicious contacts online.

But there was still the strange man. Nathan had seen the wavy haired man once or twice more, but the police hadn't been able to identify him. So far he hadn't made any direct contact or made any threats, he just showed up in odd places, a glimpse here or there. Just enough to put Nathan constantly on edge and send his blood sugar levels soaring. He was looking forward to being out in the woods, away from the man, so he could just relax.

"What are you thinking about, Bug?" Mama questioned, glancing aside at him.

"I dunno... just that it's nice to get away for a while."

She nodded. "I think it's going to be a blast," she said. "We're going to have a great time."

"You can't call me nicknames there."

"Am I allowed to speak to you at all?" Mama questioned.

"Yes, I'm sorry. Just..."

"You don't want them to think you're a baby. I know, you're a big boy, Nathaniel. I'm not going to embarrass you."

"Okay. Sorry. I think we're going to have a really good time."

At first, Mama attracted a lot of attention, and people gave her and Nathan strange looks. Mama stood out in her black and red dress, when everyone else was in blue-jeans or khakis or camo. Her voice was loud, and she was bubbly and excited to help out. Nathan was sorted into his camp group, which happily included Bly.

"Is that your mom?" Bly questioned.

Nathan's face warmed. "Yes," he admitted, looking down at his feet.

"She's pretty. Is she really going to camp in a dress?"

"Women did for hundreds of years," he pointed out.

"What if she gets it dirty?"

"She'll wash it when she gets home. She has more packed."

Bly accepted this. "Is she going to be in charge of our group?"

"I hope not," Nathan said.

"I wouldn't mind. She seems kind of cool."

Nathan flashed a look at Bly. "Really?"

"Look at the other parents," Bly pointed out.

Most of the other parents were standing to the side in a tight group, talking with each other and paying no attention to the kids or to the camp leaders who were trying to get things organized. Mama, on the other hand, was joking around with the kids in the group nearest to her, and consulting with the camp leaders to see what she could do to help.

Nathan tried to relax. Maybe it would be okay. Maybe Mama would keep her word and not embarrass him. And if the other kids got to know her and liked her, then maybe they would stop teasing Nathan about being such a mama's boy.

Nathan wasn't surprised that Mama was assigned to be the mom for his group. He couldn't see Mama letting them set it up any other way. She helped them to set up their tents, keeping an eye on Nathan but not rushing in to do it all for him. They had camped together plenty of times, and had always put up the tents together, but Nathan could do it on his own well enough. After they were all set up, they sat around the fire pit. No fire had been lit yet. Most of the other groups were still trying to get their tents up, so Nathan's group got to relax.

"Why don't we sing some campfire songs?" Mama suggested.

Nathan looked at the others, who did not look excited by the prospect. "There's no campfire, Mama," he pointed out.

"We don't need a campfire to sing, Come on, what else are you guys going to do? Y'all weren't allowed to bring any of your electronics with you, so you're pretty much crippled now."

There were grins and moans of agreement from the other kids. They were all pretty fidgety without their electronic fixes. The beginnings of withdrawal.

"So some songs," Mama repeated. "Who knows the one about gopher guts?"

Most of them looked at each other blankly. Mama looked around the circle. "Help me out, here, Nathaniel," she encouraged.

Nathan hesitantly joined in with her. The others started to giggle, and in a few minutes, they had all picked it up and were singing or shouting along. Bly swayed back and forth, bellowing away. He looked at Nathan, grinning, and nodded his approval.

It took some time to get everyone settled down for supper. The leaders tried to get the various groups of students sat down at the right tables, instead of sitting with their friends wherever they pleased. This was supposed to be about outdoor and survival skills, not about sitting with their buddies. They were supposed to do everything with their groups, on a schedule. Finally everyone was sitting down at the right tables, but there was still a lot of arguing and yelling going on. The room was noisy and chaotic, even though the camp director had a microphone and was trying to yell over top of them with the volume turned all the way up, making it squeal.

Nathan's group was sitting pretty quietly, and Mama left them at their table, working her way up to the front of the room. Nathan buried his head in his hands, trying to make himself invisible before she could do anything to embarrass him. But through the cracks in his fingers, he saw her take the microphone out of the director's hands, and adjust the volume level. Then she started to sing.

No greasy grimy gopher guts this time. It was Amazing Grace, and she sang it in a low but clear voice, far below the raucous noise of the students. But those closest to her immediately stopped talking and yelling, and started nudging each other into quiet, and the more students stopped talking, the more that could hear her. In thirty seconds, the room was completely silent, other than Mama's song. Everyone was still, watching her, listening to the faith and emotion in her voice. When she finished, nobody clapped, there was just silence. Everybody seemed to be holding their breaths. Mama looked around the room at them.

"Did y'all have someone assigned to give thanks over this food?" she asked the camp director softly.

He shook his head, apparently stunned by the turn of events. Mama scanned the students in front of her.

"Do I have a volunteer to say grace?" she questioned.

A couple of tentative hands went up, and Mama motioned to the girl closest to her.

"You, my dear. Come on up. We'll have plenty of other opportunities for everyone else."

The girl went up to the front and took the mike from Mama. She had pretty red hair, pulled back into a ponytail. She smiled at Mama and said something to her, away from the mike. Then she looked out over the students, waiting. Nathan folded his arms and bowed his head, and pretty soon just about everyone was waiting with folded arms or hands. The redhead said a brief thanks and blessing. Then she handed the mike back to Mama, blushing.

"Thank you. Now, if everyone will remain quiet for another minute, you will be told the rules and which table is going to be served first," she announced.

She handed the mike back to the camp director, who stumbled through awkward thanks, a list of 'do nots,' and motioned to Nathan's group.

"We'll call that table one, and they can take their plates up first. Then two," he pointed to another table, and continued counting them off. Nathan got up with the rest of his table, and grabbed Mama's plate as well as his own, handing it to her as they got to the buffet tables.

"I hope I didn't embarrass you too much," Mama teased.

Nathan shook his head. "That was really nice. I'm surprised it worked!"

"You just have to give people a chance, Nathan. They don't even know it, but they're starving more for the Spirit of God than for their supper. Everyone's heart is touched by music."

The next morning, everyone sat around waiting for the guest speaker. Nathan couldn't understand why they had all been pulled away from their various activities to sit out in the hot sun, when the speaker wasn't even there yet. They could have at least waited until the guy was in the campsite before insisting that everyone come in.

"This is stupid," Bly groused. "Why do we have to wait around here? He's not coming, right? So just let us go back to whatever we were doing?"

Nathan's group had been canoeing, and Nathan had just been getting the hang of what to do with the oars when they were told to come in. He wasn't even sure what the guest speaker was supposed to be talking about. Bear safety, or something. Nathan hadn't seen much more wildlife than birds and squirrels. The camp was well-used, and he imagined that all of the bigger game had been scared off long ago.

"I'm so bored!" one of the girls, Teffany, complained, laying flat on her back on the ground with her hat over her face. "And it's so hot! Can't we go back to the lake?"

Everybody was having similar thoughts, whether they said them aloud or not. Nobody was happy. Nathan heard a shutter click sound effect, and looked around.

"That better not be..." he saw Mama, holding out her phone, taking his picture. "Mama!"

"Let's see some action shots," Mama called out to them. "What are you guys doing laying around? Michael," she prompted one of the other boys. "Show me a slow-motion sprint!"

He looked at her like she was crazy, and Mama gave him *the Look*. Michael got up off of the ground, and though embarrassed and awkward in front of everybody, he gave it his best shot. Nathan could hear the shutter click going over and over again.

"I want to see archery," Mama called next. "Who can do archery for me?"

"We've got no equipment," Bly pointed out.

"Who needs equipment? Use your imaginations. Nathan?"

At least he hadn't been the first one that she had called upon. Nathan stood up, and gave her his best slow-motion no-bow-or-arrow archery shot. She nodded encouragingly.

"Okay, how about--"

"Swimming!" one of the other boys suggested, and gave her an out-of-the-water front crawl.

Teffany had taken her hat off of her face to watch them. She shook her head in disgust. "This is so stupid," she complained. "Why hasn't anyone picked horseback riding?"

Getting up, she started trotting around, holding imaginary reins as she cantered up and down the field. They all tried several different sports and poses for her, and then Mama had another idea.

"What about a pyramid? Let's get all the boys on the bottom, on their hands and knees."

They moved to obey. Mama looked at Nathan. "You're too small, I'm going to need you on the top," she instructed.

His face hot, Nathan got back to his feet. Mama moved a couple of other people out and into other positions. Then she pointed out who she wanted on the next row, and they carefully climbed on the backs of the bottom row people. The third row was pretty unstable, and people on the bottom kept collapsing. Mama kept encouraging them, taking pictures, and laughing. Eventually they got a third row that was able to stay for a few seconds, and Mama tried to boost Nathan up on top. By the time she got around to the front of the pyramid for a picture, they had all collapsed. Nathan laughed and tried to extricate himself from the pile of bodies and arms and legs.

One of the camp leaders called out to the students with a megaphone, asking them to all be seated now that their guest speaker had arrived. A little cheer went up, and Nathan and his group all sat down on the ground to listen. Nathan heard one of the girls in the group that sat closest to them whisper to her friend.

"How come group one always gets to have all the fun?"

Nathan glanced at Mama, and she gave him a smile. She looked down at her phone to thumb through the pictures that she had taken. Nathan looked around at the other parent leaders who were standing around in various bored or authoritarian stances.

Chapter Sixteen

WEDNESDAY WAS HIKING DAY. As in hiking-all-day. They had all packed their daypacks, which had to include lunches, pocket knives, emergency kits, first aid kits, extra water, and a bunch of other gear that Nathan was sure they were not going to have any need for. It was just more equipment to weigh the kids down and make sure that they didn't get too far ahead of the adults. They wanted the students to be good and tired by the end of the day so that they would be too exhausted to cause any trouble.

Mama moved around the group one kids. "Everybody got everything they need? Anyone need some help?"

Yawning, everybody mumbled and shook their heads. Mama rounded up some hats for bare heads and double-checked that a few people had extra water. The camp director came over with the hike leader for their group, Guy.

"Everything all ready to go here, Billie?" the camp director questioned.

"I think we're all set."

"I'll be the judge of that," said Guy. "I want everyone to sit down on the grass for a minute. I'm going to read off a checklist, and you have to make sure that you have each item in your pack. Everyone ready?"

They all sat down, grumbling, and Guy started to read off the list. The director walked off to talk to the next group.

It turned out that each group had a different map with a different route to take. Nathan had assumed that they would all just be hiking the same main trail, one behind the other, with no chance of getting lost or getting in any kind of trouble. The idea that each group was going a different way gave them some chance at something interesting happening, anyway. Even if it was just the sighting of a deer or a waterfall.

Once Guy was convinced that they had all packed what was required, he took a cursory look at the map, and was apparently familiar with the route. He handed the map to Mama.

"I'll take the lead. Why don't you bring up the rear? Just holler if you have any concerns."

"I'll sing out," Mama agreed.

At first, Nathan was in the middle of the group. But he ended up walking with Bly, who didn't have much stamina for hiking, and they lagged in the back. So Nathan, and Bly, and Mama walked together, bringing up the rear. After they had been hiking for a while, Bly stopped and bent over, huffing and puffing, trying to catch his breath.

"Are you okay?" Mama questioned. "You'd better take a break for a minute. Nathaniel, run up and let Guy know that we're going to stop for a break."

Nathan hesitated.

"Go on," Mama encouraged. "We don't want to get separated."

Nathan ran on ahead. "Guy, Guy!"

The man turned around and looked at him, irritated. "What is it?"

"We have to stop for a minute."

"We just barely got started. What's the matter?"

"Bly. He has asthma, and he's having trouble. Mama said we have to take a break."

Guy made a noise of disgust. "All right, everybody hold on for a minute. We're going to need to take a break." He stalked back along the trail to where Mama and Bly had stopped. Nathan trailed behind. "What's up, bud?" Guy asked Bly. "You're holding up the whole group. We've barely started, and you need a break already?"

Bly breathed heavily, nodding. He coughed. "Not in very..." he puffed, "very good shape."

Guy shook his head. "We can't keep stopping every ten minutes. Maybe you should just take him back to the camp," he suggested to Mama.

"No, no," Mama soothed. "He'll be fine in a minute. We'll just have to take it a little more slowly than you're used to."

"I'll go wait with the others. We need to go on soon."

Guy marched back up the trail to join up with the rest of the group. Mama followed him with her eyes. She looked back at Bly. "Don't you worry about that," she told Bly, who was looking anxious. "We'll be able to go with them."

She met Nathan's eyes and gave a slight twitch with her head, asking him to join them. Nathan got closer, and patted Bly's arm. "Do you need to take your inhaler?" he suggested.

"Not yet," Bly told him weakly.

"The coach said you should take it before you exercise, so you don't start to wheeze."

"He doesn't need that," Mama said. "He's going to be just fine." She rubbed Bly's back in soothing circles, like she did when Nathan was sick. "Do you want me to try laying hands on you, Bly?"

"What's that mean?" Bly questioned, still breathing heavily.

"I put my hands on you, and pray, to try to heal you." Bly looked at her doubtfully. "I have done it before. It can't hurt you, and it may help, if you have faith that God can heal you."

Bly looked at Nathan. "Can she do that?" he questioned.

"I've seen her heal people," Nathan confirmed.

Bly looked back at Mama. "It won't hurt?"

"No, of course not. I just touch you. Usually your head. Would that bother you?" Bly shook his head. Mama smiled. She nodded to Nathan. "Why don't you hold his hands, and we'll all pray together? That would work the best."

Nathan and Bly looked at each other's hands, and reached toward each other hesitantly, feeling awkward. Nathan closed the distance and took Bly's hands, holding them firmly.

"Okay," he said. "Just think about being better. Do you believe in God?"

Bly nodded, just a tiny movement.

"Then you pray that He'll heal you. And Mama will pray too. We all will."

Mama put down her daypack and put her hands on the top of Bly's head. He was nearly as tall as she was. She started to pray aloud. Nathan barely heard what she was saying. He was listening to Bly's breathing, as it quieted and slowed. The prayer was not a long one, but by the time that Mama was finished, Bly was breathing normally again.

"There," Mama said softly. "Better, huh?"

Bly nodded.

"You don't need to worry about it anymore. Your lungs are healed."

Bly took a deep breath and let it out.

"No more?" he repeated.

"You'll be just fine now. Shall we join the others?"

Bly started walking up the trail without answering. Mama and Nathan followed behind. When Guy saw that they were back, he got everyone to their feet.

"Let's go. We've got some time to make up," he encouraged. He looked at Bly. "We can't keep taking breaks every ten minutes."

Bly nodded. "No. I'm okay now."

"Good. Let's move."

They headed up the trail again. Nathan walked beside Bly, and though he breathed heavily when they were going up the steeper portions of the trail, he didn't have to stop again. Mama started singing cadence, and their hike progressed well.

The rest of the hike up the mountain was without incident. They did see some wildlife, a couple of deer here and there, woodpeckers, and other small woodland animals. They broke for lunch near the peak, and everyone sat down on the rocky ground and devoured their meals with great appetite.

Nathan moved away from the rest of the group into the trees, where they couldn't see him well, and checked his blood sugar. He gave himself a shot, and waited for a few minutes before putting his kit back away and rejoining the group. Mama watched him come back, frowning slightly. Nathan sat down beside Bly and started on his dinner.

"So... you're doing okay now?" he questioned.

Bly nodded cheerfully. "I made it all the way up the mountain without having to use my inhaler!" he said. "I can't believe that I could do that! Your mom..." he trailed off and shook his head. "I don't know... I didn't know she could do that."

Nathan nodded.

"So why doesn't she heal you?" Bly questioned. "Then you wouldn't have to take your diabetes medicine anymore."

"She's tried," Nathan said with a sigh. "It doesn't always work. If you don't have enough faith, or if it's a trial that God thinks you need to go through... then it won't work."

"Well, you have enough faith, so that must mean that God wants you to go through it," he observed. "Why would God want that?"

"I don't know," Nathan said, not correcting him on the faith issue, and feeling guilty about it. "We can't know the mind of God."

Bly nodded. "Guess not," he agreed. "Heck, half the time I don't even know my own mind!"

Nathan chuckled. They continued to eat their bagged lunches without much discussion.

It wasn't a long break, and Nathan's legs were sore and heavy after the hike up the mountain. Now they were on their way down again. He didn't think it would be as hard, but he was getting pretty tired, as were the others, and the steep portions that they had come up seemed even steeper and slipperier going back down. Nathan and Bly still hung toward the back of the group, so when a shout went up on the trail ahead, they couldn't see what was going on. Mama moved past them to see what was wrong, and Nathan and Bly followed quickly.

Nathan suspected that someone had probably turned an ankle, or suffered a fall down one of the slopes. There hadn't been any dangerous obstacles on the way up, and even thought they were going down a different route than they had come up, he didn't think there would be anything too treacherous on the way back down.

He rounded the last bend of the trail. Everyone was frozen, looking down at something. Nathan tried to look over and around them, but couldn't see. Mama gently pushed her way through the group, and they parted for her. Nathan followed close behind her before the crowd could move back together again. Guy was on the trail ahead of them, still, his face as white as a sheet. Nathan and Mama followed his eyes to the trail ahead, where a big rattler was coiled up, its head high, ready to strike.

"It's just a li'l old rattler," Mama said soothingly. "It ain't gonna hurt y'all. Why don't you back up a bit, and we'll take care of it?"

The children backed up. Guy didn't move. Mama's movements were slow and deliberate as she walked over to him and pulled him back a few steps.

"Stay away from it," Guy whispered. "We'll just wait until it goes away."

"Oh, he found himself a nice sunny place on the trail and he doesn't want to give it up," Mama said with a laugh. "You could be waiting for a long time. You just stay back here."

She and Nathan got closer to the snake. "What've we got here, Nathaniel?" Mama questioned.

"Timber rattler..." Nathan suggested. "But it's pretty far west for timber. I would've expected a prairie or western."

Mama nodded in agreement. "But, timber is what we've got," she agreed. "You want to get me a stick?"

Nathan was already scouting around for one. He found a long, weather-worn branch and brought it to her. Mama broke it in half, and approached the snake.

"Stay away from it," Guy warned. "That's a rattler! It'll kill you!"

"Oh, it's got no intention of killing us," Mama dismissed.

She continued to approach the snake, slowing down and circling when it reared its head back to strike, her movements calm and slow. She nudged the coils of the snake with her stick, and it quickly uncoiled, looking to retreat off of the path. Mama followed it, and using her stick, lifted it deftly into the air. A gasp of shock went up from the group of students. Nathan moved in.

"Can I see?"

She passed him the stick, and Nathan turned it this way and that, getting a good look at the snake. It was lovely the way its scales shimmered in the sunlight. The snake wound around the stick, not liking to be off the ground. Nathan stroked the tail and examined the rattle.

"Old grandaddy," he commented, pointing out the length of the rattle to Mama.

She nodded. "Now take it over there," she suggested, "to the rocks just beyond that stand of trees. Nobody will bother it there."

Nathan nodded and took it over to the rocks, where he laid the stick down. The rattler slithered quickly off and found a hiding place between the rocks. Nathan walked back over to the group, shrugging.

"All gone," he said. "He's not going to bother anybody."

Bly gaped at him. "It could have bit you!" he said, his eyes wide with amazement. "How could you get that close? And touch it!"

Nathan laughed. "I've handled lots of snakes," he said. "I wasn't even holding it in my hand."

"It could kill you!"

"I've been bit before. It wouldn't kill me."

Guy was getting his voice back. He rounded on Mama and Nathan. "You guys shouldn't have gone anywhere near that snake! You can't do things like that. If you see a rattler or something else hazardous, you're supposed to stay away, not play with it! What if it had bitten one of you? Or both of you? Do you know what kind of trouble you would have been in?"

"Probably better than you do," Mama said with a smile. "Are you an expert on snakes?"

Nathan giggled. By Guy's reaction, he was obviously not an expert, or anywhere near comfortable with them.

"You don't get near poisonous snakes!" Guy insisted.

"Venomous," Nathan said. "You wanted it off the trail, and we moved it off the trail. Nobody got hurt."

"I'm going to report this!" Guy said angrily, and marched off down the trail. The group followed, but Nathan noticed that he and Mama were no longer at the back of the group, but instead, most of the students preferred to follow behind them.

There was another set-to when they reached the base camp and Guy told his story to the director and other camp leaders. Then there was no end of lectures over how dangerous it was for Mama and Nathan to be handling dangerous snakes. Eventually the excitement died down, though Nathan heard the story whispered over and over again for the rest of the camp. The size of the snake grew over time, until it was the size of a python instead of a rattler. Oddly enough, the boys who had been most vocal about teasing him at school about his Mama were suddenly silent. They kept their distance, and whispered to each other.

By Sunday, though, the excitement over the snakes was old news. When Nathan got up in the morning, he put on his worship clothes like he normally would. When Bly saw him all dressed up, he burst into laughter.

"Where do you think you're going all dressed up like that?" he questioned.

Nathan shifted uncomfortably. He scratched his ear. "It's Sunday."

"Yeah...?"

"It's the sabbath," Nathan said. "I'm dressed for worship."

"Worship? Where?"

"Uh..." Nathan looked around. "I don't know."

The other students who were up were already dressed in their usual t shirts and blue jeans. There were a number of looks and giggles aimed in Nathan's direction. Nathan went to the latrine, and then wandered over by the kitchens where he thought Mama might be. It was a few minutes before he tracked her down. Mama too was in one of her Sunday dresses, and smiled when she saw him.

"There's my handsome boy," she said.

"Mama... are we having worship?" he questioned. "I don't see anybody getting ready."

She frowned. "They must be planning something," she said, "even if it's non-denominational. I'll find out."

"Okay," Nathan agreed. He could have gone back to the tents, but didn't want to be the focus of attention there. It seemed like a long time before Mama finally got back. She shook her head at him.

"There will be worship," she said. "Just give me a few minutes to get something organized!"

"They didn't plan anything?"

"Not a thing."

He shook his head. "Well, you're always good coming up with stuff."

"I will," she agreed. "Look, breakfast is almost over in there, you'd better go get a bite to eat. Then could you see if you can help clean up, so we can use the dining room for service?"

Nathan agreed and went to find something to eat. Sleeping in a tent was catching up to him, and there had been no reveille Sunday morning. He'd slept much later than he normally would, and not eating on time wasn't good for his diabetes.

Nathan was helping to bus dishes from the dining room to the kitchen to ensure that the dining room was ready for Mama to use for services when he saw the man.

Through the back door of the kitchen, left open while they carried in the last shipment of food for the camp, he saw the familiar handsome face. He had a bit of a beard now, and the hair that was usually so well-styled was a bit sweaty and messed up. He was unpacking cases of pop, and as he added another case to the stack, his eyes met Nathan's across the room.

There was a crash of shattering glass, and camp workers surrounded Nathan, blocking his view of the open door.

"Stay right there; don't move," one woman told him sternly, and Nathan stood there, not comprehending what was going on, straining to see past them to the door again. He dropped his eyes to the concrete floor, which was covered with shards of broken glasses. Nathan hadn't even realized that he'd been holding the dishes, let alone that he had dropped and broken them.

The woman came back with a little broom, a handheld brush for counters or small messes, and she moved around Nathan, brushing his clothing, and especially his pant cuffs and shoes, to remove any slivers of glass that might stick him as he moved around.

"Okay," she instructed, "take a big step over here, watch out for the glass."

They helped him out of the pool of glass, though he could see that some small pieces still sparkled all the way across the kitchen.

"Who was that?" Nathan questioned. "Who was that outside? Where'd he go?"

He couldn't see anyone there anymore. The delivery truck was gone.

"Where did who go?"

He went to the door that stood open, his hands shaking and knees wobbly. He tried to catch his breath.

"The man who was out here, dropping the food off. Where did he go?"

"To do his next delivery, I guess."

"Who was that? Does somebody know his name?"

He looked around at the kitchen staff, and they all shook their heads at him, looking at him like he was crazy.

"That guy--I need to know his name! I need to know who he is. He's been following me, he keeps showing up. You have to call the police and tell them that he was here."

"He's gone now. And you'll be gone back home at the end of the day."

Nathan smacked his fist into his hand in frustration. "Does somebody know his name? Who hired him? Somebody must know!"

"He's just a delivery driver. It's a service. You'd have to find out from the delivery company."

"What's the delivery company?"

"You'd have to find out from the grocery store," someone else contributed.

Nathan rolled his eyes. "Can you find out? Someone? Please?" he looked around at them. "Seriously, this guy is stalking me, I have a police file number and everything. Maybe they can track him down now..."

The big woman who seemed to be in charge nodded, making calm-down motions with her hands. "I'll talk to the grocery store and we'll try to track it down, okay? Now why don't you go back to the dining room and see if your mom needs help with anything."

Nathan walked slowly back to the dining room, his heart pounding. He knew he should do something to make himself calm down, or the stress would raise his blood sugar, but he was too shocked at seeing the man all the way at camp to settle down. Mama was in the dining room when he got there.

"Nathaniel? What is it?" she questioned as soon as she saw his face.

"That man. He was here."

"What? Here?" Mama's eyes got big.

Nathan nodded.

"Where?"

"Unloading food in the kitchen."

She took a step toward him. "Is he still here?"

"No, gone."

"Did anyone know who he was?"

"They're going to try to find out his name. From the delivery company."

"Okay... we'll see what they can find out. If he's gone, there's no point in calling the police until we get home." She pulled him close to give him a tight hug. "You're safe here with me. He's gone."

Nathan nodded, swallowing a lump in his throat.

"Let's focus on our worship. God will help us to put it in perspective."

Nathan nodded. Mama gave him instructions, and he moved around the dining room helping her to get everything set up.

Chapter Seventeen

NATHAN RANG CHANDRA'S BACK doorbell, and then knocked on the door so that she would know that he was at the back door rather than the front. She opened the door after a minute and smiled at him.

"Is it garbage day?" she said, looking at her watch in bemusement.

Nathan nodded. "Do you have anything else to go out?" he questioned.

"Yes, let me just get the kitchen garbage."

He watched her walk back to the kitchen, and waited for her return. When she came back with the last garbage bag and put it in the bin, Nathan had an overwhelming sense of *déjà vu*. It was so strong that he felt dizzy, and grabbed onto the doorframe for support.

Chandra's smiled turned immediately to concern. "Nathan? Are you okay?"

He knew every movement that she was going to make, every word she was going to say before she said it. He focused on the solidity of the doorframe under his hand. That was real. It wasn't a dream, or it would not have felt so solid in his hand. There was nothing vague or dreamlike about the scene. It was all crystal clear, like he had lived this precise moment before. He had seen and heard and felt all of these things before.

"Come inside and sit for a minute. Are you dizzy? Faint?"

Chandra held his arm and escorted him inside. Instead of taking him all the way to the sitting room at the front of the house, she pulled him into the kitchen and sat him down on one of the kitchen chairs, and poured him a glass of water.

"Here. What's wrong? Is it your sugar? Should I get you some juice or something?"

Nathan shook his head. "No. It's just... *déjà vu*. Really, really strong *déjà vu*." He shook his head as if he could shake the feeling off. "Man, that's weird."

Chandra smiled at him. "Been time traveling, have you?" she teased.

Nathan frowned at her. "That's not possible. Everyone says it's not possible."

Chandra shrugged and gave him a mysterious wink. "No, of course not," she agreed.

Nathan was starting to feel more grounded again. "That was just really weird," he said, getting to his feet. "It's okay now. I gotta take the bin out, and get back for breakfast."

"Are you sure you're okay?"

"Yes'm. I'm fine."

She walked with him to the back door.

"What really causes *déjà vu*?" Nathan asked.

She looked at him for a moment, eyebrows raised.

"It's not time travel," Nathan insisted. "So what is it?"

"If you're asking what the scientists know about it--not much. They don't know."

Nathan sighed and grabbed the bin.

"Thank you for helping me out, Nathan," Chandra said. "You're always so helpful."

"Yes'm. See you later."

He dragged the bin out and put it in place, then went back in his own back door. Mama was placing his breakfast on the table.

"What took you so long? Are you okay? You're white as a ghost!"

Nathan swallowed and shook his head. "I'm fine," he said. "Just had a little... dizzy turn. That's all."

"You didn't... see that man again?" she checked.

Nathan shook his head. "No. What did the police say? Did they get his name from the delivery company?"

Mama pressed her lips together. "They said he used a false name. They couldn't find anything out about him."

Nathan sighed. He rubbed his temples, a wave of vertigo going through him, making him start to shake again.

"Eat up," Mama advised. "That will make you feel better."

He nodded and sat down to eat. "I need to get more insulin," he reminded Mama. "I told you I was running out."

"We'll see."

He looked up at her, frowning. "We have to get more," he repeated. "I'm out."

"And you've been fine so far. Let's just see how you do."

Nathan swallowed a forkful of eggs, and it stuck in his throat. He took a drink to wash it down. "If I don't have insulin, I'm going to get sick again," he pointed out.

"Let's just see how it goes," she repeated.

Nathan stared at her. She gave him an encouraging smile and ruffled his hair.

"Do you want me to pray with you?" she questioned.

Nathan nodded slowly. "Yes'm."

As she prayed, he tried to focus on her words and to remember how she had healed Bly on the mountain. If she could heal Bly's asthma, why couldn't she heal Nathan's diabetes too? It must be because of his doubts. If he could just have faith in God's ability to heal him just like he'd healed Bly, Nathan could be healed too.

When she finished, Mama ruffled his hair again and smiled encouragingly.

"Now you'd better get finished up, and get ready for school. You don't want to be late."

It seemed like things went downhill much faster this time. Maybe it was because he knew how good and how normal he could feel if he was getting the right medicine. Within a few days, he could barely get out of bed in the morning. The fatigue was overwhelming; he didn't know how he'd managed to continue on before.

"Nathan. Nathan," Mrs. Davis was shaking him by the arm.

Nathan raised his head and looked at her, rubbing his eyes. "Sorry-- what?"

She kept her voice low. "Are you okay?" she questioned urgently. "Are you sick? Should I call your mom?"

"No," Nathan straightened up and blinked, trying to focus his attention. "I'm fine. Just didn't... I just didn't sleep very well last night."

She studied him for a minute, then nodded slowly. "Okay... but if you need something... you tell me, okay? If I can help..."

"I'm fine," Nathan repeated, forcing a smile. "Sorry. I'll stay awake."

"Okay."

Nathan shifted in his seat. "Can I got to the bathroom?"

"Yes. You don't have to ask me, Nathan. Just go if you need to."

He got up and headed to the boys' room, stopping at the water fountain for a long drink on the way there.

On Sunday, Bly and a couple of other school kids attended their worship with a parent or two in tow. The room was crowded, and in order to have enough room to dance, they expanded into the kitchen and hallway. Nathan didn't get up to dance even one dance. Delia tried to get him to his feet, but he just couldn't summon the energy.

After the rest of the worshipers left, Nathan sat looking at the snake in the terrarium behind the straight-backed chair he was sitting in. Mama came in after seeing the last couple of people off.

"You didn't dance today," she said. "You weren't moved?"

"I wanted to," Nathan said, resting his head on his arms on the back of the chair. "But I just couldn't do it."

She sat down next to him and stroked back the hair lying over his forehead. "Do you want to lie down for a while, sweetie?"

"Yes'm... in a bit."

She followed his eyes to the terrarium.

"I thought maybe you'd use it in the service today," Nathan commented.

"They're not ready yet. People here... aren't moved by the spirit as easily as some of the simpler areas we've lived. So much competing for their attention. When it's time, the Lord will tell me."

"Can we handle it today?"

Mama hesitated. "I don't know if you're up to it."

"I can't dance," Nathan protested, "but I can still handle. I can manage that!"

He wanted to prove to himself that he hadn't lost his faith. God just didn't want to heal him right now. It wasn't because of his lack of faith. He had to prove to himself that he was still a believer.

"I don't know," Mama was still reluctant.

"I'm *moved*, Mama. I'm moved to take it up." She didn't make any sign she would allow it. "Do you *doubt me*?" Nathan demanded.

"No, of course I don't doubt you. I know how strong your faith is."

"Then let me," Nathan insisted. He gestured toward the stereo. "Put something on. You'll be moved too."

As soon as she moved toward the stereo, Nathan had the top off of the terrarium. He was lifting the snake out before Mama realized what he was doing.

"No!" she shouted as he lifted it over the edge of the glass.

Nathan jumped and gripped the snake harder, startled by her yell. In an instant, he felt like someone had punched him in the shoulder, followed by a searing, fiery pain. He cried out, and did something that he'd never done before; he dropped the snake. It slithered quickly away from him, looking for somewhere to hide. Mama hurried to retrieve it. They only had the one snake right now, and they were not in plentiful supply like they had been back home. It would get into the walls if it could, and maybe even die there.

"Get it!" Mama yelped, chasing after it. Nathan tried to help, but he was too slow and only got in the way, tripping Mama up so that she went crashing to the floor almost on top of the fleeing serpent. She managed to stop herself from crushing it, but she had landed too awkwardly to capture it properly or get out of the way, and it struck again, sinking its fangs into her leg. Nathan saw her flinch and heard her muffled grunt of pain. But unlike Nathan, she kept her head and grabbed it just behind the head before it had finished detaching, then gently picked up its middle body with her other hand to support its weight, and took it back to the terrarium. She replaced the top and turned to Nathan once the snake was safely secured.

"I'm sorry," Nathan offered immediately, a lump in his throat. He massaged the searing bite with his opposite hand. "You scared me! I didn't mean to."

"You know it's up to the pastor to decide if the Spirit moves and the congregation is ready. It's not up to you."

"I know," Nathan agreed. Tears escaped his eyes and ran down his face. "Man, it hurts like a--"

"Mind your tongue, boy."

Nathan chewed the inside of his lip. "It hurts!" he whined.

"I know it does, baby," Mama agreed, her voice softer.

She pulled up her skirt to examine the bite on her leg. It was rapidly swelling and turning red and purple. Nathan looked at the one on his shoulder. It too was already swelling, the burning pain spreading.

"Let's get washed up," Mama encouraged. "You know how easily they can get infected."

He followed her to the bathroom, where Mama washed both wounds off with soap and water, and applied dressings the best she could. Nathan could tell by the tightness around her eyes and mouth that she was in as much pain as he was.

"I don't think I got as much venom as you did," she observed. But he thought that she probably had. "Let's go lie down. Nothing to do now, but let it work its way out."

Nathan was crying in earnest, and couldn't stop. He'd been bit before, but it always took his breath away. You always forgot from one time to the next just how badly it hurt. He managed to make it to his bed and crawl in. Mama limped after him, and though she probably intended to go to her own bed, she didn't make it that far, but collapsed at the end of Nathan's bed instead.

Nathan writhed on the bed, grasping his shoulder and groaning aloud. He kept waiting to pass out or for the pain to ease. But neither happened and the swelling kept growing, until he thought his skin would burst open. Mama moved occasionally, but she made no noise, and Nathan thought she was probably unconscious. She must have gotten more venom than he did, or else she was reacting to it worse.

He passed through a period of darkness, unable to tell whether he was awake or unconscious. The pain was ever-present, with no relief. Then the nausea started. Nathan climbed out of bed, feeling his way toward the door, everything around him fuzzy and unclear. The snakebite throbbed. He made it to the bathroom before throwing up, and then lay on the floor on his side for a long time after, appreciating the cold tile on his hot face.

Worrying about Mama more than himself, he crawled back to the bedroom to check on her. She was still, unconscious, and didn't rouse when he shook her. He pushed up her skirt and tried to focus his eyes on the snakebite site around the dressing, blue and purple, swollen like a football. It looked like Nathan's arm felt; ready to burst through the skin, it had grown so tight. Mama's face was burning. Nathan got shakily to his feet and again made the trip back to the bathroom, wetting towels and then tottering back to Mama's side to sponge her face. She was flushed, and still didn't stir at his touch. Nathan lay back down on the bed beside her and tried to figure out what to do. His brain worked sluggishly, either because of his blood sugar or the venom. He imagined his sugar, aggravated by stress, was probably soaring.

Nathan got up, unsure how much time had passed. It was dark outside the window. He was shivering, his teeth almost chattering. He felt his way to the closet and pulled a pile of blankets out, pulling them over himself and Mama. He prodded her again, but she still didn't move.

The next time he awoke, his arm felt wet. He looked at it and just about threw up at the sight. The skin had finally split, and blood and fluids were leaking everywhere. Some of the flesh was black, but mostly it was red and glistening, the split gaping wide like a mouth. Suppressing the sickness and nausea, he went to the bathroom to get a roll of gauze, and wrapped it around and around his arm, covering up the open wound. Taking another roll with him, he went back to the bedroom and checked on Mama. He was afraid to look at her wound. Steeling himself, he pulled back her skirt. Hers too had split, and as well as red flesh and blood, there were pockets of glistening yellow fat. Nathan reached for the wastepaper bin, and this time he did throw up. Then he shakily wrapped the roll of gauze around her leg, breathing through his mouth, fearing the smell of gangrene from the blackening wound.

He pulled himself back onto the bed and put both of his hands on Mama's head. He couldn't think of the words to pray, so he just knelt there like that, his hands on her head.

"Mama," he whispered finally. "Please get better."

Eventually, he removed his hands from her head, and lay down again, resting his hand on her arm to stay in contact with him, and drifted from consciousness once again.

Time continued to pass at an uneven pace, waking in sunlight, waking again at night. He became aware of the phone ringing endlessly. Then Mama stirred. Nathan tried to rouse himself to talk to her. She sat up and turned her head toward him. She pulled the blanket up to cuddle under it, and then pushed it away from her.

"Mama," Nathan murmured, unable to follow her when she got up.

She turned back toward him. "It's okay, baby. The worst is over now."

"Your leg..."

She pulled up her skirt and looked at the swaths of bandages. "How bad is it?" she questioned.

"You have to look," Nathan said. "Make sure it's not gone bad."

"I'll check it in the bathroom. I'll be back in a few minutes."

She limped away from him, out the door and down the hall. Nathan lay still, listening, straining his ears as if he could see what she was seeing if he tried hard enough. He heard her throwing up. Nathan groaned. It must be bad. He tried to get up to go help her, and blacked out.

It was light again. Nathan couldn't figure out how many days had passed. He looked at his shoulder and saw that it had been re-dressed. He prodded it very gently, and winced at the shot of pain. But he was happy that it hurt, because dead flesh didn't feel.

Mama came into the room, slowly and painfully. She cocked her head and smiled at him. It was strained, and he could see the tired lines around her eyes, but it was a genuine smile.

"Hey there, favorite boy."

"Hi."

She came over to the bed and sat down. She had a bowl of soup in her hand, and she dipped a spoonful and held it toward him.

"You have to keep up your strength," she said. "You haven't eaten."

Nathan wasn't hungry, but he took the spoonful, and she spooned up another.

"How bad is it?" Nathan questioned, looking at his shoulder and then nodding toward her leg.

"I had to cut out some flesh that died," she admitted, "on both of us. But not a lot. It will scar, but we're not going to lose whole limbs. It's good that you were unconscious at the time."

"But you weren't," Nathan observed. "And you had to do it to yourself?"

"God granted me strength."

Nathan closed his eyes. "I'm so sorry."

"Sometimes they bite," Mama said, with a shrug. "We can't stop them. They're not tame. But we are believers, and God grants that we still live. It was not our time."

"But it's my fault for taking the snake out, and for jumping and dropping it."

"You are forgiven. It's not my first snakebite, and I'm sure it won't be my last."

Nathan didn't say anything.

"Now open your eyes. You need to eat more."

Nathan complied. He ate the soup for as long as he could, then turned his head away.

"That's enough."

"You need to eat more," she told him.

He shook his head. "I want to go back to sleep."

Mama sighed deeply, then shrugged. "Okay. Get some more rest. You can eat more again after a nap."

Nathan nodded. "You should sleep too," he told her.

"I'm feeling okay now. And thank you... for taking such good care when I was out."

"I didn't do much."

"You did good."

Nathan was feeling a bit better the next time he awoke. He tried to read for a few minutes, but his vision was still fuzzy, and he put the book aside. The doorbell rang, and he listened to see if Mama was home and would answer it. There were voices at the door, and in a few minutes, Mama poked her head into the room.

"You're awake," she observed.

"Who was at the door?"

"A visitor," Mama said, and she stepped back and Chandra came into the room.

"Hello, my little friend," she said, looking him over.

Nathan motioned to the chair at his desk. "Hi. You can sit there."

He saw Mama's shadow cross the doorway, headed back toward the kitchen and sitting room.

"I was worried about you," Chandra said. "It was garbage day--or I thought it was--and you didn't come to see me."

Nathan rubbed his eyes. "Is it already?" he questioned. "I lost track. Sorry."

"Oh, don't feel bad. I was just worried about you."

Nathan nodded. "I'm doing better now," he said. "I should probably get up, but I'm being kind of lazy."

"You take your time. You know you don't have much strength. It's too bad you got sick again before you had a chance to get more of your strength back and put some meat on those bones."

Nathan nodded. Chandra studied him curiously. Her eyes travelled over his bandaged arm. "So what happened?" she questioned.

Nathan didn't know what to tell her. He knew he shouldn't lie. But he didn't think that she would understand about snake handling.

"I got hurt," he said vaguely.

"So did your mother," Chandra said.

"How'd you know that?"

"She's limping pretty obviously. What happened? You didn't hurt each other, did you?"

Nathan shook his head. "No! We wouldn't do that."

"Sometimes, even when we love somebody a lot, we end up hurting them. Or getting hurt. We get impatient, lose our tempers."

"Mama would never hurt me," Nathan insisted.

"Your mama wasn't giving you your insulin before. That hurt you."

"That's not the same. I didn't want the insulin. We don't believe in medical treatment."

"She was negligent and hurt you."

Nathan shook his head.

"So what's going on this time?" Chandra questioned. "Why won't you tell me what happened?"

Nathan's stomach was tying itself in knots. He knew that she wouldn't understand about handling snakes any more than she did about not using doctors. But if he didn't tell her something, she could end up calling Child Services, telling them that she though he was the victim of abuse or more neglect. And lying to her would be a sin. Nathan tried to keep his breathing slow, and he closed his eyes, saying a brief prayer in his head that God would help him with his answer.

"You have to promise not to tell," he said.

"I can't do that, Nathan."

"But it's not anyone else's business."

"If someone hurt you, I'm not going to keep quiet about it."

"Nobody hurt me. I hurt myself. It was an accident."

"Then tell me about it."

Nathan looked at her. Chandra's face was kind and concerned. She was worried about him, not trying to make trouble for him. If he could just make her understand about handling snakes.

"I sort of... got bitten by a snake," he explained haltingly.

"By a snake? You mean at your camp? But you were fine when you got back from the camp. Did it go bad?"

"It wasn't at the camp."

Her brows moved down and closer together. "Then... where was it? You can't get bitten by a snake in the middle of the city."

Nathan looked over at his bedside table, where his Bible lay. He looked back at Chandra. "You *could*."

"How?" Chandra demanded.

"Maybe I travelled back in time to when it was still wilderness here," he said with a weak laugh.

Chandra smiled, but it didn't reach her eyes. She knew that he was avoiding giving her a proper answer. She might be an old lady, but she wasn't stupid.

"Do you know much about the Bible?" he questioned.

"I don't see what that has to do with snakes."

"There are snakes in the Bible."

"There may be," Chandra allowed. "But what does that have to do with you getting bitten?"

"Paul put wood on the fire, and a snake came out and bit him--"

"Are you telling me a snake came out of a fire in your house?"

"But Paul was okay. It didn't kill him."

Chandra nodded, staring at Nathan. Nathan blew out his breath.

"Mark says: 'And these signs shall follow them that believe: In my name shall they cast out devils; they shall speak with new tongues. They shall take up serpents; and if they drink any deadly thing, it shall not hurt them; they shall lay hands on the sick, and they shall recover.'"

"Yes, I've heard that before."

Nathan nodded. "That's what we believe," he said. "We are the believers that it is talking about."

Chandra shook her head. "What does that mean, you are the believers?"

"In my name, they shall take up serpents," Nathan repeated.

"You take up serpents," Chandra repeated.

Nathan nodded.

"You know about snakes," Chandra said, comprehension dawning. "You liked Kenneth's snake. You knew all about how to handle it."

"Yes'm."

She raised her eyebrows, staring at him intently, as if she was trying to read his mind. "Nathan... are you telling me you picked up a snake, and it bit you?"

Nathan nodded.

"You picked it up on purpose."

"Yes'm."

"*Not* a venomous snake," Chandra said in disbelief.

Nathan nodded. "Rattler," he said.

"You picked up a rattlesnake."

"Yes. I didn't mean to get bitten, though."

"Well, I don't expect so... but if you are handling a poisonous snake with your bare hands..."

"We do it as part of our worship," Nathan said. "When the Spirit moves on us."

Chandra sat there, silent. She leaned back in the chair, raising her eyes to the ceiling. She rubbed her temples. "You believe that God manifests himself through snakebites, but you don't believe in the possibility of time travel?" she demanded.

Nathan rolled his eyes. "Time travel isn't possible," he said firmly. "Everybody says so."

"Do you believe the people who tell you there isn't a God, or the people who believe there is?"

"The people who *know* there is," Nathan said firmly.

"There are plenty of people who say that God isn't real. That he couldn't exist. Why don't you believe them?"

"I feel him," Nathan said. "When I dance."

"And I know time travel is possible because I can do it," Chandra said.

Nathan looked at her, frowning. He could never figure it out. He always thought that she was teasing him, just making an extended joke about time travel. But she was so serious this time, not smiling. She sounded like she really did care that he didn't believe it.

But Mama said that time travel wasn't possible.

Everybody said so.

Chapter Eighteen

NATHAN WAS STANDING AT the door looking out while he waited for Mama to finish tracking down her coat and gloves. She came up behind him.

"Christmas is coming," she observed.

Nathan turned slightly to watch her pull on her shoes and tie them up. "Is it going to snow?" he questioned.

"It's not cold enough yet. You'll have to ask your friends, but I don't think there's usually snow here for Christmas."

They had lived in quite a few different places, most of them too warm for snow. But Nathan remembered one year they'd been further north and it had snowed. And snowed, and snowed. He didn't really like the cold, but he'd loved the snow. He and Mama had gone sledding, and he remembered her face, happy and flushed pink, and the excitement of sliding down the hill at crazy speeds, snow flying up in his face and getting down his neck and under his gloves.

Mama was the only parent who was sledding. There were other parents standing around supervising the little kids, helping them to drag their sleds back up the hill or yelling at the older kids to be more careful. But Mama was the only adult sledding, whooping and squealing and enjoying it just as well as any kid.

"What are you thinking about?" Mama questioned, noticing Nathan's smile.

"Sledding. Remember that year...?"

She laughed. "I remember," she agreed. "We were so cold and soaking wet when we got home!"

"But it was worth it," Nathan said. "And we had hot chocolate."

"Yes, we did, Bug. That was a fun day."

Nathan nodded. They walked out to the car together.

"So what do you want for Christmas this year?" Mama questioned.

"I dunno. Nothing."

"You must want something," she pressed.

Nathan shook his head. "I've got everything I need."

"But you must *want* something."

Nathan sighed. The only thing he really wanted was to be well again. But that wasn't something that she could give him. She looked at him, frowning slightly, and started the car.

Christmas morning dawned. Mama was undeterred by Nathan's claim that he didn't need or want anything. He had seen, when he got up to the bathroom in the middle of the night, the mountain of presents in the sitting room. He was almost afraid to get out of bed in the morning to go open them. He lay there in bed, waiting for Mama to wake up, thinking about all of the kids who went without for Christmas. Some of them didn't even have enough to eat or somewhere to live.

Eventually, as the room started to get brighter, he heard Mama start to move around. He heard her door squeak open, and then her soft 'oh!' when she saw the other side of the bedroom door. She shuffled down the hall toward him. She still limped from the snake bite, and he wondered if she would for the rest of her life. They were healing, the flesh knitting back together, not that painful anymore unless they bumped the injured limbs. But the flesh that had died and had to be removed had left deep indentations, and Nathan didn't know if they would ever fill back in and look normal again, or would be left misshapen permanently, like his finger.

Mama appeared in the doorway. "Are you awake?" she whispered.

"Happy Christmas," Nathan whispered back.

She came the rest of the way into the room and sat on the edge of his bed. "I love the stars," she said.

Nathan had filled her doorway with cut-out paper stars, each one with something written on it in his neatest printing. Something about how he loved her or a trait that he admired, or about Christmas. Seventy-two stars in all. He'd produced them over the weeks leading up to Christmas, cutting them out until his fingers ached from holding the scissors. Writing out the messages without a mistake. It had taken a long time and a lot of work.

"I love you, Mama."

"You too, Bug."

She cuddled up to him and kissed him on top of the head. Then she reached over and turned the lamp on, brightening the room a little more. She picked up his Bible, and turned to the traditional Christmas reading, and in the early-morning stillness of a new Christmas morning, read the old words again. Nathan was still, listening to her and feeling the warmth of her body. He closed his eyes and just let the words and the hope wash over him.

After Nathan finished opening presents, he sat there looking at the pile of motorized and electronic toys, games, and other stuff that he'd probably never use. There were a couple of books that he thought he might read. She'd gotten all of the popular stuff advertised on TV, but they weren't really the kinds of things that Nathan would use. Their Christmases were usually pretty modest, but this year Mama had both the money left over in Nathan's birthday account and the collection taken up at their worship services. She should have been putting that money aside to rent a hall now that their little congregation was growing too large for the house.

Mama was taking pictures of the toys and Nathan. He looked at her. "Mama..."

"I know, you don't want me to post pictures of you," she sighed. "But I can post the presents, anyway."

"No, not that," Nathan said. "I just wondered..."

"What, Bug?"

"Could we give some of my presents away? You know, to kids who don't get anything..."

She snapped another picture of him, then lowered her phone, looking thoughtful. "Well, I suppose we could..."

"Not all of them," Nathan said, not wanting her to feel bad about him not appreciating the presents. "But I don't need so many..."

"I'll make some phone calls to see where we can take them," Mama decided. "Why don't you go through and decide which ones you want to keep, and put the others in a bag?"

Nathan nodded. "Okay," he agreed.

A few hours later, not only had the toys been given away, but Nathan and Mama were busy helping to serve Christmas dinner at a soup kitchen downtown. Mama had on a hair covering and grinned at him as she served out steaming vegetables onto the plates of patrons moving down the counter with their plates held out in front of them. There were a lot of families there. Nathan was surprised. He thought of the dirty, ancient-looking men and women that he sometimes saw begging when he was out with Mama. That was what he thought of when he thought about homeless people and the clientele of shelters and soup kitchens. But there were a lot of children. A lot of men and women younger than Mama, with two or three children and tired faces. There were lots of smiles as they went through the line at the counter and as Nathan directed them to tables with space, but he noticed that when they sat eating, no longer interacting with the friendly staff and volunteers, their faces fell into sad, beaten expressions.

He tried to keep an eye on the families that were leaving, who were being given toys from the pile that included Nathan's donated gifts. He enjoyed seeing the smiles of the little boys who got his presents.

Mama had volunteered herself and Nathan to help with the Christmas dinner without really thinking about what Nathan's limits were. He was exhausted, and the room was steaming and sweltering hot. He was dizzy and his thoughts were getting foggy, unable to direct people to the right tables anymore. One of the staff caught him by the arm.

"You look like you need a break. Why don't you go out and get a breath of fresh air for a minute or two?" he suggested, propelling Nathan toward an open door.

Nathan staggered out the door, relieved to feel the cool outdoor air on his flushed skin. There were a few other people out there, talking quietly or having a smoke. They nodded to Nathan but didn't say anything to him. He found a crate to sit down, and collapsed, not sure when he was going to be able to get up again. He rested his elbows on his knees, hunched over, head bowed down.

"You okay?" one of the idling men asked.

Nathan grunted. He closed his eyes and just focused on breathing, trying to get his strength back. It seemed like he was sitting there a long time. A woman nudged him.

"You should be getting back to work," she suggested.

Nathan shook his head. "Can't. Not feeling good," he told her, without looking up.

"Are you sick? Where are your parents? Who are you with?"

"My mama. She's in there serving." Nathan raised his head slightly. "She has dark hair, and she's wearing a dress."

The woman left again. In a few minutes, Mama was by Nathan's side. "You okay, baby?" she questioned. "I didn't see you go out. How long have you been sitting out here?"

"I dunno," Nathan said.

"You not feeling good? Ready to go home?"

Nathan nodded.

"Okay. Come on then, Bug. Up and at'em."

She took him by the arm, helping him to his feet. Nathan stood still for a moment, getting his bearings, and then she walked him back through the hot, humid room, out the other door to the car.

"Poor boy, you're all in," she observed, as he slumped in the seat of the car. She grabbed his seat belt and pulled it around him, fastening it in place.

Nathan just closed his eyes and tried to fall asleep to the drone of the car engine.

‡ ‡ ‡

Chapter Nineteen

H<small>E HAD TOLD</small> C<small>HANDRA</small> repeatedly that he didn't believe in time travel, that it wasn't possible. He didn't know whether she was teasing him about the whole thing, just playing games, or whether she really believed it. People could believe really crazy things.

But when he woke up, it was obvious that he'd gone back in time. He was in a different house, a different Christmas. He must have been six or seven. It was so exciting when you were that age. Everything was sort of magical. He didn't get a lot of presents, but he enjoyed being with Mama, and the decorated Christmas tree, and all the little surprises that she arranged for him throughout the day.

Mama came into his bedroom. "Did you take the tree?" she demanded. "Where did you put it?"

Nathan stared at her. "What?"

"Come back, Nathaniel. What are you doing all the way back there? I told you that time travel is impossible!"

"But here I am," Nathan insisted. "How can it be impossible?"

"With God, all things can be impossible," she pointed out.

Nathan tried to make sense of this. He looked at the tree in the corner of the room, wondering how he could have gotten it in there. It was a bigger tree than they had managed to get in the present time. It was always easier to get big trees when you were living in an area that was almost wilderness anyway. You didn't need a permit or a tree lot, you just went and cut one down.

"It's beautiful," he told her.

"It's nonsense," she snapped. "This whole thing is nonsense, I told you that."

Nathan licked his lips. "I'm thirsty, Mama. Are you going to water the tree?"

"Are you just going to lay there while I have to move everything? You need to get up and help me."

Nathan tried to move his heavy, uncooperative limbs, but failed. He felt like his body was set in concrete.

"Maybe... maybe I could use some help," Nathan said.

"What can I do?" another voice questioned. This time it wasn't Mama's voice. Mama seemed to have faded away. But it was a voice that he knew.

"What can I do?" Chandra repeated, as Nathan opened and closed his mouth like a dying fish, looking for the words.

He tried to focus his eyes on her. To keep both his body and his mind in the present. Grounded. "I think I need help," he said.

She sat down on the bed next to him, pushing his hair back from his face. "I'm here to help you," she said. "Your mama is at work, but she asked me to check in on you."

Nathan held her hand, holding on tightly to avoid slipping back into the past again. "I did it. I travelled back too," he told her.

She stared back at him, her eyes fathomless. "You too?"

He nodded. She touched his face.

"You're hot. I think you might have a fever."

"I need..." Nathan's voice petered out.

"What do you need? What can I do for you?"

"I need insulin," he admitted, his voice cracking.

He didn't want to cry in front of her, but the tears started flowing down his cheeks. He wanted so badly to be well again, even if it meant taking medicine.

"You don't have any?" Chandra demanded.

He shook his head. She turned to go. "I'll call an ambulance."

"No!" He gripped her hand tighter, no. letting her pull away. "You can't call an ambulance. They'll take me away from Mama."

"If she won't get you your insulin, then they're going to have to."

"No, please."

She squeezed his hand. "Then how am I supposed to get you insulin? I can't just go to the drug store and pick some up."

Nathan struggled to sit up. Chandra put her arm behind him and supported him. "If you take me..." he said. "If it's an emergency, they'll give us some."

"You're not in any shape to go anywhere. Let me call an ambulance."

"No. I can get up. I can come."

Nathan swung his feet over the side of the bed and tried to get to his feet. He could get insulin, and he could stay with Mama, if he could just walk with Chandra. He knew she had a car, even though she rarely used it. Chandra steadied him, but was reluctant to let him come with her.

"You're sick, Nathan."

"I'll get it sooner if I come."

Holding himself up with the dresser, he pawed through the various items on top of it, knocking things to the floor.

"What are you looking for?" Chandra asked.

"Empty bottle."

He knew he had left one on top of the dresser. They'd have to have something to prove to the pharmacist that he had a prescription for insulin. Chandra looked over the junk on top of the dresser, pushing stuff gently around. Then she plucked out the empty vial.

"Is this it?"

She looked at the label, while Nathan nodded. "Yes'm, that's it."

He staggered toward the door, and Chandra caught him and helped him across the room. With her cane and her limp, he didn't want to lean too much on her, but his legs were weak and wobbly, and he knew that she was taking most of his weight. It was a good thing that he was so thin, or they couldn't have managed it. When they got to the front of the house, Chandra steered him into the sitting room instead of to the front door. Nathan tried to protest.

"You can't walk all the way to my car," Chandra pointed out. "You sit here and get your breath, and I'll bring the car to the front of the house. You'll never make it otherwise."

Nathan knew she was probably right. She helped him onto the couch.

"I'll just be a minute. Stay there and rest."

"Yes'm," Nathan agreed, breathing hard. He felt like he'd run a race, when all he'd done was walk to the other side of the house. With help. He closed his eyes and rested, waiting for Chandra to return. After a while he heard the noise of the engine, and the car door slam. He felt like it was very far away, and realized that he was slipping from consciousness again. He tried to sit up and rouse himself.

Chandra returned to the room, and leaned on her cane, getting ready to help him up. She suddenly froze, looking past Nathan, and he turned to follow her gaze. She was looking into the terrarium, where the snake was moving around, probably hearing or smelling them in the room.

"Is that--" Chandra shook her head, not believing her own question. "That's not--that's not the snake that bit you, is it?"

Nathan nodded. He put his hand lightly on the glass in front of it, but didn't tap. "Yes'm. Pretty, isn't it?"

Chandra shook her head in disbelief. "You keep rattlesnakes in your living room!"

"Only one," Nathan pointed out.

"Only one," Chandra repeated, still shaking her head in wonderment. "Well... come on. Are you ready to walk to the car?"

Nathan heaved himself out of his chair, and tried to walk without her aid, but only got a couple of steps. She didn't censure him, just moved over beside him and offered her arm again. Nathan took it, and they walked to the door. The steps outside the front door were a bit of a challenge, and Nathan ended up having to crawl down them, then after a short rest, got back to his feet and with Chandra's help, kept going. It seemed like ages before they finally reached the car, and Nathan collapsed into the seat. Chandra lifted his feet into the car and shut the door.

"Are you sure, Nathan?" she questioned, once she got in herself. "I think I should just take you to the hospital."

"They'll just give me insulin. We'll get insulin... at the drug store. It's faster," Nathan insisted.

Chandra sighed, and pulled the car away from the curb. She drove carefully, as if Nathan was a basket of eggs she was afraid of breaking. The nearest pharmacy was a little corner store, not part of a big chain in the mall or superstore. Nathan thought that was good. He knew about trying to fly below the radar of the authorities, and knew they'd have a better chance not getting Mama investigated if they used a small independent pharmacy than a big chain, with a big computer system that might flag him somehow.

"Can you make it?" Chandra asked, looking at him.

"Yes'm," Nathan assured her. He had to. He had to get insulin, and he had to get it without making anyone suspicious. He got out of the car, and leaned against it, gulping for breath. "You say you're my gramma," he told her. "You take care of me while my parents are out of town. Nobody realized that I was down to my last dose."

Chandra nodded, and took him by the arm, easing his weight back onto her again. They hobbled together into the pharmacy, into the back of the store where the pharmacist stood behind the counter. He looked away from the customers that he was serving, and looked alarmed. He hurried out from behind the counter to give them a hand.

"What's wrong?" he questioned. "How can I help?"

He was focused on Chandra at first, assuming that she was the one who was ill, but quickly realized that it was Nathan who couldn't stay on his feet without help. He and Chandra lowered Nathan into a chair in the small waiting area.

"I was babysitting," Chandra explained. "I didn't realize he was down to his last dose. Nobody realized."

"Last dose of what?" the pharmacist questioned.

Chandra handed him the empty bottle, and he looked at it.

"Insulin." He looked at Nathan, worry lines etched deeply into his forehead. "How long since he finished his prescription? How long has he been off?"

Chandra stammered for an answer.

"I should have gone back," a voice said, and Nathan was so disoriented that it took him a few seconds to realize that it was his own voice, hoarse and breathless. "If I went back in time, I had insulin *then*."

The pharmacist swore.

"Is he hallucinating?"

He cursed again, hurrying back behind the counter. His other customers started to ask questions or protest the interruption of their transactions, but the pharmacist waved them off impatiently. He grabbed a blood glucose monitor off of the shelf and tore the box around it open. He prepped the little computer swiftly, and returned to Nathan's side. The pharmacist pulled up Nathan's shirtsleeve, and scowled at Nathan's wasted forearm, switching instead to his fingers, and finally selecting one of his thumbs to prick to draw the blood. They all waited for the monitor to beep. The pharmacist's face was pale. He looked at the display on the monitor.

"Stay there," he ordered, as if Nathan might suddenly get up and wander off. He went back behind the counter and disappeared through a doorway.

"I'm sorry," Nathan said to Chandra. "I didn't mean to cause trouble."

"You haven't caused any trouble," Chandra soothed. "We're going to get you some help. You'll feel better soon."

The pharmacist soon returned with a syringe and vial, and Nathan breathed a sigh of relief. He barely felt the prick as the pharmacist injected the insulin. Then the man rubbed the injection site. Nathan waited for it to take effect. The pharmacist pushed a bottle into his hand. Nathan looked down at it. It was a bottle of water.

"You need to get your fluids up," the man told him. "Drink that. And we should get an ambulance or take him to emergency," he told Chandra. "He should be on IV and have his electrolytes monitored. He could have organ damage."

"Oh." Chandra looked at Nathan. She swallowed and nodded. "I'll take him to emergency," she said. "Once he's had a chance for that to take effect."

Nathan tried to communicate with her through his eyes, without the pharmacist catching on. Chandra could not take him to emergency. She had to take him back home. She looked away from Nathan.

The pharmacist went back over to deal with his other customers, and once getting them off, he handed Chandra a box of vials.

"Keep those in the fridge. And keep track of them. Get him to a doctor so they can monitor his levels." He shook his head, eyes dark. "Don't let him get like this again."

Chandra nodded. The pharmacist looked at Nathan.

"Feeling any better?" he questioned.

Nathan was breathing better, and starting to feel the effects of sugar reaching his cells. His brain was clearing. He nodded. The pharmacist prepared the monitor and pricked his other thumb this time. His eyes stayed on the monitor until it beeped. Then he nodded.

"It's starting to come down. Do you have a monitor?"

"Yessir."

"Make sure you use it. How old are you?"

"Twelve."

"You're old enough to watch your levels. If you don't, you're going to end up dead," he said baldly. At Chandra's gasp of shock, he scowled. "You have to understand that. You can't fool around with this. Look at the boy," he commanded Chandra. "He's barely keeping body and soul together. Neglect his insulin, and you will have killed him just as surely as if you shot him with a gun."

Chandra nodded, her eyes wide and alarmed.

"Make sure the hospital checks his levels every hour."

"Okay."

Nathan rose unsteadily to his feet. Chandra reached for him. "Take it slow. Are you sure you're ready?"

Nathan nodded. "I'm okay."

They both watched him standing there for a few moments. Nathan didn't collapse back to his chair or grab at Chandra for support.

"I'm okay," he repeated. "I can walk."

"Thank you so much for your help," Chandra told the pharmacist.

"Just take care of him. Take him to the hospital."

Chandra nodded. Nathan reached for her hand, and led her toward the door before she could talk anymore. He was out of breath again when he got to the car, but not ready to collapse. Just out of breath. Chandra let him into the car and Nathan got in. She got into the driver's seat, and they both looked at each other.

"No hospital," Nathan warned.

"He said that's what you need. I don't want you to die."

"I won't die if I'm taking insulin. I can check my own levels every hour, like he said."

"But you can't give yourself an IV, or check your electrolytes or for organ damage. You need a hospital."

"No," Nathan insisted. "Just take me home."

Chandra looked at him. "Please, Nathan."

"No."

She started the car and pulled out. Nathan watched her worriedly. He started to relax as they started on the route home. He leaned his head back against the back of the seat, and closed his eyes.

Nathan was dozing when they pulled in front of the house. Chandra got out of the car before Nathan could pry his eyes open. She went around the car and as she opened his door, Nathan heard another voice. Low and quiet. Male.

"Is he okay?"

"He's... doing better," Chandra said, her voice hesitant.

Nathan rubbed his eyes and opened them. He saw Chandra's face as she leaned across him and undid her seatbelt. She smiled at him. "Wakey wakey, sleepyhead."

Nathan tried to see past her. "Who was that?" he questioned.

Chandra looked back over her shoulder, and shook her head. "I don't know. A man. I didn't recognize him."

"Where is he? Where did he go?"

She looked around, and shook her head. "I don't know. He's gone now. What's wrong?"

"It wasn't *him*, was it? The man we saw that day, when you called the police?"

Chandra looked back at Nathan again. "Your stalker?"

"Was it?"

"I... I don't know. I never saw his face, that day. Just... from a distance. It could be..."

"What did he look like? What did he want? Why did you talk to him?"

"Brown hair, kind of mussed. Nice eyes. A bit of a beard. He just asked if you were okay. I didn't know what to say."

Nathan climbed out of the car and looked around. The man had vanished.

Once inside, Nathan headed for his bed, still tired and needing to rest. Chandra followed him. "Where do you want me to put this?" she questioned, holding up the box of insulin.

"It's supposed to go in the fridge," Nathan said.

Chandra turned to put it in the kitchen, and Nathan held up his hand. "No, wait--you can't. If Mama sees it..."

He was afraid she would just throw it out. Chandra frowned and nodded. "Do you want me to keep it at my house?" she questioned.

Nathan nodded. "Yeah. Just give me one vial, I'll hide it in the drawer. And you can take the rest, keep it in your fridge."

"Okay. You're going to sleep?"

Nathan nodded. "I feel a lot better, but... still tired."

"You come over whenever you need it. You can keep other supplies there as well. Whatever you need."

"Yes'm." Nathan thought about it. "I might need more needles. And my sharps box is almost full." He nodded to the red needle disposal box.

"What do you need to do with it?"

"Just take it to the drug store. A different one this time."

"Okay. And they'll give me a new one?"

Nathan nodded.

A couple of days later, Mama looked at Nathan as he came into the kitchen for breakfast. She smiled broadly. "You're looking better," she observed. "I think you're starting to get better again."

Nathan nodded. "Yes'm," he agreed.

"Thank the Lord. I was really getting worried about you."

"What's for breakfast?"

"It's getting pretty cold out. How about some oatmeal to warm your belly?"

"Sure."

"Have a seat."

Nathan instead wandered over to the sink and started to wash up the dishes that had been left there. She watched him for a minute, smiling.

"Thanks, Bug."

"You do too much work. I should help you out more."

She shook her head. "I know you do what you can. You've been sick."

After breakfast, Nathan yawned and stretched. "I'm going to go over to Mrs. Mullenny's. To tell her thank you for coming to check on me when I was sick."

"That's very thoughtful. I'll see you in a few minutes, then. Maybe we can play a game or something when you get back."

"I don't know if I can yet... maybe there will be a good movie on."

"I'll check."

Nathan headed over to Chandra's. Delia stopped him on the way. "Why are you going to see the witch again?" she demanded.

"Delia, she's not a witch," Nathan insisted, rolling his eyes.

"How do you know?"

"Because there isn't any such thing as witches."

"Yes, there is. That's what your mom said."

"She didn't mean *that* kind of witch. It's different."

"Well, I still think she is. She always wears black."

"Her son died. I think she wears black because of that."

"And she has a black cat. Dominic says that she has other creepy animals in there as well. His mom went over to help clean when the witch hurt her leg."

Nathan shook his head. "There's nothing creepy. Just her son's pets, that she still takes care of."

"What does she have?" Delia demanded.

Nathan sighed. "A boa and a tarantula," he said.

It took a moment for Delia to process this. Her mouth fell open. "She has a black cat, and a spider, and a snake? She's a witch for sure! Your mom said she's a witch!"

"My mom doesn't think that anymore. That was just a mistake. Mrs. Mullenny isn't a witch. She just a... a normal person."

Nathan felt a little dishonest saying that she was a normal person. Did a normal person claim to be able to time travel? But then, Nathan was normal, and he had been thinking some pretty weird things while he was sick. He had been confused.

"She's not a witch," Nathan reiterated. "And I'm just going over there to tell her thank you for helping me the other day."

Delia made a cross with her fingers, and Nathan shook his head. He started back on his way over to Chandra's house.

She didn't answer right away when he rang the doorbell. Nathan knocked on the door, trying to rouse her. It didn't usually take that long for her to get to the door. Nathan walked to the side of the house and looked to make sure that her car was there. He could see it parked behind the house. He went back to the front door again and rang the bell. Maybe she had gone out for a walk. Though he had never known her to, with her bad leg. She could have gone to visit someone.

Eventually, Nathan decided that she was out, and there was no point in ringing the doorbell any longer. He walked back down the sidewalk toward his house. Delia watched him come back.

"Do you know if Mrs. Mullenny went out?" Nathan asked her.

"No, she didn't go anywhere. She never goes anywhere."

"She's not answering the door."

Delia shrugged. "Maybe she's busy cooking a potion or doing a spell, and doesn't want to be interrupted."

Nathan rolled his eyes and went back to his house. Mama was in the sitting room. "Everything okay with Mrs. Mullenny?" she questioned, flipping through the guide on the TV.

"I don't know. She didn't answer the door."

Mama looked up at him, frowning slightly. "Do you think there's something wrong?"

"No... I guess she just went out or something. I'll try again later."

She nodded. "Come and cuddle," she invited. "We'll watch a movie together." She patted the seat next to her. Nathan sat down with her. She put her arm comfortably around him, and they watched the show.

He hesitated at first about going back to Chandra's place later in the day. If she was home and just didn't want to see him, he didn't want to keep disturbing her by ringing the bell. But she'd never given him any indication before that she didn't want him to come by. She'd always encouraged him to come any time. So, after debating with himself for a while, he decided to try once more.

This time, Chandra answered after the first ring. It still took her a few minutes to get to the door, but he expected that. Her face was a little pale and her hair mussed, but she smiled at him.

"Were you laying down?" Nathan questioned. "I didn't mean to get you up."

"Oh, no. I'm fine."

Nathan entered, and they went to her sitting room. Nathan looked around. "Could I hold the snake again?" he asked.

Chandra looked hesitant, but she nodded. "Of course. I'm sure she misses people."

Nathan led the way to the bedroom and opened the terrarium. He lifted the sleepy snake out, and wrapped her around his shoulders. Chandra watched him carefully at first, then relaxed a bit, and sat down on the edge of the bed.

"Were you out this morning?" Nathan questioned.

"Out? No, I was right here," Chandra said, frowning slightly.

"Oh."

She blinked at him. "Why do you ask?"

"Oh, just, you didn't answer the door. So I thought you were out." But obviously she simply hadn't wanted company at that point. She was entitled to her privacy; she didn't have to open the door to visitors if she didn't want to.

"I didn't hear you ring," Chandra said.

"I rang a whole bunch of times. And knocked. I looked to make sure your car was here, because I thought you might have gone out."

Chandra pondered this for a moment, then she brightened. "I was traveling earlier," she said. "So I was here, but not in this time. That must be what happened."

Nathan tried to figure out if she was being serious. He wanted to argue again that she couldn't time travel, but he had told her that he had gone back in time, and if now he said he didn't believe her, she would just throw that back at him. Nathan didn't know what he thought about it. He watched the snake coil around his arm, and stroked her scales.

"You should take her out more often," he said. "Boas aren't dangerous. They don't have to be cooped up all the time. You could get her one of those trees and a heat lamp. She'd like that, and she'd stay close to the heat."

Chandra shuddered. "It's bad enough having it in the house," she said. "I couldn't bear the thought of her slithering around free!"

"You wouldn't keep a dog kenneled all the time."

"She's not a dog," Chandra shuddered again. Nathan stepped closer to Chandra.

"She's not scary," he said. "Here, touch her."

Chandra gingerly touched the snake's mid-body, and quickly withdrew. "Kenneth was always trying to get me to hold her," she said. "I just can't do it. I don't know why I ever even let him buy her."

The snake was trying to reach itself out to Chandra, and Nathan redirected her. "She wants to go to you. She probably knows your voice and your scent."

"She just wants lunch," Chandra teased.

"It would be good, if she did. She's too thin."

"Like someone else I know."

Nathan looked at his arms, sighing. "I know."

Chandra looked out the bedroom window. "Your mother didn't say anything? You didn't get in any trouble?"

Nathan shook his head. "No. She doesn't know."

"I don't know how she could not figure it out," Chandra said, with a laugh. "It's like night and day. It's obvious you're feeling a lot better today."

"Yes'm. But maybe she thinks I'm just getting better on my own. Or God is healing me."

"She seems like such an intelligent woman. I can't understand why she would believe some of the things that she does."

Nathan raised his eyebrows at her. This from the woman who kept trying to convince him that she could travel through time? Chandra laughed and looked away.

Chapter Twenty

KEEPING HIS CONTINUED INSULIN use from Mama did not become any easier. Nathan was adept at hiding his supplies, moving them every so often, keeping everything he could at Chandra's house. He kept his room spic and span so Mama didn't have any reason to poke around while cleaning. Mama had never been particularly respectful of Nathan's privacy; opening doors without knocking, taking pictures when he didn't want her to, and posting embarrassing things about him online, and she didn't appreciate his increased desire for privacy now. There was no lock on his bedroom door, so to be sure that she wouldn't interrupt him while he was giving himself a test or injection, he had to put his supplies in his pockets to go down the hall to the bathroom, then lock the door so that she couldn't walk in on him. Mama kept muttering about how he thought he was getting so grown up now, but Nathan remained firm. He had to be able to keep taking his insulin without her finding out about it. He had no choice. The pharmacist and the doctors at the hospital had said that he would die if he didn't keep taking insulin, and he believed it. He knew that if he didn't take insulin, one day he would just lie down on his bed and be unable to get back up. Mama wouldn't call an ambulance even if he was critically ill, and Nathan would die there.

Nathan was trying to read his Bible, but thinking about death led his mind down pathways he'd refused to go down before. He had tried to keep it out of his mind, to squeeze it out with other thoughts and by refusing to acknowledge it. But now he couldn't stop the trickle of memories that were pushing their way into his consciousness.

Mama wasn't the only pastor he'd ever had. There had been others too. Many of the congregations that they had attended had multiple pastors, and they would trade off weeks, or all lead worship at different points during the service, or split up duties according to demographics, with different pastors teaching the children or youth or some other special group.

Pastor Dan had been a big man. He was taller than anyone else in the congregation, and had a big belly to go with it. He had a booming voice that tended to scare the children, until they got to know him better and found what a gentle soul he really was at heart. But his sermons were fiery. Loud shouts and haranguing filled the little country chapel. It reverberated off of the walls and reached into your soul. The services were lively, never neglecting singing and dancing and demonstrations of signs--snake handling, drinking poison, fire handling, speaking in tongues--the signs always followed.

But that wasn't where Nathan's mind kept taking him. His mind took him to the last day that Pastor Dan preached a sermon. It had been on repentance. Pastor Dan delighted in calling mankind down to repentance. 'I'm a simple man. If it was good enough for our Lord, it's good enough for me.' And it had been good enough for the congregation. The 'amens' and 'hallelujahs' rang out. Many had been moved upon to dance, to testify, and even to speak in tongues.

When the volume of the music overtook the preaching, Pastor Dan threw his hands up in the air and danced. He danced over to the snake crates and threw several open. Without pausing, he plunged each hand into a different crate, and grabbed a handful of snakes. Their heads moved in different directions, and they twisted and writhed in his hands as he sang out and danced. Several snakes escaped the crates and were picked up by the congregants. Pastor Dan lifted the snakes over his head, praising God, and lowered them again.

That was when one struck. Mama said she didn't know which one it was, but Nathan had been watching, had seen it rear back and then dart in, biting Pastor Dan on his fleshy neck. It was a beautiful tricolor snake. A coral snake. Usually they handled rattlesnakes and copperheads, sometimes a cottonmouth. But corals were harder to get, not native to the area. A beautiful, highly toxic snake.

The snake didn't bite and release like a rattler, which was always more interested in getting away than further aggression. Instead it struck and it hung on. Pastor Dan froze as stiff as a board, his mouth forming a shocked 'O'. The color drained from his face. The snake finally dropped away and slithered across the floor, looking for somewhere to hide. Paster Dan made croaking noises, and dropped the other snakes. He held his hand over the bite mark on his neck.

Everyone kept dancing and singing at first. Not everyone noticed that Pastor Dan had been struck, and even those who did kept dancing and praising. It wasn't Pastor Dan's first bite. Several of the congregants had been bitten before. Sometimes a bite hardly even registered, it was so commonplace. Pastor Dan dropped to the floor; facedown at first, and then rolling himself onto his side, almost his back. His mouth opened and closed, and he looked like he was trying to swallow a particularly big bite of food, his Adam's apple bouncing up and down. Foamy spittle flecked the corners of his mouth.

The music died down. Pastor Dan's limbs began to shake. There was a noise in his throat like he was attempting to speak, but no recognizable words came out. Nathan watched in horror as Pastor Dan shook harder and harder, then stopped, stiff, all of his muscles straining and standing out. Then his body relaxed. His eyes stayed open, staring, but Nathan knew his soul had left. His eyes were dull and dead. Everyone stood around, looking at him and at each other. Nathan watched a snake slither across the floor toward him, its tongue flicking out, tasting the air. He bent down and picked it up gently. He looked at Mama questioningly, wondering what to do next. She looked down at him, her eyes filled with tears.

"Put it in one of the crates," she said softly.

Nathan walked up to the front of the church, and put it into one of the empty boxes. He closed the lid. Walking back toward his seat, he picked up another snake, and again took it to the front of the church. Others now started to follow suit, picking up the escaped or dropped snakes, and putting them back into the crates. Nathan watched for the coral snake that had bitten Pastor Dan, but didn't see it again.

That was death. He'd seen Pastor Dan die before him, seen the life fade from his eyes. Mama said that he went to a better place. He was in heaven now, with Jesus. He'd been a good man, one of the believers, so he was guaranteed a place in heaven. That was where they all wanted to go. They all needed to be like Pastor Dan.

Nathan remembered more. It hadn't just been Mama with him in the church that day. Daddy had been there too. Nathan had looked up at him for reassurance, and Daddy had forced a tight smile, and ruffled his hair.

Nathan went out to the kitchen, where Mama was bent over her computer. He couldn't tell from where he sat down at the table whether she was researching something for a sermon, or posting on a discussion board or social network. He folded his arms on the table and put his chin on top of them, and watched her.

After a few minutes, Mama turned around and looked at him. "Hi, Love Bug. How are you doing?"

"Fine," Nathan said.

"Good. You look like you're thinking deep thoughts."

Nathan didn't move. Mama turned back to her computer to press a few more keys, and then she turned and looked at him again. "Are you staring at me?"

"Sorry," Nathan said, dropping his eyes to a group of crumbs on the table where Nathan had eaten his breakfast earlier. He hadn't realized he'd left a mess behind.

She continued to look at him for a moment, then turned back to her computer.

"Mama... what happened with you and Daddy?" Nathan questioned finally.

Mama froze, with her fingers hovering above the keyboard. Seconds passed. She turned around and looked at him. Her expression was blank.

"What made you think about that?" she asked.

"I was just wondering," Nathan said. "I was remembering... when we lived with him."

"You were pretty young when he left," Mama said. "You're probably remembering sometime he came by for a visit."

Nathan shrugged.

"Maybe," he said. "I don't know. Why did he leave?"

"He wasn't a good daddy to you," Mama said. "He wasn't there when you needed him. Only I was."

"Why? Did he work too much or something? He didn't hurt me, I don't remember anything like that."

"No, he never laid a hand on you, thank the Lord. But a child needs more than just someone who doesn't hit them. You needed someone who was there, who could provide for all of your needs. Someone who understood you. I was the only one who could do that."

Nathan shifted, getting a slight headache from the worry lines that creased his forehead. "Why doesn't he visit anymore?"

Mama licked her lips, and pressed them together, considering her answer. "He visited for a while," she said slowly. "But the visits got further and further apart. He just kind of... drifted away."

Nathan felt the knot in his stomach tighten. He had a feeling that this wasn't quite the whole truth. Of course she would shade it in her own favor, remember it a certain way, but he had a feeling that his daddy would tell him a different story.

"Do you know where he lives now?" he questioned.

"Well, if he's like us, he's probably moved around a bit. Who knows where he lives now."

"You don't know?"

"I didn't keep track of him. I don't know his address. Where are all of these questions coming from?" Mama asked. "That man is not a part of our lives anymore. Why are you even thinking about him?"

Nathan rubbed his forehead. "It's just been a long time since I've seen him. I was wondering what happened to him."

"We don't need him. You and I do just fine together, don't we? You and me, that's how it's always been."

Nathan nodded.

"I know," he agreed. "You're a good mom, and you support us, and we have a good time together. Sometimes, you know, a guy just wonders about his daddy."

And sometimes, Nathan thought, maybe a daddy just wondered about his son.

Nathan blamed the mushrooms. Most of the time, he could sense Mama's moods, and he could cheer her up when something was bothering her. She was generally a happy person and loved to spend time and do things with Nathan, but sometimes black moods overtook her, and she could get very low, beyond his reach. It could be scary, looking into her eyes and not being able to connect with her. He could never judge what she might do when she got like that.

He supposed that there were worse things that she could take. She didn't drink a lot of alcohol or do illegal drugs or anything like that. But the mushrooms were natural, and they had been used for hundreds of years by the natives seeking visions, and sometimes when Mama hit one of her dark times, she would take them to enhance her sensitivity to the Spirit; to seek the mind of God. Nathan supposed that the mind of God must be a pretty scary place to be. How could humans even begin to comprehend the infinite without losing their sanity?

Nathan got home from school and was surprised to see Mama's car in front of the house. He had thought that she was supposed to be putting in a shift at work. When he walked into the house, he could smell something sort of earthy and musty hanging in the air. It was a smell that made him feel sick and afraid, even before he could identify what it was. He followed it into the kitchen, and when he saw the teapot and hit the stronger scent in the kitchen, he knew what it was. She had made a tea from the mushrooms. Nathan swallowed hard, feeling sick. He glanced around.

"Mama? Are you okay?" There was no answer. Nathan went down the hall to her room. "Mama?"

Nathan tapped on her door lightly, wanting to be reassured, but not really wanting to go in. There was no answering assurance. He hesitated, not sure whether to go in without being invited, or just to leave her alone.

"Mama, are you okay?"

He turned the handle of the door slowly, hoping that it wouldn't squeak. The doorknob remained silent, and he pushed the door open a couple of inches and peeked through the crack. He didn't call her again.

Mama was kneeling next to the bed. Just praying, Nathan realized with relief. That was why she hadn't answered. Nothing was wrong. Everything was perfectly all right. Nathan shut the door again quietly, and went to his own room.

He opened his window slightly, even though it was nippy out, to try to clear some of the smell of the mushrooms. It always made him feel sick. He pulled out his school books and spread them on his desk to work on his homework. Nathan would be finished his work early, so that he could spend some time playing games or watching TV with Mama after supper. And if she wasn't done praying when he was done his homework, he would start making supper for them. That would make her happy. She always liked it when he helped out or volunteered to do things.

He was so focused on his schoolwork, on getting it done and out of the way so that he'd be able to start on supper, that at first the noises didn't really reach his consciousness. But eventually he looked up, frowning. Mama was moaning, or talking to herself, or something. Nathan frowned, and tried to go back to his work. But the noise continued, and he couldn't ignore it any longer, couldn't focus on his spelling or his reading. So he finally got up from his desk and went back to her door. He didn't knock, but opened the door surreptitiously again, to see what was going on. Mama was still kneeling beside the bed, but she was groaning, holding her face and making noises like she was in pain.

Nathan breathed in a couple of times, feeling like it was a strain to get enough air. He cleared his throat.

"Mama, are you okay?"

She didn't look up, didn't respond to him. As far as he could tell, she didn't even know that he was there. Nathan opened the door further, hesitating before stepping into the room, her sanctum.

"Mama?" She still didn't look at him. Nathan went up to her side, and touched her shoulder tentatively. "Mama," he pleaded. "You're scaring me. Are you okay?"

He pulled up on her shoulder a little, and she straightened up, taking her face up out of her hands, off of the bed. She didn't look at him. He still wasn't sure that she was aware of him being there. Her eyes were dark and distant; far, far away. She groaned again. Her face was scratched and gouged, like she'd been trying to tear it off with her fingernails.

"Come on, Mama, get up," Nathan encouraged. He put his hand under her arm and tried to lift her. He didn't have to put his strength into it; as he pressed her, she stood up of her own accord.

"Do you want to lie down, Mama? Maybe you'd feel better if you had a sleep," Nathan suggested.

She stood there, staring blankly ahead of her. Finally, very slowly, she turned her head and stared through him. Nathan bit the inside of his cheek and tried to keep a calm, reassuring expression. She would be okay. There was nothing to be worried about.

"Let's get you to bed," Nathan suggested again, and he directed her, nudging her gently. She responded to his movements, climbing into the bed as if she was going to sleep. Nathan pulled the blankets over her, and stroked her hair. "Atta girl. You just have a sleep; you'll feel better soon." The mushrooms would wear off, and she would be fine, back to normal. No worse for wear.

Still feeling anxious, his stomach writhing, Nathan went into the kitchen to start on supper. He didn't feel like eating, and Mama probably wasn't up for it for a while, but it was all he could think of to do. He was just about done preparing a pot of macaroni, when he heard Mama moving around again. Nathan looked up as she wandered out of the hallway into the kitchen. She looked at him, but obviously wasn't herself yet.

"Hi, Mama. Are you feeling better now?" he asked with forced cheerfulness, "Do you want something to eat?"

Her eyes were focused on him, but there was still something wrong. He could tell that she wasn't really seeing what was in front of her. She wasn't really on the same plane as he was.

"And signs shall follow..." Mama said, her voice hoarse as if she hadn't used it for a long time.

Nathan nodded. "Those who believe," he finished gently. "That's right, Mama."

"Signs follow," she echoed.

"Do you want some macaroni, Mama? I made you some."

"No... poison..." she murmured.

"It's not poisoned!" Nathan said, shaking his head. "It's all okay. I just made it for you."

She reached out and touched Nathan's face, her eyes wide. It was as if she didn't even know who or what he was. Her fingers brushed his face briefly, and then she withdrew.

"No," she murmured again, and turned back around, leaving the room.

Nathan watched until she was out of his sight. He was careful to turn off the burner on the stove to avoid any accidents, and dished up two plastic bowls of pasta. He put spoons in them, and put them on the table.

"Mama?" he called. "Do you want to come eat?"

She returned a few minutes later, her feet making a dragging sound as she shuffled into the room. Nathan was relieved that she had come back on her own and was responding to verbal prompts. He indicated the dishes on the table.

"Here's some supper, Mama. Sit down and have some."

She ignored him, walking by him to the counter. She rifled around in the cupboards, and he thought maybe she was craving something different to eat. But it soon became apparent that she was not looking for something else to eat.

Mama pulled out a box of needles. Some of the straight syringe insulin needles that Nathan had been given in addition to the pen needle, which he preferred. She also retrieved the box of mouse poison that he had seen back when they first moved in. Nathan gulped.

"No, Mama. Let's put that away," he suggested. He grabbed the box and attempted to put it back under the sink. Mama grabbed his arm, pulling it back. Her face was fierce.

"Unclean!" she spat. "You are unclean. Don't touch that which is holy!"

"No," Nathan wrestled to pull the box away. "It's poison, Mama. Let's put it away. Come have some pasta."

She shoved him away, holding onto the box of poison tightly. Nathan stood back from her, wary. She turned back to her project. Nathan didn't know what to do. He went back to the table, hoping to distract her.

"This is really good," he offered, taking a few bites of the macaroni. It was hard to swallow, even though it was the same salty, creamy concoction as usual. He just couldn't seem to get it down his throat without straining. It stuck like a big lump in his throat. "Mama, come have some with me."

She paid him no attention. Nathan didn't want to watch what she was doing. It was too bizarre. Too horrific. He sat at the table, eyes closed, wishing he could make it all just go away. Why did she have to take those mushrooms? Why couldn't she just stay with him, in the real world, instead of seeking visions?

He was shaking, and wondered if his sugar was too high. He'd completely forgotten to take his insulin before sitting down to supper. But he'd only had a few bites. His sugar shouldn't be that high yet.

He heard Mama's feet shuffling again behind him. She came up to stand alongside him. Nathan opened his eyes and looked at her.

"Do you want some dinner now, Mama?"

She caught hold of Nathan's arm and held onto it tightly. Nathan didn't pull away at first, wondering what she was doing. Then he saw the loaded syringe in her other hand, and tried to jerk out of her grip.

"No! Mama, no, don't!" he pleaded.

"You need to be purified," she told him without emotion.

Her grip on him was like iron. Nathan's stringy muscles, wasted by the diabetes, were no match for her bigger, healthy ones. He strained to get away from her, but couldn't get out of her grip. She held his arm pinned with one hand, and brought the needle closer with the other. When it was almost touching him, Nathan kicked out, desperate, his body going wild. He would never hurt his Mama, never lay a hand on her, but his body seemed to have a will of its own, and self-preservation overrode all. But even his kicking and writhing had no visible effect on her. Her grip just tightened, and she pushed the needle into his arm. Nathan watched the plunger going down, and tears ran down his face.

"Mama, no!" he wept.

He expected it to burn like the snake venom, but it didn't. It felt uncomfortable, but not painful like a bite. Maybe she had diluted it too much to have any affect. Mama let go of his arm, and shuffled back over to the counter. Nathan sighed in relief. It was okay. It was all going to be okay. She had diluted the poison too much for it to hurt him. And by taking it by needle, he had bypassed the horrible bitter taste.

Nathan laughed in his relief. He'd been afraid it would hurt. It would kill him instantly, or in a long, painful, terrifying ordeal.

Mama turned and looked at him.

"If they take any deadly poison, it will not hurt them," she recited.

"No," Nathan agreed, grinning, and laughing again. His smile felt tight and strained, almost painful. He rolled his head and arched his back, trying to shake the tension. He couldn't stop smiling.

Restless and unable to sit still, Nathan got up and paced across the room.

"Do you want to go for a walk?" he suggested. "I have to get out of here."

Mama made no response.

"We can't just sit around here," Nathan pointed out, jiggling impatiently. "We need to get out." She still didn't respond. Nathan scratched the back of his head, agitated. "Mama? Mama..."

His arm where she had injected him was starting to hurt, the muscle cramping painfully. Probably because he was holding it so tense. Nathan tried to relax it, and massaged it, but it stayed hard and tense.

"Ow. That's sore."

He rubbed his mouth and jaw as well, becoming aware that he was grinning so widely that it hurt, but he couldn't relax his face and jaw any more than he could his arm. He arched his neck and back again, trying to find relief. He was starting to get scared. He'd never had any of these symptoms before. What if it was the poison working on him? What if he was, after all, going to die an agonizing death?

"Mama, I'm scared."

"It will not harm them," she repeated mechanically.

"But Mama..."

She looked toward him, and swiped her hand through the air in front of her, as if trying to catch a ghost. Nathan's back arched, and he rubbed it, trying to relieve the muscle cramp.

"I guess I... I guess I'll go lie down," Nathan said, spit dribbling down his chin. He wiped at it with the back of his arm, and walked, legs stiff, down the hall to his room. He lay down on his bed and moaned. All over his body, his muscles were cramping or twitching. A feeling of horror and dread started in his middle and spread out over his whole body. He tried to rub the sore muscles, to just count to ten and relax and laugh at himself for getting so worked up over nothing. He was starting to sweat, and didn't know whether it was from the stress or the poison.

Nathan writhed on the bed, unable to find relief. The tears that had started when Mama injected him returned. He didn't call out, but sobbed to himself, helpless and hopeless.

$$ \text{⚕ ⚕ ⚕} $$

Chapter Twenty-One

NATHAN GRADUALLY BECAME AWARE of the room around him. He had come through a long, dark tunnel of nightmares and pain and confusion, and this awakening was different. He could feel the soft blankets under him, and cooling cloths on his head and limbs. The air smelled of steamy chicken noodle soup. The room was only dimly lit, and he wasn't sure at first whether it was morning light, or if the blinds were closed and it was lamplight.

"Drink, Nathaniel," Mama's soft voice encouraged.

Nathan turned his eyes to focus on her. She sat on the edge of the bed, looking very concerned. She held a straw to his lips. Nathan sipped it, gagging at first when it hit his throat, then relaxing and taking a long sip. His mouth, lips, and throat were very dry and sore.

"That's my boy. We've got to get some fluids into you."

Nathan took a few breaths, then another long drink. Mama stroked his hair.

"That's right," she crooned.

Nathan rubbed his eyes. "I was sick," he said foggily.

"Yes, you were."

"Was it the food?" he questioned, not quite remembering the sequence of that last day. "I made you macaroni."

Mama laughed.

"Yes, you did, and it was delicious. It wasn't the macaroni. Just a bug, I think." She paused. "When I came into the room, you were writhing around, hot with fever. It lasted a very long time."

"What day is it?"

"Don't worry about that," she soothed. "You're fine now. Mrs. Mullenny has even been by and sat with you for a while so that I could get in a shift at work."

"I don't remember," Nathan said, trying to reach back through the confusion and darkness.

She studied him. "You spoke in tongues," she said.

"I did?" Nathan was surprised. "What did I say?"

"Well... I don't know. I don't have the gift of tongues," she said with a laugh.

Nathan smiled and shook his head. "Well, that's not much use, then."

"No. Just as a sign." She ruffled his hair. "Oh, I love you, my Love Bug. I was so worried."

Nathan nodded. "I'm sorry," he said. "I don't know what made me so sick."

"Well, you got through it, anyway. It was quite the trial."

Nathan reached for the water, and Mama held the straw to his mouth again, letting him drink all he could. "Do you think I could go back to sleep for a while?" Nathan suggested.

"Sure. I'll leave you alone--" She got up to leave. Nathan reached for her.

"No... could you just sit with me?"

"You're going to be asleep."

"I know... but I don't want to be alone. I was scared when I was alone."

She sat back down. "All right, Bug," she agreed. "I'll hang out with you for a while. But if you wake up and I'm gone, and you're scared again, you just holler out for me. I'll be around."

Nathan swallowed. His throat hurt. "Okay," he agreed.

Nathan moved around restlessly. The doorbell had awakened him, but he wanted to go back to sleep again. He closed his eyes more tightly and snuggled down in the blankets.

There was a tap on his bedroom door, and Nathan opened his eyes, startled. Mama looked in the doorway.

"You have a visitor," she announced.

Nathan expected that it was probably Chandra, but when Mama stepped back, he saw that it was Summer. Nathan hurried to sit up, embarrassed. He patted at his hair, wondering how bad it looked after the length of time he had been sick in bed. His face warmed, and he didn't meet Summer's eyes. Mama came into the room and put Nathan's desk chair a little back from the bed for Summer.

"You can sit *there*," she said sternly, as if Summer had asked to climb into bed with Nathan. Nathan's face got still hotter.

"Thanks, Mrs. Ashbury," Summer said with a pretty smile.

Mama nodded, and left the room after shooting a warning glance at Nathan. She needn't have worried. He clearly remembered her previous warning about Summer chasing after him. He rubbed his forehead, hiding his gaze from Summer.

"We've missed you at school," Summer said. "I just wanted to come by and see if you were okay."

Nathan nodded. "Yeah. I'm all right. Probably be back at school in a day or two. Thanks."

"So was it your diabetes again?" she questioned. "I know some people really have trouble controlling their levels."

"Uh, no. Not this time. I just... I dunno. The flu, or food poisoning or something. I'm a lot better now."

Summer nodded understandingly. "Good. You've missed a lot. Mrs. Davis is worried about you getting caught back up again."

"Yeah. Maybe I'll have to get a tutor or something. I don't want to be kept back."

"That would totally suck. You need to graduate with the rest of us."

Graduate. Nathan hadn't even thought about moving from the elementary school to the bigger school. His heart sank as he realized he'd probably be the smallest, scrawniest kid in the school. Not a great position to be in. At least at the elementary school, he looked like he belonged in one of the younger grades. He wasn't the smallest.

"Your mom is really cool," Summer observed, looking for another topic of conversation. "She seemed like she was a lot of fun at the outdoor education camp."

"Yeah. People kept complaining about how our group was more fun than the others. She thinks of a lot of good things to do."

"Yeah. She wasn't self-conscious about singing in front of other people, or concerned about doing the same thing as everyone else. She was comfortable in just doing whatever she thought was good. She's really self-confident. That's pretty cool."

Nathan traced one finger through the folds in the blanket over his legs. "I bet your mom would have had a lot of fun with it too," he said. "She brings you to see me when I'm sick and stuff. So she must care about other people."

Summer agreed, pushing some of her hair back over her shoulder. "She does. I know it's inconvenient for her sometimes, but she doesn't act like she minds. She just says 'let's go, then,' and we go. We both think that people are pretty important."

"That's cool," Nathan said.

He thought about Mama. She didn't really seem to care a lot for other people, which might seem really strange in a pastor, who was supposed to be concerned with saving souls. Souls *were* important to her, but it seemed like counting up how many she could claim was more important than the actual saving. She loved Nathan, and she loved God, and other people were just... numbers to her.

That was pretty harsh, and probably unfair of him. What had she ever done to make him think that she didn't really care about people? She'd left a lot of congregations behind in their moves, but that had been out of necessity, not because she wanted to leave all of those people without the guidance of their pastor. They had to move to stay safe.

"We finished that science fiction unit," Summer said, looking at the books still on Nathan's dresser. "Everybody presented their projects, and we're doing Shakespeare now, I guess."

"Shakespeare," Nathan repeated, and wrinkled his nose.

"We're mostly watching old movies of Shakespearean plays, and reading modern translations, so you don't have to figure out all of the 'whithers' and 'wherefores'. Then we're going to talk about modern movies and songs based on Shakespeare. I think that part will be fun."

"Doesn't sound too bad," Nathan agreed.

Summer was quiet for some time, watching a bird hop around in one of the bushes outside of Nathan's window. Nathan couldn't think of any other topic of conversation to bring up, and sat there looking down at his lap, embarrassed.

"So you're okay?" Summer questioned finally. "I'm glad you're feeling better."

"Yeah, I really am. I should be back at school soon." He gave a little laugh. "I'm actually looking forward to school. I'm tired of laying in bed all day."

Summer snorted. "Yeah, rough life, huh?"

Nathan smiled a bit. He hadn't smiled in a while, and it felt a little unnatural. He flashed back to the effects of the poison, pulling his smile unnaturally wide and refusing to let it go, and felt a lump in his stomach. He swallowed, his smile fading.

"What?" Summer questioned. "I didn't mean it. It was just a joke. I know it's no fun being sick."

"No, not that," Nathan said quickly. "I was just thinking of something else. It wasn't you."

"Okay," she said uncertainly. "If you say so... I'll tell everyone that you'll be back soon. Bly will be glad, he hasn't had anyone to hang out with lately."

"Yeah. Tell him 'hi' for me."

"I will," Summer agreed. She got up, and didn't seem to know how to say goodbye. She gave an awkward little wave.

"I'll see you soon, then," she offered.

"See you later," Nathan agreed.

She gave him a warm smile, and then left.

A few days later, Nathan returned from school loaded down with homework. Mrs. Davis said that he didn't have to make up all of the assignments that he had missed, but he had to make up some of them, and he had to read over the stuff that they had learned while he was gone to try to get a handle on what he had missed. It was an overwhelming amount of work, and he had missed so much over the past weeks and months, and been so foggy half the time that he was there, it felt like there would be no catching up. Mrs. Davis promised that the resource room would help him. But he might have to go to summer school to brush up, or get a tutor or something. It felt like the whole year had been a wash.

With a sigh, Nathan put his book bag down and looked longingly at the bed. The day had wiped him out, and a nap sounded like a really good idea. Except that he had so much work to do. He really couldn't spare the time.

"You don't have to do everything at once," Mama said from the door.

Nathan startled and turned to look at her, not realizing that she had followed him in. "I know," he said, "but there's so much to do."

"You can only do one thing at a time. Why don't you come get a snack to start with, and sit down and rest for a few minutes? You'll work better once you've had a bit of time to recover."

Nathan looked at his bulging book bag, and nodded. "Okay," he agreed, putting it off for now. Maybe she was right. "I'll be right out."

She smiled at him and nodded, and went out to the kitchen. Nathan grabbed his glucose monitor and insulin pen and locked himself in the bathroom. When he was done, he dumped them back in his drawer and went out to the kitchen, where Mama was preparing an after-school snack of apples and peanut butter for him.

There was a hard rap on the front door as she put the plate on the table in front of Nathan. They both looked at each other, but neither was expecting company. Mama sighed and went to the door to see who it was.

Nathan heard another woman's voice, and figured it must be a salesperson or a neighbor. But Mama's voice grew tight and clipped in response. She wasn't happy about something. She didn't talk like that even to door-to-door solicitors. A few minutes later, she walked back into the kitchen, with a woman in a blazer and skirt following her. She had a lanyard around her neck with a plastic ID sleeve hanging in the center of her body. Mama's face was a thundercloud. Nathan put down the apple he was eating, swallowing the last bite unchewed, scraping his throat all the way down.

"Nathan, this is Mrs. Something-or-other. She's a social worker."

Nathan looked at Mrs. Something-or-other. "Mrs. Beckon," the social worker advised with a rigid smile.

"Hi," Nathan said.

"Could I talk to Nathaniel alone?" Mrs. Beckon questioned.

Mama didn't look too keen on this. "I supposed I don't have much choice," she growled.

"Nathaniel, maybe we could go to your room for a few minutes," Mrs. Beckon suggested, ignoring Mama's irritation.

Nathan got up. He glanced at Mama, trying to reassure her with his gaze. She pressed her lips together. Nathan led Mrs. Beckon out into the hallway.

"I take good care of Nathaniel," Mama said to their backs. "I wouldn't do anything to put him in danger. I love him more than anything."

"I am sure you do," Mrs. Beckon agreed. But her tone of voice contradicted her words.

Nathan took her into his room. He gestured with both hands and shrugged. "This is it."

"Why don't you have a seat? Relax," she suggested, indicating the bed.

Nathan sat down, and Mrs. Beckon pulled the desk chair over to face him, uncomfortably close. "Do you like Nathaniel or Nathan?" she questioned.

"Nathan," he told her.

"Or maybe Nate?"

"No. Nathan."

"Well, I'm glad to meet you, Nathan. I'm just here to make sure that everything is okay, that you're being taken care of properly, and there's nothing going on here that shouldn't be. I know you've been pretty sick lately; pretty sick a number of times since you moved here, in fact."

Nathan nodded. "Yeah, I guess."

"You've lived in some other states before."

"Yes'm," he agreed.

"You've had social workers talk to you in other states too."

Nathan swallowed. She had searched his name in other states. "Yes'm."

"So you kind of know the drill," she said, her voice taking on a flinty tone.

"Yes'm." Nathan breathed. "There's nothing wrong. Mama takes good care of me. A lot of people just don't like single moms, or our religion, or that kind of thing. They call for no reason."

"I think the call is justified in this case. I've talked to the school about your attendance record, and to one of the doctors who treated you at the hospital."

Nathan looked down at his hands. He tried to fold them so that the woman didn't see his misshapen fingers. They always wanted to know about his fingers; how he had hurt them, why they were so deformed like that.

"The doctor at the hospital says that you have diabetes."

Nathan nodded. "Yes'm."

"But your diabetes wasn't being treated. Your mother doesn't want to give you insulin."

"We don't believe in medical healing," Nathan said.

Her eyes were sharp. "But you need insulin to treat your diabetes, or you are putting your life at risk."

Nathan nodded. "I'm taking it now," he said. "But it's against our beliefs."

"How can it be wrong to save your life?"

"That's our religion. You can't pressure me about my religion."

She considered that for a minute, and left it alone. "Show me your insulin," she said.

Nathan opened his drawer and took out his equipment and the insulin vial. She looked at the insulin, which she could see was only half full. "When is the last time you took some?"

"A few minutes ago," Nathan said.

He pulled the blood glucose monitor out of the pouch, and after turning it on, brought up the history, which he showed to her. "See, that's my last test. It has the date right there."

She studied it, squinting at the tiny numbers. "So does that satisfy you?" Mama demanded.

Nathan jumped so violently that he nearly dropped everything on the floor. He looked up and saw her watching from the doorway. Clutching his supplies against him, he stuffed it all into the pouch. Mrs. Beckon looked from Mama to Nathan, and back again, slowly, calculating.

"I'm glad to see that Nathan has the medicine that he needs," she said. "Did he see a doctor during his last illness?"

"No," Mama said flatly.

"If he's going to miss more school, he will need a note from a doctor. Or we will be investigating further."

"You can't force us to take him to a doctor when his life isn't in jeopardy," Mama challenged.

"If you prefer to have us involved," Mrs. Beckon said with a shrug. "Your choice. But you have a history of neglecting his medical care, so we will be keeping an eye on the situation."

Mama moved into the room, her eyes narrowing. "You have to report that you didn't find anything wrong here," she said, "and close the file. You can't keep it open because you think that something might happen in the future based on another state's file. You came here, he's fine, and he has his insulin. You have to report your lack of findings and close the file."

Mrs. Beckon considered this, and shook her head. "My investigation is inconclusive," she said. "Nathan wasn't getting his insulin before, and that put his life at risk. He now appears to be getting it, but I am not convinced that is a permanent state of affairs."

The two women stared at each other, neither backing down.

"I'd like a couple more minutes alone with Nathan," Mrs. Beckon said.

"I think you're done."

Nathan swallowed. Mrs. Beckon turned back toward him, and handed him a business card.

"Nathan, if you are worried about anything, or you're sick and need help, you call me. You don't have to suffer with no medical treatment. We will help you to get the care that you need."

Nathan froze with the card in his hand. He couldn't hand it back. He couldn't say that he would call her if he got sick. He didn't know what to do. Mrs. Beckon nodded.

"Anything," she repeated.

She stood up off of the desk chair and took a very slow look all the way around the room. She ended up facing Mama in the doorway again.

"You have a lovely home," she said. "I know you guys just moved in recently, and probably didn't have much to start with, but it's a nice, homey place to live. You wouldn't believe the squalor of some of the places I have to visit."

Mama's expression did not relax. She didn't simper and say thank you for the compliment. She just stood there, her face frozen in a blank expression, and waited for Beckon to leave.

Mrs. Beckon walked to the front door, and Nathan heard Mama shut and lock the door behind her. She returned to Nathan's room. Nathan clutched the little pouch of supplies against his body, worried that she would take them away. Mama stood there for a minute, looking at him.

"You've been lying to me," she said. "Sneaking around taking insulin behind my back. That's not honest and upright."

Tears filled the corners of Nathan's eyes. He held onto the supplies tightly. "I know," he admitted.

"How could you do that? How could you pretend that you were getting better on your own, and not tell me that you were taking medicine?"

Nathan stared at the floor, sniffling. "I didn't want to," he said. He wiped at his nose with the back of his hand. "But it was so bad... I was dying, Mama. I didn't want to die."

"How did you get insulin?" Mama questioned, her eyes narrow and suspicious.

"I just went to the pharmacy. They gave it to me, because it was an emergency."

"They gave you insulin, all by yourself, just because you asked?"

"I took my last vial with me," Nathan said.

Mama looked at him, frowning. He was afraid that she could see right through him. Right through all of the lies and half-truths. She would know that the pharmacists hadn't just helped a kid off the street without a responsible adult there. She would know that it was Chandra. Mama came in closer, right up to him, looking at the medical supplies.

"So you don't believe our faith anymore."

"I... I do... but I guess I don't have the faith to be healed. I really tried. I tried really hard to believe." Nathan swallowed, sniffling. "But... I just couldn't do it."

She looked at him for a long time. "Lots of people have children who go astray," she said finally. "I love you anyway, Bug. Always. This..." she flicked a finger toward his insulin. "This isn't you. I hope you'll have the strength to come back."

Nathan nodded, gulping. Mama sighed, and turned away, leaving the room.

Chapter Twenty-Two

NATHAN WAITED FOR A few days before going over to see Chandra, worried about making Mama suspicious of Chandra's part in Nathan getting insulin. Then Mama was at work after school one day, and he thought it was safe to go over to see her, and tell her about the social worker's investigation and what had been going on.

Chandra opened the door and smiled. "Nathan. Come to visit the snake again?" she questioned.

Nathan smiled. "I wouldn't say no," he admitted.

"Why don't you come in and visit her, then? You and I can talk in there."

Nathan followed her into Kenneth's bedroom, and he bent down and looked at the snake through the glass before opening up the terrarium to take her out. "Did she eat?" he questioned.

Chandra nodded. "One mouse. Not much, but more than she's had since... Kenneth... left."

"Good," Nathan approved. He slid his fingers around the cool body of the snake and lifted her carefully out.

"So... what's been going on with you lately?" Chandra asked.

Nathan looked at her, and then back down at the scales of the snake. "I guess you were around while I was sick," he said.

Chandra nodded. "I wish that there was something I could have done for you. But you know your mother... she won't let anyone help."

Nathan wound the snake behind his neck and let her slide down his arm, investigating, tongue flicking out curiously.

"I don't know why you were sick," Chandra said. "It wasn't the diabetes this time, was it? Was it a snake bite?"

"Just a bug, or food poisoning or something," Nathan said.

Chandra walked slowly over to the window and looked out. "I don't see our friend today."

Nathan looked out. "Has he been around?"

"Not that I've seen. I'd call the police if I did."

"I think..." Nathan stopped himself.

Chandra cocked her head. "What...?"

"Nothing. I forget what I was going to say."

She sat down on the edge of the bed. "*Was* it a snake bite, Nathan?" she asked again.

"No."

"I don't want you to lie to me."

"It wasn't."

"Okay." She lowered her voice, as if afraid that she might be overheard there, in her own house. "I gave you insulin a couple of times, when I could, if I was checking in on you while your mother went to work. I felt sort of guilty about it, when she trusted me to come into the house while she wasn't there, to see to you... but I knew that I had to."

"Oh. Thanks. You didn't have any trouble?"

She shook her head. "It's a pretty cool system, with that monitor and the pen where you just set the dose. The hardest part was actually injecting it. I didn't want to hurt you. But I got used to it."

Nathan nodded. "Thank you... I don't know how bad it would have gotten, if my blood sugar was all messed up too."

"Well, you probably didn't get as many doses as you should have. The monitor was always giving dire warnings. But I got you as much as I could, without her finding out."

Nathan sighed. "She knows."

"What?" Chandra's eyes widened in alarm. "What? About me giving it to you?"

"No, just that I've been taking it. She doesn't know that you were the one who helped me get it. But... she might suspect."

"Did she find it? What happened?"

Nathan explained to her about the social worker coming, and Mama finding out that he was still dosing himself with insulin.

"I guess she wasn't too happy about that," Chandra said.

Nathan shook his head. "No. I keep worrying about what she might do... take it away... or something." He swallowed. "I don't want to die."

"If she takes it away, we still have more here. You just tell me. I won't let anything happen to you."

It was comforting to Nathan to have someone looking out for him. He felt safer knowing that Chandra was only a couple of houses away, that she would know if something happened to him. Unless they had to move again. If they had to move, he would be alone again, with no guardian angel and no insulin. He couldn't let that happen.

He stroked the snake's back. The scales were soft, and smooth, and delicate. Nathan couldn't understand how anyone could think that snakes were ugly or disgusting. To him, they were always beautiful and mysterious. Dangerous, maybe, but not repulsive. The snake's skin made a whispering sound as she glided over Nathan's shoulders and arm, and she poked her head into his shirt. Nathan laughed and pulled her back.

"No, you don't, you can't go in there," he chuckled.

Chandra smiled. Her eyes were distant. "I remember, when she was smaller, and Kenneth would let her curl up inside his shirt."

Nathan couldn't help feeling sad for Chandra and the snake. Kenneth was gone, and he couldn't come back again, to hold his mother or to let the snake slide into the warmth of his shirt.

"You miss him," he said to Chandra.

"I can still see him," Chandra said, shaking her head.

Nathan opened his mouth, trying to find the words, but he never got anything out. Chandra's body suddenly flung back, so that she was stretched rigidly across the bed, like she was playing some bizarre planking game. For a moment she was still, and he wondered if she'd fainted. Then she started to shake, bouncing the bed violently. Nathan put the snake back in the terrarium as quickly as he could, latching the top securely, before running to her side. He tried to take her hand, but she was unresponsive. Her eyes were rolled back, showing only the whites, and spit gathered at the corners of her mouth. She started making a loud groaning noise.

"Chandra... Chandra, are you okay? What should I do?" Nathan demanded, panicking.

She didn't respond to him. Nathan didn't shake her, she was already shaking so much he was afraid she was going to bounce herself right off of the bed. He caught a glimpse of a medical bracelet on her wrist. A staff with a snake wrapped around it. He had to leave the room to look for the phone. His heart pumped hard and fast as he dialed 911. He couldn't catch his breath and didn't know what to say. The emergency operator answered and asked what kind of emergency it was.

"She's having a seizure," Nathan said. "I don't know what to do!"

"What's your name?"

"Nathan."

"How old are you, Nathan?"

"I'm twelve. Please help me!"

"We're dispatching an ambulance to your location." She read off the address. "Is that right?"

"Umm, yes, that sounds right."

"Can you tell me about who is having a seizure? Is it your mom?"

"No, a neighbor."

"How old is she? Is it a child?"

"No, she's older. Like a grandma."

"Are there any other adults around?"

"No. Just me. I don't know what to do!"

"Is she breathing?"

"I don't know," Nathan said in frustration. "She's in the other room."

"Okay. I understand. I want you to do a couple of things for me, Nathan. Stay calm."

Nathan breathed out and tried to calm himself. "Okay. What?"

"I want you to put down the phone, but not hang it up. Then I want you to go to the front door and make sure it is unlocked for the paramedics. Then you can go and see how your friend is doing. Don't try to stop her from seizing or put anything in her mouth. She might bite her tongue and it might bleed, but it's okay, just let it be. I just want you to sit with her until she stops seizing or the paramedics get there. If she starts to turn blue, or if she stops seizing, but isn't breathing, I want you to come back to the phone. Okay? Can you do all of that for me?"

Nathan nodded. "Okay. Yes'm. I can do that."

"Put down the phone, open the door, and then just sit with her. Okay?"

"Okay," Nathan agreed.

After unlocking the door, he went and sat with her, watching worriedly. In a few minutes, she stopped shaking, and Nathan leaned close to her, listening for her to breathe. She seemed to be asleep, her breathing natural and even. Nathan breathed a sigh of relief, and just sat looking at her, afraid to even touch her or speak.

He heard the ambulance siren growing louder and louder before it cut off with a squawk outside the house. In a few minutes, there was a knock, and the front door opened.

"Paramedics!"

"Over here!" Nathan called back, and he went to the door of the bedroom and looked down the hallway. The two paramedics, a man and a petite blond woman, came toward him. Nathan moved out of the way and let them come into the room.

"How long was she seizing?" the woman questioned.

"I don't know... it seemed like a long time."

The man put on his stethoscope and took Chandra's vitals.

"Does she have any medical conditions?"

Nathan shook his head. "I don't know. She has a bracelet."

He took a look at her wrists and found the medical bracelet. "Epilepsy. Has she been taking her anticonvulsants?"

"I don't know... I don't live here, I was just visiting."

"Okay. She'll probably come around before very long. What's her name?"

"Chandra. Mullenny."

"Chandra," the paramedic spoke in a loud voice, near her ear. "Chandra, wake up. Can you hear me?"

Chandra started to move. At first her limb movements seemed random, then like she was trying to climb a ladder. Eventually, she opened her eyes and tried to sit up.

"Are you okay, ma'am? You had a seizure. How are you feeling?"

"I saw him," Chandra said.

Her eyes found Nathan, but she still seemed confused and disoriented. "Kenneth? Did you call me?"

"It's Nathan, Chandra," he told her. "Kenneth isn't here."

"He was here," she said, frowning. "Or was I there? I just saw him."

The paramedic tried to get Chandra's attention back. "Mrs. Mullenny. You had a seizure. How are you feeling?"

"Where did he go?"

The paramedic looked at Nathan. "Was there someone else here? Do you know who she's talking about?"

"Her son. He died. This was his bedroom."

The paramedic glanced around. "How's your head, Mrs. Mullenny?"

She touched her forehead. "Did I hit my head?"

"No," Nathan said. "You just fell over on the bed."

Chandra's eyes stayed on him. "Nathan."

"Yes'm," Nathan said, relieved that she recognized him.

"Nathan. Oh, I'm sorry. What happened?" she looked around. "Did I go back? I travelled? I'm sorry..."

"You had a seizure," Nathan said, his mouth dry. "You didn't go anywhere."

"But I did," she insisted. "I know that's what happens to my body, but you have to understand, my soul, my brain--it's different."

"She's still disoriented," the paramedic told Nathan.

He nodded.

"There's no one else here to help look after her?" the man questioned.

"No."

"Okay. We'll take her to the hospital until they're sure that she's okay to be on her own."

Nathan nodded. "Thanks."

They seemed to take a long time getting the gurney and moving Chandra onto it. Nathan was standing outside watching them put Chandra in the ambulance when Mama arrived home. She came over to see what was going on.

"Nathaniel? What's going on, Bug?"

"Mrs. Mullenny had a seizure."

"A seizure?" Mama repeated.

Nathan nodded. "She has a bracelet that says she has epilepsy."

"I never noticed that."

Nathan shook his head. "Me neither. I didn't know."

They watched the paramedics close the ambulance doors, and the man, who was driving, nodded to Nathan. "Thanks for your call. You'll lock up the house?"

Nathan nodded. "Yessir."

The medic gave a little wave, and got into the cab of the ambulance. They watched it drive away, lights on, but no siren. Mama turned and looked at the house.

"I'll help you lock up," she said.

Nathan uneasily let her step ahead of him into the house. Mama walked around the house, taking a look around each room.

"We just need to lock the door," Nathan said.

"I'm just making sure that all of the windows are shut, and the stove and dryer and everything are off."

"Oh," Nathan hadn't even thought about any of those things.

Mama took a little longer to look around Kenneth's room. "Her son," Nathan said. "He died."

"She has a snake," Mama noted.

"Yes'm. It was Kenneth's. She doesn't like to handle it, though. I come over and hold it sometimes."

She watched the snake for a minute. "You didn't know that she has fits?" she questioned.

"No. I knew her son was dead, and that she thought she could see him... I didn't know it was when she was having seizures."

She gazed off into the distance. "I thought that she was a believer..." she said.

"She is," Nathan insisted, worried. "She's a believer. She is."

"You've read about devils in the Bible. Jesus healed people with fits that were possessed with devils. The boy who threw himself into the fire? Remember? And the one about the pigs."

"That's different," Nathan protested. "She just has a sickness. Epilepsy. It isn't a devil."

"That's what it is," Mama insisted. "Medicine tells you that it's just your body, and they can fix you with a pill. But a pill doesn't heal your spirit. It doesn't get rid of the devil. It's just a sham."

Nathan shook his head. "She's good, Mama. I know she doesn't have a devil. She's a good person."

"Good people can still be fooled, they can still be possessed. If she's talking with her dead son's spirit while the devil has possession of her..."

"No..."

Mama looked at him, and didn't say anything. Nathan swallowed. "We should go home."

She followed him to the door. Nathan locked the handle, and they walked back to the house.

"She's had a bad influence on you," Mama commented. "I thought that she was a believer, and that she would support our beliefs... but she's been leading you astray, influencing you when I am at work, or when I'm at home and you're over there. She's something completely different from what I thought. I was completely misled. I haven't been listening to the Spirit..."

"Mama..." Nathan could see that he had lost her. She didn't even hear his voice. She picked up her Bible and walked to her room.

Nathan went to his room to start on his homework, but he was distracted and couldn't focus on anything.

$ $ $

Chapter Twenty-Three

NATHAN HAD MISSED THE bus, and Mama was already gone to work. That only left one option, and that was to walk to school. He was going to be late. With the insulin, he at least had the energy to walk. If he'd missed the bus before he was on it, he probably would have just gone back to bed. But he couldn't miss any more school now. The school would call Child Protective Services, and the social worker would show up at their door making all kinds of threats just because he'd missed the bus. He had to get there.

Nathan gradually became aware there was a car trailing behind him. He glanced over his shoulder, trying to get a look at it without being obvious. He waited for it to go past him. But it didn't, it kept just driving behind him. Nathan looked for a shortcut, a way to get away from the road to where the car couldn't follow him. But he didn't usually walk to school, and he was nervous about getting lost if he took a different route. Nathan glanced back again, and decided to cut through the houses to try to lose it. He might have to jump a couple of fences, but maybe he could get away before something bad happened.

"Nathan!"

Nathan froze.

"Nathan, it's okay," the man's voice said.

Nathan turned slowly, afraid of what he was going to see. He was both scared and relieved to see the familiar face looking back from the driver's window of the car. The wavy hair. Handsome face. Nathan swallowed. He couldn't think of what to say. His mouth was dry and he couldn't find his voice.

"I'm not going to hurt you," the man said.

Nathan nodded. He licked his lips. "I figured out who you are," he said hoarsely.

The man got out of the car slowly, as if he expected Nathan to run if he moved too fast. But he didn't need to worry. Nathan's feet felt like they were nailed to the ground. He should probably walk away. But he couldn't.

"You know who I am?" the man questioned.

Nathan nodded. "You're my daddy."

Neither of them spoke for a long time. Harv Whit was standing just a few feet away from Nathan. Harv opened his arms hesitantly, an invitation. Nathan wasn't sure. He breathed, looking into his daddy's blue eyes. Harv let his arms fall back to his sides again. Nathan took a step toward him, reaching out his arms. Harv took him into an embrace, pulling him close. His arms were gentle, careful not to squeeze Nathan too tight or make him feel trapped. Nathan hugged him tightly in response. Harv bent down and picked him up. Like he was still a little boy. Nathan pushed his cheek against Harv's smooth neck below his ear. Harv's smell was familiar, bringing a flood of disconnected images to Nathan's consciousness. He couldn't put his finger on any one of them. But he felt warm and safe and protected.

"Nathan," Harv whispered, his big hand cupping the back of Nathan's head and stroking his messy hair.

"You're my daddy," Nathan repeated.

"Yes," Harv agreed.

"You're my daddy, and I haven't seen you for a long, long time."

Harv pulled back a little, so they could look at each other face-to-face.

"I'm so sorry, Natey," he whispered.

"Where have you been?" Nathan questioned.

"I've been trying to keep track of you, when I could."

"Really?" Nathan touched one of the lines on Harv's face, following the crease from the edge of his nose down to his mouth. Harv didn't used to have lines like that.

Harv nodded. "You guys move a lot. I try to stay out of the way, so your Mama doesn't get spooked and run again. But sometimes... I just have to see you."

"Why don't you visit?" Nathan questioned, not understanding. "Can't you ask for visitation?"

"What are you, a lawyer?" Harv teased.

Nathan shrugged. "Lots of kids have divorced parents. Everybody knows about visitation."

"Billie was okay with visitation to start with," Harv said, putting Nathan down now, but still holding onto his shoulders, as if afraid to break the connection they had. "But they got further and further apart, and then she started refusing to let me see you. Making things up about me to prevent me from seeing you. And then she ran, and told everybody that I was abusive, so that they wouldn't tell me where she had gone."

"I didn't know that," Nathan said.

"No. How would you?" Harv stared off somewhere over Nathan's head. "Any time I tried to contact her, to try to reconcile or make arrangements to see you, she would get a restraining order, or disappear."

Nathan thought about all of the moves. Sometimes he knew why they moved; a Child Protective Services investigation or trouble at the church. But other times, he would come home to packed bags and have to get into the car to leave it all behind, without any idea what they were running away from. How many times had it been because his daddy had tried to make contact with him?

"How did you know we were here?" Nathan questioned. "We haven't been here that long."

Harv shook his head. "Eight million people saw you. More than that. International news. You think a practiced investigator or hacker couldn't track you down with all of that attention?"

Nathan grinned, his face getting warm. Of course Harv had been able to figure out where the posts had originated. They had gotten lots of calls and visitors. Lots of people with less interest in him than Harv had figured it out.

"It was nice to be able to see your twelfth birthday," Harv said, smiling, his eyes crinkling up at the corner. "I even sent you money."

"You were at the house that day," Nathan said.

Harv looked startled. "You knew that?"

"That's the first day I saw you. But I didn't know who you were then. You were with the reporters."

"When did you figure it out?"

"Not long ago. And I wasn't sure. It's been a long time."

"It has. I'm surprised you remembered at all."

Harv squeezed his shoulder and looked intently into Nathan's face. "You're okay?" he questioned. "How are you feeling?"

Nathan nodded. "I'm good," he said. "I've been sick lots this year... but I'm good now."

"Good." Harv slid his hands from Nathan's shoulders to his hands, and looked at his stick-thin arms. "I'd never forgive myself if... if I let something happen to you."

"I'm okay," Nathan repeated. "Nothing will happen to me."

Harv shook his head. "You've been too close too many times lately. We have to do something..."

Nathan withdrew his hands from Harv's, feeling queasy. He knew instinctively what Harv meant. "I can't," he objected. "Mama needs me."

"Billie will survive without you. But I don't know if you'll survive with her."

"No. No, I can't leave Mama. I help her. She needs me."

"Children need to be able to rely on their parents. It's not up to you to take care of her."

"I'm the only one," Nathan said. "You don't take care of her. You left."

An expression like pain crossed Harv's face. "I didn't leave," he corrected. "She kicked me out."

"Why? Mama wouldn't do that without a reason."

"She had her reasons," Harv admitted. "But they weren't what she said they were."

"She wouldn't lie."

"Do you really think that's true? That she always tells you the full truth?"

"We're honest with each other," Nathan insisted. "One hundred percent."

"Like you were honest with her about getting insulin after she cut you off?"

"Mama is honest with me," Nathan amended.

"Did she tell you that she was keeping me away? That I wanted to see you?"

"No..."

"Why would she tell you that she'd kicked me out? Sometimes I wonder if she even understood herself what was going on."

"What?" Nathan questioned. "What do you mean?"

"Why don't we go sit in the car?" Harv suggested. "It's a bit chilly out here to be standing around."

Harv wasn't wearing any gloves. Nathan looked at the car nervously. How many times had he been told not to get into strangers' cars? Even if he was Nathan's father, Harv *was* a stranger to him. A stranger who wanted to take him away from Mama.

"We'll just sit here?" he questioned.

"Right here. I'm not going to take you away."

"You promise not to drive anywhere?"

Harv nodded. "I promise."

Nathan walked over to the car with him and got in. It was an old car, the interior worn, but clean. Lots of leg room. Nathan settled into the seat. Harv fiddled with the buttons and knobs of the heating system. Eventually he sat back. He stared out the front windshield and didn't look at Nathan.

"We were very happy the first few years," he said. "Your mama a junior pastor. Newly married and having fun playing house. Just two kids wrapped up in each other and in God."

"You went to the church too?"

Harv nodded. "That's where I met her. It was rare to see pastors so young, and lady preachers were practically unheard of. And there Billie was, confident, holding her own, a real leader. The services were fun. Lots of music, everyone participating and testifying. Things could get pretty wild sometimes." He paused, pursing his lips. "I never was big on the snakes."

Nathan laughed. Harv smiled, his eyes crinkling up again. Then his face got serious, all of the humor fleeing. "We wanted a family right away. We both felt like that was what God wanted for us."

Nathan watched him intently, nodding.

"Billie had a miscarriage. She had been so happy when she got pregnant. She just glowed. She floated everywhere she went. It was a dream come true. When she miscarried, it was like God had struck her with lightning. A bolt from the blue, totally unexpected. One day she was pregnant, and the next she was empty, totally devastated."

Nathan pictured his Mama a young bride, transformed from a happy mother-to-be to a shattered shell, mourning the loss of her baby. He knew the depth of her feelings. He knew how much she loved Nathan, loved interacting with other children in her congregation. The loss of the pregnancy would have been crushing.

"Poor Mama."

"That wasn't the worst," Harv said bleakly.

Nathan swallowed, looking at him.

"People said all of those things that people say. It wasn't meant to be. The baby wouldn't have survived birth, or would have been handicapped. You can get pregnant again. At least it was early in the pregnancy." Harv sighed deeply. "There's really nothing you can say. Nothing that makes a mother that just lost her baby feel any better. Anything that you say is just going to hurt her."

Nathan nodded. "After a few months, she did get pregnant again. We were more cautious this time. Didn't tell people until she was starting to show. Were really careful of her activity. Did everything that we could to ensure a healthy pregnancy, to make sure the baby was okay. After getting past the first trimester, we were cautiously optimistic. Then when the baby was old enough to be viable... we were overjoyed."

He swallowed, and stared down the street. Nathan waited for him to continue.

"She made it to her due date, and then overdue. She didn't go into labor. Billie went in to see a doctor, and he said that she had to be induced right away. There was something wrong with the baby. We went to the hospital, and they brought on her labor and delivered the baby."

Harv's voice cracked. Nathan glanced over at him surreptitiously. There were tears in the corner of Harv's eyes. Nathan knew this story was not going to have a happy ending.

"He died," Harv said. "Our perfect little son, that we have prepared for and prayed for over all those months. He just died. They wrapped him in a blanket, and put a little blue hat on him, and let us hold him."

His voice was raw with grief. It had been years ago, but it was still an open wound.

"That's so sad," Nathan said. "Mama's never told me about that. She never even mentioned it."

Harv sighed. "Then you finally came along," he said. "We were afraid to get pregnant again. So scared of losing another baby. It hurt so much. Billie read about Hannah in the Bible. How she promised God that she would dedicate her son to him, if she could have a baby. So that's what Billie did. She told God that if he would just let her have a baby that lived, she would raise him to God. To his glory. She felt guilty for going to the doctor when the other baby was overdue, felt that it was her fault. If she hadn't gone to the doctor, and to the hospital, the baby would have lived. So with you, she refused to see any doctors. Not a single doctor's visit or ultrasound. She had a home birth with a midwife. And you..." Harv looked at Nathan with an affectionate smile. "You were healthy. Big and strong and hearty."

Nathan smiled.

"And she poured all of her love into you. All of the love that she had saved up for those two lost babies."

Harv fiddled again with the buttons and dials of the heating system. "Throughout the pregnancies, we had grown apart. It was hard on the marriage, losing those babies. It should have brought us closer together, but it hadn't. Finally having you, I thought that we would be able to fix it. A perfect little family. Just what we had always wanted. But Billie poured all of her love into you. She didn't have any left for me. Not that I was jealous. But there was nothing left for me, or anyone else."

Nathan ran his finger along a line of stitching in the door. "Is that when you left?"

"I didn't leave you," Harv insisted. "I told you. I never left you. I would have stayed, even if Billie had no time for me. But she kicked me out. She made up stories, said that I wasn't a supportive husband and father, that she couldn't stand living that way anymore, and I had to leave. Forced out of my own house. I thought that she'd change her mind, and we'd be able to get back together again once she realized what it was like to have to live by herself and support herself."

Nathan thought about this. "How old was I?" he questioned. "When she kicked you out?"

"I think you were about three. I was still able to keep up visits for a couple more years, before she disappeared."

"I remember you once, when I was older. I guess it was sometime you came back to visit. You went to worship with us."

Harv gazed at him. "I went to church with you?" he repeated, his expression blank.

Nathan nodded. "It was... it was when Pastor Dan was there."

Harv licked his lips and didn't offer anything.

"Were you there?" Nathan questioned. "Do I remember right? Or did I dream that?"

Harv scratched his chin. "Maybe. I knew Pastor Dan."

Nathan stared out the window. He should be getting to school by now. It seemed strange that it was just a regular school day. That it could be just a regular day for everybody else.

"Were you there when Pastor Dan died?" Nathan questioned, without looking back at Harv.

He didn't answer at first. Nathan could feel Harv looking at him, but Nathan didn't look back at him. "Yes," Harv said finally. They sat there in silence. Nathan remembered the music. The bright colors of the snake. The instant that it struck. "I never held with the snakes," Harv said. "I couldn't understand the need to handle them. And taking children to services like that."

Both of them looked at Nathan's hand at the same time. Nathan curled his fingers up, hiding the deformed one away.

"I was furious when I heard about that," Harv said. "Letting a baby be bit by a snake. She shouldn't have even had you in the service, especially so close to the snake. But..." he shook his head. "She was ecstatic. Your faith was proven. You were a believer, and only a few years old. It proved that she had done the right thing, dedicating you to God."

Nathan glanced over at Harv, and then down at his own knees. "I wonder what she thinks of me now."

"You've lived through all of the trials she's put you through so far," Harv pointed out. He cleared his throat. "But I'm worried you might not survive the next."

"I should get to school," Nathan observed, looking at the clock on the dash. "I'm late."

Harv put the car in gear. "I'll drop you off," he said.

Nathan breathed a sigh of relief. In spite of Harv's assurance, Nathan had been worried that Harv was going to try to take him away. Harv drove in silence, and stopped just down the street to let him out.

"You can tell them you missed the bus," Harv suggested.

Nathan nodded. "Thanks," he said, and got out of the car.

Chapter Twenty-Four

NATHAN TOSSED AND TURNED, his mind going a mile a minute. The meeting with his daddy had stirred up all kinds of emotions and fragments of memories. He tried to focus on something that would help him to sleep. Thinking about school, working through the math problems that they'd been working on, trying to fool himself into being bored and falling asleep. But that wasn't working. His mind kept jumping back to Harv. The things that he could remember about when Harv had lived with them, or had visited him after that. The way that he smelled and the feeling of the rough skin on his hands.

Mama had noticed he was distracted after school, but Nathan had brushed it off as being worried about homework and trying to get caught up.

Nathan turned over, trying to settle himself into a comfortable position. One that would bring sleep quickly. He flipped over his pillow, the other side of the pillowcase cooler on his face. But he still couldn't get comfortable.

Mama had never liked to talk about Nathan's daddy. She always said that he had left, he had abandoned them, and Nathan had not had any interest in tracking him down or meeting him. Now it was Harv's word against Mama's. Nathan had lived with his Mama his whole life, and he knew how much she loved him. He should believe her over Harv. He ought to believe his Mama one hundred percent.

But he didn't. If Harv had abandoned Nathan and Mama, then what was he doing now, tracking Nathan down, following him, and watching him? It wasn't just idle curiosity about how his son had turned out. He wasn't just drifting through town and thought he'd look into Nathan before he left again. Nathan couldn't help but believe the emotion in Harv's face and in Harv's voice. That was real. That was the truth; Nathan knew it when he heard it.

Mama, on the other hand, avoided his questions, brushed them off, and fudged her answers. She might not exactly be lying to him, in her mind, but she wasn't being honest and open with him. And she had never told him about the babies that she had lost before Nathan was born. Nathan had no doubt that Harv's story was true. And it had finally explained why Mama poured so much love into Nathan. Why she was so close to him. Not like other mothers were with their children.

Nathan sat up, frustrated, and ran his fingers through his hair. He had to get some sleep. He couldn't let the mixed-up feelings get in the way of his sleep, or he'd be sleeping in class tomorrow. And if he was foggy or sleepy in class, Mrs. David was going to think that he was off his insulin again and call Child Protective Services. Nathan didn't know how he was going to keep fending off the CPS investigations. Sooner or later, they were going to stop believing him, and try to take him away from Mama. He couldn't let that happen.

He let out a noise of exasperation, and flopped back down on his back again. Sleep. He had to sleep. He had to stop thinking about Mama and Daddy and just go to sleep. Nathan decided to focus on his classmates. He would think of each student in his class, starting with the desk nearest the door, and going through each desk in each row. Picture their faces, remember their names, try to list everything that he knew about them. If he thought about school, instead of Mama and Daddy, he could get to sleep.

It was kindergarten. The first day of kindergarten. Nathan watched the faces of the other mothers and children as they waited for things to begin. Everybody looked happy and excited. Nathan was enthusiastic about being a big kid and going to school at last.

Mama gave him a tight hug, picking him up off of his feet and snuggling him close. Nathan realized that her face was wet, and looked at her in confusion and concern. Tears leaked steadily out of her eyes, welling up endlessly.

"Mama, what's wrong?" he questioned, wiping her face.

"Oh, Nathaniel," she wept, her voice breaking. "I just don't want to have to leave you alone. I can't let you go to school all day without me."

"I'll be home after school," Nathan said.

"I know, but that is so long away. I'm going to cry the whole time you're gone, sweetie. Oh, Love Bug. Give me a squeeze."

He hugged her tightly. "It's okay, Mama. I'll be okay," he assured her.

"I know you will, sweetie. You'll be fine, won't you?"

The tears continued to pour down her face. Nathan looked around at the other children. Their mothers all seemed happy to let them go to kindergarten. They pointed out different features of the brightly-colored kindergarten classroom to their children, encouraging them to explore. One mama, with a younger child hanging off her leg and a gangly baby on her hip, kept pushing her kindergartner away from her with her foot, repeatedly telling him 'go on, John. Leave me alone and go do something!' Nathan felt sorry for the other children, that their mamas didn't love them as much as his mama did. None of the other mamas were going to miss their children like Nathan's.

As he looked around the room to see what interesting things he would be allowed to do now that he was a big kid, Nathan's throat started to get tight. If he was staying home with Mama, they could go out in the woods looking for wildlife, and interesting rocks, sticks, and leaves. They would return home with pockets full of rocks for the garden out front. Maybe they'd go down to the grocery store or the convenience store to get a special treat together. Mama would make him a hot lunch, instead of sending him off to school with a cold sandwich. She'd been crying as she made it that morning, but she had said it was just the onions. If Nathan was staying home instead of going to kindergarten, they would watch Nathan's afternoon shows together, and he'd fall asleep curled up in her arms as they laid on the couch. When he woke up, they would play a game or make a craft, or maybe go for another walk if he was restless.

Now he would miss all of those activities. And more than that, he would miss Mama. They would never be able to have carefree days like that again. Because school was taking him away from her.

"Don't cry, baby," Mama sniffled, wiping at a couple of tears that escaped from Nathan's eyes. "It's okay, Bug. Really it is. I don't want you to be sad."

"Mama, I want to go home with you," Nathan said, his throat hot and tight. "I don't want to stay here. I want to go home."

"You can't, Nathaniel. You have to stay here. I'm sorry, but that's the rule. You have to go now that you're old enough. They won't let you stay home with me anymore."

"But I want to," Nathan protested, bawling now. Why were they taking him away from Mama? Why couldn't he stay with her anymore? Why did he have to be so big?

He clung to her, and she held him tightly, rocking back and forth, patting his back and trying to soothe his tears, while her own still tracked down her face. She sniffled.

"I need to take pictures of you your first day of school," she pointed out. "So you have to stop crying now and smile for your pictures. You'll want to remember this day. It's a happy time, not a sad time."

He didn't know how she could even say that. She didn't think that. She was sad. She knew it was a horrible, sad, tearful day. They couldn't be happy about being separated every day for the rest of their lives.

Mama made him go stand in front of the classroom door, and gave him a tissue to wipe his eyes and blow his nose. But more tears had just leaked out again after being wiped away. Nathan stood there miserably, feeling alone and isolated, his heart already aching for Mama, who was going to cry all day long, and would keep crying every day that he had to go to school. The other kids watched him with wide eyes, pointed and whispered with their parents. A couple of others started to tear up as they saw his distress.

"Okay, it's time for the parents to say good-bye and head out," the teacher announced, seeing how the tears would spread to all of the students before long. They had to get rid of the parents before it was too late.

Mama was the last to go. She clung to Nathan again until all of the other parents had left the classroom, and one of the teacher's aides gently pried Nathan out of her grip, murmuring that he would be fine, and forget all of his sadness once she was gone.

"Nathaniel. Time to get up, Bug."

Nathan awoke from the dream, and lay there disoriented for a minute, trying to remember what day it was and what he was supposed to be doing.

"It's time to get up," Mama repeated. "You don't want to miss the bus again today."

She hadn't been happy to get a call from the school about him being late because of the missed bus the day before.

"I'm up," Nathan agreed, moving to sit up, pushing the blankets away from him. "I'm getting up."

"Are you sure?" Mama studied him, frowning, wanting to make sure that he didn't go back to sleep the minute that she left the room again.

"I'm sure. I'm up," Nathan promised. "I'm staying up."

"Okay. Get showered and dressed quickly, so you're not late."

"Yes'm. I will."

She left him alone and went back to the kitchen to get his breakfast on the table. Other kids just had cold cereal for breakfast, but Mama always prepared a hot meal if she could be home for breakfast. If she wasn't home, then sometimes he had a muffin or cold cereal, but he always preferred a hot breakfast. And she preferred to make it for him.

In a few minutes, he was showered and dressed, and had taken his insulin. He sat down at the table, while Mama dished up for him. Nathan said grace when she nodded to him, and then he dug in.

"Mama...?"

"Yes, Bug?"

Nathan concentrated on keeping his expression blank, and kept his eyes on his breakfast, not looking at her. "Did I ever have any brothers or sisters?" Nathan questioned, keeping his voice carefully casual.

The serving spoon that Mama was holding clattered to the floor. She bent down to get it, and he saw that her face was as white as a sheet. Nathan quickly averted his eyes, looking back at his plate.

"What?" she demanded.

"I just... wondered," Nathan said. "I just... I don't know... sometimes I have dreams, or memories... when I think you had other babies sometime." He shrugged. "It's nothing, I guess. Everybody probably dreams that."

Mama stood by the table, staring down at him. She was not easily dissuaded. "You can't remember any other babies," she challenged.

"No," Nathan agreed. "I guess not."

But she still stood there. The conversation was over, and he had agreed, but she still stood there, looking down at him.

"Why would you ask me that?" she questioned. "What would make you ask me a question like that?"

"Just a dream," Nathan said lightly. "Last night I dreamed I was back in kindergarten again too. Maybe because I've been worrying a lot about my schoolwork."

"Your schoolwork is just fine. You'll get through grade six okay, and then wonder what all of the fuss was about, because they're going to reteach it all to you again in grade seven. That's the way it always is, because kids forget stuff over the summer, and because you've got kids coming from all different schools and have to make sure that they all have the same base. You'll get it again in grade seven."

Nathan nodded. "Good," he agreed. He hoped that it was true. Maybe if they started over, he'd be able to understand it the second time around.

He continued to eat, and Mama stood there over him, staring at him. "I had other babies," she said finally. "But they all died."

Nathan stopped eating. He could barely even chew and swallow what was already in his mouth. "What?" he questioned around the mouthful. "Was that before me?"

"There were two before you that didn't survive," Mama said, her voice curiously flat and emotionless. "And three that came after you."

Nathan tried to close his mouth and swallow. "Are you sure?" he questioned.

That was just how it came out. Of course she was sure. A mother would know these things. A mother would remember them. But Harv had said nothing about three babies that came after him.

"What happened to the ones who came after me?" he asked. "I don't really remember much about them..."

Mama finally sat down. She put the serving spoon down carefully on the table. "Sometimes pregnancies don't go so well, or babies don't live for long after they are born," she said.

Nathan nodded. "So... you lost them when they were still in your belly?" he asked. "They died before they were born?"

"How could you remember them if they died when they were still in my belly?" Mama demanded logically. "Of course not. You know better than that. But... they weren't very old."

Nathan looked down at his plate. "Why did they die, then?"

"Sometimes God sends us tests," Mama said. "To see how we'll act, if we'll still be faithful. And sometimes, he lets the devil have his own way. Like in the book of Job."

Nathan remembered the story of the man who Satan had been given permission to afflict. How he'd lost his wife and children and everything he owned, and then been made sick and frail, and his friends had argued against him, had accused him of being evil.

"So that was your test?" Nathan said. "God took away your babies?"

Mama stared off into space for a long time. So long that Nathan had to turn to see what she was looking at, to see if there was something physical that had caught her attention. But there was nothing. It was just her memories.

"That was my test," Mama said finally. "But I got to keep one baby." She reached across the table and stroked his hair. "One baby I dedicated to the Lord, and he's always been faithful." She tucked a lock of his hair back behind his ear, and smiled. "And who needs a haircut," she observed.

On the way home from school--which had, of course, been disastrous after his restless night--Nathan saw his daddy's car again nosing up beside him. He looked over at him. Harv rolled down the window.

"Want a lift?" he offered.

Nathan shook his head hesitantly. "Mama would see," he pointed out.

"She's not home. She's at the store."

Nathan considered. "She wasn't supposed to be working today."

"I guess she got called in, then."

Nathan stood there for a minute, uncertain. Then he nodded. He went around the car, and Harv leaned over and opened the passenger door. Nathan got in and buckled up. He leaned back, closing his eyes briefly.

"I couldn't sleep last night," he said. "My brain wouldn't stop going."

"Sorry. Was that because of me?"

Nathan shrugged. "Then when I finally got to sleep, I kept dreaming about kindergarten."

Harv laughed. "Well, I hope you didn't dream you had to go back to kindergarten. I always have dreams where I have to go back to junior high to finish some course that I didn't get for some reason."

Nathan wondered if Harv was being intentionally light-hearted, not wanting to get into any painful subjects like the day before. He didn't say anything. After a while, Harv looked over at him.

"And...?"

"I had other dreams too. Weird. I had little brothers and sisters. I guess because of you talking about the babies Mama lost before I was born."

Harv looked briefly at Nathan, and then ahead at the road again. They drove in uncomfortable silence. Harv rubbed the back of his head, his forehead wrinkled into a worried frown. Nathan let him sit and stew.

"Billie had other children," Harv admitted finally.

Nathan swallowed. "And they died when they were babies?" he suggested.

Harv's lips trembled. Nathan waited. "They were older than babies," he said slowly. "But still very young..."

"What happened?" Nathan questioned.

"I don't know..."

Nathan frowned. "You lived there. You must have known."

"I wasn't home all day. I had to work, do other things."

Nathan shook his head, his anger rising. There were too many secrets that had been kept from him. "But you must have known! You don't just come home from work one day and find your kids dead and not ask what happened! So what happened?"

Harv pulled up to the front of the house, and sat there, not moving. "Steven died of something called crib death," he said. "They don't know what it's caused by, exactly... babies have immature respiratory systems... sometimes they just stop breathing."

Nathan raised his eyebrows.

"That's what it was," Harv insisted. "Billie loved all of her babies. She wouldn't have done something that hurt them or put them at risk."

Nathan didn't even try to counter that one. "What about the others?" he questioned. "There were two others. Did they die of crib death too?"

Harv rubbed his face, covering his eyes briefly. "Natey," he said. "What is the point in digging it all up again? It just... hurts, so much."

"Why wouldn't Mama ever tell me? How could you have that many children die, and not ever even mention it?"

"What's the use of going over it? *You* survived. You were the one that survived."

"You're not going to tell me?" Nathan questioned, and reached for the door handle to let himself out.

"Wait." Harv touched him on the arm. "Stop."

Nathan waited.

"We lived in the back country," Harv explained. "We didn't use doctors, and there were a lot of hazards. There were a lot of old traditions, old beliefs. There was a high infant mortality rate. Do you know that that means?"

Nathan gazed at him. "It means that all of the babies in our family died, except for me."

"Yeah," Harv said, swallowing and looking away. It was a few minutes before he spoke. "Amy ate something poisonous," he said.

Was it a plant outside? Rat poison inside the house? In her food? Or was it really something she didn't eat? A spider or scorpion? Or a snake? Nathan didn't ask aloud. Harv was looking very gray, and the lines on his face were more pronounced. That was two. There was still one more. One more child for Harv to tell Nathan about. Harv rubbed his forehead.

"I came home one day," he began, his voice already breaking. He struggled to control it, wiping his forehead and closing his eyes in pain. Nathan wondered what he saw when he closed his eyes. "Baby Hannah... everything was quiet when I got home. When you've got little ones, things are never quiet like that. I called to Billie as I came in the door, and she didn't answer. She was laying asleep on the couch, with a blanket pulled over her. She didn't look good. Her face was gaunt, her eyes looked like someone had blackened them. I knew she was sick. I went to look for you and Hannah. I thought maybe she had put you down to nap so that she could rest. So I went to your room, and you weren't there. And I went to Hannah's room." Harv cleared his throat. He made little sobbing noises with each breath, like a wounded animal in a trap. He breathed with his mouth open, trying to get the air and the courage to go on. "I can't, Nate. I can't!"

Nathan just waited. Either Harv would tell him, or he wouldn't. An argument would just get them off track. It would just be an excuse for a fight that would end in Nathan never finding out the truth. So he just stared straight out the windshield ahead of him, and said nothing. Harv covered his face, crying harder now. Nathan felt sorry for him. But he *needed* the truth. He needed Harv to get himself under control and tell Nathan the rest of the story. Harv eventually pulled out a wad of tissues and blew his nose. He stared straight ahead of him, like Nathan. There was moisture under his nose and in the corners of his eyes, but he forged on ahead. He kept his voice even and emotionless, telling the story as if it had happened to someone else, and hadn't torn the heart out of him.

"Hannah was in her crib. There was blood everywhere. Spattered on the walls and the crib. Soaking into the mattress under her little body. Her clothes were soaked with it. You could barely see the places that the knife had stabbed through her little pajamas. It was just all bloody."

"Was she dead?" Nathan asked.

Harv nodded.

"What happened to her?"

Harv didn't answer the question directly. He continued on as if he hadn't been interrupted.

"At first I couldn't find you. I was frantic. I looked under the crib, in the closet, in your room, calling to you all the time. I went to the door and looked outside and called you and called you. But you didn't come. I was afraid that you had been kidnapped. I went--" he gulped. "I went back to Billie in the sitting room, on the couch. I wondered if she had been hurt too. That someone had come into the house and done this horrible, unthinkable thing, killing Hannah and Billie and stealing you away. I touched Billie's face. She was still warm. Hannah--" Harv shook his head. "Hannah hadn't been warm. When I touched her, she was cold as ice... and stiff." He sobbed a few times, and then got it under control again. "But Billie was alive. And I pulled the blanket away from her body to make sure that she was okay. To see if she had injuries too. Her face looked so... haunted. I pulled back the blanket, and there was blood everywhere. She had spatter and stains all over her dress, and her hands. She had cuts on her hands, and I thought that she'd been attacked, that she'd fended the attacker off with her bare hands, trying to protect herself and her babies. And then... I pulled back the blanket the rest of the way, trying to see where else she had been injured. And there you were, under the blanket, cuddled up to Billie like a chick under a hen's wing. You were unconscious too, and at first I thought that you were dead like Hannah. But you were warm when I picked you up."

He stopped talking and breathed again for a few minutes, trying to find the words, trying to stay calm enough to tell the story.

"You had been stabbed too. You were soaked in blood. But you were alive. I got to the phone, and called for help. It was back country. There was no ambulance, no 911 service. Just neighbors. They came to help. They drove me down the mountain, with you in my arms, praying that you would live. Before I left, others told me that Billie didn't seem to be injured, other than in her hands, that she must be unconscious with exhaustion and grief, or she was hit over the head by the intruder, or something. They told me that she was alive and that she was okay. I had to get you to care. It was the only hope."

"And you did," Nathan said. Because he had survived. He had scars. Mama told him they were from an accident, but she had never explained. Why not? Why did everything have to be a secret?

"I got you to the hospital, and to the doctors. They treated you, gave you blood, stitched up the wounds. They said that you were very lucky. That it was a miracle that nothing vital had been injured."

They both sat there for a few minutes. Nathan wiped at his own eyes and found them wet. Who was he crying for? Baby Hannah that he couldn't even remember? Himself? His Mama, attacked in her own home, trying to defend her helpless babies?

"Who was it?" he said finally. "Did they ever find out who it was?"

"The police officers who went up to the house to investigate said that the kind of cuts that Billie had on her hands were not 'defensive wounds'. They said that they were the kind of cuts you get on your hand when you stab something with a knife that has no hilt or cross guard. Because your hand slips down to the blade."

Nathan thought about the scars on Mama's hands, not really processing what Harv was saying. The kind of cuts you get when you stab something. He looked down at his own hands, imagining holding a kitchen knife.

"She had a hallucinogen in her blood," Harv went on. "She had brewed an herbal tea to boost her energy, and it had... it had a kind of mushroom in it that can give you hallucinations."

Nathan wondered if it had really been an accident. Maybe it was the first time that she had tried mushrooms. Maybe she hadn't known what it would do. Or had it been intentional, seeking after visions, like the other times? Harv was a little naive, believing the best of his wife. Perhaps everyone had preferred to look the other way and accept her story. Harv went on gently with his explanation.

"When she took this mushroom tea, she had visions that a devil had entered the house, and that it had gone into Hannah. And when she was stabbing Hannah, it was to try to get the devil out of her."

Nathan swallowed. "And me?"

Harv shrugged helplessly.

Mama had stabbed Nathan with a knife. Had nearly killed him. Had killed one of his siblings. Nathan couldn't fathom it. Mama loved him so much. How could she have done anything to hurt him? Mama always protected him. Always did what was best for him. It was inconceivable that she would ever attack him, try to hurt him.

"I'd better go do my homework," he told Harv.

Harv looked at him, surprised. "Natey... don't you understand? It's too dangerous. You can't stay with her."

Nathan wrapped his arms around his backpack as he got ready to get out of the car. He leveled a look at Harv.

"That was a long, long time ago," he pointed out. "I'm not a baby anymore. Nothing like that is going to happen again. If you thought Mama was a danger to me, you would have done something about it years ago, wouldn't you? You wouldn't just let her keep me, and just come for visits now and then. The police didn't think she was dangerous. Nobody put her in jail. All these years... you haven't been there. Maybe you tracked us down now and then, but you never did anything about it. Never tried to get custody. If you thought she was going to kill me, you would have done something."

Harv's face was gray. "Nathan. I did everything I could. No one would listen. No one understood how dangerous she was. But *you* understand. I see how sick she keeps making you. The next time, you could die."

"Mama's not going to do anything to hurt me," Nathan insisted. "Mama loves me more than anything."

"I know she does. That's what makes it so crazy. Nathan, you have to listen. Stay with me. You can live with me. I can keep you safe from her. So that you get a chance to grow up, a chance at life."

"I have faith," Nathan said. "I'll be protected. Just like I always have."

Harv shook his head. "He can't protect you from her evil. She has the freedom to make her own decisions, and they are putting your life at risk. You have to know that."

"Her evil?" Nathan repeated, shocked by the suggestion. "She's more righteous than anyone I know. She has more faith and belief in God than anyone else. That's why you don't understand. You can't understand that kind of faith, because you've never had it. That's why you couldn't keep living with us. Because you were an unbeliever. She had to keep me away from you."

Nathan pulled the door handle to let himself out, before Harv could decide to just run away with him.

"Nathan. Hold on. Let me give you something."

Nathan turned warily. Now what? Harv patted his pockets and came up with a stack of business cards and a pencil. He wrote on the back of one of the business cards.

"That's my cell number. I'll... I'll be close by. If you need something, please call. I'll come right away. I'll be here in five minutes."

Nathan took the card from him, swallowing. He looked at the front, which was an advertisement for a realtor. Not Harv's name.

"And if you just want to talk," Harv said. "That's okay too. I'd love to just talk with you."

Nathan put it into his pants pocket. "Bye, Daddy," he said softly, and shut the car door.

Chapter Twenty-Five

NATHAN THOUGHT THAT HE could go back to the way that things had been. Harv's insights into the past did not really affect anything in the present. Harv hadn't been part of their life for many years. And all of those things that he knew had happened in the far distant past. Mama was still Mama. She hadn't changed. Nathan's schedule was still dictated by the school calendar, and his home life by Mama's work calendar. When they were both home, they could watch TV, play games, study scriptures, or do any of the other things that they enjoyed doing together. Nothing had changed.

Mama left Nathan's insulin alone, but Nathan still left the extra supplies at Chandra's, not wanting to risk a change of heart. Things between them had become strained. Nathan felt it, but he didn't know if Mama felt it too, or was aware of his feelings. Nathan couldn't look at her without thinking about the dead babies. His siblings. If they had lived, he would have had little sisters and a brother. Maybe Steven had died of crib death and Amy had accidentally eaten something poisonous, but Mama had killed Hannah. Nathan couldn't get that out of his mind. He kept hearing Harv warning him over and over again that it wasn't safe. That even though he had survived all of his trials so far, he was still in danger. He might not survive the next one.

It made him look at everything differently. He was suspicious of the food that Mama prepared for him. Worried that she was going to buy more of the hallucinogenic mushrooms. Worried that she would take away his insulin, and he would die before Chandra could help him to get more again.

God protected the believers. Nathan firmly believed that. Mama had always taught him that faith would protect him from the snakes, from poison, and from other dangers. It said so in the Bible. But more and more, Nathan found himself doubting. Would God protect him from another knife attack, as he had once done? Or had that just been luck? God didn't stop people from making wrong choices. And at some point, every person would reach the end of his life, even if he did believe. If it was Nathan's time, nothing could stop that. But he wasn't ready for his life to be over.

Sunday after worship, Nathan found himself growing increasingly anxious. Mama kept looking at her Bible, and thumping her finger down on the page, and pacing around. Then she came to look at it again, pounding it with her finger, and pacing. Nathan walked casually past the open book and looked down at it, scanning the page in the quadrant where he had seen Mama tap it.

Exodus. Nathan's eyes found the verse immediately. 'Thou shalt not allow a sorceress to live.'

He instantly knew it was Chandra. Mama had been obsessed with Chandra since the older woman had gotten back home from the hospital after her seizure. Mama took a plate of cookies over to wish her a speedy recovery. Nathan didn't tell her that Chandra wouldn't eat them, because she couldn't eat wheat. But Chandra would be graceful to Mama and thank her and not let her know that she wasn't actually going to eat them. Nathan worried a little that she might give them to someone else to eat, but the fact that she was a recluse meant that she wasn't in contact with a lot of other people. Hopefully she would just toss them in the garbage.

Nathan was afraid to go over to Chandra's house unless he had to. He was afraid to upset Mama further. So lately, he had only been going over there if Mama was at work and wouldn't know.

Mama continued her agitated pacing. Nathan made them a light supper out of leftovers in the fridge, and Mama hardly even smiled. She sat down with him to eat, but barely touched the food she put on her plate. Without excusing herself, she was up again, pacing back and forth as she tried to get her thoughts straight.

As the evening wore on, Nathan hoped that Mama would settle down, and let herself be distracted by the TV or some other diversion. But Mama looked at her watch.

"You should go to bed early tonight," she told him. "You've been dragging in the mornings lately."

It was still pretty early. But the tension was wearing on Nathan, and he had to admit that he was tired. Maybe his bedtime routine would not just help get him ready for sleep, but would help Mama to calm down for the evening as well. She tucked him in and read from the Bible to him, and before long, Nathan's eyes were drooping. She leaned over and kissed him.

"Sweet dreams, Love Bug," she told him.

Nathan nodded slightly, closing his eyes. "You too," he told her drowsily.

"You stay in bed," she advised. "I have to go out for a bit."

She drifted out of the room. Nathan dozed for some time. Then he woke up, his heart pounding. Did she say she was going out? Nathan sat up. But even as he was getting ready to put his feet over the side of the bed, he could hear her moving around. It was fine. She hadn't gone out. That part must have been a dream. Nathan put his head back down and dozed some more.

When he awoke again, he knew the house was empty. He got up and wandered around, looking for Mama, or maybe a note saying where she had gone. All he saw was the Bible on the table, still open to Exodus. Nathan went back to his room and pawed through his clothes, eventually retrieving Harv's phone number. He called the number, feeling a little silly, like a child who had just woken from a nightmare and wanted his parents, even though he knew it was just a dream.

"Hello?" Harv's voice sounded sleepy, disoriented.

"Daddy, it's me," Nathan said.

"Nathan?" Harv cleared his throat and sounded more alert. Nathan could hear him moving around. "What's wrong?"

"Mama went out... I think... I'm worried..."

"She went out? What for?"

Nathan could hear a car starting in the background. Was Harv sleeping in his car? He couldn't have gotten out of bed, and gotten dressed, and gotten into his car that quickly.

"I don't know. I think... she might do something."

"I'll be right there, Nathan. In five minutes, remember? I'll be right there."

"Okay."

Nathan hung up. He looked out the window to make sure that Mama wasn't coming back. Where had she gone? What was she doing now? And what was she going to do if she got back while Harv was still there? It wouldn't be pretty.

The minutes ticked by. It seemed like an hour. It certainly didn't feel like five minutes. Harv got out of his car and came up the house. Nathan opened the door. Harv seemed reluctant to enter.

"What's going on, Natey?" he questioned. "Tell me what happened."

Nathan showed him the open Bible, and told him how Mama had been so agitated. Then he explained about Chandra, and her seizures, and talking to her dead son, and how now Mama thought, once again, that she was a witch. Harv nodded, taking it all in.

"We should call the police," he suggested.

"What are you going to tell them?" Nathan demanded. "We don't know what she could be doing! We don't have any proof of anything."

"Still, we have to let them know. Don't you think? Even when you just have suspicions? If you're wrong, then fine. No harm done. But if you're right, and she might be trying to harm Chandra, we should tell someone."

"That's why I called *you*," Nathan said.

"But I can't do anything on my own. I think I should call the police."

Nathan sighed and shook his head. Harv pulled out his cell phone and started to place the call. Nathan went to the door and looked out again. Still no sign of Mama. Nathan breathed in the crisp night air. It was a little cool to be standing at an open door without shoes and a jacket. But Nathan found the fresh air to be invigorating. Somebody had lit a fire, and the woodsmoke drifted through the air, tantalizing Nathan's nose, making him crave sweet, chocolatey smores. It was strange to have a fire on a Sunday night. Usually it was a Friday or Saturday night, when the neighbor didn't have to go into work the next morning. Those lazy Friday or Saturday evenings, when a person could huddle up to the fire as late as they liked and sleep in the next day.

Then Nathan's nostrils flared. A wood fire? On a Sunday night? He knew who would do that. *Thou shalt not allow a sorceress to live.* In the middle ages, the prescribed method to kill a witch was burning at the stake.

Nathan's feet barely touched the ground between his house and Chandra's. He rang the bell wildly. Somewhere on his sprint from one house to the other, he had observed that smoke was drifting over from Chandra's house, and he had been able to see bright flames through the kitchen window. Nathan pounded on the door wildly, tried the handle, and kicked the door.

"Chandra! Chandra, wake up! Your house! Chandra! It's on fire!"

About that time, an alarm started up, and it drowned out Nathan's voice. The noise was accompanied by flashing lights. Nathan kept ringing the bell and pounding on the door. Chandra opened the door, bleary-eyed. Her hair was mussed. She had on a thin nightgown. And she didn't have her cane. Nathan grabbed her arm.

"It's on fire!" he told her. "Come over to my house. We'll call 911."

He'd forgotten that Harv was already calling for help. Keeping a hold on Chandra's arm, he escorted her back to his house.

"What's going on?" Chandra questioned. "I don't understand! How did it start?"

Nathan shook his head. "I don't know," he said, and hoped that it was true, even though he knew it was not. He knew how the fire had started.

He helped Chandra up the steps to his house, and guided her in.

"Nathan, what's going on?" Harv demanded.

"Chandra's house is on fire!" Nathan told him, his voice cracking and squeaking. Harv should know that without being told. Couldn't he smell the smoke in the air? Hadn't they just talked about what Mama might do?

Harv started to talk into the phone again, asking them to send a fire engine right away. Nathan guided Chandra to a chair in the sitting room. Harv hung up his phone and gave Nathan a hug. Nathan could feel him shaking.

"And I guess you're Mrs. Mullenny," Harv said to Chandra.

She looked at him with wide eyes. "Yes... and who are you?"

"I'm Nathan's daddy."

Chandra looked at Nathan. "Truly?"

Nathan nodded and shrugged. "Yes'm. Really," he agreed.

"Nathan's my son," Harv said, looking down at him.

Chandra smiled. Then her face suddenly went sheet white. She jumped out of the chair and she started moving very quickly back toward the door. Nathan tried to stop her.

"Chandra, no. You have to wait here," he said.

But she was gone. He had never seen her move so fast. Nathan followed her to the door, panicking.

"Chandra!" he called out to her. She looked back to him.

"I have to get the animals!" she yelled back. "My cat and Kenneth's pets are still in there!"

"Chandra--"

Nathan tried to follow after her. He couldn't let her go back into a burning building. Her life was more important than those of her pets. But Harv grabbed Nathan before he could get out the door.

"No," he ordered. "You stay here. The fire fighters will be here soon. They will help. I don't want you in the way or in danger."

"But she can't do it by herself," Nathan insisted, and tried to pull away from Harv.

Harv held on with fingers like steel. He was not going to let Nathan go. Nathan struggled with him, but couldn't get anywhere. Harv was way too strong for him. Nathan had no chance, with the wasted muscles that he hadn't begun to build up again yet.

"Sit down," Harv ordered, pushing Nathan into a seat in the sitting room.

"No, I need to help."

"I need to keep you safe. That's the first priority."

Nathan slumped in the chair. He couldn't see the burning house from there. Couldn't see Chandra's progress, if she'd even been able to get back in through the door. Surely the other neighbors wouldn't let her pass. They'd be watching the house burn, and they wouldn't let her back inside.

"You're safe here," Harv told Nathan. "You've got to just stay here and let the firefighters do their job. You shouldn't have even gone over there alone like that."

"I had to wake her up! I had to tell her!"

Harv nodded. "I know. And you've done everything that you could. Now you need to just wait for the professionals."

Nathan's eyes leaked.

"I know, Nate. I understand," Harv soothed.

How many times had Harv stood by and waited for the professionals to do something, while Nathan lay in danger's path? Had he been the one to call Child Protective Services, too afraid to do anything himself? How many times had he been the voice behind those calls?

Harv stood there, between Nathan and the door, and looked around for something to talk about. "You have a snake?" he questioned, looking at the terrarium.

Nathan nodded, not looking at it. Harv wandered over and peered through the glass. "A boa?" he said.

Nathan stared at him. The man couldn't tell the difference between a boa and a red diamond rattler? Harv had said that he'd never been big on snakes, but anyone could tell the difference between a boa and a rattler that close up. Nathan got up out of his seat and walked over to the terrarium. He looked into it to point out to Harv that it was a rattler. But instead of their red diamondback, he saw a sleepy boa curled up under the light. Nathan gasped and grabbed Harv's arm to steady and orient himself. He knew that boa, too. It was Kenneth's boa. Who had swapped the rattlesnake for the boa? Who would do that? And why? It didn't make any sense.

In his mind's eye, Nathan saw Chandra shuffling into the house, feeling her way through the smoke-filled house back to Kenneth's room. The tarantula terrarium was easy to carry, small and plastic, lightweight. But she couldn't carry out the snake terrarium. It was too big, heavy glass and metal construction. Chandra couldn't carry it on her own. The only way to save the snake was to reach into the terrarium and pick it up.

Her eyes full of smoke, she wouldn't be able to see the snake, and if she could, only its general shape. The house was dark, the smoke alarm lights were strobing. She would reach in and feel around and grab the snake to take it out of the house to safety. The rattlesnake, blinded and frightened by the smoke, would strike.

Chandra was old and frail. Her heart was already pumping fast in her panic, and adrenaline was speeding through her veins. It would pump the venom through her body before she could even get back out of the house. She was not coming back out. Mama had made certain of that.

They could hear the sound of the fire engines approaching.

Harv had no idea. Harv simply thought that Nathan had a pet boa. He looked down at the terrarium with only casual interest, looking for something to pass the time while they waited for the professionals to do their job.

"No!" Nathan protested, and he made a break for the door. Harv had moved too far away from it to stop him this time.

P.D. WORKMAN

Nathan felt like his legs were pushing through wet concrete. They were heavy and sore and moved far too slowly. Every second counted, and he couldn't get there in time. The fire engines were noisy, their engines revving and their sirens so loud Nathan thought that his eardrums would burst.

He got to the house at the same time as the firefighters were getting out of their trucks, unloading the fire hoses and surveying the fire inside the house. It was still contained within the house, not spreading to the outside or the neighboring homes. Nathan tried to rush into the house, but strong hands caught him, pulling him back.

"Whoa, there. You can't go running into a burning house," the fireman told him, looking down at him with amused eyes and a friendly smile. "Why don't you let us take care of that?"

Nathan struggled to free himself. "She's in there. She went back in to get the snake," he explained. "Please, I have to help her. She doesn't know!"

"Who went back in there, buddy?"

"Chandra. Mrs. Mullenny. She's an old lady. She can't move very fast. I have to help her with the snake!"

The fireman called over to his buddies that there was someone inside. "Why don't you slow down," he told Nathan. "And tell me what you are talking about. Your Mrs. Mullenny went back inside *why*?"

"The animals! Her cat and Kenneth's pets--a spider and a snake."

"Who is Kenneth? Is he in there?"

"Her son. He's dead. She had to go save his animals."

"Okay. Don't you worry. We'll find her and get her out, okay? It doesn't look like there's any structural damage yet, the fire is mostly contained in the kitchen in the back of the house. It's mostly the smoke that we need to worry about. Especially with an old woman. Just leave it to us, okay?"

"It's the snake," Nathan protested. "She doesn't know. It's a rattler. She'll reach into the cage and she'll get bit!"

"A rattler?" the fireman repeated, several expressions flashing over his features. Amusement, disbelief, fear. "Why would there be a rattler? How would she not know about that?"

"Somebody swapped them. Somebody swapped the snakes and lit the fire. They wanted to kill her. They put the rattler in there to kill her when she went to rescue it."

"Come over here and sit down," the firefighter sighed, and led him over to the front of the firetruck. Nathan sat on the steps where he indicated. The firefighter faced Nathan, looking him sternly in the eye, his forehead wrinkled.

"Now what's going on here? What do you mean someone swapped the snakes and is trying to kill her? You? Were you playing tricks?"

249

There wasn't time to explain. Nathan couldn't say that it was Mama. He wouldn't get her in trouble like that. So he just nodded his head and did his best with the suggestion.

"Yes, it was me. We caught the snake up in the hills. Mrs. Mullenny, everyone thinks she's a witch. And she was always getting after us for playing in her yard. So I put the rattler in there, because I was mad, but now I'm not, and I don't want her to die!"

The firefighter looked doubtful, but it was believable enough to pass initial muster. He motioned to someone outside of Nathan's vision. "You'd better stay here and explain. Meanwhile, I've got a burning house and an old lady to save."

Someone else came around the side of the firetruck. A policeman. The fireman motioned to Nathan.

"Suspected arsonist," he said succinctly. "Keep him here."

The policeman looked down at Nathan, his eyes dark and hard. Nathan felt a wave of fear, but he pushed it away. It was Chandra that was in danger. If Nathan got in trouble, even if Nathan got thrown in jail, it was worth it if they could save Chandra.

"You want to tell me what's going on?" the policeman questioned, as the fireman walked away, calling out to his colleagues and coordinating everyone for the entrance into the burning building.

Harv managed to push through the crowds to get to Nathan in the fire truck, under the watchful eye of the policeman.

"Natey," he said with relief. "There you are. I'll look after him now," Harv told the policeman, moving in to get Nathan out of the truck.

The policeman pushed him back. "The boy's not going anywhere until this is sorted out," he said in a hard voice.

"Oh... well, okay..." Harv said uncertainly. "He didn't have anything to do with this, he just knows the victim."

"Are you the father?"

"Yes," Harv looked at Nathan. "I'm his father."

He looked as if he was afraid Nathan might disagree with the statement, but Nathan said nothing. Nathan wished that he could see what was going on in the house. How long would it take them to find Chandra? To put out the fire? She might have already been struck, and the clock was ticking a countdown on whether they could get the antivenin to her in time. She might have had a heart attack and already be dead.

A few minutes went by; a couple more police cars arrived, and then an ambulance arrived as well. Nathan stood up and tried to see where Chandra was. Did they have her out of the house? He couldn't see anything, and the policeman moved closer to him as if worried that he might bolt.

"Sit down," he ordered. "Unless you want me to put you in handcuffs."

Harv's eyes widened at the threat. Nathan sat back down on the steps without protest. The ambulance had pulled in right beside them, and Nathan watched the paramedics unload the gurney and push it toward the house, out of his sight. Harv was standing further back, with a better vantage point. Nathan watched Harv watching the action, studying his expression for indications of what was happening. Then the paramedics rolled the gurney back into Nathan's line of sight. Chandra was lying on the gurney, strapped down, mid-seizure.

Nathan was standing up again without realizing it, trying to step down from the firetruck steps to go to her. The policeman grabbed him and prevented him from going any further, pushing him roughly back against the firetruck. The back of Nathan's head hit the truck, making him wince in pain.

"Hey, take it easy," Harv protested. "He's just a kid."

"Suspect," the policeman corrected.

"She's my friend," Nathan said, his throat choking up as he watched the paramedics load Chandra into the ambulance, convulsing against the straps of the gurney.

The policeman said nothing, studying Nathan's face.

The firefighter returned to the truck. He looked down at Nathan as he unstrapped his helmet and breathing mask. His face was smudged with smoke. He glanced at Harv and said nothing to him.

"Now then, how about you tell me, nice and slow, just what went on here tonight?" he suggested.

"Did she get bit?" Nathan questioned in a hoarse whisper, trying to keep the tears from escaping his eyes.

"No. She didn't get that far. I suspect her epilepsy was triggered by the strobing alarm lights. That kept her on the floor away from the worst of the smoke, and away from the snake cage."

Nathan breathed out a sigh of relief. His legs shook, and he tried to wiggle away from the policeman's hold to sit down on the steps again. The officer tightened his grip on Nathan, then seemed to recognize that Nathan was very nearly fainting, and lifted him up. He put Nathan back on the steps and pressing his head down.

"Put your head between your knees," he advised. "Just breathe. Nice and slow."

Nathan tried to obey. Harv tried to move toward him, but the policeman pushed him back with a growled command.

"He's diabetic," Harv said. "He could be hypoglycemic. Nathan, are you okay? Do you need anything?"

Nathan shook his head, still hunched over with his head between his knees. "No," his voice was muffled. "No... I'm okay."

They were all silent for a while, waiting for Nathan to recover. He was so relieved that Chandra was okay, that she hadn't been bitten, and hadn't died in the fire. He kept hearing the scripture run through his head, like a command. 'Thou shalt not allow a sorceress to live.' But Nathan didn't believe that she was a sorceress. She was just an old lady with seizures who missed her son. Nathan raised his head back up, taking a deep breath. He looked toward the house, but couldn't see it around the side of the firetruck.

"How is the house?" he questioned. "Is it bad?"

"There's lots of damage in the kitchen, in the back," the fireman said. "But just smoke damage throughout the rest. It will be expensive to fix, but the house is at least not a write-off. They won't have to demolish and start over."

Nathan nodded. He rubbed his eyes, stinging from the smoke or his tears.

"Now," said the fireman, "did you start that fire?"

"What?" Harv demanded. "Of course Nathan didn't start the fire! He ran over to warn her, and he tried to go follow her when she ran back in. Why would he start it?"

The fireman ignored Harv and looked steadily at Nathan. "Well?"

"No," Nathan said. "It wasn't me. I just... smelled the smoke, and saw the flames. I was just trying to help her get out."

"You did more than just see the flames. You know a lot more than you're letting on here. Was it your father?" he jerked a thumb toward Harv, whose mouth dropped open. He was so shocked that he couldn't speak.

"No," Nathan shook his head.

"How did you know about the snake?" the fireman asked.

Harv and the policeman both looked puzzled at this, and frowned at the fireman.

"What's going on?" a familiar voice questioned. "Nathaniel, what are you doing over here? Are you okay? I told you to stay in bed!"

Nathan looked up, his stomach tying in knots. Why did she come back? Why had Mama come home in the midst of the action? Why didn't she stay away, until all of the chaos had settled down, and the emergency vehicles had gone home?

Mama looked around the circle of men surrounding her son, and her eyes stopped on Harv, widening in shock.

"You! What are you doing here?" she demanded, her voice screeching upward.

"Nathan called me," Harv said calmly.

"Nathan called--?" her eyes turned to Nathan. "How did Nathan have your phone number? You're not supposed to be making any contact with him!"

"I never agreed to that," Harv countered. His voice was calm and measured, while Mama was obviously falling apart. She'd already been upset and on edge. Now with her ex-husband thrown into the mix, she was rapidly losing control of herself and the situation.

"You've been stalking him! We've had the police called. They've been looking for you. Do you know how much you terrified him, following him around like that? Showing up places? Messaging him online pretending to be someone else?"

Harv looked uncomfortable and guilty, but he fastened onto the last accusation, shaking his head.

"I never messaged him online. I never pretended to be anyone else. Has someone been giving him trouble...?"

Mama pushed her way toward Harv, shoving past the firefighter.

"Like you don't know! Trying to lure him away, get him alone. You know that's illegal!" she turned to the policeman. "You should arrest him. Arrest him for luring a child online. False pretenses. Hacking our accounts."

"Ma'am," the police officer said, his brows drawn down in concentration. "What's happened here tonight is a lot worse than some online shenanigans. We're talking about arson."

"And attempted murder," the firefighter added.

They all looked at each other.

"Nathan didn't start that fire," Harv said. He looked at Mama. "You left him alone tonight. Where did *you* go?"

"I told him to stay in bed."

The officer and firefighter looked at her for further explanation.

"I want him arrested for stalking," Mama said, pointing to Harv. "Do it now!"

The policeman wasn't in any hurry to comply.

"What was this about a snake?" Harv interrupted, looking at Nathan. "What was he asking you about a snake?" He glanced sideways at his ex-wife, suspicious.

Nathan pressed his lips together and swallowed. He didn't want to say anything else about the snake. Now that he knew that Chandra was safe, he didn't want to chance getting Mama in any trouble. She looked at him now, her eyes wide.

The fireman looked at Nathan, then looked at Harv and Mama and answered Harv's question.

"He said that *someone* had swapped the owner's snake with a rattlesnake. He said that he did it, but I think he's probably covering for someone else."

Harv turned on Mama. "You--"

"Daddy, no!" Nathan protested.

"A child's story," Mama said, shaking her head. "Why would you believe a little boy's overactive imagination? A rattlesnake?" She forced a laugh.

"It will be easy enough to figure out what kind of snake is in that cage," the fireman said. "The fire was contained in the kitchen. There is no damage to the snake cage."

Mama's look was furtive.

"That's why Nathan came running over here," Harv realized. "He saw that the snake in your cage was a boa, and he knew that meant that you had swapped the snakes. Because *you* had a rattler. Of course you would. Why would you have a non-venomous snake? Your whole ritual is based on poisonous serpents."

"What ritual?" demanded the police officer, starting to get the gist of the conversation now. His eyes were focused now on Mama and Harv, and he edged gradually closer to Mama.

"This whole thing is ridiculous," Mama said. "You're here because of a fire, what is all this about snakes?"

She made a break for it. The firefighter and police officer were both expecting it, and even in full gear, the fireman was fast. They both tackled her to the ground, and the policeman put his knee on her back as he handcuffed her wrists.

"You have to arrest him too," Mama yelled, determined that she was not going to be arrested and Harv allowed to go free. "He's been stalking my son! He's not supposed to be making contact with him. I have restraining orders in three jurisdictions!"

Other policemen were coming over to help control the situation, and two big men confronted Harv, making sure that he wasn't going anywhere. Nathan looked at his parents, looked at all of the police, and ran.

Chapter Twenty-Six

WHERE WAS HE GOING to go? Nathan knew that he couldn't go home. There was no one to go home to. Mama arrested for arson and attempted murder, Daddy arrested for stalking and breaking restraining orders. Who would take care of him now? The only person that he could think of that could help him was Chandra. She always helped him. She was his friend, and she was always willing to help him out. He wanted to see her anyway, even if she couldn't help. He had to see that she was all right, that Mama had not succeeded in hurting her.

Nathan didn't run for long. He couldn't. Even now that he was on insulin, he didn't have the energy to run far. Maybe once he had managed to put on some more weight, he'd have the reserves to run for longer. As it was, he'd only had enough energy to get himself out of sight while the policemen and firefighters were distracted by Mama and Daddy. Now, he needed to figure out how to get to Chandra. They would have taken her to the General, that was the closest hospital. That's where they had taken Nathan. But he wasn't sure exactly how to get there. It was to the west, so he started walking west. He knew he'd made a mistake within a few minutes, but he didn't know what else to do. He had left the house after dark, straight out of bed. He was in a pair of thin sweat pants and a t shirt, and had nothing on his feet. He hadn't stopped to get shoes on in racing over to Chandra's house to save her from the fire and from the snake. Now he was walking in the dark, in his bare feet, freezing cold on the pavement.

He walked for a long time. He did the best that he could to steer by the landmarks he saw. The hospital wasn't that far away. But it took a very long time, even after he had it in sight, to reach the big, brown building.

Once inside, he had the challenge of trying to find Chandra. The hospital seemed to be built like a maze, intentionally confusing, with bits and pieces added on over time, with sections that didn't connect to other sections, elevators that led you to the right floor, but the wrong wing. They had attempted to help with colored lines painted on the floor and numerous 'you are here' maps, but Nathan was beginning to wonder if he would ever be able to find the unit that Chandra was being held in.

When he reached the hospital room with the right number and Chandra's name on the plate outside, he was confronted with a new problem. A policeman stood in the closed doorway, blocking the entrance. He didn't see Nathan initially. Nathan stood there, staring at him, all of the remaining energy draining out of him. He had walked all night to get there, only to find his way barred. It was hopeless. There was nowhere else to go.

As he slumped over, trying to hold back an exhausted sob, the cop's eyes turned to him. His eyes widened slightly in surprise. "Are you Nathan?" he asked softly.

Nathan nodded, defeated. The man took a couple of steps toward him, then swept Nathan up in his arms as, spent, frustrated and hopeless, Nathan crumpled. The man's arms wrapped around him and picked him up, holding him close in a comforting hug, rather than accusing him, perhaps even arresting him for his part in Chandra's attack. Or for running away. Nathan sobbed aloud, so tired and helpless, lost and alone. He wrapped his arms around the policeman's neck, and just sobbed in despair.

"You poor kid," the cop murmured. "It's okay, Nathan. It's going to be okay."

Nathan shook his head. He knew better. Both of his parents had been arrested. He had no one left. Orphaned. They'd put him in a home, or in foster care. He'd never have a permanent place to live again.

He didn't hear what the policeman said to the nurses. He didn't really know what was going on, but in a few minutes he was sitting in a soft chair, with his feet in a warm pan of water, a young intern examining the damage he'd done to his feet in walking all the way to the hospital.

"You have to be really careful," the doctor told him, carefully cleaning any debris out of the cuts and abrasions on Nathan's feet. "You have diabetes, right? So the circulation to your feet isn't so good. You might not feel it if you have injuries on your feet that need to be treated. Did your doctor tell you that? You should be checking them regularly to make sure that they are healthy and don't have any sores or discoloration."

Nathan just watched, as the doctor used a brush to make sure that all of the dirt and foreign matter had been removed from his feet. Then he dried them off and looked at them again. A few bandaids later, the doctor pulled some warm white socks on over his feet, and rubbed his toes soothingly. They started to warm up, the numbness turning to pins and needles and then normal feeling. Nathan pulled the blanket that he'd been given around his shoulders, snuggling down. He was getting drowsy now.

"Where's my boy?"

Nathan forced his eyes open, and rubbed them with both fists. He blinked at Harv, standing in the doorway smiling at him.

"Daddy?" he questioned, in disbelief.

"What are you doing, running off like that?" Harv remonstrated gently. He bent over and picked Nathan up, holding him cradled in his arms.

"How did you get away?" Nathan demanded.

Harv squeezed him. "I didn't have to get away, Natey. I didn't break any laws. It just took a little time to sort things out."

"But you were following us!"

"Yes, but that's not criminal stalking."

"Mama said she had restraining orders!"

He nodded again. "Expired ones," he agreed. "In other jurisdictions. Temporary orders that she never pursued in court to make them permanent."

Nathan put his arms around Harv's neck, and pressed his face to Harv's chest. "You're not leaving?"

"No. I'm not leaving. Now why don't you tell me what you're doing here?"

Nathan sighed. "I wanted to see Chandra. I want to make sure she's okay. And I thought that if you and Mama were both going to jail, maybe she could take care of me." He paused. "I don't know anyone else who would," he explained.

Harv shook his head, and shifted his grip on Nathan, holding him close. "You don't have to run away anymore," he said. "And you don't have to live with strangers. Your Daddy's here to take care of you."

Tears started in Nathan's eyes, and he wiped them away, feeling his face flush with embarrassment. "I'm sorry," he sobbed, trying to stay in control of his emotions.

"There's nothing to be sorry for," Harv soothed. "Now why don't we go see how your friend is doing?"

Harv was sitting in the visitor chair beside Chandra. Nathan was in Harv's lap, wrapped up in the blanket, dozing off and on, listening to the steady beep and hiss of the machines hooked up to Chandra. It had been a long night, and Nathan wasn't ready to wake up yet when the doctor finally came in.

"Are you family?" the doctor questioned, smiling down at them.

"Friends," Harv said, straightening up. "Nathan is her neighbor. We called for help for her tonight. Nathan saved her from her house burning down. Didn't you, bud?"

Nathan sniffled and rubbed his eyes. "Is she going to be waking up soon?" he questioned. He wanted to talk to her about what had happened. To explain that it wasn't really Mama's fault; that as Harv had told him, Mama hadn't been the same since she'd lost that second baby. It had affected her mind badly. Although, Harv had made a face as he had tried to explain, maybe it had all started even before that. She'd always been... very passionate. God and religion had always meant more to her than they did to other people. That could be good. But it could also be bad, if she let it swallow her up.

The doctor sighed, looking down at Nathan, and then turning to look at Chandra. He looked at the clipboard her records were kept on, but Nathan didn't see his eyes move back and forth to scan the lines of information. He just looked at it, not really seeing what was written there.

"Your friend had a seizure," he started out.

Nathan nodded. "She's had them before," he agreed. "She has a bracelet. She takes medicine for it."

"Well, from the levels in her blood, she hasn't been taking her anticonvulsants for some time."

Nathan thought about Chandra seeing Kenneth during her seizures. Maybe she had stopped taking her meds because she wanted to see him more often.

"But a seizure can't hurt you," Nathan said. "Once it's over, you're just normal again."

The doctor touched Nathan on the shoulder briefly. "I can't really talk to you about her case, since you're not her next of kin," he said carefully. "But... let me tell you about something called 'status epilepticus.'"

Harv frowned at this. Nathan looked at his face, and then at the doctor. "What's that?" he questioned.

"When a seizure lasts for more than a few minutes, it's called status epilepticus. And it can cause permanent brain damage. The longer it lasts, the worse it is."

Nathan looked at Chandra. "How long was her seizure for?" he questioned.

"We don't know how long she was seizing before she was brought in. From the timeline we got from the firefighters, it could have been half an hour or more."

"But she's not doing it anymore. So when she wakes up..."

The doctor shook his head. "Sometimes you can't tell that someone is having a seizure. It isn't always a tonic-clonic seizure, where you can see the person convulsing all over. Sometimes, it is just electrical activity in a certain part of the brain. You can only see it on an EEG." The doctor gestured at one of the machines that was hooked up to Chandra. Nathan looked at the wildly spiky lines that ran the length of the display. Was that a seizure still going on in Chandra's brain?

Nathan looked at Harv's face.

"You're trying to reach next of kin?" Harv questioned.

The doctor nodded. "In a case like this, we need instructions on how long to continue life-sustaining measures," he said gently.

"She's still having a seizure?" Nathan questioned.

The doctor didn't answer. Harv took Nathan's hand in his own big, warm fingers, and held it firmly. Nathan took a deep breath. "She told me that when she had a seizure, she travelled back in time to see her son," he told Harv.

"Her son?" the doctor repeated hopefully.

"He's dead," Nathan said. "I don't think she has anyone else, anymore."

"Ah." The doctor nodded. "Well... people with epilepsy can have funny feelings when they have a seizure. It can make them see, or smell or taste something particular. They might have a strong sense of déjà vu, like they've seen or done or experienced something before. It could invoke particular memories or emotions."

Nathan slid off of Harv's lap. He touched the thin, smooth skin on the back of Chandra's hand. "So if she's still seizing, in her brain," he said slowly. "Then maybe she's been seeing and visiting with Kenneth all night."

Harv nodded. The doctor cocked his head and shrugged. "Maybe," he agreed.

"That would make her happy," Nathan said. "Is it... do you mean... if nobody tells you to keep the machines on..." he looked at them, swallowing hard. "That you'll shut them off? And then she'll die?"

"No, Nathan," Harv protested.

But the doctor didn't deny it. "When we turn the machines off," he said. "It will be because we don't believe that her brain is alive anymore."

"And then she'll be in heaven," Nathan said. "And she'll be with Kenneth again forever. She won't have to leave him anymore."

In his head, he saw Chandra's pictures of Kenneth, and imagined that he could see Chandra and Kenneth greeting and hugging each other, up in the bright clouds, happy once more.

He held her lifeless hand to his cheek for a moment, then kissed her fingers, and put it back down again.

Epilogue

"ARE WE GOING TO visit Mama today?" Nathan questioned. Harv shuffled to the fridge and started pulling out milk, juice, and eggs for breakfast. Nathan knew Harv wasn't fully awake yet. It always took him a while to get his motor running first thing in the morning. After some food, coffee, and a hot shower, he'd be more alert and cogent. Harv put the food down on the counter and rubbed his eyes.

"Today's Sunday, isn't it?" he questioned. "Don't I always take you to see your Mama on Sunday?"

Nathan nodded. "Yessir... I was just making sure."

"Yes, I'll take you to see her today. What time do we need to be there? Is she leading worship today?"

Nathan shook his head. "No, it was her turn last week. They'll have one of the outside preachers today."

"So do you want to be there for services, or not until after?"

Nathan liked sitting with Mama for Sunday services, but the other inmates made him nervous. There was his Mama, so neat and pretty, looking like a beautiful young woman even in her penitentiary uniform, and then the other women... women with ugly tattoos, unkempt hair, faces deeply lined with scars and scowl marks. He found them a little bit scary, even if there were guards close by to take care of any problems that arose.

"After," he decided finally. "Is that okay?"

"Of course it's okay."

Nathan went up to his father and hugged him. Harv squeezed him back, then looked down at him. "What was that for? Are you okay?"

"Yes... I just... I just love you, Daddy."

Harv smiled. "I love you too, Natey," he said. "Always and forever."

Sign up for my mailing list at pd.workman.com and get
Diversion, Breaking the Pattern #2 for free!

"fast-paced and
intense, with a great
climax and
conclusion!"

SIGN UP AND GET IT FOR FREE!

Sneak Preview

BOBBY WATCHED THE SCENERY flash past the window, feeling a little car sick. He swallowed and glanced at Elsie. "What are they like?" he squeaked. He swallowed and cleared his throat. "I wish I didn't have to l-leave Devonish's."

"I know," Elsie agreed in a low, soothing voice. She fiddled with the radio dial, looking for something to provide background, something to help Bobby stay calm. "But I really think this is going to be good for you. And at your age... it could even be your last foster home."

Bobby shook his head. Sometimes you stayed in one foster home for a few years, but you always got moved again sooner or later. He wished that this *could* be his last foster home, but he wasn't going to count on it.

"Katya is the mom," Elsie told him. "I really think you'll like her. She seems really nice, very warm and outgoing. She's single, no husband or boyfriend on the scene."

Bobby sucked his cheeks in, thinking about that. Elsie knew that he'd had conflicts with foster fathers before. It didn't seem to matter whether they were nice or abusive, he always butted heads with them over something. The sporty ones hated how uncoordinated and hopelessly unathletic he was. The brainy ones thought that he should work harder and not be so concerned about his social life. And the abusive ones... well, it didn't matter what you did, they just didn't like you out of principle. There was always something.

"That's good," he agreed. "And other kids?"

"Just one. A little girl. She's Katya's natural daughter. You're her first foster child."

"She's just s-starting out?" Bobby questioned, surprised. Usually the homes he went to, they'd been fostering for years. All of the rules were set up, and they could be as hard-nosed as any social worker.

"Yes, but don't you go trying to take advantage of her," she warned. "Show her how much fun it can be."

Bobby rested his head back against the headrest, closing his eyes.

"Yeah. Fun."

"Now come on," Elsie remonstrated. "You've had some good families. Some good experiences."

"Yeah. But when you get the g-good ones... then it's that much worse when you have to l-leave."

She sighed, tapping her nails on the steering wheel.

"I suppose."

Bobby looked out the window again, looking at the neighborhood.

"I haven't been around here b-before," he observed.

Elsie nodded.

"It's kind of a funny area. Close to downtown. There's a real mix of inner city families that struggle to make ends meet, and then there are the... sort of yuppie families, I guess. Professionals who want to be close to the office. Nice condos, single family dwellings, all that. Quite a combination."

Bobby nodded.

"Which is Katya?" he questioned.

He'd lived with poor families. Some families that really struggled. Families that fostered kids just to have the extra money to try to put food on the table for everyone. Or that they gambled away, trying to make it big.

"Katya would be the latter," Elsie said, looking like she was trying to hold back the smile that tugged at the corners of her mouth. "She's not hurting. It will be a nice change for you."

"Sure," Bobby agreed.

He was used to Elsie trying to push him into liking a family before he even saw them. Telling him how great they were, trying to hype it up so that he would be excited about meeting them. But Bobby wasn't excited about meeting anyone new now. He wanted a permanent home. Somewhere he could stay until... until he aged out of the system, he supposed. That was as much as a guy could hope for from the system. Semi-permanent permanence.

"I'll give them a ch-chance," he assured Elsie.

She nodded, giving him a warm smile.

"I know you will. You're a good kid."

Bobby shrugged, and felt the warmth of a blush filling his ears and creeping up his face. He flipped down the visor and opened the flap for the vanity mirror and examined himself. He did want to make a good impression on the new family, however much he might hate starting out somewhere new again. But what he saw in the mirror wasn't too impressive. He looked too short, thin, and gawky. His hair was messy. Again. Even though he had combed it and pressed it down before leaving the Devonish house and getting into the car. He hated its tendency to curl. He should have worn a cap or something, to keep it pressed down and keep it from getting messed up. But he didn't even have a cap to put on. All of his clothes were carefully folded and stuffed into his back-pack. Anything he couldn't fit in the backpack was free-for-all for the other kids. All of his worldly possessions were in that one bag.

In the visor mirror, his teeth were too prominent. No one wanted to give foster kids braces. It was hugely expensive. And the system wouldn't pay for it. You could always get braces once you were older, an adult looking after yourself. Assuming that you actually were looking after yourself and not in jail or homeless or something. A lot of foster kids ended up in dead-end jobs. That's just the way it was.

Bobby sighed and pushed the visor back up again. He didn't need to see any more. He could pretend that he didn't see the rest. The glasses. The slightly misaligned eyes and crooked smile. All the things that made it painfully obvious to the rest of the world that he would never be popular or a jock. He pushed up his glasses as they slid down his sweaty nose, then changed his mind and pulled them off, sliding them out of sight into his shirt pocket.

"You look fine," Elsie said. "You just smile and be friendly, they'll love you."

"Uh-huh."

"You always get along somehow."

Bobby chewed on his bottom lip.

"Yeah."

She turned the music up a bit, and looked ahead as she drove, leaving him to mentally prepare himself.

They pulled up in front of a big white house with dark green trim and shutters. Bobby looked at it, his eyes pulling open wide. That was quite some house. He looked over at Elsie.

"This is it?" he questioned. "Are you s-serious?"

She nodded.

"Nice, eh?"

"Ho-o-o-ly," he drew the word out long.

She grinned.

"Like I said. She's not hurting."

"And only three people l-live here," Bobby said, shaking his head in wonder.

"That's right. Just you and Katya and the little girl."

"Man. Do I get a whole wing to m-myself?"

Elsie laughed. She opened her door and got out of the car. Bobby pushed himself out of his seat, and coming around the car, she put her arm around his shoulders and gave him a friendly squeeze.

"Give them a chance," she reminded him.

"I've got incentive," Bobby commented.

They walked up the sidewalk together. Not just a sidewalk with big square slabs of concrete. A beautifully crafted cobblestone, laid out in patterns, lined with bright flowers and greenery on either side. Everything looked like it had been trimmed to perfection with nail scissors. Bobby adjusted his backpack on his shoulder, inching it up a bit further.

"Okay," he whispered.

Elsie rang the doorbell.

It was a couple of minutes before the door was opened. Bobby stared up at the tall, blond woman, slack jawed. She had to be some kind of model. She was slim, wearing clothes that clung to her curves. And despite her already significant height, she was also wearing some kind of platform shoes with long spiked heels, making her tower over both Bobby and Elsie. She gave them a brilliant, wide smile.

"Hello! I am so excited to meet you!"

Elsie nodded.

"Katya, this is Bobby Thomas. Bobby, Katya Bernosky, your new foster mom."

Bobby was still gaping at her speechlessly. He thrust his hand out toward her to shake, unable to find any words. Katya laughed and took his hand, not in a firm, businesslike handshake, but in a sort of soft caress, then pulling him to her and giving him a welcoming hug.

"Come in, come in and see your new home," she invited.

Elsie remained on the doorstep as Bobby was dragged in the door.

"I'll just leave you to it, Katya," she said, "I don't need to stick around."

Katya made a careless motion with her hand.

"Of course," she agreed. "We've already signed all the papers. Unless you want to see...?"

Elsie smiled.

"All right. Bye, Bobby. You behave yourself."

He nodded.

"B-b-bye," he stammered, as Katya shut the big, heavy door.

His stomach was cramping, and he felt sick. The first word he said in front of her. Almost a decade of speech therapy, you would think he'd have the stammer licked by now.

"Come with me, Bobby," Katya invited, pulling him along to keep up with her long strides, "I am so excited to show you your new bedroom."

Bobby picked up his pace to avoid being dragged behind her. She released his hand, but put her hand on his back, guiding him along. Up the grand staircase from the front lobby, whisking past various rooms that he only caught a glimpse of, until she stopped in front of a door with a little wooden name sign mounted on it that said: 'Bobby's Room, Keep Out!'

"You like it?" Katya laughed, nodding to the sign. "I know how much teenagers need privacy. Especially teenage boys!"

"Yeah--" Bobby started.

But he didn't get a chance to finish. She grabbed the door handle and pushed the door open with a whoosh, propelling him inside with the other hand. Bobby stumbled into the room, and looked around.

He didn't know whether she had hired a professional decorator or if she had done it all herself. All he knew was that he had never had a room like that before in his life. Not in any of his foster homes. He had rarely even had a room to himself, for a few days or a week in between other foster children transferring out of the home and new ones transferring in. Usually, it was three or four to a room, in bunk beds, squeezed claustrophobically close together. But this... he'd never even seen something like this.

The ceiling was painted a deep blue, almost black, with stars dotting it. Not just random stars, but apparently a real picture of the night sky. Bobby didn't know a lot of constellations, but he recognized the big and little dippers and Orion's belt. The bed was piled deep with white and red sheets, blankets, and pillows. There was a work desk with a computer set up on it and 'Welcome Bobby' running in a banner across the screen. Shelves full of books, including graphic novels, and a dictionary and thesaurus for reference. There was a display shelf with various miscellany. It included a baseball on a display plaque. Bobby took a closer look at it and could see that it was autographed, but he wasn't sure whose signature it was. He smiled tentatively at Katya, sure that he was supposed to be impressed by it. There were framed posters on the wall, actors and athletes. He could see from the door that there were already clothes hanging in the huge closet on his right. Katya looked at Bobby expectantly.

"Th-th-this is..." Bobby fumbled with his words. "Wow. Wow."

"You like it?" she prompted.

Bobby nodded vigorously.

"I d-do," he agreed.

"Good. I put a lot of work into it for you," she commented.

Bobby continued to nod. He swallowed and licked his lips.

"It's g-great," he assured her.

"Well, I guess I'll leave you to make yourself comfortable." She indicated the computer. "There are movies on there if you want to watch something, and some music, but I didn't know what you would like. You have your own bathroom," she pointed to a closed door beside the closet. "Please try to keep it clean."

"Yeah," Bobby agreed. "I will."

She gave him another impulsive squeeze around the shoulders.

"It's going to be so much fun having you around, Bobby," she said, showing off her perfect, even teeth in a broad smile.

Bobby nodded and gave her a half-hearted pat on the back, wanting to return the affection, but not sure what to do. She was obviously a touchy person, and he wasn't that into hugs.

"Thanks," he said.

Katya giggled, and retreated from the room, shutting the door behind her. Bobby looked around the room slowly, taking in more details that he had missed the first time. A hand-held gaming system on the bedside table. A fancy-looking watch beside it. A beanbag chair in the corner with a set of headphones lying beside it. Bobby dropped backward onto the bed, landing with a poof in the pile of soft bedding.

This was going to be the most incredible foster home ever.

It turned out that even the bathroom was fancy, and decorated for a teenage boy. He had his own shower, the curtain covered with footballs, baseballs, and basketballs. The liquid soap dispenser, towels, and cloths were in coordinated navy blues and maroons. She had even included an electric toothbrush and various toiletries that featured in megabuck TV commercials.

Bobby used the toilet, then washed his face and brushed his teeth just for the heck of it, thoroughly enjoying the experience of his own space and his own things. It didn't look like he was going to have to share anything here. His own room, clothes, shower, and computer. It was luxury like he had never even considered before. He fiddled with the computer for a few minutes before finding the movie library and putting something on, then he laid stomach-down on the bed, resting his chin on a couple of fluffy pillows hugged in front of him, and watched it.

The time passed quickly, and it didn't seem like long before he heard voices and divined that Katya's daughter was home from school. Bobby's nervousness returned. What would she be like? And how would Katya behave in front of her daughter? Some foster parents treated you fine, but they treated their own children differently. When their own kids were around, you were decidedly second-rate. It was always awkward, going to a home where they had their natural children at home too.

Bobby swallowed and took a few deep breaths, trying to slow his heart back down again and relax his clenched stomach. Nothing bad was going to happen. Katya was nice. They lived in a mansion. Nothing was going to ruin this, even if the daughter was a spoiled brat who always got into his stuff. At least Bobby had his own stuff for her to get into. He should be glad about that.

Bobby opened his door and followed the voices, arriving downstairs in the front lobby where he had first entered the house, where Katya helped her daughter to remove her backpack and outdoor clothing.

"There he is," Katya said, turning to look at Bobby. "There's your new foster brother."

Bobby smiled tentatively. The little girl was five or six. She had mid-length white blond hair framing her face. Her face was heart-shaped, making her look like a little pixie. She smiled at Bobby, her face taking on a mischievous look as her eyes danced.

"Hi, Bobby," she greeted.

Bobby nodded, smiling at her. She was cute. She was dressed pretty fancy, but she didn't look like a spoiled brat. And she wasn't turning up her little pixie nose at him or scowling about her space being invaded by a teenage boy.

"Hi," Bobby acknowledged. "I d-don't know your name..."

"It's Xenia," she said, pronouncing it ZAYN-yah.

Bobby looked at her closely.

"Xenia," she repeated, and she spelled it out for him. "X-E-N-I-A."

"Oh," Bobby acknowledged, "Z-z-zane..."

Xenia and Katya nodded.

"Xenia," Katya repeated.

Bobby didn't try it again. He just nodded as if it wasn't a problem. Maybe it wouldn't have been so bad if Xenia hadn't spelled it out for him, and he'd only heard it phonetically, but knowing there was an 'X' in there made it seem so exotic that he was immediately tongue-tied.

"It's okay," Xenia said wisely. "It takes people a while to get used to."

Bobby nodded. It seemed like that was all he could do right now. Just keep standing there, bobbing his head up and down like a dummy. He needed to figure out a way to get out of the situation, to break the ice and help him to get more comfortable.

"Can we have a snack?" Xenia questioned. Bobby was inordinately pleased that he seemed to be included in the 'we'. They had just met, and she was already including him like family.

"Let's see what is in the kitchen," Katya agreed.

Katya led the way, eating up the floor of the large entrance hall with her long, gazelle-like paces, which left Bobby just staring after her admiringly. Xenia took Bobby's hand in her small one and led him after her mother. Bobby closed his mouth again and walked with her, happy to stick to her short stride and get a better look at everything between the front lobby and the kitchen.

It certainly wasn't like any kitchen that Bobby had ever seen before. It was what Katya referred to as a 'great room,' a combination of a sort of a living room with a big stone fireplace and furniture that you sank down into, a big dining room table with a white lace tablecloth and silver candlesticks, and a slate-tiled kitchen with a big, long, green-marble-topped island. The kitchen itself had at least two ovens. There might have been more, Bobby couldn't identify for sure what all the appliances were. The fridge was more like a walk-in closet. The stove-top embedded in the island had eight elements. Eight elements to feed a family of three! Everything was sparkling clean. Xenia led Bobby over to the island, not the dining room table. There was a series of bar stools along the counter, and she climbed up into one of them and put her elbows on the island, resting her chin in her hands.

Katya went around the other side of the island and looked around. She opened one cupboard that had a big rotating lazy-Susan shelf in it, which appeared to be filled with every kind of popular snack carried by the grocery store.

"What do you children want?" Katya questioned. "Granola bars?"

Bobby nodded.

"Sure, that would be g-great," he agreed.

"No," Xenia objected, shaking her head. "Fruit snacks."

"Which ones?" Katya questioned.

"The gummy ones. Dinosaurs."

Katya got out a couple of packages of dinosaur candies flavored with real juice and placed them on the counter in front of Xenia and Bobby.

"Do you want a granola bar too?" she asked Bobby.

He shook his head.

"This is f-f-f-fine," he said, tearing the corner off of the package.

Katya threw a chocolate chip granola bar on the counter in front of Bobby anyway. Xenia handed Bobby her fruit snack, and he knew intuitively what it was she wanted. He tore the corner off of her bag, and handed it back. She smiled at him as she took it back. She was missing both of her top front teeth. Her gap-toothed grin was endearing. Bobby started eating his fruit snacks, and opened up the granola bar as well, nodding at Katya.

"Thank you," he said.

She nodded her head in acknowledgement.

"And what about drinks? I'll get you some milk," she suggested. "Growing kids need lots of calcium for strong bones."

Bobby and Xenia nodded at this. Xenia watched her mother disappear into the fridge.

"We have pink milk," she confided to Bobby.

"Oh? Pink?"

She nodded, smiling.

"My friends all say their moms make them drink white milk, and they're only allowed pink milk now and then, for school lunch. If you bring your own money to buy lunch, the white milk and the chocolate and the pink are all the same price. So sometimes they get it at school, but at home they have to drink plain *white* milk."

She said it with a tone of disdain.

Katya drew back from the fridge with a carton of fake-strawberry-flavored milk. She poured them each a glass and put it in front of them.

"Thank you, Mommy," Xenia trilled.

"You're welcome, sweetie."

"Thank you," Bobby echoed awkwardly. He ran into this problem at every new home. What to call the foster parents. Some of them insisted on Mom and Dad. Some of them went by mister and missus. And others casually went by their first names. Katya had only been introduced to him as Katya, but he worried that she would not appreciate him calling her by her first name. So was she a missus, or a 'mom'? He swallowed and let it hang there, waiting to see if she would jump in and tell him what to call her. She did not. Bobby picked up his strawberry milk and drank it, hiding his gaze from her as his face flushed warmly.

"Do you like pink milk?" Xenia questioned.

Bobby put his glass down and wiped his lip with the back of his hand. It was sickly sweet.

"Yeah, it's good," he agreed.

Katya handed him a cloth napkin. Bobby looked at it blankly for a moment, and then dabbed at his mouth. She nodded her approval. Xenia shot Bobby a mischievous look and continued to eat her dinosaurs and drink her milk.

"We'll get you registered for school tomorrow, Bobby," Katya said. "I didn't think there was any point in taking you over for half a day today."

Bobby nodded. Another new school. New faces, new rules, teachers he wasn't familiar with. Another mid-year change. It would make so much more sense if all foster family transfers could just be done at the beginning of the school year or current semester. Mid-term transfers were always so awkward and embarrassing, and it felt like it took the rest of the semester to get caught back up to where everyone else was. No matter how long you were there, you would always be the outsider. Always the mid-year kid. Other kids knew each other since kindergarten, or since they had started junior high, but a transfer didn't belong anywhere.

"It's a combined school," Katya advised, "elementary and junior, so you and Xenia are in the same school. They go to different parts of the building, of course, but you're in the same building."

"I c-can walk her to school for y-you," Bobby noted.

"Oh, no. I'll drop the two of you off."

"Oh." Bobby nodded. "Sure."

"It's too far to walk," Xenia explained to Bobby, "and it's... in a neighborhood you're not allowed to walk in."

Bobby frowned at her, trying to figure out what she meant. A neighborhood you weren't allowed to walk in? Katya nodded at what Xenia had said.

"It's not a particularly safe neighborhood," she enlightened Bobby. "I wouldn't want either of you wandering around there by yourself. But the school itself is safe. There's a fence, and metal detectors, and everything."

Not unusual. Bobby had gone to plenty of schools with barbed wire fences and metal detectors. It seemed to be the norm these days.

"I've thought about putting Xenia in a private school," Katya offered, "but I wanted her to learn how to get along with... all types of people. And you don't really get those experiences at a private school."

"Oh," Bobby shrugged. "Yeah, I guess."

Xenia slurped her milk, attracting a frown from Katya.

"Yeah," Xenia agreed. "We have poor people, and black people, and everything."

Bobby restrained a snicker and tried to nod seriously in understanding. But it was a stretch, and Xenia saw the humor in his eyes.

"What?" she questioned.

"Nothing. I just had lots of p-poor people and black people at my last s-school too."

She pursed her lips, and then nodded.

"You'll make lots of friends," she told him. "Do you think you'll make lots of friends?"

Bobby glanced at Katya. She was looking at him expectantly. Bobby nodded slowly, taking a bite of his granola bar.

"Yeah. I'll make l-lots," he said.

Katya nodded, and got out a glass for herself. Bobby watched curiously to see if she was going to have pink milk. She did not. She went to a glass-fronted cabinet and poured a glass from out of a fancy liquor bottle.

"I prefer something a little stronger," she told Bobby with a smile.

He realized he was staring, and looked away. When he glanced back at her, she was putting her glass down, the pink imprint of her lipstick on the edge.

"Do you have any homework to do, Xenia?" she questioned.

Xenia shrugged.

"I'm supposed to read," she admitted.

"Bobby, why don't you go read with Xenia?" Katya suggested. "You can help her if she is having any trouble."

"Sure," Bobby agreed. "I'll help her."

Xenia popped the last of her snacks into her mouth and swallowed the last gulp of pink milk, then slid down from her stool.

"Come on," she invited, taking him by the hand again, "I'll show you my room."

Bobby's room was a decorator's dream 'boy room,' and Xenia's was a girl's. It was overwhelmingly pink and frilly. There were china dolls lining shelves, a lacy canopy over the bed, a porcelain-white dressing table, an incredibly detailed doll house, and pink everywhere. Xenia looked up at Bobby expectantly, smiling.

"Wow," Bobby complied, "it's like a room for a princess."

Xenia bounced, smiling widely.

"That's what Mommy says!" she exclaimed, her voice squeaky with excitement. "She says I'm her princess, and this is a princess room."

"She's right," Bobby agreed. He looked around for somewhere to sit down. "Where do you want to read?"

Xenia considered.

"On the bed," she decided. She bounded across the room and jumped into the nest of pillows arranged at the headboard. Bobby followed her over. They arranged the pillows behind their backs, and sat side-by-side. Xenia pulled a book out of her pink Disney Princess backpack and snuggled up to Bobby.

"I like you, Bobby," she said.

He was surprised that she had attached to him so quickly. Foster kids could be pretty stand-offish. They kept cool and watched to see what kind of damage the others might have before getting too close. Burned too many times. So he wasn't used to the immediate acceptance.

"I like you too," he said after a moment. It sounded a bit too tentative in his own ears, and he was afraid that Xenia would hear it and would be hurt. But it didn't seem to bother her.

"I like you too, *Xenia*," she prompted.

Bobby swallowed. Sooner or later, he was going to have to be able to say her name without stammering.

"I like you too, Zay-zay-zane," he stuttered.

"It's not that hard," Xenia said.

Bobby pressed his lips together tightly and ground his teeth. He could feel his face getting red.

"Some words are just hard for me," he explained slowly. "It's just... it's just my p-problem."

She studied his face, her eyes wide and innocent.

"Why?"

Bobby shrugged.

"Some people stutter," he said.

"And you can't stop?" she questioned.

Bobby shook his head.

"No. I've t-tried. Lots."

She nodded.

"You can say Zane," she pointed out.

"Zane," Bobby repeated, without fumbling it.

She smiled at him, her fair hair framing her delicate cheeks like a pixie.

"You can call me Zane," she said.

Bobby scratched his chin, trying to hide his embarrassment.

"You don't mind?" he questioned. "Really?"

"I like Zane," she said.

"Th-thanks."

The newly-dubbed Zane opened her book and held one side, letting Bobby take the other side. She started in on the story. Her voice was soft and hesitant, but she didn't have much trouble with the words. Bobby helped her out when she got stuck, but mostly she was able to get through it on her own.

"Do you want to read another one?" Bobby questioned.

Zane shook her head. She leaned against Bobby's shoulder.

"Would you read me one?"

"Sure," Bobby agreed.

She got off of the bed and went to her bookshelf, pulling a handful of books off and bringing them back to Bobby. She snuggled back into the pillows and against him, and they read for a while.

They got through the last book, and Bobby looked at Zane to see what she wanted to do next.

"You don't stutter when you read," Zane observed.

"No. Not usually," he agreed.

"Mommy talks funny sometimes," she offered.

Bobby raised his eyebrows at her.

"What do you mean? She d-doesn't stutter like me?"

"No. She just talks in a funny way."

Bobby shrugged.

"Hmm. Okay. When she drinks?"

Zane shook her head.

"When she drinks, she just gets... happy. But sometimes she talks... like she's someone else."

"Oh." Bobby frowned, but accepted this. He would find out more about Katya in the coming days and weeks. Then he would figure out what Zane was talking about.

"What do you want to do n-now?" he questioned. "Do you have to do any m-more s-schoolwork?"

"No. I can play now."

Bobby got up.

"Okay. I'm going to go b-back to my room."

Zane's face fell.

"Aren't you going to play with me?"

Bobby didn't really have anything better to do, but he felt a little self-conscious about playing with a five-year-old.

"I don't know... what do you want to p-play?"

"Dress-up!" Zane announced immediately. She jumped off of the bed and darted into her closet. Bobby followed her and peeked around the doorway.

He hadn't really done more than glance at his own closet. When he looked into Zane's, his jaw dropped. It was at least as large as her bedroom, with a crystal chandelier sparkling in the middle of it. Again, the predominant color was pink. There were rods and shelves full of clothes, racks of shoes, drawers of accessories. Lots of mirrors, and places to sit while you dressed. The carpet was a deep, lush rose.

"Do you like my dressing room?" Zane questioned, eyes sparkling.

"Wow. Yes. I think you really are a p-princess," he teased.

She nodded, smiling broadly.

"What am I going to d-dress up in?" Bobby questioned.

"You go to your room and find a suit. Then come back here," Zane instructed.

Bobby agreed, and stepped back out into the hallway.

"Umm... Zane?" he called back over his shoulder.

"What?"

"Where's my room?"

She came out of the dressing room, laughing. Her cheeks were flushed pink.

"That way," she pointed, "three doors down."

"Okay."

He followed her directions and return to his room. How long was it going to take before he didn't get lost in his own house? He'd gotten turned around in new foster homes before, ended up opening the door to someone's bedroom instead of the bathroom, or something like that. Hadn't been able to find the laundry because it was in the garage and not the basement. But this house brought a whole new dimension to the problem.

Bobby opened his closet door, prepared for the worst. It wasn't as big as Katya's dressing room, and there was no chandelier, but it was still nothing like he had ever had before. It was a walk-in closet, very masculine with glass and black accents, bright halogen lights giving even light to the room. Long black-framed mirrors, rows of clothing. He'd lived with entire families that didn't have that much clothing all together.

Zane had said to find a suit, so he examined a row of suits carefully. He had a pretty good idea that she was going to dress up as a princess, so he was going to have to dress in something pretty sweet to complement her. He found a frilly tuxedo shirt that he would never wear out in public, and a black suit. He wasn't sure whether it was a tuxedo or not, but it seemed to go well with the shirt. It wasn't so formal as to have tails, but he thought it might be silk. He pulled it on and straightened the lines carefully. It was just a bit too big for him, as if Katya had estimated that he would be bigger than he was. But it still looked pretty good. There was an assortment of pre-tied bow ties, cummerbunds, and pocket kerchiefs, and Bobby selected three that looked like they matched. He examined himself in the mirror. If he didn't look like such an awkward geek, he might actually have been pretty handsome in this get-up. Bobby picked up the brush and comb on the dressing table and tried to tame his hair into order. Not bad. For a geek.

He wasn't sure how long Zane would take to get ready. Girls always took longer than guys, but he wasn't sure if a five-year-old girl took longer than a fourteen-and-a-half-year-old guy. He went back down the hall to Zane's room and tapped on the door.

"Are you ready?" he queried.

"Come in. I'll just be a minute," she invited.

Bobby re-entered the candy floss room. He hadn't noticed the cloudy blue sky painted on the ceiling the last time he was in. Zane was still in her change room. Bobby didn't want to sit down and wrinkle anything or not be ready for her, so he stood there, waiting. In a few minutes, Zane made her entrance.

She stepped into the room and paused for a moment to allow him to get the full effect of her outfit. Then she slowly twirled so he could see all sides. She stopped and held a pose, chin lifted up, waiting for his comment.

"You're beautiful," Bobby obliged. "I tried to d-dress up, but..."

She immediately abandoned the haughty pose and rushed him, smiling.

"You look very handsome!" she insisted, giving him hug. "Just like Prince Charming."

"And you look..." Bobby hunted for a comparison. She wore a red kimono, sleek and satiny, with complicated embroidery. She had picked out a sparkly tiara to go with it. She had on a pearly pink lip gloss, and he wasn't sure whether she had makeup on her cheeks, or if they were just that bright from excitement. "Like that girl," he said awkwardly, trying to remember the name of the girl on the Disney movie who had been a samurai soldier, "on that movie..."

Zane looked delighted.

"Do you think so?" she questioned excitedly. "I love that movie."

Bobby smiled and nodded.

"You look just like her," he agreed.

He wasn't sure that she was thinking of the same movie that he was, but if she was happy about it, he'd done his part.

"Let's dance," Zane suggested, "and then we'll have tea."

When Katya came looking for them, Bobby and Zane had gone through several costume changes, and he was no longer in the tuxedo, but in a navy pinstripe suit that looked something like a prohibition gangster's outfit. And Zane was in a pretty green, frothy dress with a bunch of netting under the skirt. Bobby grimaced and scratched his head, a bit embarrassed to be caught playing dress-up at his age.

"You both look very nice," Katya approved.

Zane launched into an excited recollection of all of the outfits they had tried on, and Katya nodded, waving off the conversation.

"We are going out for dinner," she announced.

Bobby looked down at his suit.

"What should I wear?" he questioned. "This probably isn't..."

"No, no, keep what you have on," Katya interrupted. "Both of you. You look just fine. We'll go to Enrico's. Just give me a moment to get myself ready."

Bobby and Zane nodded. Katya left the room. Zane jumped into the bed with a poof of her dress and the quilts.

"She only goes to Enrico's when she's in a good mood," Zane told Bobby. "That's good."

"Is she in a bad mood very often?" Bobby questioned, teasing. Katya didn't seem like the kind of person who let herself get into a bad mood. She was kind and cheerful and upbeat.

Zane's expression changed. Her smile disappeared, and she looked at Bobby, her lips pursed as she considered his question.

"Well, *sometimes*," she said. "Sometimes she gets really mad. Or sad." She let out her breath in a long sigh. "It's better when she's happy."

Bobby nodded.

"Well then, I'm glad she's in a good mood."

Zane rested her chin on her fist, elbow propped on her knee.

"Do you have a real mom?" she questioned.

"Mmm," Bobby searched for an appropriate answer, "I used to have a biological mom. But it was a long time ago. I don't really remember her any more."

"Was she nice? Did she get mad and sad?"

Bobby nodded.

"Mostly sad," he said. "She'd get so sad that she couldn't t-take c-care of me anymore. So then I would have to go to a f-foster family. But then... she died. So I didn't have a real h-home to go back to anymore."

"Oh." Her brows drew down in a cute frown of concentration. "That's too bad. Did she die because she got too sad?"

That was an interesting question. Bobby shrugged, unable to answer it.

"I don't know much about it. I guess so."

"I hope my mommy doesn't get so sad she dies," she worried.

"Oh," Bobby hurried to repair the damage, "I'm sure she'll be okay. Most p-people don't get *that* sad. We'll keep an eye on your m-mom, okay? Make sure that she's happy m-most of the time."

"Okay," Zane agreed. "You'll help me?"

"Sure."

She nodded, and they were both quiet, thinking about it. Bobby didn't know how to change the subject to happier things. He expected Zane to be distracted by other more interesting and immediate subjects, but she continued to sit, brooding on it thoughtfully. Katya appeared in the doorway.

"All right, children, time to go," she invited.

She had changed into a simple white sheath dress, with a diaphanous blue scarf tied in some complicated knot around her shoulders and collarbone. She had on a different pair of shoes, but these too added inches to her height. She clutched a tiny purse in her hand. She was so incredibly beautiful, Bobby found his heart pounding hard just looking at her. Katya smiled at Bobby, waiting.

Bobby shook his head in amazement, his cheeks getting hot and sweat breaking out on his forehead.

"You look so... st-stunning," he breathed. "You're so b-beautiful."

Katya nodded, smiling approval.

"Let's go," she repeated, holding her hand out for Zane.

Zane took her hand, and they preceded Bobby out of the room. Bobby wondered, as he followed them, what sort of car they had. He was determined not to be surprised by anything this time. He was leaving his mouth open just a little too much since he got here.

They went through the door to the garage, and Bobby looked around. He kept his mouth shut, but his eyes were probably almost popping out of his head. There was a shiny, fire-engine-red convertible, and a long black town car. Katya gestured to the black car. Bobby followed Zane to get into the back seat.

"Bobby," Katya snapped.

He turned his head so quickly he almost got whiplash, surprised by her tone.

"S-sorry?"

"Open the door for your sister, please."

Bobby glanced at Zane, standing just behind him, waiting. He pulled up the handle of the door and opened it for her. Zane smiled sweetly.

"Thank you."

Bobby nodded. Looking at Katya, he shut the door as quietly as he could, and went around the car to the other side, letting himself in. Katya nodded, sliding into the driver's seat. She started the engine and it purred to life. Bobby found his seatbelt and clicked it into place. He glanced at Zane, and she smiled reassuringly.

The car was luxurious, and spotless, which Bobby expected by now.

Bobby was not surprised that Enrico's was a high-end restaurant. He got out of the car, and with a glance at Katya, went around the other side to open Zane's door for her. They followed Katya into the restaurant. At the entrance the maitre d' smiled in a friendly way, and glanced down his nose at his reservations book.

"Reservation in the name of...?" he prompted in a smarmy voice.

Katya looked at him and didn't say anything. The man looked at her questioningly, a little surprised. Katya waited for another moment before saying anything, making all of them shift uncomfortably.

"Madam?" the maitre d' prompted.

"Is 'Rico in?" Katya demanded.

He swallowed, and looked her over.

"Err... yes, madam. I will go get him," he agreed.

Katya nodded, not smiling. Zane looked at Bobby and smiled at him. Obviously this sort of behavior was not unusual and she was not worried about it. Bobby nodded and waited. In a couple of minutes, the maitre d' and another man, in a sharp black tuxedo, came back to the lobby, voices and heads lowered in conversation. When the new man saw Katya, his face broke into a wide, approving smile.

"Ah, my dear Ms. Bernosky," he greeted, lengthening his stride to meet her.

They joined hands between them, not a handshake, but the man holding Katya's hands warmly in his, and they air kissed, both cheeks.

"I am so delighted that you decided to join us today," Rico said.

"Thank you," Katya allowed. She took off her gloves and readjusted her scarf over her shoulders. "Is there a table free?"

"For you? Always, my dear," he agreed.

He turned to the maitre d'.

"I'm sorry, this is Mr. Douglas. He has only been with us for a couple of weeks, and he has not yet had the pleasure of meeting you. Mr. Douglas, this is Ms. Bernosky. And we always have a table for her." Mr. Douglas looked as though he might say something, but Rico cut past him. "*Always*," he reiterated.

Mr. Douglas nodded, looking properly put in his place.

"Delighted to meet you, Ms. Bernosky," he said.

Rico nodded, and putting Katya's hand in the crook of his arm, he led the family to a quiet booth in the corner of the dining room. Bobby looked around, uncertain. He didn't want to end up knocking anything over or doing anything stupid. But he wasn't always at his best in situations like this. Rico pulled out a chair for Katya, and Bobby wondered if he should do the same for Zane, but they were in a corner, and Zane slid in along the wall of the booth, so he couldn't hold her chair. He slid in beside her. He swallowed and looked around.

It wasn't crowded. The tables were far apart, and it seemed like only half of them were filled. There were candles on each table, and a series of cutlery on either side of the plates. One of his friends at school a few years ago had advised him that you could tell how expensive a restaurant was going to be by the number of forks and spoons you were given. All the way from a fast food restaurant where there were none, or a plastic spoon or fork that you had to get yourself, all the way up to fancy-shmancy restaurants that seemed to have a countless number of forks and spoons and other implements. This restaurant, if he hadn't already figured it out, was obviously very expensive.

Bobby shifted in his seat. Rico handed each of them a menu placard, one sheet on a leather board. This wasn't a burger joint. Bobby looked down at the cursive writing to see if there was anything that he recognized.

"Rico, I want to introduce you to my new foster son," Katya said, motioning to Bobby.

Caught in the glare of the headlights, Bobby froze. He looked at Katya, and looked at Rico, looking for the proper response to the introduction.

"I'm so pleased to meet you," Rico said. "I had no idea that you were interested in fostering, Mrs. Bernosky."

"No, well I thought I should do my part. So many needy children in the world. All I have is Xenia, and so many children have no one to look after them. So I decided to take on Bobby here. Give him a home. Show him what it was like to really be loved and belong."

Bobby swallowed. That was laying it on pretty thick. But her tone was sincere, and Rico didn't act like she was exaggerating at all.

"Yes, of course," he agreed. "Such a generous person. Well, Bobby, you have certainly picked up a gem, with Ms. Bernosky as a foster mother."

Bobby nodded.

"Th-thank you. S-sir."

Rico smiled down his nose at Bobby.

"Delightful," he said, and patted Bobby on the shoulder. He looked at Katya. "I'll leave you to decide what you would like, unless you have decided already?" he questioned.

Katya glanced at the menu card and shook her head.

"Mmm. I don't know. You don't have any fresh fish today?" she suggested.

"I am sure we have some salmon. If that would do...?"

Katya nodded.

"Lemon juice, capers, something light," she suggested.

"Certainly, Ms. Bernosky," he agreed. "I will speak to the chef."

Katya nodded. She looked at Zane.

"What do you want, sweetheart?" she questioned.

Zane glanced around the dining room at other people's meals, and shrugged.

"Chicken?" she said. "In that sauce?"

Rico nodded again.

"Of course, miss. Would you like some fries to go with it?"

Zane nodded up and down several times and smiled up at him, handing him her menu.

"Yes. Fries with ketchup," she directed.

"Yes. And the gentleman?" he faced Bobby and cocked an eyebrow.

Bobby looked down at the menu, and over at Katya. He certainly wasn't confident enough to order something that wasn't even on the menu. He hadn't really had a chance to read through it to see what he liked. He glanced over at Zane.

"I'll have the chicken too," he said.

"Excellent choice. Fries like Miss Xenia? Or do you want mashed potatoes? Scalloped? Something else in mind?"

Bobby handed his menu to Rico.

"Uh--fries p-please. That would be g-great."

He nodded and favored them all with a benevolent smile. Then he retreated and disappeared out one of the side doors. Bobby breathed out in relief. He looked at Katya for approval.

"Is that okay?" he questioned.

"Of course, dear. You can order whatever you like."

"Okay. Thanks. It looked really g-good," he said, looking over at one of the other tables. "This is a really n-nice place. Thank you for taking m-me out."

She smiled thinly and nodded.

"I don't do much cooking myself," she said, "so we do go out... perhaps a little more than most people."

Zane looked at her mother, eyes shining with mischief.

"You don't cook ever," she pointed out.

Katya arched an eyebrow.

"I don't cook ever?" she repeated. She looked over at Bobby. "You've seen my kitchen. You think I would have a kitchen like that, and never cook anything?"

Bobby shook his head, feeling a flush rise up his cheeks.

"No ma'am," he said quickly.

Katya laughed.

"Well, it's probably more true than not," she admitted. "Maybe not never... but even when I do cook, it is usually just warming up a frozen meal, and maybe you can't really call that cooking."

Zane nodded. Bobby shrugged.

"That sounds good," he said lamely, not knowing what else to say.

The conversation before the dinner arrived was stilted. Bobby wasn't sure what was expected of him. Katya watched him closely, and he found it unnerving. He tried a few times to deflect conversation over to Zane, and she helped him out the best she could, but often Katya would just cut across whatever Zane was going on about, and start a new conversation with Bobby. Bobby was a bit embarrassed for Zane. But she seemed to take it in stride. Bobby supposed that was nothing new, that she was used to it, having grown up with Katya. Eventually, their dishes came, and Bobby sat back while the waiter arranged them on the table. Bobby looked at the array of forks and knives and watched Zane to see which ones she picked out to use. He copied her. But he was too busy watching her, and knocked over his water glass, sending is splashing across the table.

"Oh!" Bobby jumped up and reached for a cloth napkin, trying to stop the flow and quickly mop it up. "I'm sorry. I didn't m-mean t-to. Let me..."

He wasn't doing much good, and his elbows seemed to get in everyone else's way as the waiter attempted to help and Zane tried to save her chicken, which Bobby had just drowned.

"Bobby," Katya's voice had a snap to it. He looked up. "Sit down!" she ordered. "And put your hands in your lap."

Bobby sat down abruptly. He wanted to keep trying to get it cleaned up, but he forced himself to pull back his hands and put them in his lap. He watched with dismay as the waiter mopped up the mess and gazed at the dishes.

"You can have mine," he told Zane, nudging his plate over toward her. "I'm s-sorry! It was an ac-accident."

"It's okay," Zane said in a small voice.

"You have mine. I'm... n-not hungry any more," Bobby said, his voice cracking.

"I will get a new one," the waiter assured him. "It won't be very long."

The waiter left the table, and Bobby sat looking down at his hands, not wanting to see the expression on Katya's face. He'd been trying so hard to do everything right, and now he had ruined the meal.

He could hear Katya's fork clinking, and stole a glance at her. She was not looking at him; her attention was entirely on her dinner. Zane and Bobby didn't eat, waiting for the return of the waiter. He was only a few minutes, and then put a new dish in front of Zane, and a new glass of water in front of Bobby, a few inches further away than the previous one had been. Zane and Bobby started to eat again without comment.

Katya insisted that Bobby have a chocolate brownie for dessert. He was stuffed, and he already felt embarrassed and queasy about the whole incident, but she waved off his protests.

"We are celebrating tonight. This is your first night here, and you need to have dessert. You like chocolate, don't you? Do you want something different? A malt, or pie, or something?"

"The brownie is the best," Zane said reverently beside him. "It's drizzled with chocolate sauce, and then whipped cream, and curls of chocolate and a cherry on top of the whipped cream. It is soooo good."

Bobby had to smile at this.

"Will you at least share it with me?" he suggested to Zane. "I couldn't eat the whole thing, I'm really full."

She nodded, eyes wide with pleasure at the suggestion. She looked at Katya for permission.

"Can I, Mommy?" she questioned.

"Yes, you may have a little," Katya agreed. "But you must only have a little bit. You have to watch your weight."

Bobby was surprised by the remark. He looked at Zane.

"She's not fat," he pointed out.

"No. She's just perfect," Katya agreed. "And that's the way that she's going to stay. My friend Annabelle's daughter is overweight, and I think it is just *terrible*. That poor child. Nothing she wears fits properly. The children at school make fun of her. And of course, she can't participate in any beauty shows or anything. The doctor says that it is not dangerous, so Annabelle doesn't care, but if that was my daughter... there is no way that I would let her just go on eating so much and not getting any exercise. I would make sure that she went on a diet and got back down to an appropriate size."

"Oh." Bobby nodded. "Okay."

Zane looked at Bobby.

"I can have a few bites," she said. "Maybe... three."

Bobby looked back at Katya.

"Is it okay if I don't eat it all?" he questioned. "I don't think I can... and I don't want to get fat either."

Katya nodded her assurance.

"You don't need to finish it. We are not members of the 'clean plate club' here. That is a silly tradition that just encourages children to eat more than they should. We believe that you should stop before you are full. Just eat what your body needs, and no more."

Bobby was already overfull. He probably shouldn't have finished all of his fries. And helped himself to Zane's too. He should have left half of them on the plate. Maybe if he knew he was going to get dessert too, he would have. But he was used to eating out being such a rare treat... he just ate everything that he could... he never knew when he might be going out again. He got in all the enjoyment that he could, while he could.

When the waiter brought out the chocolate brownie, Bobby had to admit that Zane had not been exaggerating. It was a work of art. He put it between them, and they each took small bites.

"Do you want the cherry?" Bobby offered.

Zane gave him a brilliant smile.

"Yes!" she agreed. "Are you sure you don't want it?"

"No. You go for it."

"Thank you!" Zane scooped the cherry off of the top with a fair amount of whipped cream and chocolate shavings, and put it into her mouth. "Mmmm. That's really good!"

Bobby pushed the plate away from himself a fraction of an inch.

"I really can't eat any more," he said, sighing and putting a hand over his belly. "That was so great."

When they got home, Bobby figured it would be time for bed. Foster parents tended to like to put kids to bed early so that they would have the evening to themselves. Especially if they had a lot of kids. Sometimes the bed routine started as early as six or seven.

But it didn't look like Katya was ready to send them off to bed when they got home. She looked at Zane.

"What do you want to do?" she asked the girl. "Shall we put on a movie? Play a game?"

Zane considered for a moment.

"Watch a movie," she decided.

Katya nodded.

"You want to join us, Bobby?" she invited.

Bobby had been wondering whether he should just head off for his room and hide there. It had been a busy day and he wasn't sure how much more newness he could handle. It was all a little bit overwhelming, even if it had been good. But a movie didn't sound too bad. He could just veg out, and he didn't have to be on his best behavior.

"Umm, yeah," he agreed. "That sounds g-good."

"Xenia will take you to the family room. I'm going to change into my grubbies before sitting down. Actually, why don't we all change? You're not going to be comfortable watching the movie in that suit, are you?"

Bobby agreed. He followed Zane back toward the bedrooms, though he was getting a better idea of the layout of the house now, and might have actually been able to find his room by himself.

"See you in a minute," he whispered to Zane, and they each went into their own rooms.

Bobby carefully hung his clothes back up again. He had a pretty good idea that Katya would not be a mom who would overlook clothes strewn on the floor even for a minute. He put everything away neatly and looked for something to change into. What did Katya mean by grubbies? Sweatpants? Jeans? Something else? Bobby picked out a soft track suit and put it on, then went down the hall to Zane's room and tapped on the door.

"Zane?" he called lowly. "I don't know what I should wear."

The door opened, and she peeked out through the crack.

"Whatever you want," she giggled.

"But I don't know. What's Katya going to wear? What are you going to wear?"

"I'm putting on my jammies," Zane whispered through the crack.

"Oh. Good. Okay. I'll see if I can find some too," Bobby said.

He went back to his room and looked through the various drawers before picking out a pair of pajamas that looked like a baseball uniform. He felt a little silly. Most places he lived, he just slept in an old, holey pair of sweatpants, maybe a ragged, faded t-shirt thrown over top, for those moms that didn't like 'immodesty'. The baseball jammies were just a little juvenile for him, but he put them on anyway.

He went out into the hall, and Zane joined him and took his hand again in her little one.

"That's cute," she commented.

Bobby felt himself blush. Zane was wearing a pair of... surprise, surprise... pink pajamas. With feet. She ran her fingers through her hair and scratched her scalp.

"Okay," she said. "Let's go watch a movie."

"What are we going to w-watch?"

"I don't know. Mommy will pick something," she informed him.

They walked together, Zane leading him to the family room. In spite of Bobby's constant assurances to himself that he wasn't going to be surprised by anything else, he couldn't help but be astonished by the family room. It was really more of a private screening room. The screen took up an entire wall. There were rows of theatre seating, but Zane ignored them and led him to the bottom, where they pulled over some beanbag chairs and blankets, and made themselves comfortable. Katya was a few minutes more getting there. Bobby studied her, trying not to stare. This was the first time that he saw her without shoes, and could see her real height. She was tall even without heels. Probably six feet all by herself. She had put on some sort of leisure suit or pajamas that were white and satiny. Certainly nothing Bobby would have ever called "grubby." Katya smiled at the children.

"All set, then?" she questioned.

They both nodded. Katya went to the projector and tapped on the computer there for a few minutes, before starting the movie showing. Bobby was full from the restaurant, but had a sudden craving for fresh popcorn. He ignored it and turned to the screen to watch the animated feature that Katya had chosen. He expected her to sit in one of the big, comfy theatre chairs, but she did not. She grabbed another big beanbag, and plopped it between the children, falling into it and making the children's beanbags rebound. Zane giggled, and settled again, leaning back against her mother. Bobby readjusted his posture, and looked up at the screen.

They hadn't been watching for long when Katya shifted, and Bobby felt her hand on his back. To start with, she rubbed it gently. Bobby tried to relax and enjoy the massage. After a while, she just laid her arm across him, and they watched the movie, cuddled up together. Zane readjusted and laid partly across her beanbag and partly across Bobby's legs. She was snoring lightly before the end of the movie, and Bobby was afraid to move and wake her up. By the time the movie ended, he was almost asleep too. He shifted carefully and looked at Katya.

"Thanks, that was g-great," he said.

"It was good, wasn't it? Now what are we going to do with sleepyhead here?" Katya surveyed her daughter.

"Do you want me to carry her to her b-bed?" Bobby suggested.

"Won't she be too heavy for you?"

"No... but I might w-wake her up. I don't know if she'll s-stay asleep."

Katya shrugged.

"Well, she'll wake up if I take her to bed, because I am not carrying her. You might as well give it a try."

Bobby nodded. He shifted his position to slide his legs out from under Zane and laid her gently across the beanbags. Getting up to massage his legs and get the feeling back, he stretched and walked around for a few minutes. Zane continued to just snore, oblivious to what was going on around her. Bobby went over to her and picked her up, one arm under her legs and one behind her back. She was light. Bobby straightened up.

"Which way back to our bedrooms?" he questioned after a moment of consideration.

"I'll show you," Katya offered. She went out what he thought was a different door than they had come in. Bobby followed her. In a few minutes they arrived at the familiar hallway.

"Thanks," Bobby said.

"Of course. Have a good sleep, I'll see you in the morning."

Bobby nodded.

"Do you need anything?" she questioned.

"No. I'm g-great, really."

"Night."

Bobby continued on to Zane's room and pushed the door open. He had to juggle her a bit to get the blankets back, lay her down, and then cover her up again. She shifted and turned onto her side.

"Night, Bobby," she said softly.

"Night," Bobby told her.

He left, pulling the door shut behind him, and headed back to his own room. The baseball jammies would do for the night. He brushed his teeth and crawled into the soft, warm bed. No broken springs or sleeping bags here. With a sigh, Bobby closed his eyes, expecting to fall asleep instantly.

Time passed, and Bobby wasn't asleep. He opened his eyes and turned restlessly, looking at the window. He should have closed the blinds, a streetlight shone directly in his eyes. He turned again and pulled the blanket over his head, but sleep still eluded him. The events of the day replayed over and over. When he tried to shut them off and stop processing them, he started thinking about school the next day. A new school. Another mid-year transfer.

Bobby tossed and turned, his body comfortable, but unable to settle his mind and find sleep.

By-Pass, Breaking the Pattern #3
is coming soon!